"Please, Eliz[...] leave. I didn't m[...] out of this even[...]

She stared do[...] overwhelmed. "[...] tain everyone was staring at them.

Gavan was disheartened. He didn't want the evening to end so poorly and was all too aware of her dismay. He was determined to have her reconsider.

"There is no judge at this table. I do not want to crucify you, okay? Just calm down and give me a chance. Will you? Please," he begged.

Their eyes locked for an eternity before Elizabeth blinked and chose to interpret his plea as authentic. She sedately slid back into her seat, brushed her hair out of her face, and moistened her lips with a quick dart of her tongue. She had made a fool out of herself threefold and wanted nothing less than to crawl under the table. Instead she gave Gavan a direct stare and said with a calm that she didn't actually feel. "This was a mistake."

Gavan was quiet a moment, staring at his empty liquor glass before finally bestowing a wayward smile upon her. "Yeah, maybe. I shouldn't have pushed you so fast," he admitted. "But I don't want you to leave here upset. Have dinner with me and we can talk about something else. What do you like? Seen any good movies lately? Anything, Elizabeth, just don't leave."

His tone indicated nothing of the turmoil he had felt when she nearly flounced off. He was smiling, but if she declined his offer he would lose the battle of composure and she would see how disappointed he was in the awkward turn of events.

Elizabeth was silent, digesting his statement. She would have to be honest with herself. He was more than attractive. His earlier arrogance had only been one side of him. Tonight he was charming and kind, engaging and attentive.

She sighed with regret, raised her eyes to peer at some inconsequential image over his shoulder, anything to avoid his gaze, and said in a barely audible whisper, "But that's the problem, Gavan. I am guilty."

INTUITION

DIANNE MAYHEW

BET☆
BOOKS

BET Publications, LLC
http://www.bet.com
http://www.arabesquebooks.com

ARABESQUE BOOKS are published by

BET Publications, LLC
c/o BET BOOKS
One BET Plaza
1900 W Place NE
Washington, DC 20018-1211

All Kensington Titles, Imprints, and Distributed Lines are available at special quantity discounts for bulk purchases for sales promotions, premiums, fund-raising, and educational or institutional use. Special book excerpts or customized printings can also be created to fit specific needs. For details, write or phone the office of the Kensington special sales manager: Kensington Publishing Corp., 850 Third Avenue, New York, NY 10022, attn: Special Sales Department, Phone: 1-800-221-2647.

ISBN: 1-58314-540-4

First Printing: September 2005

10 9 8 7 6 5 4 3 2 1

Printed in the United States of America

I dedicate Intuition *entirely to my mother-in-law, Dorothy Morgan, for her support during the process of completing this novel. Thanks, Mom, for ensuring that my son, daughter, and husband had more than peanut butter and jelly sandwiches for dinner!*

CHAPTER 1

"Did I hear you right?"

Elizabeth leaned forward in her chair, absorbing his words with incredulity. Reflexively her slender fingers clutched the iron arm rails of her chair. Her hold was steadfast as if she was fearing she would fall off the chair.

Her attorney was not surprised by her reaction. Her dazed happiness made his unusual early rising, his rushed breakfast and weak coffee, and even the downtown traffic that he hated any day of the week, well worth it. He had felt much the same way when he received the unexpected news. And although it was Saturday morning, although he had been awakened by the district attorney's office before the dawn had filtered across the morning sky, he was thoroughly satisfied in delivering the message that Elizabeth Wilkins was free.

"Yes, Elizabeth, you did."

"I can't believe it," she murmured.

She blinked rapidly but she could not quell a suppressed sob that constrained her throat, rendering her remark barely audible. She was simply too overjoyed by the news. Her eyes welled with unshed tears that harbored all of her frustration and disbelief at being so unjustly accused. Attempting to regain her poise, she stared at the floor as she fought to control a rush of foolish sobs. She was so happy, so incredibly thankful that she was practically hysterical. It was all so startling, so unexpected, and so very just.

She had prayed and, in the same breath, cursed her cousin for his lies. She had wanted to die with mortification that the authorities had believed in her guilt. But she was strong. She was a Wilkins and her grandmother never let her forget it in her twenty-nine years. Carrying the Wilkins name meant there was no room for spinelessness.

It was the biggest challenge of her life to sit for three days in a cell *and* not cry. But she had done it. She had survived the ordeal and instead of hiding in shame, for nearly seventy-two hours she had maintained her innocence *and* her composure.

And she was innocent. No one could take that from her and she intended to prove it to the world. She never dreamed that it would be done for her, that her prayers would actually be answered, and that the truth would come to light, all within a span of three days. It was practically a miracle that on a Thursday she was arrested, booked, and held prisoner in a cell smaller than her master bathroom, and by Saturday she was being set free. She was cleared of any wrongdoing. She sent up a grateful prayer, before releasing a long sigh of contentment.

To her lawyer, it had the sweet sound of a purring, and rather well-fed, cat. "Believe it, Elizabeth, you are free to leave. You're free," he emphasized, spreading his brown hands wide to represent the whole expanse of his tiny office.

Elizabeth's eyes shimmered, showing signs of moisture that she no longer attempted to conceal. She found the courage to look at her lawyer and bestowed a wide smile upon him. Henry Miles paused in midthought, momentarily awestruck by his client's smile. It was a dazzling display of even, white teeth against a honeyed complexion that glowed with happiness. He was charmed by her gratitude, thinking it enhanced the depths of her dark brown eyes, the velvetiness of her smooth golden complexion, and the serenity of her shapely mouth.

Henry recalled their first meeting and that it had been anything but pleasant. Rather, he had encountered an angry, distraught woman vehemently declaring her innocence and ready to claw down the walls of the courthouse in her desperation. Yet, even in her state of discord, her inborn poise somehow managed to subdue her hysteria. Never a man to make rash decisions, he felt his gut telling him that she was innocent. Like a besotted puppy, he had longed to ease her distress and simply see her smile, as she was doing now, and he was not disappointed.

He'd had a hand in making her happy, he thought smugly. He resisted the urge to swivel in his chair. If he were a young man, he doubted he would have been able to maintain self-control. He chuckled softly, then cleared his throat and assumed an authoritative air, although his brown eyes, covered by prescription glasses that seemed to require more and more thickness over the years, twinkled with mirth at his outrageous thoughts.

Despite himself, he grinned with her, before recalling his other news. "There is just one other matter I wanted to discuss, Elizabeth," he began.

"Yes?" she responded so swiftly that he sensed her panic.

"Oh, it's nothing bad," Henry hastened to assure her. "Actually, it's rather a favor for a friend of my son. He's an author by the name of Gavan T. Ward. You may have heard of him? Yes, well, he happened to hear about your situation. Actually, my son told him. I hope you don't mind but he was fascinated by Mikel Wilkins. He thought Gavan would be interested in it, you see. And lo and behold, Gavan is interested in speaking with you."

"Don't tell me he wants to write about me?" Elizabeth gasped, her cheeks burning with indignation over public awareness of her disgrace. It was a blessing indeed that her fate had not made the press. She had no intention of encouraging it now that she was free.

Henry paused, wisely taking note of her discomfort. He decided to proceed with caution. He adjusted his posture, shifting in his seat until he was comfortable. "I think that's the idea. I believe he writes—"

"About broken families, family murders, anything bad about a family, is what he writes," Elizabeth finished for him. Her regard was steady, her initial bewilderment under control as she added, "I'm familiar with Mr. Ward's work, Henry. I won't be a part of his theories."

"I don't believe he plans to vilify your good name, Elizabeth," Henry suggested gently.

"No? I suppose he wants to write a glowing picture of my innocence. Not likely," Elizabeth scoffed.

"I could be mistaken," Henry said while absently tapping his pen against his chin. "But my impression was that Gavan was interested in writing about your cousin and the Liberty Sutton affair. He was hoping he could meet with you and get your input. Perhaps you could give him the benefit of the doubt."

Elizabeth was silent, not missing his emphasis on doubting Gavan's intent. She refrained from rolling her eyes heavenward with impatience. Because Henry had proven to be a friend, mainly due to his friendship with Sonya, Elizabeth's personal assistant and dear friend, she would consider his request. She could not envision giving anyone, particularly a crime novelist or whatever he considered himself, an interview. But what harm would it do if his focus was on Mikel and not her?

Henry was patient, allowing Elizabeth to ponder his words. After a few moments, he was certain she was less wary about Mr. Ward's interest in her. He got up, walked around his desk, and stood in front of her. The back of his thighs pressed against the desk to support his body while he spoke. His brown eyes stared down at her with understanding.

"You'll have time to consider his invitation so you don't have to feel any pressure, Elizabeth. I believe he'll be in town on Monday. You can decide then if you're interested or not."

She nodded, then tensed when she realized he was not going to sit back down but was heading toward the door. "Are you leaving?" Elizabeth asked, failing to mask her panic.

Henry appeared confused and no wonder, she thought with worry. He was well beyond the retirement age. She guessed he was near seventy, her grandmother's age, and although he was a dear friend of Sonya's, he did seem distracted more often than not. Sonya had insisted that Henry Miles was the best lawyer for Elizabeth *and* had insisted that she accept his services. Elizabeth had been distraught, barely listening to Sonya's glowing portrayal of the lawyer. But it hadn't mattered. Sonya was more like a mother to Elizabeth than an assistant, and if she wanted Henry to defend Elizabeth, Elizabeth was confident that he was more than qualified.

It wasn't as if she could discuss her case with her family, who now only consisted of her grandmother, Anne Wilkins. Her grandmother was still in the hospital since her nephew, Mikel Wilkins, who was also Elizabeth's cousin, had attacked her. At that thought, Elizabeth could not help feeling old resentment stir. Her grandmother was by no means in a coma, but she was recovering from the trauma of the attack, according to Sonya and Liberty Sutton. Elizabeth had been visited once by Liberty Sutton, who was clearly sympathetic toward her as recently as Friday night. And naturally Sonya called at every opportunity, faithfully coming to the courthouse daily. Elizabeth half expected Henry to say Sonya was outside the door waiting for her.

"My apologies, Elizabeth, I thought I told you. I need to get your release papers. I was so surprised by the call this morning I actually forgot to inquire about them. And with it being Saturday, I expect there'll be limited help. I'll be back shortly," he added before hurrying from his office.

Elizabeth stood slowly, staring at the closed door, feeling suddenly closed in. She glanced down at her slender wrist, then at the door again. She was not shackled. There were no handcuffs or bonds or even a policeman about to keep her confined in Miles's tiny office. All that stood between her and freedom was the door. She had an urgent need to breathe the air outside the room, to know in every way that she was truly free and that it was not a malicious, twisted jest. Something Mikel had concocted.

She took a deep breath and swallowed. She was being foolish. Of course it was not a joke. She could walk right out that door and never have to see another precinct or courthouse or jail in her life; at least, once she signed the papers Henry was gathering.

Slightly dazed by the reality of her new circumstances, she moved in a trancelike state until she was in front of the door. Putting her hand on the doorknob, she flung the door open with an abruptness that indicated her expectation that it might be locked or barred somehow. She hastily stepped outside and closed it with a decisive snap, her heart racing frantically. Breathing at an exaggerated rate, she leaned against the door, her pulse racing so fast she fully expected to faint. It was a ridiculous notion but she closed her eyes, her lips parting slightly as she took deep, shuddering breaths and fought the telling lump that formed in her throat while she attempted to recover her equilibrium. She was so emotional that she wanted to cry. But she would not, especially not now when she had every reason to shriek with joy.

CHAPTER 2

Gavan's breath caught at the sight of her.

It was obvious that she had not seen him. Before he could react to her unexpected emergence from the office, she closed Miles's door, leaned against it, and squeezed her eyes shut. Mystified by her odd behavior, Gavan watched in fascination, momentarily unable to turn his regard elsewhere.

Then he knit his brows together and instinctively glanced at his Blackberry. The name Elizabeth Wilkins stood out like a warning beacon within the subject line of the directions to the courthouse that he had received from his friend Tyke Miles.

It couldn't be her, he thought in disbelief. She couldn't be *the* Ms. Wilkins. He raised his head sharply, examining the tall, slender woman with more thoroughness. She wasn't cuffed, was unescorted and not at all what he had anticipated. Perplexed, he reread the name on the office door that reached above her head, glanced again at the message on his Blackberry, and confirmed that he was, at the very least, in the right place.

It was Miles's office all right. But if this woman was Elizabeth Wilkins, where was Miles?

Tyke could have gotten the information wrong. He had received it secondhand from his father and it could have been distorted by the time it reached Gavan, leaving out the fact that Elizabeth Wilkins was released. Unsatisfied with this reasoning, he could not resist a closer inspection of her, his perusal trailing down the length of her. Beneath her loose-fitting and rather faded blue-jean long-sleeve shirt and pants, a prison uniform no doubt, she was slim with just enough fullness in the right places to make her appealing. He looked away, disturbed by his train of thoughts, his confusion growing by the moment.

The long, gray corridors of the courthouse were nearly empty. He mentally counted the number of people that came into view, which amounted to only seven, including the officers and suited men who passed one another without comment. He turned his attention back to the woman before him and thought, if she was supposed to be a prisoner, no one was taking notice. Miles had clearly left her unattended.

There was the possibility that she could have been released on bail, but it didn't seem likely. According to Tyke, the Wilkinses were planning to leave the country when the police caught up with them. Bail would not be given to individuals who were irrefutably fleeing, not even if it was an exorbitant amount.

He thought the tall beauty at least fit the vague description he had gotten from his brief conversation with Henry. She was wealthy, independent, educated, and pretty. Her attire was prison uniform. No judgement of wealth could be determined there. He certainly couldn't judge her independence. And as she had not yet spoken, he had no way of discerning the credibility of her education. But the trivial mention that she was pretty, he could judge and it was an understatement.

Tyke obviously had not met the lady for himself. She was more than simply attractive; she was stunning, leaving Gavan to reason that if Tyke had described her to him, her striking personage wouldn't have been articulated properly. Her skin was a flawless golden honey tone, her bone structure delicate and almost handsome in its perfection. Her eyes were closed, but he suspected they were wide from the expanse of her thick eyelashes that lay on her high cheeks. Her eyebrows were finely arched and were as dark as her long black hair that was pulled in a ponytail, giving him an unobstructed view of her face. Her lips were full and wide with a hint of an upward curve.

He shook his head, unable to fit this woman into the character of a notorious impersonator, forger, and kidnapper. It was a foolish thing to do and if looks were any indication, this woman was not a fool. There was an air about her, a confidence and poise and . . . He scowled. She was a stranger to him, barely in his world for five minutes. He didn't know her well enough to make *any* judgments. She was a beauty, yes, but he was no freshman. In his line of work, he was all too familiar with the reality that looks meant nothing when determining a person's innocence or guilt.

Having no doubt now that she was none other than Elizabeth Wilkins and unhampered by politeness as she was yet unaware of his presence, he was free to check her out at his leisure and did so from head to toe.

He had a lifetime of dating attractive women, attracting them by the droves, and yet he could not recall ever being so fascinated. Particularly by one fresh out of jail, he thought in mockery. Still he could not help appreciating the appealing picture she made standing a few feet away from him. In an experience rare for him, he simply couldn't believe how incredibly lovely she was and how he, a man familiar with being in the presence of beautiful women, was enamored by her. He kept staring. He couldn't help it.

As he watched, her mouth curved upward in a slight smile. He caught himself smiling in an unconscious response. She wore an expression of pure pleasure and looked as if she had been fed the most delicious meal and was well satisfied. He had never seen a more tempting woman. Suddenly, he detected the tension within her as she literally held her breath.

She was aware that he was staring, he was sure of it, and he was deeply embarrassed. If he didn't want to make matters more awkward, he would have to say something and fast. He straightened to his full height of six four, cleared his throat, and then spoke.

"Ms. Wilkins?"

His voice was masculine, resonant, and remarkably cool despite the confusion her presence had stirred within him. She was slow to respond, which caused him to fret. He had a strong desire to see her eyes, to complete the picture. He wanted the vision to come alive. And as if she had heard his silent petition, she finally opened her eyes.

Elizabeth was unprepared for the sight that greeted her. Her breath caught the moment she saw him, as much from discomfort at the sight of a stranger watching her as the fact that he was incredibly good-looking. He leaned nonchalantly against the wall as if he belonged there, his stare telling her nothing of his thoughts. She released a soft gasp that sounded exaggeratedly loud to her ears and swallowed hard, all the while her dark brown eyes staring into intense, light hazel orbs.

He was so near that a few steps would have her standing directly in front of him. She went from a moment of fear at being alone with the stranger—although she was as safe as she could be within the courthouse and with police officers roaming all over the building—to being annoyed that her private moment had been shattered by his rudeness.

The man was watching her intently; a slight frown creased his forehead, causing Elizabeth to wonder if he had spoken to her when she initially came from the office. She had been so engrossed in reveling in her lack of restrictions that she hadn't noticed anything or anyone else. Mortified at the thought, she managed to nod a response even as she said, "Yes, I'm Elizabeth Wilkins," in a voice so breathless she wanted to crawl away. Where was her composure when she needed it?

He was very stoic, not even a smile in greeting, as he said, "Gavan T. Ward. It's a pleasure to meet you."

Ah, so this was the infamous author. She nodded again, failing to see any visible indication of his stated pleasure.

Watching her closely, he cleared the space between them with a few swift steps, his tall form overpowering her space. He offered his hand and absurdly she stared at it, noting its size and strength with uncommon interest. Finally, she accepted his handshake, managing to keep her expression bland despite the shock that soared through her during the fleeting contact.

Gavan shook her hand firmly before releasing her so abruptly she was insulted. It was one thing for the man to be indifferent, and obviously he was unimpressed by her, but rudeness was not necessary. She may have spent two nights in a prison cell, but that did not declare her as guilty or, Lord help her, infectious.

As she debated what she would say to express her displeasure, something witty that would put him in check, she realized that he had already made haste to separate them by returning to *his* wall. He treated it like an invisible barrier, a protective one, and once again he leaned casually against it, the expression on his face nothing less than disillusionment. She gave him her profile, suddenly self-conscious and stared down the hall as she muttered, "I don't rub off."

He leaned forward, knitting his brows in confusion. "What was that?"

"Henry," she said quickly, thankful that he had not heard her childish and far from witty comment.

Gavan looked down the hall and saw no one. His frowned deepened. "Henry?"

"Yes, he informed me that you would be calling. On Monday, that is?" she added. She glanced at him, adding, "We were speaking of you."

"Really?" he said slowly and, to her sensitive ears, doubtfully. "Is Henry in his office then?"

"No," she said, imitating his tone. "He actually stepped away."

"Ah, I see." Gavan's tone indicated he knew something she didn't. She bristled with annoyance. "Were you, uh, stepping away as well?" It was the wrong question, the wrong emphasis, and he knew it immediately.

Her eyes narrowed, her nostrils flared slightly, and she retorted, "Not quite. I was escaping."

Gavan was tempted to believe her, but the fire in her eyes warned him that she was daring him to challenge her further. He wouldn't. Not when it could very well affect his ability to get to Mikel Wilkins and to find out for himself what her role was in the Wilkins scandal. Hindsight was a killer and he now wished he had gone to visit Mikel first, rather than Elizabeth. She had baffled him from the moment he saw her. He could have kicked himself. First he had gawked at her like a schoolboy and now he was grilling her, and it was no way to get her to warm to him.

"I realize the question was inappropriate—"

"I concur," Elizabeth agreed with cool reserve.

"But I . . . it was inappropriate," he repeated. His words faded off.

He was confounded. Now how was he to fix the breach he created? It was a new situation for him and he was failing miserably in making her acquaintance. For several moments, Gavan fumbled through the best way to ask if she was a prisoner or free. And if she was free, would she be willing to have lunch or dinner with him? He would accept anything, but he did not want her to kick him to the curb. He had behaved poorly and was just about to apologize when Henry Miles came rushing down the hall.

Gavan exhaled a sigh of relief. Elizabeth heard him and narrowed her eyes in growing irritation.

He ran his hand over his head, scratching in bafflement. He was never as clumsy with a woman as he was with Elizabeth Wilkins. Between his fumbling and her current censure, he anticipated she would require a lot of coaxing to get an interview out of her, or anything else. Then he felt a surge of anticipation that he refused to recognize as anything more than adrenaline at the thought of changing her mind. He grinned, buoyed at the prospect.

Perhaps all was not lost.

CHAPTER 3

"Elizabeth!" Henry called when he spotted her outside his office.

"Great," Gavan said, his voice laden with a relief that Elizabeth found suspect.

She eyed the older man's approach and with her chin raised proudly, thought she could not agree more with Gavan's sentiment. Gavan T. Ward was handsome in the extreme with his tall, bronzed good looks, but beyond that, she was not impressed. Henry's timing was perfect. It would put an end to what was fast becoming a collision of wits.

"Henry." She smiled, masking her distress with genuine appreciation that he had returned.

Henry raised both of his black eyebrows and peered at his office door in silent inquiry.

"I only stepped out to test the waters," she explained with a laugh at his comical attempt to be subtle.

"Fair enough," Henry said with a nod. He was slightly out of breath from his exertion, having quickened his pace the moment he recognized Elizabeth and Gavan waiting outside his office. Catching his breath more fully, he inquired, "I take it you've met Gavan?"

"I sure have," Elizabeth confirmed with a mocking drawl that only Gavan picked up. He wasn't offended, his natural optimism having returned with Henry's presence. Besides, he could understand Elizabeth's disapproval, having insulted the woman when a blind man could have seen that she was free.

"You're looking good, Henry," Gavan said.

Henry was short, barely five eight, but his shortness was more pronounced beside Gavan, who fervently shook his hand. With her not being a woman of average height herself at five nine, Elizabeth had to admit that Gavan's height did make a commanding figure. She monitored their amicable greeting, not missing how Henry couldn't seem to wipe a pleased grin off his face. It was a firm indication that he admired and respected the younger man. Elizabeth was unconvinced that Henry's esteem for the author was so deserving.

"Thank you, Gavan," Henry said warmly. "Didn't expect you today. How did you know Elizabeth was released?" he asked, leading them into his office. His back to them, he didn't see Gavan's slight frown at his question or witness Elizabeth's hasty retreat to the chair she had occupied earlier.

Gavan lingered near the door. Sensing Elizabeth's discomfort, he decided to be prudent and keep his distance until she was less disagreeable toward him. Besides, he was unnerved by her and needed time to regain his composure. Their eyes met and he could tell her censure had not lessened. He sighed. It seemed he was going to be standing through the entire meeting.

"Have you seen Tyke yet?" Henry asked.

"No," Gavan answered, grateful for the distraction. "He doesn't know I'm here yet. My brother and I are supposed to meet him for drinks later."

"Ah, I see," Henry responded absently as he fumbled

through a stack of forms he had gathered for Elizabeth's release. He looked up and frowned at Gavan when he noticed the younger man was still standing. He pointed to the only other seat in his office. It was appallingly near Elizabeth, and Gavan held a groan in check when Henry said with the impatience of one self-absorbed and heedless of the strain surrounding him, "Have a seat, man, no need to stand there like a statue."

Gavan was left with little choice, knowing a refusal would only stir Henry to badger him until he got what he wanted. He accepted the offered seat. He chanced a glance at Elizabeth and was not surprised that she was staring steadfastly at the papers on Henry's desk.

Elizabeth forced herself to breathe evenly, to ignore the impulse to hold her breath and not to stiffen when Gavan sat next to her.

"That's better," Henry continued once Gavan was seated. "Where were we?" he asked, considering first Gavan and then Elizabeth.

"You were inquiring about Tyke," Gavan offered.

"But you're here to see Elizabeth, correct?" Henry probed, neatly positioning the papers on his desk.

"That's correct," Gavan said and then, smiling, he faced Elizabeth. "I came here to meet you, Ms. Elizabeth Wilkins."

Elizabeth felt his eyes upon her and only intended to steal a peek at him. Not anticipating the most appealing smile on a male she had ever seen, she paused and stared a near ten seconds at his mouth before she looked upward. His eyes were a light brown, hazel, she concluded absently, and they twinkled knowingly. The tip of her tongue dabbed her suddenly dry lips. How aware was he of his far too sensual mouth? Likely he was very much aware.

"Did you?" she managed to ask.

"I most certainly did, as I mentioned earlier. But," he added smoothly, "first I must apologize for my unannounced visit."

"No problem," Henry said easily, completely unaware of the discord between the man and woman sitting across from him. "You weren't expected any more than I was, was he, Elizabeth?"

Elizabeth tried not to appear vexed. "No, Henry, neither you nor Mr. Ward were expected today."

"Gavan," Gavan corrected quickly.

"Excuse me?" Elizabeth asked.

"Please, call me Gavan. I insist," he added with another charming smile.

Despite her flustered response to the impossible author, Elizabeth managed a nonchalant shrug and said, "Then Gavan it is."

"Good, good. I see you two are off to a good start. It's been a good day," Henry chimed in, finally having settled his papers. "Elizabeth was released today," he added proudly.

"So I gathered," Gavan responded. He wouldn't remind Henry that he had already pointed out that fact.

"She's been exonerated of all charges, mind you," Henry said sternly, leaning back in his chair and crossing his arms firmly over his chest. "That means that no evidence or support of any kind could determine her guilt or participation, direct or indirectly, with Mikel's scheming. Got that, Gavan?"

Gavan laughed, undaunted by the old man's protection of his client. "Got it," he answered. "I would like to add that I by no means am attempting to write a book defaming Ms. Wilkins," he told Henry. His expression carefully bland, he continued speaking directly to Elizabeth. "I thought we could talk, discuss the case, or the circumstances rather. It's the state of mind of Mikel

Wilkins that I think will make an interesting story, not the ordeal you went through. I don't want to do that to you."

Ooh, he could be convincing. Her cheeks grew warm beneath his perusal and she chastised herself for being so aware of his every look. She would not be duped so easily, she resolved, and as a result, responded far more tartly than she had intended. "Sure you don't."

"I absolutely don't," he agreed, choosing to ignore the sarcasm.

"And how do you plan to get in Mikel's head? He'll never let you interview him," Elizabeth pointed out.

"I'll worry about that." Gavan smiled. He leaned into her and asked softly, "Does this conversation mean you have forgiven me?"

"For the incident earlier?" she asked flippantly. "I hadn't even thought of it. It was no big deal." She shrugged. She would never admit the humiliation she had felt by his assumption that she was attempting some foolhardy escape. It was killing her to be in the position she was in to begin with. She didn't want to deal with the reality that he was yet another person who assumed her guilt so easily.

"What incident?" Henry asked, peering at them over the rim of his eyeglasses, at last discerning the tension surrounding them.

Gavan settled back in the narrow chair, his tall physique uncomfortably cramped, but he ignored the discomfort as he explained to Henry, "I made the mistake of questioning Ms. Wilkins's intent before you arrived."

"Yeah? Thought she was escaping, did you?" Henry joked, not really expecting Gavan to admit that it was actually the situation. He laughed outright when Gavan nodded regretfully.

"Something like that."

"And I would have made it, too," Elizabeth said with dry humor.

Gavan cut his eyes at her, expecting defiance, and was floored by her smile; tempered, a little mocking, but it was a smile nevertheless. He was reassured. She was actually making light of their unfortunate clash. There was a chance she wouldn't kick him to the curb after all.

"You're as innocent as a newborn babe, Elizabeth. Anyone could see that. I'm just glad you didn't have to stay another moment behind bars," Henry continued in all seriousness.

"Oh, let's not discuss that now. I might embarrass us all and cry." Elizabeth laughed, although she was sincere in her warning. She was not sure how much longer she could control the rampant emotions bombarding her senses. And her bizarre encounter with Gavan had increased the mayhem trying to burst forth.

"Then let's not," Henry agreed. "Let's get you signed and then you and Gavan can be on your way."

"Gavan?" Elizabeth gasped. She wasn't leaving with Gavan. Where in the world had Henry gotten that notion?

"You agreed to talk with him," Henry said, surprised by her outburst.

"No, I did not," she stated pointedly. "I simply dismissed an embarrassing moment we shared. That's it."

Gavan was instantly deflated. She *had* kicked him to the curb.

"What would it take for you to agree?" Gavan asked, unwilling to accept defeat. It could be his only chance to convince her to allow him an interview. Otherwise, he fully expected that he would have to make a bunch of inquiries and calls to change her mind and even then there was no guarantee that she would accept his offer. It was an intolerable situation. He had no idea why, but he could not allow Elizabeth Wilkins to dismiss him. Not yet.

"I don't know, Mr. Ward," Elizabeth answered, first startled by his desperate question and then thoughtful. After a brief pause, she added, "Although, I guess you could agree to sign an affidavit stating that you will not . . . what was that term you used earlier, Henry?" Elizabeth deferred to her attorney for assistance.

"Uh, vilify?" Henry guessed.

"Yes, that. I don't want you to vilify my name," she said to Gavan.

"That's an incredibly easy request as I have no intention of doing so. What else?" Gavan asked.

"I don't know," Elizabeth admitted. "I haven't decided yet. I need to think about it, Mr. Ward."

"Gavan."

"Gavan," she acquiesced. "You must understand that I'm in a state of shock, happy, but shock that I'm going home. Frankly, right now, that's all I can think about."

"Fair enough," Gavan relented. He tried another angle. "Then may I call on you?"

"Call on me?" she repeated, clearly confused.

"Tomorrow or Monday, if tomorrow is too soon. But tomorrow is what I'm hoping for. We could have brunch," he suggested with enthusiasm.

"I'll have to think about it," she repeated.

"Lunch?" Gavan asked for clarification. His tone was teasing, but somehow an underlining desperation caught her attention.

"The interview," she corrected, even as her own curiosity grew with his doggedness. He didn't actually need her to write about Mikel, so why the desperation?

Gavan finally accepted defeat. He rose from the miserable chair, reached across the desk, and shook Henry's hand again. "Well, Henry, I tried," he said pleasantly, but she could detect his disappointment. "Warn Elizabeth that I don't give up easily, will you?" he added brightly.

Her first impression of him was sorely lacking. He should have expected nothing less than her refusal to do an interview and he doubted if he would have another opportunity, at least in person, to convince her to speak with him. He dismissed the thought, literally shaking his head to clear it just as Henry was asking him to dinner the following weekend.

"Ah, that's too bad. I was hoping you and Elizabeth could both come," Henry added.

"What . . . Oh, I wasn't saying no to dinner, Henry," Gavan explained quickly.

"Then you can make it?" Henry asked hopefully.

"I'm certain I can," he said, trying not to appear anxious. To say he was positive would have been more accurate, especially if Elizabeth would be there.

"I don't know, Henry. I have so much to do," Elizabeth said. She didn't want to have dinner with Henry and his family. She didn't know them and she certainly didn't want to be forced into the same room with Gavan while he was trying to get an interview, and nothing more than that, she thought, a bit vexed.

"But it's a week from now, Elizabeth, and on a Sunday. And Sonya is going to be there," he pushed.

"Sonya will be there?" Elizabeth repeated in delight.

"Certainly, she's been a regular for dinner at our house for years."

"I had no idea," Elizabeth admitted. She did not know as much about her longtime assistant as she thought. Sonya and Elizabeth had dined together many an evening and not once, until Elizabeth was wrongfully imprisoned, had Sonya ever mentioned the Miles family. And now Henry was telling her that Sonya Brown was a regular dinner guest. How obtuse could she be to know so little about a woman whom she adored?

"I'm sure you have an idea that she's an excellent cook?" Henry smiled, sensing Elizabeth giving in. "And fried turkey is on the menu. Between Sonya and my wife, Terri, you don't want to miss out. Not to brag, but Terri has to be the best cook in the city. Tell her, Gavan."

"She is that," Gavan confirmed, grinning at Henry's pride over his wife's cooking. He had dinner at the Mileses' on occasion and although Terri's cooking was nothing to complain about, he doubted if she was in the running for the best in the city. But if that was what it would take to get Elizabeth Wilkins to agree to have dinner with the Mileses, Gavan would say Terri Miles's cooking was worthy of an award.

"Henry," Elizabeth began, with as much patience as she could gather. She did not want to hurt the elder man's feelings and she certainly had no plans for next Sunday, which at the moment was as far away as next year, but she would not be pressured into answering him while Gavan stood expectantly over her and was causing havoc on her sanity. "Can I sleep on it? I would love to just sign those papers and go home," she declared.

"Naturally," Henry relented. "I fully understand. Let's get you released. Gavan," he added, suddenly all business, and Gavan knew what was next. "Will you please excuse us?"

"Of course," Gavan said, then took a step toward Elizabeth. He offered his hand, and once she shook it, he smiled, saying, "It was a pleasure meeting you, Elizabeth. I hope you will consider my request and I hope to see you at Henry's next weekend. But," he added with emphasis, "what I'm really hoping is to see you as early as tomorrow."

"I'll think about it," was all she could promise. Her

hand was fairly burning in his and she wanted the distraction gone.

"Fair enough." He nodded. Before departing from the office, he added, "By the way, congratulations on your release."

"Now, about those papers," Gavan heard Henry say as he closed the door.

Gavan paused thoughtfully. He was tempted to wait around, to offer Elizabeth a ride home, but he suspected she would not only reject him flat out at that point but would accuse him of stalking her. He grimaced at that distasteful idea and briskly headed toward the exit. He would simply have to bide his time and wear her resistance down with persistence and charm.

CHAPTER 4

Elizabeth was alone at last.

After receiving her few belongings, which consisted of a silk blouse, black slacks, a pair of Prada sandals, and a Seiko watch, she insisted on changing. Feeling more herself and more than happy to return the prison-issued wardrobe, Elizabeth was released. Henry escorted her from the building and insisted on driving her home. She had been anxious to escape the proximity of the courthouse and it had taken little encouragement on his part for her to accept.

She would never forget how, having expressed her desire to get home as quickly as possible, Henry had all but crawled down the road. Initially she had experienced annoyance and then impatience and finally resignation. It was Saturday and Henry was in no hurry. His pace was so decelerated she actually nodded off to sleep twice. When they finally arrived at her house, Henry had redeemed himself by proving very understanding when she kindly voiced her need to be alone. He had smiled with compassion and left without delay, promising to call before the end of the week.

Handling a glass of red wine—she had consumed a

full glass before leaving her kitchen—Elizabeth sat on the throw carpet in front of her fireplace. It was warm and midsummer, so the fire was not lit, but it was her favorite spot in the house. She crossed one leg over the other, rolled her head in slow circular motions to relax the tension in her neck, and then took another sip of wine, enjoying the warmth that had long since begun flowing through her veins. Gingerly she leaned her head against one of the full, white armchairs that decorated her seating area, closed her eyes, and finally allowed her thoughts to drift.

She knew she would never feel the same about her house after having been informed that it was there that Liberty Sutton had been held captive by her cousin. Once Henry was gone and she was truly alone, her first objective had been to inspect her house, which she'd lived in for eight years. And in all that time, she had taken it for granted, never giving the house the proper acknowledgement it deserved. Perhaps, she thought sadly, it was because of how she had gained the house. Elizabeth couldn't help wondering what her grandmother had been thinking to purchase such a huge house just for her granddaughter. It was more suited for a family of four than a single woman living alone. For the first time, Elizabeth wondered if it had been a subtle message that her grandmother expected her to marry and have children.

The house had five bedrooms, three that had never been used and were more like showrooms than livable spaces in both design and comfort. The kitchen was huge, with an island that served as a center focal point and seated six, a bar whose sole purpose was decoration, and a stove to rival any restaurant's even though she was a very poor cook. The house also had a breakfast nook that led out to a sunroom and farther to an unfurnished patio and a huge yard that Elizabeth could not recall having actually ever explored.

After checking the house, she had chosen the coziness of the fireplace because of its relaxing environment. Before the harrowing trouble with Mikel, she had recently discovered scented firewood. She inhaled deeply of the cinnamon fragrance, thinking that if the house weren't so large, the fragrance could more easily have filtered throughout each room and into the basement.

Elizabeth groaned, recalling that was exactly where Liberty had been held. And it was ultimately the reason Elizabeth would have to relocate. She would put the house up for sale, find something smaller and less conspicuous. Her grandmother would simply have to understand. The house was now tainted, which was ironic as she had just come to appreciate its warm design.

Elizabeth didn't want to dwell on it. She sighed, enjoyed another taste of wine, and curbed the impulse to call her grandmother. She didn't want to do that yet as she was in no mood for her grandmother's daunting temperament. It was getting late, too, and even if it wasn't, her grandmother was bound to have a ton of questions, definitely some scolding, and certainly no sympathy.

She stared at the logs in the fireplace, feeling her eyelids grow heavy. She set her glass on the table stand and then lay back on the rug and began following the ceiling pattern.

Her thoughts trailed away, inevitably falling on Gavan T. Ward and the discomfort surrounding their introduction. She mulled over the events that led up to her meeting the author. From the moment Mikel forced her to help him embezzle the Wilkins-Zonnick funds, to the hysteria she had felt at nearly being shot during Mikel's attempted getaway, right up to the moment she came forward and admitted her part, albeit forced, in the whole sordid affair between Mikel and Liberty Sutton, her life had been a nightmare. She recalled the dismay, no, the devastation she had felt when the police informed her that she was being detained and then the bigger, but pleasant shock at being released three days later. And to confound her further, the very man she had refused to see was not only waiting for her outside Henry's office but had witnessed her most vulnerable moment. To make matters even worse, he was not only the most attractive man she had ever met but she had never met a man more charismatic.

She squeezed her eyes shut, stifling the embarrassment that the moment had created, and refused to allow any fascination with the author to test her resolve to keep the traumatic episode involving Mikel Wilkins private. The problem was, from the moment Gavan had left Henry's office, she could not completely dismiss him from her thoughts. He was always there, lurking in her subconscious, even as she tried to concentrate solely on Henry. She laughed lightly, concentrating on Henry and how he had been excruciatingly precise in the final processing of her release.

"Now, about those papers," he had said after Gavan's departure. He stood, took the vacant seat beside her, and scooted it closer to her chair, then adjusted the papers on the desk so that they both could look at them. After checking the tip of his pen, he handed it to Elizabeth.

"Sign here," he said. "And here." She signed her signature swift and sure. "And here," he finished. When she was done, he carefully placed the pen in the pen holder on his desk, picked up the papers, and taking distinct small steps went to the copier machine to photocopy a second set of papers for Elizabeth. To Elizabeth's hypersensitive ears, considering her eagerness to leave, the machine whimpered like a sick puppy with each sheet it spat out. But, with teeth gritted in firm resolve to be patient, she had silently waited out the ordeal. Copies made, he placed the papers inside a folder and turned to Elizabeth. She was on the edge of her seat, her barely contained agitation pinching her face.

"Ms. Elizabeth Wilkins, it's my great pleasure to inform you that you are officially released and free to go." He had been dramatic, at least for him, and offered his hand to her with all the pomp of an Oscar award winner. Impulsively, Elizabeth ignored the gesture. She swept to her feet and flung herself into his arms, giving him an affectionate hug. And even at that moment, and quite anomalously, the path of her thoughts had strayed to Gavan.

He'd invaded—or rather crashed—into her concentration, unbalancing her generally exceedingly controlled feelings. There had even been an instant when, in suppressed panic—an emotion alien to her prior to the sordid affair with Mikel—it had dawned on her that Gavan had no means to reach her. And he certainly hadn't given her his business card, e-mail, phone number, or any forwarding information. True, she had stated her disinterest in allowing him to interview her. But still she wondered if he was aware that they had not exchanged contact information.

Elizabeth sat up, reached for her wine, and pursed her lips thoughtfully. She didn't want to think about Gavan or his book and she especially didn't want to think about his charming smile and handsome face. But she could not stop images of him, particularly her first perusal, from racing through her head.

She gave in to the visions. What else could she do? She guessed that he was at least six four or five because he towered over her and she was no average-height woman. His physique was appealing, too. His muscular arms and trim torso were complemented by a white, short-sleeve shirt that was thoroughly starched and black slacks neatly finished with a black unassuming belt. He wore no watch but he sported a number of other gadgets from a high-tech earpiece trailing to a cellular phone clasped on his belt, to the Palm Pilot or Blackberry he tucked into his back pocket before he approached her. There was another gadget inserted in his shirt pocket that she suspected was an iPod or some other similar device and she wondered when he had time to actually write with so many gadgets to manage.

His hair, smartly cut close to his head, was of a fine, wavy grain that she guessed would prove unruly if he allowed it to grow out. His coloring was almost bronzed and accentuated his heavy eyelashes that shielded the most magnetic hazel eyes she had ever seen. He was exotic, from his coloring to his finely chiseled jawline, his full mouth, and his captivating eyes.

Then their eyes had locked and she realized that she had been appallingly brazen in her ogling of him. Even now she was burning with shame, having no doubt that while she had been assessing him, he had examined her in unveiled curiosity.

A grimace crossed her face. She could only imagine what he must have thought in those brief moments. Her clothing had been prison standard and a sadly ragged uniform. With her face devoid of makeup and her hair pulled into a spinsterish ponytail, she didn't blame him for ignoring her beyond the opportunity she presented to meet Mikel.

She refused to dwell on the memory. It only traumatized her more. She forced Gavan from her thoughts, declaring aloud that she had more important things to deal with, such as deciding whether or not to call her grandmother. Henry did mention that Anne would soon be released from the hospital and Elizabeth hadn't spoken to her grandmother since the incident with Mikel. She would have to call her grandmother soon and should have hours ago. And then there was Sonya to consider.

She sighed. Exhaustion was settling in, as was the wine, and she didn't want to actually fall asleep on the floor, carpeted or not. Finding her resolve, Elizabeth stood and made her way into the kitchen. She emptied the remains of her wine in the sink. She was starting to feel its lethargic effects and didn't dare have more.

Aware that she should accept the fact that she was tired rather than force a phone call to Sonya or her grandmother, she reached for the telephone anyway. It rang with a blaring screech that caused her to immediately snatch her hand away and jump back, startled by the unexpected ring. Then she burst into laughter, the surprise and the effects of the wine causing her to giggle at the ridiculousness of her reaction. It was just a phone, for crying out loud.

Attempting to control her mirth, she answered the line before the caller could hang up.

"Elizabeth here," she said with a chuckle heard clear through the receiver.

"What's so funny?" a familiar feminine voice demanded.

"Oh, hi, Shannon," Elizabeth answered. Her laughter subsided and with it, her energy. She leaned against the bar and momentarily closed her eyes. Man, she was tired, she thought, sobering.

"'Oh, hi, Shannon'? That's it? I was worried about you all day! I just got off the phone with Sonya. *She* at least thought to call me. Of course it was early this morning, an afterthought, mind you—"

"Shannon," Elizabeth interrupted. "I'm tired, girl. Can we talk later?"

"No. I was told you were locked up one moment, and then the next thing I hear you're released, and all in one day."

"Not quite," Elizabeth drawled.

"Well, I'm coming over." Shannon was determined. So was Elizabeth. "You are not coming over."

"Oh, come on, Elizabeth. I just found out what happened to you. You should sue, by the way, but thank God those idiots recognized your innocence. I knew Mikel was a nut, but how could he have behaved so stupidly?" Shannon ranted.

"My exact sentiments," Elizabeth said dryly. "But not today, Shannon. I'm tired beyond belief and only want to revel in the reality that I'm home." Elizabeth left the kitchen and slowly walked up the stairway toward her bedroom.

"Well, yeah, I guess, but I need to see you," Shannon said stubbornly.

"Not today, you don't," Elizabeth retorted. "I just got in. I'm tired and I'll see you Monday." Elizabeth was firm.

"Monday?" Shannon was disappointed. She released an exaggerated sigh into the phone and then relented. "What's wrong with tomorrow?"

"I'll be resting."

"Elizabeth! Come on—"

Elizabeth refused to bend. "Monday, Shannon."

"Fine. Are you going to work?"

"I see no reason why I shouldn't," Elizabeth responded.

"Only you would say that. I would need a month to get over getting locked up."

Elizabeth cringed at Shannon's ease in referring to her imprisonment but was silent.

"Oh, all right. I'll see you Monday. But I mean it, Elizabeth, don't ditch me," Shannon insisted.

Elizabeth smiled affectionately, unable to stay annoyed

with her friend. She looked at the telephone, hit the Off button, and dropped it on the bed. A moment later, fully clothed and still on the edge of the bed, she fell asleep, a fleeting image of Gavan her last thought.

CHAPTER 5

From the moment Gavan met Elizabeth Wilkins everything had gone awry.

He had gotten in his car and was starting the engine when he swore aloud. In that moment, it dawned on him that he had failed to take measures to ensure future contact between himself and Elizabeth.

He grunted in disgust. He couldn't believe what was happening to him. That woman had thoroughly unsettled him. And now he was behaving like a novice. He would simply have to go back. He didn't like how inept it would make him appear, but it could not be helped. Decision made, he briskly returned to Henry's office. Upon reaching the office, Gavan tried to dispel the nagging suspicion that they were gone and rapped firmly on the door. There was no answer. He knocked louder. When no response came, ignoring the impropriety of his actions, he tried the door handle. It was locked. And judging from the silence within, he accepted that they were gone.

He peered down the halls of the courthouse. The building was practically empty and neither Henry nor Elizabeth was one of the few occupants in sight. He had missed them. Elizabeth had been unpretentious in her readiness to depart. He couldn't blame her for wanting to flee, he just wished he had been more on his game and less absorbed by her astonishingly pretty face. He exhaled a defeated sigh and headed back to his car.

For several minutes he simply sat behind the steering wheel, staring distractedly at the pedestrians crossing the street as he digested the situation. He could go back inside and look around. They could have gone elsewhere to finalize her release papers. But he rejected the notion. He had already gone inside. Once was enough.

He could wait until Monday, call Henry, and get Elizabeth's information then. He pursed his lips, instantly rejecting the thought. Although it was only a two-day delay, it worried him. She had not been responsive to him. Experience had taught him that allowing too much time to pass before confirming an interview could result in the negative. And Elizabeth Wilkins was a key interview. He couldn't allow her to simply walk away, not without some kind of an effort to make contact. It would have to be today or at the very latest, first thing in the morning. But he needed a plan of action. One that would aid him in reaching Elizabeth without hinting of desperation on his part.

Deciding to give Henry another try, he opened his cell phone and scrolled to Henry's office number. The call went directly to voice mail. He tried Tyke, first on his cellular phone and then on his home line. Neither proved fruitful.

Gavan was annoyed. What good was it to have a cellular phone if the person never answered it?

Impulsively he drove to Henry's house. His condo was not that far from the Miles residence and even if Tyke wasn't at his parents' home, Gavan doubted that he would have long to wait for Henry, if Henry wasn't already home. Either way, he was willing to wait in his car if he had to.

Henry actually grinned when he saw Gavan sometime later. He was fully aware that the younger man had been patently dismissed by Elizabeth and had been flustered by it.

Gavan had waited less than an hour for Henry, which was fortunate. He had been left to his own devices but did not have to wait in his car. Terri, Henry's wife, had chastised Gavan for coming over without calling first, a small matter he hadn't thought of. He was vastly aware that he had intruded when Terri, in a no-nonsense mien that accompanied the confidence that came with aging, informed him that she was busy and refused to play hostess. She expected him to entertain himself until either Tyke, who wasn't actually expected, or Henry got in. It made no difference to her so long as he didn't step on her toes while she cleaned and prepped for dinner. In a gesture Gavan took as sympathy after her initial tirade, Terri offered to allow him to watch the basketball game in the basement until her husband arrived. Gavan readily agreed.

Henry, directed by Terri, went to the basement. Gavan scarcely exchanged a greeting before he explained, "I know you've never worked with me, Henry, but let me assure you I am usually more professional than I've been today. I didn't actually intend to meet Elizabeth when I went to the courthouse. I only thought I was going to get her information, Mikel's, the grandmother's, et cetera, but running into her threw me off, you understand."

"I understand." Henry smiled.

"Yeah, well, Elizabeth's unexpected release distracted me and, like I said, I was distracted and—"

"You were distracted," Henry agreed, his smile widening.

"Uh, yeah. I didn't get her number. Hell, I didn't give

her mine either. I was hoping you could give me her information so that we can set up a meeting," Gavan finally managed. Henry was a far more intimidating figure than Gavan had realized. It wasn't by far their first meeting, but never before had he noticed how keen and direct Henry's gaze could be. What he saw made him uncomfortably aware of how important it was to him to reach Elizabeth. He wondered what Henry was thinking and was reassured when Henry answered kindly:

"I have no problem with that."

"Great," Gavan said, his enthusiasm rising by degrees.

Henry sat down in the brown leather Lazy Boy chair that Gavan had vacated upon his entry. "However, son, I can't just give out phone numbers. Client privacy and all."

Gavan hesitated, not having expected that answer, then asked ever so smoothly, "Could you call her?"

"Of course I can call her." Henry shrugged.

Gavan first thought Henry was being facetious, but the older man proceeded to ignore him and began flipping through the ESPN channels with his remote control. Gavan was forced to inquire further. "Yes, sir. I know you can call her, but I meant would you call her for me? If you could get her permission, that would be helpful."

"Can't wait until dinner next week?" Henry asked rather dismissively. He was leaning forward reading the basketball games time and channel list.

Gavan suppressed his growing exasperation. "No, sir. Next week is not a guarantee. Besides, I would like to get a draft of *The Wilkins Affair* started. I was hoping I could talk to Elizabeth right away." Gavan kept his expression bland. Even to his own ears, it was a poor excuse. In that moment he accepted that it was more about not losing a chance to see Elizabeth again than getting an interview for his book. With an effort, he managed to remain stoic beneath the knowing glance Henry shot him and felt a surge of annoyance at the nagging inkling that Henry Miles had deliberately made him grovel for Elizabeth's number.

Henry took pity on him and said, "That's fair. Hand me the phone, will you?" He pointed to a cordless phone haphazardly left on the seat of the sofa. Gavan hastily got it. A moment later, Henry was on the line with Elizabeth, his eyes on Gavan as he spoke.

"Well?" Gavan asked after Henry hung up the phone, his disappointment well hidden.

"Sorry, son. She wasn't in," Henry stated sympathetically. "As you heard, I left her a message."

Gavan was torn. He could wait for Elizabeth to return the call or go home and wait for Henry to call him. The decision was made for him.

"I'll call you the moment I hear from her," Henry promised.

Dissatisfied with the results of his efforts yet having no other recourse, Gavan went home. Half an hour later he tossed his house keys on the dining table, went into the living room, and hit the Playback button on the answering machine. As the messages played, he headed for the kitchen and took a Pepsi from the refrigerator. Snapping it open, he sat on a bar stool at the kitchen counter that also served as a separator for his dining room. He gulped down half the Pepsi while listening with amusement to three consecutive messages from his mother and another from his brother inviting him out to the sports bar. And then Henry's voice filled the room and Gavan rose sharply, coming alert. He set the Pepsi can on the counter and walked over to the answering machine, listening intently.

He paused at the machine before going to his second bedroom, which served as his office, and grabbed a pen. As an afterthought, he took a sheet of paper and went back to the living room, swiftly writing as Henry read off Elizabeth's home and work phone numbers. When he was done, a wide grin hovered on Gavan's face, and he read over the phone numbers vaguely aware that Henry was rambling on about Sunday dinner.

Absently Gavan tapped the pen against his chin, his mind racing. Elizabeth had not done the office-number-only routine. She had actually given him her home number. Henry's message ended and Gavan reached over to end the recall. His hand paused in midair. Elizabeth had left him a message too.

"Hi, Gavan, this is Elizabeth Wilkins. We met earlier today." She paused. An uncomfortable small laugh was audible before she continued. "Henry asked that I call you. He said you wanted to know the best time to call me. Obviously now is not a good time. Actually, I can't really say at the moment when will be. But I'm rambling." She sighed into the phone. "Anyway, I am usually in the office about eight a.m. and generally leave about four p.m. I guess it's fair to say before noon on Tuesday is the best time to reach me. Well, okay, thanks and have a good evening."

Gavan's smile faded. He was uncertain how to decipher her message. Was it a subtle way of letting him know she was making a courtesy call and nothing more was possible? It was no coincidence that she specifically mentioned Tuesday while she was at work and likely inaccessible as the best time to call her. Was she even aware that Henry had provided her house number? Nonsense. Henry was by the book. Elizabeth would have to know.

Well, he thought resolutely, he was going to use the number despite her message. She didn't say he couldn't. And one thing was certain, she had been too close to declining any form of communication for him to allow any unnecessary delays between their next conversation. At least now she was willing to be civil. He grimaced at the expression. He wasn't overly concerned. He had successfully dealt with more obstinate people than her and gotten his interview. Nevertheless, there was no way he was going to wait until Tuesday to call her but, relenting somewhat, he would bide his time until Sunday.

Hours later, baffled at how difficult it was to stick to his resolve, Gavan became thoughtful. When was the last time he had been so preoccupied, so utterly taken by a woman? Never, he realized.

It was a revelation.

One Gavan could not fathom. So what if she was incredibly attractive? So what if she had floored him with her breathtaking stance outside Henry's office and startled his senses? He had dated plenty of attractive women and frankly, none of them had been incarcerated or accused of a crime. And here he was, fascinated by a woman who could have been accused of being a major corroborator in a conniving and deceitful scheme. Henry may have declared her exoneration, but she could turn out to be every bit the conspirator. Even as he thought it, he rejected it, but then only time would tell.

Thinking of the time, Gavan glanced at the clock. It wasn't even six o'clock yet. It was her first evening home and he was acting like a youth unable to contain himself. He considered accepting Tyke's and his brother's invitation and even started to call them but changed his mind in mid-dial. He was too tired to go out and his fascination with Elizabeth Wilkins did not alter his exhaustion. In fact, it made it more pronounced.

After a week in New York, which was always grueling in itself, and having avoided his mother's persistent calls, a warning pattern that always raised his guard, he only wanted to relax and get back into his groove, one that was sidetracked from the moment he looked into Tyke's claim that the Wilkins fraud story would be a good addition to his family series.

He distracted himself by making notations examining the persons involved in the Wilkins case. Hours later, having written several draft summations off the vague information he had on the Wilkins encounter, he quit and went to bed, at last shelving all thoughts of Elizabeth Wilkins.

He rose before six a.m., surprisingly refreshed and no less enamored, his first thought to call Elizabeth. He heaved a sigh and shook his head in misery. What had gotten into him?

"I'll make the call and get it out of my system," he muttered as he prepped his coffeemaker. But he couldn't very well call her at six o'clock in the morning. He would look like an idiot. Frankly, he wasn't even sure why he was up so early. He should have gone out last night instead of ignoring Tyke's and Lance's invitation. His eyes narrowed and he pinched his lips, not sure whom he was more cross with, himself for not controlling the direction of his thoughts or Elizabeth for invading them.

"I'll give her until noon," he grumbled. And then he would make the blasted call and that would be that. He managed to get past 10:00 a.m. before dialing Elizabeth's number. No answer came and he was disappointed to get her answering machine. Concealing his letdown behind a cheerful tone, he left his message.

"Good morning, Elizabeth. This is Gavan calling. I was pleased that you agreed to meet with me. I'm sorry I missed your call yesterday. I thought we could get together today, brunch or dinner if you prefer, to get dialogue started. It will be preparatory of course. Give me a call back. Here's my number if you don't have it."

He repeated his home number, cellular number, and

added his e-mail for good measure. When he was done, he set the receiver down and stared at the telephone. There was nothing he could do now but wait.

Hours later he was awakened to the shrill ringing of the phone. He fumbled for the phone, nearly falling off the sofa, where he had dozed off, and fighting a yawn, gave a muffled "Hello?"

"Oh, I'm sorry. Were you sleeping?" a feminine voice said in distress at having disturbed him. He sat up, suddenly alert, and rubbed his eyes.

"No. Yeah, I was sleep but I'm glad you woke me," Gavan said smoothly.

"Uh, yes, well, this is Elizabeth Wilkins. You called." Elizabeth was hesitant.

Gavan sensed it and quickly stated in a clear voice, "Sure did. Thanks for calling back. I apologize for falling asleep. . . ."

Elizabeth laughed, asking, "Why in the world are you apologizing for that?"

Gavan chuckled. "I honestly don't know," he admitted. He stood up and paced the living room. "I wasn't tired, I just fell asleep. I got up way too early this morning."

"How funny is that? So did I . . . it must have been six-thirty. Actually, that's why I missed your call."

"What?" Gavan asked, confused.

"I was up so early I decided to run a few errands. I was actually at the Home Depot before I realized it was Sunday and after being, uh, detained, time has gotten away from me."

Her discomfort was unmistakable. How many times had he awakened after being on the road and forgotten what day it was? He could only imagine how time would have crawled for her over the three days she was held, and suddenly being released would only have disoriented her more. "I understand," he said, all gentleness now. He sat down, and a long silence filled the air before Elizabeth prompted awkwardly, "Well, I got your message. I can't do brunch. . . ."

"Yeah, it's a little late for that," Gavan agreed, glancing at the clock.

"Yes . . . well, I've given some thought to your book and everything. I can't say that I'm agreeing to an official dialogue, but I will consider it."

"Have dinner with me and let's discuss it."

"Your whole purpose will be to persuade me to an interview," she accused him.

"Not my whole purpose," Gavan denied instantly. He questioned what on earth drove him to make such a rash declaration. He was going to scare her away.

"What does that mean?" Elizabeth asked him carefully.

Gavan hesitated. "It means it's an opportunity for us to learn a little about one another and maybe build some trust."

After a brief and uneasy moment for him, she replied, "I'm not so sure one meal can instill my trust in you, Gavan, but since I don't think you'll give up until I agree, I'll have dinner with you . . . for the book," she added almost questioningly.

Gavan wasn't going to make the same error twice, so he confirmed, "For the book."

"Well, don't be surprised if I decide against the interview," she warned.

"All I'm asking is a chance to discuss it. That's it. The decision will be all yours," Gavan asserted. "I can pick you up at six—"

"No," Elizabeth rejected in haste. It was bad enough she was confused by his approach. It wasn't a date and she wouldn't allow him to treat it as if it were. She would drive her own car. To him she stated, "Don't you think it would be better if I met you at the restaurant?" Besides, if it was as awkward as the call was she wanted to get out of there with lightning speed.

"If that's your preference," Gavan said slowly. "Where would you like to meet?"

He was disappointed and trying to control it. She wondered what had caused it. "I'm not exactly a restaurant connoisseur. Where would you suggest?"

"There's a small restaurant that I think is perfect to converse in. It's just off Route One. Chaney's."

"I'm familiar with it," Elizabeth said.

"Good. Let's say six?" Gavan asked.

"I'll see you at six," Elizabeth agreed.

Gavan was relieved and a bit more excited than he cared to admit. He was having dinner with Elizabeth that evening and it had taken only a little coaxing to get her to agree. It was an interview, only an interview for his book, he tried to convince himself. But he was grinning uncontrollably and anticipation caused his fingers to fly over the keyboard with renewed energy. There was no curbing his enthusiasm and he wasn't even going to try. He whistled an offbeat tune as he drafted an outline for *The Wilkins Affair*.

CHAPTER 6

Dinner was an intimate affair and Elizabeth was perturbed.

On the one hand, she had known what to expect, having dined at Chaney's on occasion. She supposed she had never noticed how small and private a setting it was. At least she need not fear anyone would overhear their conversation as there was no telling which way Gavan might direct it, and for that she was grateful. On the other hand, it was exactly what she had tried to avoid by choosing to drive: intimacy with Gavan.

There were maybe twenty tables in total. There was ample space between each table, which she actually liked about the seating, but it seemed to her that the table arrangements were more for lovers than friendly chats. Scented flowers or floating candles were silhouetted beneath small lamps that managed to illuminate only the table and its occupants, casting off cozy warmth. Had she not been so flustered during their earlier conversation, she would have flat-out rejected his choice. Certain that Gavan patronized the restaurant with his dates, and uncomfortable at the image it evoked, she wondered what he was thinking in bringing her there.

Gavan was already seated when she arrived. Unprepared for the sight of him—she was nearly twenty minutes early, having misjudged the distance to the restaurant from her home—she felt a flutter of nerves knotting her lower abdomen, the vision of him sitting nonchalant at the table, drink in hand, and his hazel eyes on her momentarily staggering her senses.

He had seen her immediately and, composure now in check, she managed to curb the impulse to primp. Still, she couldn't help feeling disoriented beneath the distant perusal that was so potent it could have been a smoldering caress.

Did he look at all women that way or was it reserved for her?

She reasoned that it was no more than the habitual response of a man given to admiring women. Any woman, she concluded, within his view.

Unaware that she had seen him, Gavan looked her up and down with such thoroughness that she congratulated herself for having the prudence to inspect her makeup and hair before she exited her car.

The host directed her to their table. Gavan greeted her with an engaging smile that only served to unravel her more. And before she could protest, he leaned over and gave her a light kiss on the cheek. She looked at him, weighing him with uncertainty. But there was no lechery in his stance, no mocking glint in his eyes, and she finally accepted that it was only a warm greeting.

"I'm glad you made it," Gavan said, then produced a colorful floral display that had been hidden on the seat that would serve as hers.

Elizabeth was surprised. "Thank you. They're lovely." It had been some time since she'd received flowers. It was too bad it wasn't a real date.

"Not as lovely as you," Gavan murmured.

Flustered by his flattery, she held on to her composure by threads. Gratefully she accepted the seat the host pulled out for her, discreetly taking in Gavan's changed appearance as she eased into her seat.

She had replayed his image in her head more than she cared to concede and yet, implausibly, he managed to outdo her imagination. She guessed that he was in his late thirties and she wondered if it was the confidence that maturity afforded, the opulent setting, or his attire, although simple in concept, consisting of a black Ralph Lauren T-shirt and black slacks that were devastatingly flattering on his tall, well-proportioned physique and made him stand out with unrivaled prominence. He was completely unadorned, his trusty gadgets the only addition to his wardrobe.

On closer examination she was able to admire the smoothness of his skin, amazed that not a blemish or shadow of hair marred the dark, bronze complexion. His features were so chiseled a sculptor could not have more perfectly set them. His jawline was strong, his nose slightly flared, giving him a rugged edge. His hazel eyes seemed darker, an odd mixture of brown and green that caused her pulse to run away from her. He was incredibly handsome, made even more so by the uncomplicated look he sported.

Elizabeth concentrated on bolstering her composure, no small feat beneath his careless appraisal. Her initial intent was to dress down rather than up. At the time she had thought by wearing her well-worn but favorite old black jeans and a plain blouse, there would be no room for misinterpreting her acceptance of his dinner invitation. Had she done so, it would have amounted to no less than humiliation for her. Next to him she would have been dowdy and gauche if her feminine vanity hadn't kicked in. Instead, she had dressed with painstaking care to affect a natural allure.

She wore a pair of brown flat-front slacks that complemented her sleek figure. Her blouse was a camel cashmere lightweight pullover trimmed with silver beading along the collar. It was a little snug and artfully accentuated her slender waist, pert bosom, and sleek arms. She had washed her hair and wore it in long, loose curls. Her makeup was minimum and not that far from her normal application. She added a light powder to soften her skin tone and an earthy cream eye shadow to highlight her dark brown eyes. She wore a neutral shade of lipstick that was more gloss than matte and completed the look with delicate gold orb-shaped earrings. Otherwise, like Gavan, she wore no jewelry, and judging by the gleam in his eyes, she had chosen her wardrobe appropriately.

Gavan had just received his drink when Elizabeth made her entrance appearing radiant and exuding confidence. He was instantly captivated, never having considered how she would look outside her prison garb, mostly due to his suppressing the more wanton path his thoughts tried to take from the onset. Still, she was a knockout and her attractiveness was so protruding she would stand out in any setting, plainly garbed or decked out.

Gavan had to jar himself out of the trance she had cast. He set aside his drink, smiling with genuine pleasure to see her. Then he was at a loss for words, unable to stop gawking. The host saved him, asking Elizabeth if she wanted to begin with a drink. She did. While she provided the host with her preference, Gavan attempted to regain his composure and avert his gaze, but like a magnet he was drawn back to her tempting profile.

Her face was tilted upward, showing off the graceful curve of her jawline and trailing down the length of her long, slender neck that was a tempting silkiness he could only imagine sampling. Her voice was breathless as she queried the host in regard to a Chardonnay.

Gavan's gaze fell to her full mouth and he was captivated by the soft curve that hinted at a smile. He watched as she innocently but far too provocatively for his sanity licked her lips as she concentrated on the host's recital of wine choices. He was stoic when she at last faced him and caught him.

Her long, velvety-lashed dark brown eyes fell on him, at once widening in inquiry and then with amusement at catching him so engrossed in watching her. A saccharine smile greeted him.

She leaned forward and asked with a hint of sarcasm, "Conclude anything?"

"Seems I have," Gavan responded, and to his credit he didn't falter.

"Really, and what have you concluded?" Elizabeth asked mischievously.

She was surprisingly relaxed now and attributed the fact to pleasure at his unconcealed admiration. It wasn't as if she weren't used to men admiring her, but in Gavan's case it was altogether a different matter. He wasn't actually interested in her, the woman. No, he wanted to get close to write his bashing book. To see the spark of manly appreciation from him was gratifying, especially after his complete dismissal at Henry's office.

"That I have never seen a more beautiful woman. You're like a superlative painting, unreal and impossible to describe," Gavan stated, his words so sincere that Elizabeth was dumbfounded. It was the last thing she had expected him to say. How did one respond to a compliment of such monumental proportions? She managed to swallow and force a blithe response, her ease swept away by his startling declaration. "Superlative? How unique."

Gavan chuckled and gave her a lopsided grin that took years off his face. "I'm usually more eloquent in my speeches."

"More eloquent? That's hard to believe," she scoffed, choking in disbelief at the understatement of his prowess. Then she laughed, refusing to take him seriously. With a shrug, she added, "Well, at least you're off to a good start."

Gavan had gathered his wits. There was no excuse for his rambling or his bemusement. What had gotten into him? Normally a master at disguising his true feelings—but then he had never experienced the sensations he was muddling through before Elizabeth—he managed to forge a reserve that turned the whole affair back to his supposed purpose for dining with Elizabeth Wilkins.

"That's my goal," he said with a wayward smile and took that moment to down the remains of his drink.

Elizabeth was a bit disappointed at his dry admission but not at all surprised. He wanted to use her as research for his book.

Nothing else.

She had chosen to be there knowing full well his intent. But, well, she was disappointed.

"Gavan, you're still staring," she stated dryly, her attention captured momentarily by the approach of their waiter with her drink.

"You'd tell me if there's a blemish on my face, wouldn't you?" she asked mockingly.

"I would tell you anything you want to know," Gavan responded.

Elizabeth had to laugh at that and suddenly at ease, she said teasingly, "That is the corniest thing I've ever heard."

Gavan grinned, nodding his agreement. "Yeah, it was rather bad. I've got to admit, Elizabeth. Seeing you like this . . . well . . . you caught me by surprise," he confessed.

"Uh-huh," Elizabeth murmured, a tantalizing smile curving her lips. "Did you expect me to be in the ward-of-the-state outfit? If so, I'm sorry to have disappointed you. I had to return it. If I could have, I would have burned it," she added in all sincerity.

"I'm sorry you had to go through that," Gavan said with genuine sympathy.

She was uncomfortable with the sympathy and was grateful for the interruption when their waiter introduced himself to them. Minutes later, alone and with each wary of the other, Gavan decided to ease her discomfort.

"So, what can I tell you about myself?" he asked lightly.

"Well," Elizabeth said thoughtfully, "you can start by telling me what the T stands for, Mr. Gavan T. Ward."

Gavan grinned and pretended to consider her question. Elizabeth laughed and said impatiently, "Come on, it can't be that bad."

"Theo," he answered. He was forever explaining his middle initial and regretted having ever used it. Elizabeth grinned, fighting a bout of giggles.

"Go ahead. Laugh. I know where this is going," he said, a smile spreading his mouth.

"Theo? I'm sorry," she said between laughs. "I just imagined, oh, I don't know, something like Tyrone or Thomas. Oh, wait." She stared at him, her laughter dying. "Theodore?"

"No, Elizabeth, just Theo," Gavan assured her. He wasn't offended when she pealed with renewed laughter.

"Gavan Theo Ward. How cool," she said, struggling

to cease her laughter, afraid she would insult him if she didn't get herself together fast.

"My mom apparently thought so," Gavan responded lightly not at all offended by her humor. "And you, do you have a middle initial?"

"No. It's just Elizabeth Wilkins. Nothing fancy." His eyes were on her mouth and she slowly stopped grinning.

"But it fits you perfectly. It's a beautiful name," he added with emphasis, his gaze raised to her eyes as he spoke. That cooled her humor completely. She lowered her eyes, feeling awkward. A lull of silence gave her time to reclaim her composure, and then Gavan asked, "So, did you have any other questions for me? Do you want a family history? A bio? Often I find that people I interview are more comfortable when they know all about me."

"I guess I just want to know why you think this book is worth exploring. What you know, Gavan, is all that you'll find," she added calmly.

"That would be the first," he replied gently. "I've heard that line many times over and not once has it been true."

"Maybe not, but I don't know. I mean Henry doesn't think it'll hurt to talk to you, but I do."

"How so?" Gavan asked, attentive and ready to deflate any intransigence with veracity and a generous dose of coaxing.

"For one thing, it isn't as if the world knew about Mikel's deviant behavior. It never made the press, the news. There is no public awareness. Now I ask you, why would I want to see it written down in a long, drawn-out book for the entire world to see?" Elizabeth hissed, her ire rising as she considered the negative aspects of allowing Gavan to write about her most infamous moment.

Gavan was patient, took a swallow of his bourbon, and then answered, "Totally understandable, Elizabeth. First, my books are not long and drawn out. Second, no one would know who you are. It would be anonymous—"

"Are all your books based on anonymous characters?" Elizabeth interrupted pointedly.

"No," Gavan answered frankly. "But several of them are."

"I didn't know that," Elizabeth murmured. She paused thoughtfully, then inquired further, "What determines if they are anonymous?"

"What you described," he verified easily. "Was it newsworthy before I wrote it? Did the press hound the story? How guilty the characters are . . . that type of stuff."

"So you act as judge and crucifier," Elizabeth accused querulously.

"No. I am always neutral," he stated quickly. Then, as if it had never occurred to him, he asked, "Why are you so afraid? I am not against you, Elizabeth."

"But your books . . ." she murmured.

"Have you even read any of my books?" Gavan asked, his tone gentle, his gaze probing.

Elizabeth flushed. She knew of him. Who didn't? But she had not exactly read his work. It didn't matter, she thought stubbornly. It didn't take a rocket scientist to know what was in the material he gathered. "No," she admitted slowly. "But I am familiar with your work."

"Now how is that possible if you haven't read any of it?" he asked with a smile that softened the rebuke.

"It's about the justice system, Gavan. I've heard people discussing your books and how you always seem to uncover some interesting twist that the police never, ever guess existed." She was getting worked up as she spoke, the memories of her three-day stunt in a lonely, small jail cell overwhelming her. "Well, let me tell you something, there is nothing to uncover about me or my family—"

"Calm down." Gavan tried to interrupt, keeping his

calm and hoping to soothe her increasing distress. He was unsuccessful.

She continued as if he had not interrupted, her tangent taking a direction he could not have predicted and she certainly hadn't intended. But she couldn't stop herself, swept up in the tirade that was building in her. "What happened is what happened and nothing more. Mikel Wilkins is a malicious bastard full of irrational hate and he, not I, created this . . . this fiasco. I was a victim, a role I will never play again. God, it was a mistake for me to come here!" She ended on a gasp, upset that she had made the outburst, disgusted that she felt so vulnerable and exposed before him, and furious that he seemed oblivious of the ordeal she had experienced. She stood sharply, her purse in hand, and was jolted by the shock wave that spread like lightning through her veins beneath his firm touch on her forearm.

"Please, Elizabeth," he whispered imploringly. "Don't leave. I didn't mean to upset you. It was the last thing I wanted out of this evening."

She stared down at him for a moment, feeling uncertain and overwhelmed. "I must go," she murmured finally. She was certain everyone was staring at them.

Gavan was disheartened. He didn't want the evening to end so poorly and was all too aware of her dismay. He was determined to have her reconsider.

"There is no judge at this table. I do not want to crucify you, okay? Just calm down and give me a chance. Will you? Please," he begged.

Their eyes locked for an eternity before Elizabeth blinked and chose to interpret his plea as authentic. She sedately slid back into her seat, brushed her hair out of her face, and moistened her lips with a quick dart of her tongue. She had made a fool out of herself threefold and wanted nothing less than to crawl under the table. Instead she gave Gavan a direct stare and said with a calm that she didn't actually feel, "This was a mistake."

Gavan was quiet a moment, staring at his empty liquor glass before finally bestowing a wayward smile upon her. "Yeah, maybe. I shouldn't have pushed you so fast," he admitted. "But I don't want you to leave here upset. Have dinner with me and we can talk about something else. What do you like? Seen any good movies lately? Anything, Elizabeth, just don't leave."

His tone indicated nothing of the turmoil he had felt when she nearly flounced off. He was smiling, but if she declined his offer he would lose the battle of composure and she would see how disappointed he was in the awkward turn of events.

Elizabeth was silent, digesting his statement. She would have to be honest with herself. He was more than attractive. His earlier arrogance had only been one side of him. Tonight he was charming and kind, engaging and attentive.

It was painful indeed to meet such a man under the circumstances they had met in. He was not interested in her, even if he gave the front that he was.

He had thought her a con artist. He had found her bedraggled and in distress. And he wanted only one thing, not the usual male conquest that she would expect to fend off, but a conversation. She would have to live with that and stop pretending that she hadn't wanted his attention from the moment their eyes locked.

She sighed with regret, raised her eyes to peer at some inconsequential image over his shoulder, anything to avoid his gaze, and said in a barely audible whisper, "But that's the problem, Gavan. I am guilty."

CHAPTER 7

Gavan didn't know what to say. Guilty?

He was confused.

He was devastated.

She had just declared her guilt and through no persuasion on his part. He had not anticipated it. He didn't want it. And what was he supposed to do now? The silence between them lengthened and didn't cease until the arrival of their waiter minutes later. With interest akin to that of zombies, they placed their orders, neither taking note of the prying look the waiter gave them before departing.

Alone again, Gavan was unable to accept the bald confession at face value. Desperately wanting there to be more to the ambiguous statement than the surface exposed, he proceeded to inquire with caution.

"Care to elaborate, Elizabeth?" he asked calmly. Somehow he was able to keep his tone dry and his expression bland, but his head was still reeling in the aftermath of her disclosure. If it was a real confession, one that would involve the authorities, he wished she had saved it for someone else. It would excite his publisher, yes, but it left a hollow ache in his gut.

Elizabeth's expression was strained and Gavan suspected she had been holding her breath when she released a long sigh before finally responding.

"Mikel was fixated on acquiring my grandmother's assets. That being only the Wilkins-Zonnick Fund." She considered Gavan and explained further. "There used to be more, the house in Savannah, acres of land down there, and other investments my grandfather and Mikel's dad had built upon. But after my father died, my grandmother decided there was no one to hand everything to.

"She divested some of the interest my granddad had built and about ten years ago she sold her house in Savannah, which was no small surprise. She loved that house. Anyway, everything she had she poured into the fund, which is itself an investment fund. We offer loans more so than investment interests. At any rate, with Grandma's steady hand it's grown to a value of more than many of the investments my grandfather had bought into. And Mikel wanted to head it up, or more accurately run everything."

Elizabeth added empathetically, "He wanted it all his life. First he was mad at Grandma for getting rid of so much that he felt was his by right and then he was angry because he felt shut out from the fund. And I guess he was, but Grandma didn't trust him. She gave him a stipend and that was it. I always knew about Mikel, but I did nothing."

"How does that make you guilty? There's nothing you can do about an obsession, Elizabeth. Just what do you think you could you have done?" Gavan was gentle, but his tone had an underlying urgency that caught Elizabeth's attention. She looked at him, fixating on the golden flecks of light that seemed bright in the midst of his hazel orbs.

She raised her eyes to the ceiling and mused aloud,

"How can I explain this?" She wanted to formulate her words with more care and deliberation than her earlier artless confession. Had it been anyone else, the police would have been called instantly and she had little doubt that what kept Gavan in his seat was his wretched book.

Gavan was patient, allowing her to gather her wits. As if engrossed in some faraway moment, she spoke softly. "I have mixed parentage. My mother died when I was three years old. My father was Anne's son."

"Anne?" Gavan asked.

"She's my grandmother. Mikel attacked her before going after me and Liberty."

"I see," Gavan responded, wondering why she called her grandmother Anne. He would inquire another time, he thought, not wanting to distract her from her narrative.

"He was furious with Anne. I mean that in the literal sense, too. My grandmother told Mikel that he was no longer on the board of directors. I didn't really understand it at first, that happened about six years ago, but once I completed my economics degree, Anne shocked me with a gift I had expected her to give to Mikel. She told me I was going to run everything for her. It wasn't that it was odd, I had been working with her for years."

Elizabeth shrugged, then added with a hint of awe, "She already had a house picked out for me and a car, a BMW." She pursed her lips in an awkward smile. "Naturally I said yes. But Mikel was hot. Over the years his outbursts became more frequent, his fury more pronounced. When she told him what she was doing, it was awful, and yet I guess I didn't think him capable of more than that. So when I said I was guilty, Gavan, I only meant that I saw all of this coming a long time ago and I ignored the signs. I did nothing. Even when he started grilling me a few weeks before he attacked Anne I didn't sense how deviant he had become, but it was because it was easier that way. And what happened because I turned a blind eye toward Mikel's growing antagonism? Several people, including myself, nearly got killed."

Gavan, normally stoic and indifferent to the emotions of the people whose lives he depicted for the world to scrutinize, sat upright in his seat and stated with measured emphasis, "That does not make you guilty, Elizabeth." He had grown frustrated as she spoke. It was ridiculous for her to carry the burden of guilt when Mikel Wilkins from all accounts had driven himself insane with his own sense of injustice.

"Maybe not, but I *feel* guilty," Elizabeth said, not sensing his agitation. "When he attacked my grandmother I was too scared to react. I wasn't thinking and I kept my beliefs to myself."

"What beliefs?" Gavan asked.

"That Mikel had done it. The police and Anne's neighbor thought it was a robbery, at least at first. But then Mikel had seen Liberty Sutton and got the brainy idea that she could impersonate me. He didn't trust me to actually go into our corporate account and transfer the funds to him so he got Liberty to do it. We're not a bank, you understand."

"I get that," Gavan concurred.

"I kept my silence even then. I wasn't a hostage, at least not at first. But things got out of control . . . and then he kidnapped her son and his father and . . ." She broke off, disconcerted at the memory of the Liberty Sutton kidnapping. "I never wanted any part of it or this!" she hissed.

"It's all right, Elizabeth. I swear I didn't mean to upset you. It's too soon," Gavan said hastily. "Hell, I didn't even expect to really discuss Mikel yet."

"It's not that, Gavan," she denied even as she worried that uncontrollable sobs would soon surface. She needed to get her composure back. "I'm all right with the discussion. Other than Henry, no one has really believed me. I was devastated. Do you know that bastard actually locked me in my own basement, then forced me to go to the airport with him on that ridiculous ransom chase? Until these past few weeks I had never considered him a fool, just an embittered bastard."

Gavan was pensive in light of her unfettered contention against Mikel Wilkins. When Tyke first informed Gavan that Henry had accepted a wild case about a man who attacked his own grandmother, kidnapped her neighbor, and used his cousin to extort funds from their family business, Gavan never would have guessed it would lead to such an emotional moment for him. Her confession proved false. She was not guilty. Guilt-ridden, yes. But not of any criminal act, and for that Gavan was immensely relieved. She had verbalized enough for him to recognize the bout of internalized chiding she was experiencing. That was actually a common reaction he encountered when interviewing family members of the guilty. Interestingly, she was supposed to be one of the guilty ones. It was ironic that his initial interest hadn't even been on Elizabeth Wilkins or Mikel Wilkins.

His intent had been to write *The Wilkins Affair* based on the point of view of the victim, Liberty Sutton, who as far as Gavan could gather, under the belief that Elizabeth Wilkins was in danger, had assisted Mikel in his scheme. Elizabeth turned herself in, confessing that she had assisted Mikel with using Liberty to impersonate her. She had also insisted it was due to Mikel's threat on her life, her grandmother's life, and the life of a woman Elizabeth did not know, Liberty Sutton.

Unable to resist a family mystery, Gavan was intrigued by the tale Tyke spun for him two days before he arrived in Washington, D.C. He had thought her claims of innocence were crap, total bull, frankly. Fully expecting Elizabeth Wilkins to be imprisoned, he had gone to the courthouse, planning to interview Wilkins first and then both Mikel and Elizabeth.

Well, he met Elizabeth Wilkins and that had changed everything.

"Gavan?" Elizabeth murmured, bringing him out of his revelry when he did not speak. He concentrated on Elizabeth, offering a wan smile that tore her to the core. He didn't believe her story and she was hurt. She lowered her gaze, twirled her fork over her untouched linguini, and said softly, "Dinner was a disaster, huh?"

"I take full responsibility for that. I pushed you into coming here tonight," Gavan stated magnanimously.

"Yes, you did," Elizabeth agreed miserably. She set her fork down and stared at him. "But I wouldn't have come if that small edge of guilt hadn't been nagging at me. I don't want to be a part of your story, Gavan. I know you're going to write it. And that's fair. But despite all that I said, please . . . I can't involve myself."

"Will you think about it?" Gavan asked, unable to relinquish hope yet.

"I doubt it. Just thinking about the mess Mikel created is bad enough, but talking about it sickens me."

"I'll give you time. Besides, you don't write a book overnight." He laughed uneasily and she gave him a weak smile, the sadness in the curve of her mouth tearing at him.

"Indeed you don't," she agreed. With actions curt and marked with purpose, Elizabeth stared boldly into Gavan's eyes as she set her fork down, placed her napkin on her untouched plate, and pushed away from the table.

He knew what was coming before she said a word.

"I have to go." Her words were matter-of-fact and without emotion.

Gavan was silent. He didn't want her to leave. He wanted her to stay, to eat and be merry. He wanted her to smile, and to see her eyes sparkle with pleasure as he made her laugh and lifted her spirits. He wanted to wash away the last hour and start over. But it was too late. He had no idea how it had happened, but the evening had definitely taken a turn for the worse. And there was nothing he could do but accept her decision or he would lose any hope of making the evening up at a later time. What a mess he had created!

"Give me a moment, please? I'll escort you to your car," Gavan said, waving for the waiter. A few minutes later, the silence heavy between them, Gavan watched as Elizabeth got in her car, waved good-bye, and without further exchange, drove away.

Ignoring the couples strolling to their cars, he lingered in the parking lot and watched her car until it disappeared into traffic, a sense of melancholy overcoming him when she was no longer visible.

She had actually left him without any preamble or further ado. She hadn't even taken the flowers with her.

And what was it she said when she got in her car?

A mumbled good-night, a good-bye wave, and then she shut him out.

Twice now he had put her on the defensive. Twice she had rejected him in turn. He shoved his disappointment aside. But with her abrupt departure came a heightened awareness that the book had gone from prominence to a minor factor in his desire to know more about Elizabeth.

He wanted to see her again and the fact had nothing to do with *The Wilkins Affair*.

CHAPTER 8

"No call, no anything," fussed Sonya Brown the moment Elizabeth walked through the office door.

She didn't look up at Elizabeth's entrance, but she knew who it was.

Elizabeth smiled, considering Sonya with fondness. For as far back as she could recall, Sonya had never held her tongue when displeased. She was a spunky woman although she was plump from head to toe. Her thick, brown natural-style hair was enormous, making her chocolate-brown face appear even rounder, a visual that Elizabeth had long since gotten used to as it never varied. Her eyes were small, beady dark brown pupils, but so full of warmth that when she looked at Elizabeth they shone with beauty. Watching Sonya summoned a memory of her first heartbreak and how it was Sonya who had soothed her, nestling Elizabeth's head against her full bosom.

Anne would never have done that. Sonya was everything that her grandmother was not. With her mother's tragic accident followed years later by her father's painful death, Elizabeth had craved tenderness from Anne as a child. As a woman she had accepted the reality that although Anne might love her she would never be overtly affectionate toward her.

Sonya had no such problem.

Years earlier, when Elizabeth first started working officially with her grandmother, Elizabeth had kindly suggested that Sonya might want to retire, but Sonya had flat-out refused. She wanted to keep busy and frankly she wasn't ready to settle down to the easy life of sleeping late hours and going nowhere fast. Remarkably agile and energetic for her sixty-six years, she accompanied Elizabeth on trips both personal and business. They had cultivated a relationship that extended beyond friendship. And here they were, still together having suffered a very trying period, and Elizabeth would respectfully accept any scolding Sonya administered.

Sonya was sitting at Elizabeth's desk. Elizabeth had arrived a full hour later than usual. She had not been to the office in nearly two weeks. During that time, Sonya had successfully kept their clients, a small, intimate group, from being aware of the ignominious events surrounding the Wilkinses. Thus, a chastisement for her forty-eight-hour lapse in communication was no more than she deserved after the important role Sonya had played in assisting Elizabeth to clear her name. Ready to accept whatever remonstrations Sonya meted out, Elizabeth chose the comfort of one of the full-back white leather chairs to await the scolding.

"If it weren't for Henry," Sonya continued without pause or nary a glance at Elizabeth, "I wouldn't have known what happened until this very moment. And I had to call him three times before *he* returned my call, mind you. You just disappeared Saturday. Poof! I thought you would've at least called me, child." She was arranging files from one electronic folder to another, her round face half blocked by the computer screen while she chattered away at how insensitive Elizabeth had been not to call her and ease an old woman's worrying.

"You're right, Sonya, but I was so disoriented . . . I wasn't myself. And I guess I wanted a little time to myself," Elizabeth admitted, carefully omitting the fact that she had had dinner with Gavan the night before.

Sonya peered at her over the screen, measured Elizabeth's sincerity, and then returned to her ministrations on the computer. "Henry said as much." She was thoughtful. "But I was worried. Fortunately Anne was unaware that you were taken into custody, no thanks to those pathetic excuses for police officers, mind you. Why, I had to insist they wait until she was fully recovered or at least until they were even sure they were going to press charges against you before telling her such a horrid thing. Anyway, she's better now and all ready to go home. I told her everything, you understand, but only because she would have found out."

"Of course," Elizabeth agreed.

"Well, you're free and Anne is well. All has turned out superbly, despite that little leech you call cousin. Isn't it good that she didn't have to deal with the initial distress? Let's face it, honey, Anne isn't getting any younger." Sonya grinned at her own keen insight. Then just as spontaneously she frowned, poking her head around the computer again, and added with a raised eyebrow, "And neither am I. Don't distress me this way again," she added firmly.

"It won't happen again," Elizabeth asserted. "I apologize that you were distressed, too."

"Accepted," Sonya said.

She fell into a long silence and Elizabeth recognized the warning signs. Years of intimate propinquity and tête-à-têtes so personal even Anne wasn't aware they had taken place had given Elizabeth the ability to detect when her older friend was experiencing an inundation of emotions. Elizabeth was dismayed that she was the cause for Sonya's vulnerability; her only consolation was in the knowledge that Sonya was a strong, independent woman. It was that identifying strength that had attracted Elizabeth as far back as she could remember.

At Elizabeth's prolonged silence, Sonya openly considered her. There was no doubt in her mind that the young woman was reliving the anguish she had experienced with Mikel. Feeling a wreck herself after the reality of what had nearly happened to Elizabeth and Anne finally settled in, Sonya decided not to mention Mikel again.

"Now what's bothering you? Are you expecting Henry to tell you he made a mistake?" Sonya asked.

"Actually I did at first. It was like a dream and I was so afraid of waking up. But, no, that's not bothering me, Sonya. I'm feeling a bit of guilt on multiple levels, I guess."

"Nonsense, child. You've done nothing wrong," Sonya said impatiently. She decided it was time to switch their conversation to something more neutral, if not somewhat unpleasant. "Now, are you going to have a driver meet Anne or are you going to do it?"

"What?" Elizabeth asked, peering at Sonya in confusion.

"Anne is being released today." Sonya spoke slowly as if speaking to a child.

"She is?" Elizabeth asked dumbly.

"She is." Sonya smiled indulgently.

Elizabeth had been unable to communicate with anyone for nearly a week, going from the threat of Mikel's vengeance to the custody of the authorities, all while Anne was recouping from Mikel's attack. And during all that time, Anne had been only a passing thought, made even more so upon her highly charged and circumspect meeting with Gavan T. Ward. Sunday had arrived and Elizabeth had not thought of visiting Anne until the opportunity to see her had passed and then, shamefully, she had gone to dinner with Gavan, much to her chagrin and regret. She wouldn't be surprised if he gave up his book and ran as far and as fast as he could, as her emotional display had been such a pathetic debacle of poor taste and judgment. She sighed, forcing her thoughts from Gavan to focus on Sonya's message.

"The wonder of voice mail. I left you a message yesterday," Sonya stated in a gentle murmur.

"I didn't get it," Elizabeth confessed. She wouldn't have gotten it either, because she was so upset after her failed dinner with Gavan that she had gone straight to bed, falling asleep from the sheer exhaustion of maintaining her bearing.

"You mean you didn't check your message," Sonya corrected, then happened to glance up. She hesitated, then said, "You look upset. Being held unjustly will do that to anyone, child. Would you like me to come with you?" she asked, softening in the face of Elizabeth's dejection.

"No, I think I can handle it alone. Is there a release time?" Elizabeth inquired, rising to her feet with a wariness that tugged at Sonya's heart.

"Do they ever?" Sonya scoffed. "The message was only that she's being released. You didn't check *any* of your messages at home?"

"No, no, I didn't." She had been afraid to check her messages after her disastrous evening with Gavan. Whether he called or not, she expected no less than bafflement from him if not a new reserve on his part after her undignified behavior during dinner. She had avoided checking her voice mail and cringed when her line rang before she headed for work, her relief only halfhearted that it was Henry checking on her and not Gavan.

"Well, if they gave a time, perhaps they did so at your house. It's almost nine-thirty, Elizabeth. Why don't you just run along to the hospital and collect your belongings?"

Elizabeth stared at the clock on her desk with a frown. She really had gotten a late start. "My grandmother is not belongings, Sonya," she said in distraction.

"She's something." Sonya whooped with laughter.

Elizabeth glanced at Sonya with a grin, shook her head in amusement, then picking up her purse headed for the door.

"I better get going. Just in case," she said.

"Good idea. And, Elizabeth, do check in this time. You've much to go over when you get back."

"Yes, ma'am," Elizabeth complied and hurried from the office before Sonya's keen regard recognized her moodiness as stemming beyond the events of the past few weeks. The last thing she wanted to explain to anyone, and in particular Sonya, was the unusually potent affect Gavan T. Ward had had on her from the start.

CHAPTER 9

"Elizabeth, wait!" a petite woman called from the opposite end of the office hallway. Elizabeth narrowed her gaze, and a delighted smile crept across her face.

"Shannon?" She laughed.

"Who else would I be?" Shannon asked impatiently. Shannon was a small woman for such a big voice. She was slender and petite with a mound of light brown hair that practically hid her face, causing her exceptionally huge brown eyes to stand out against her petite features. She was smiling, her even white teeth beaming at Elizabeth as she raced down the hall, mindless of two suited men she nearly toppled in her haste. "You were leaving," she accused the moment she reached Elizabeth, breathless from her exertions.

"Hi, sweetie," Elizabeth greeted her, ignoring the accusation, and bent to hug her friend.

"Endearments won't save you," Shannon huffed but returned the embrace with an enthusiasm that belied her retort. Elizabeth was the first to pull free.

"I'm on my way out to get Anne," Elizabeth stated, a pang of guilt stinging her conscience that she had forgotten Shannon's planned visit. She was glad she had not missed her spirited friend but dreaded the flood of questions that were sure to follow.

"Where is she?" Shannon inquired, falling into step with Elizabeth as she got on the elevator.

"She's still in the hospital in Silver Spring," Elizabeth answered. "She's been there nearly ten days. It's a blessing that she's all right."

"It certainly is," Shannon agreed, then impulsively asked, "Care for company?"

"You want to go with me to the hospital to pick up Anne?" Elizabeth emphasized each word. "Are you ill?" she joked.

"Almost," Shannon murmured, then ignoring Elizabeth's questioning gaze, added with a shrug, "It's nothing physical, just emotional. But never mind that right now. I had planned to take a taxi to the airport after seeing that you were okay with my own eyes. But I can do that from the hospital."

"You're going to the airport?" Elizabeth asked, her curiosity rising. She now raked Shannon with a more thorough inspection and immediately noticed she carried no luggage, just a small black clutch.

"Yes, the airport."

When Shannon didn't elaborate, Elizabeth accepted the vague answer and said with a lighthearted laugh, "Well, if you can stomach the hospital visit I don't see why you shouldn't come."

"I can manage the hospital. It's Anne that's not so easy to stomach."

"Anne's never done anything to you, Shannon," Elizabeth stated somewhat defensively.

"No, she hasn't. She's just so cold. And when those blue eyes stare at me . . ." Shannon shivered. "It's . . . well, unpleasant. Do you know what I mean?"

"No, I don't," Elizabeth drawled mockingly. "What it

is, is your vivid imagination. I know because Anne's eyes are green."

Shannon shrugged. "Whatever."

"I couldn't believe it when I heard you were jailed," Shannon said once they were in Elizabeth's car.

Elizabeth cringed at Shannon's tactless remark and responded with open sarcasm, "Trust me, Shannon. I know exactly how you felt."

"So," Shannon inquired cautiously, "is this a temporary release or are you really free?"

"I'm really, really free. They were supposedly holding me, but no charges were ever brought against me."

"Isn't that against the law?" Shannon pondered aloud.

"No. I was being held on conspiracy to commit fraud, at minimum. I went to them, like an idiot, and they held me. It was all very legal."

"Well, you're sure taking this in stride," Shannon muttered.

"What else should I do? Break down and cry? I already did that," Elizabeth murmured.

Shannon shifted in her seat, a signal that she was uncomfortable, then said brightly, "Well, you're free now and that's all that matters."

"Yes. Totally," Elizabeth agreed.

Ten minutes later the freeway sign read HOLY CROSS HOSPITAL, NEXT EXIT. Shannon was thoughtful, glanced at Elizabeth and then her watch before stating, "I don't think I'll go inside, to see Anne that is."

"You plan to sit in the car?" Elizabeth asked dryly.

"No, I plan to hail a taxi and go to the airport, remember?"

"Ah, that's right. Well, I don't blame you for not wanting to come inside," Elizabeth said with ease. She paused; then, taking her eyes off the road for a brief scrutiny at Shannon, she asked, "So what's going on? You didn't have to check on me and why are you going to the airport? Are you leaving or meeting someone there?"

"My, my, such curiosity." Shannon grinned. "It's no big deal really. I actually called you because I needed to talk to you. My parents are splitting up."

"Get out!" Elizabeth gasped.

"While you're driving?" Shannon asked glibly.

"You know what I meant," Elizabeth said, reeling from the unexpected and bluntly delivered news.

"Yeah. Well, hey, we saw it coming."

"I didn't," Elizabeth disagreed.

"I did. I'm not mad or anything. So, anyway, my mom is moving. Can you believe that?" Shannon fell silent.

"I'm sorry," Elizabeth said sadly.

Shannon shrugged. "No need to be. I'm only surprised it didn't happen years ago. I'm twenty-seven years old, Elizabeth. It's time I accept the truth around me. My parents have been unhappy for years and years. It's for the best."

"Where is she moving?" Elizabeth probed.

"Atlanta. That's where I'm heading. I promised to finalize some papers for her, settle her closing and stuff like that."

"It's generous of you to do that for her."

"If you say so." Shannon laughed lightly. "I'll be back in a few weeks. I'm going to help her move, get settled in."

There was a long lull before Elizabeth sighed. "When it rains, it pours, doesn't it?"

"It sure does," Shannon agreed emphatically. "I have had a really awful week," she said softly. Elizabeth was silent, allowing Shannon to collect her thoughts. "Not only are my parents divorcing, but I broke up with Steve—"

"You're kidding!"

"Who would kid about that?" Shannon demanded.

"Yeah," Elizabeth agreed, then inquired, "So, how broke up are you?"

"Very! It's over. Really, really over," Shannon stressed.

"And your wedding was in two months," Elizabeth sympathized.

"It could have been worse. We could have gotten married. At any rate, I called Friday to tell you. And, then lo and behold, Sonya told me about Mikel's retarded scheme to bankrupt you. Why didn't you call me?" Shannon ended plaintively.

"As if I could have," Elizabeth retorted. With measured patience, she added, "I wasn't thinking about you or anyone else. Do you realize that Mikel held me hostage?"

"No!" Shannon gasped. "Sonya only told me that the police were holding you for questioning. And that you might have to do time and . . . my God, Elizabeth, I had no idea. Did he hurt you?"

"No, it wasn't anything like that," Elizabeth quickly reassured her. "Mostly it was an emotional, psychological imprisonment. It was crazy and I was . . . I guess I was in shock. If it weren't for his raggedy scum partners confirming my story, I would still be imprisoned," she spat out in disgust.

"Amazing," exclaimed Shannon.

"Yes, well, there's more," Elizabeth said hesitantly, an image of Gavan popping into her mind.

"Really?" Shannon breathed, fascinated that something so bizarre had actually happened to her friend.

"Some writer wants to put the whole sordid affair on paper."

"No way!" gushed Shannon, her eyes wide in awe at the prospect of Elizabeth's life coming alive in a dramatic tale.

"Yeah, my thoughts exactly," Elizabeth mumbled.

She was far from awed and was actually appalled by the
swift and unpleasant memory that surfaced at the mention of Gavan. Her outburst the evening before had
been asinine, at best inappropriate, and she regretted
it more than she cared to admit. It didn't matter, she
tried to console herself. She had scared him away and
the likelihood that she would see him again was slim
indeed. She fell into a sullen silence, not at all soothed
by the prospect.

A thoughtful silence hovered over them, the only
conversation for some time emanating from the radio.
Upon arriving at the hospital, Elizabeth followed the
signposts to the visitors' parking lot. She pressed the
button on the automated machine for a parking sticker
and continued in search of a parking space. She was
backing into an available space when a far too familiar
face grabbed her attention. A startled gasp escaped
her, causing Shannon's head to snap upward in alarm.
Though she was fully expecting a collision, the only
impact Shannon felt was the stunning vision of pure mas-
culinity facing them.

"Wow!" she whispered, her brown eyes round in her
gaping appreciation of the tall man who, dressed in an
all-white linen shirt and like pants, could have stepped
off the pages of an advertisement for a tropical island
resort fantasy. His outfit suited his physique and the stark
white against his brown skin enhanced his deeply
bronzed coloring. It took her a moment to realize he
was staring back at them. "He's watching us. No, he's
watching you. He's coming this way. Do you know him?"
Shannon inquired, glancing from the impressive figure
to Elizabeth with incredulity.

"Sort of," Elizabeth admitted. She finished parking,
cut off her ignition, and tried to settle her wildly beating heart. What was Gavan doing here?

"Sort of?" Shannon probed, peering at Elizabeth suspiciously.

Elizabeth avoided the disbelieving stare of her friend and offered a mumbled "He's the author I spoke of."

Elizabeth's author was an attractive man and from the moment Shannon spied him he had been focused on Elizabeth. Elizabeth put on an indifferent act, but Shannon was not fooled. It was easy to discern that Elizabeth was not immune to the author's good looks or his unwavering attention. Sparks were flying between those two, Shannon thought in delight, and grinned broadly. "Tell you what, why don't you just give him the interview and then tell me all about it? Better yet, go out on a date with him, because, girl, the way he is staring you down, I don't think it's a book on his mind right now."

"Shannon, please," Elizabeth hissed, embarrassed by the comment although Gavan couldn't possibly have heard or even guessed what was being said between them.

Shannon shrugged. "Hey, one of us needs to have fun. I can't imagine anyone who deserves a moment's distraction more than you. And don't even deny you're not interested, because you're looking, too. Go out with him and have a good time, if not for you, then for me."

"He's a writer, Shannon. Nothing more," Elizabeth insisted, all the while she was fighting a rising panic. Gavan was moving toward her vehicle. He had recognized her in the same instant she had recognized him. But his approach was cautious, his expression full of the same wariness she had first identified when they met outside Henry's office. Lord, what was he thinking? she worried.

She groaned aloud. Shannon heard it and chuckled. It was amusing how Elizabeth had grossly understated her interest in the infamous writer. The woman was practically spellbound. A teasing smile curved Shannon's mouth. "Somebody's interested in somebody," she sang sweetly.

Elizabeth ignored her. She had to get out of the car and meet Gavan halfway. It was the only way to stop Shannon's teasing and an opportunity to dismiss the absurdity of the previous evening.

Act as if nothing had happened and perhaps he would, too.

She was trembling. She concentrated on calming her nerves.

Shannon watched with growing interest the man and woman so intent upon each other that they took no notice of anything or anyone else. She exited the car as well but lingered politely in the background to give them a bit of privacy even if Elizabeth wasn't aware that it was needed. She wasn't fooled by Elizabeth's supposed disinterest. If Gavan's laser-beam focus was any indication, he wasn't any more indifferent to Elizabeth than she was to him.

CHAPTER 10

Elizabeth managed to portray an outward reserve. Internally she was in shambles. Her pulse had increased and her cheeks burned with a rising heat that had nothing to do with the morning sun. She was breathless and uncomfortably warm even as a whisper of a light breeze caressed her.

Don't think about last night. He's just a man, she kept repeating to herself. An excitingly magnetic man who had seen her at her worst, but still he was only a man. One thing was for sure, she would never allow him to see how mortified she was to see him so soon after the debacle she had made of dinner. And what *was* he doing here? she wondered in dismay even as she gave him a brilliant, wide smile.

Gavan nearly tripped from surprise when Elizabeth dazzled him with an act as simple as smiling. She was the last person he anticipated seeing. He was en route to meet with her grandmother, thanks to Henry's assistance, and after a brief telephone introduction, Anne Wilkins had agreed to see him. She had made no mention that her granddaughter would be there, but then Gavan had not confided that he had already met

Elizabeth. Interestingly, Henry had not mentioned that Elizabeth would be at the hospital either.

That morning Gavan spoke with Henry, partially to make contact with the elderly Wilkins and partially to inquire about Elizabeth. He had not slept. Guilt-ridden and baffled by the sudden turn of events, he called Henry the moment the hour was reasonable, explaining how he had upset Elizabeth. They had parted badly, Gavan admitted to Henry. But Henry was unconcerned, insisting Elizabeth was fine. She had gone into the office and would likely be there all day.

Only slightly relieved by the news, Gavan promised himself he would ease off for a moment. She was carrying a huge burden tainted by guilt and suspicion. His dogged insistence that they meet immediately had only served to incite her infuriation over the wrong that had been done to her. Grudgingly but with no less resolve to be patient he had decided to back off from approaching her, especially on the subject of his book, until Elizabeth's misgivings eased. But he was pleased, actually energized at the sight of her. Encouraged by her smile, he smiled warmly in turn.

"Elizabeth. We meet again." His eyes raked over her with such swiftness and thoroughness that she had the sensation he had seen more than her simple attire. Her stomach did a somersault. She wore pink sandals, a white-and-pink-striped pencil-cut skirt, and a flowing white blouse, but beneath his perusal it was as if she wore a full-length fur, she was so flustered.

"Is this coincidence or planned?" she asked calmly, but her fingers itched to adjust her blouse and smooth back her black hair. Was it in disarray? Did he notice that she had not gotten a pedicure? Oh, she thought, groaning, she should not have worn sandals.

"A very nice coincidence," he confirmed with a lop-sided smile that warmed her already heightened senses.

Gavan would have said more but was interrupted by loud laughter. His brother, Lance Ward, and Henry's son, Tyke Miles, were having a boisterous exchange. Gavan heard his name and that of Wilkins clearly. He shot a quick worried glance at Elizabeth. Her expression hadn't changed, but those of the two men approaching did when they realized that he was not alone but was accompanied by a beautiful woman. It wasn't unusual to see Gavan with exceptionally attractive women, but Lance, if not Tyke, instantly guessed the woman's identity was Elizabeth Wilkins. It made sense. She fit Gavan's vivid description, she was at the hospital where the elder Anne Wilkins was being nursed, and Gavan was mesmerized by her presence.

As they neared Gavan, Lance's brown-eyed gaze slid impassively over Elizabeth. His brother rarely expressed interest in a woman with any level of animation and certainly none that were practically strangers. She was exceptional, he decided, but he was withholding further judgment beyond that. Anything was possible. Thirty-six years of living, in particular the latter year, had taught him to never trust a woman's desirability as anything but precisely that.

Gavan wanted to strangle his brother and Tyke. He had overhead their comments regarding his interest in the Wilkins affair and was not pleased. A swift glance at Elizabeth assured him that she had not caught the gist of their dialogue. The knowledge didn't appease his annoyance with the two men and he acknowledged them without actually looking at them.

"Lance, Tyke, this is Elizabeth Wilkins," he said smoothly although his eyes never left Elizabeth's face.

"Elizabeth, allow me to introduce Tyke and my brother, Lance," Gavan added.

Elizabeth graciously turned to the men, ready to smile and greet them with cordiality despite her taut nerves. Her smile wavered precariously when she absorbed Lance's disposition. Momentary baffled, she hesitated. The coolness he exhibited was as biting as a full blast of March winds. Her gaze narrowed and she pulled herself together, giving him an equally aloof perusal.

She had to wonder what Gavan had told his brother to cause such an austere greeting, or could it be that the two brothers were simply very different men? He *was* a shocking contrast to Gavan. He was darker in complexion by several shades, not nearly as tall as Gavan, nearly a head shorter at around six feet tall. He was leaner in build although as well formed and his expression was far more severe, so much so that she felt scorched by his very presence. His facial features were the only similarity between the brothers. They were both exceptionally handsome. But where Gavan's eyes were an interesting hazel mixture of gray and green and danced with a teasing light, Lance's eyes were dark brown, keen, sharp, and full of distrust.

She shifted her focus to Tyke, a younger version of Henry, and she was instantly soothed. He, at least, was harmless. Tyke barely stood an inch over her, but he was all smiles and the light in his eyes was something more common with men looking at her than the indifference she had experienced beneath Lance's stoic scrutiny. Lance Ward, she decided, was as unpleasant as a bear and she didn't care for him at all. Her hellos came out disjointed due to the continued inspection from the younger Ward. She fought against grinding her teeth and was saved by Shannon's vivacious advance.

Shannon started talking before she fully reached the

small group. "All right, I can't wait any longer. I hate to intrude, Elizabeth, but I really must bolt," she said sweetly once she was upon them. Her smile was gregarious, her glance easily rolling over the three men, unperturbed by Lance's stern regard or Tyke's wide-eyed stare. She tugged Elizabeth's arm with the impatience of a child when Elizabeth was slow to respond.

"I'm sorry, Shannon," Elizabeth said, disconcerted by the whirlwind of events. "Gavan, this is Shannon. Shannon, meet Gavan T. Ward. And I only just met"—she turned apologetically to Lance and Tyke—"Lance and Tyke, correct?"

"Correct," Lance answered for both of them, shifting his attention to Shannon with no less gravity.

"Hello, everyone," Shannon said brightly and in contrast to Elizabeth's cool greeting. In fact, Gavan thought, she was everything opposite of Elizabeth. She had a mass of long brown hair with gold highlights. It was beautiful hair but it hid her face. She had huge, doll-baby brown eyes but they took up so much of her face it was too transfixing to look at her. She was pretty, petite, and a sharp contrast to Elizabeth, to whom Gavan was instantly attracted. He returned her smile even as she passed her gaze over him, paused on Lance, and then grinned at Tyke all in a matter of seconds. He was fascinated by the energetic cheerfulness that enveloped them by her mere presence.

"I see you have much going on right now." She addressed Elizabeth directly, her tone insinuating, but only Elizabeth understood the innuendo. "Besides, I have a flight to catch. I'll call you in a few days."

"Wait. Where are you going?" Elizabeth asked, trying to stop Shannon from hurrying away.

"To the taxi stand, where else?"

"I'll walk with you," Elizabeth offered, hesitant to

separate so abruptly from Shannon. Shannon paused, pulled Elizabeth aside, and murmured for her ears only, "You okay? They're cool, right?"

"Yes, of course. But why are you rushing off?" Elizabeth whispered back.

"I have a flight, remember? I'll call . . ." Then Shannon allowed her voice to rise, stepped away from Elizabeth, and added cheerfully, "I see several taxis waiting, so I've got to flee. I'll call," she promised again; then with a quick squeeze of Elizabeth's hand, she hastened away with a wave, blithely unaware of the pair of eyes watching her spirited exit.

"What was that?" Tyke asked with a laugh once the exuberance of Shannon's brief introduction and swift departure wore off.

"A very dear friend of mine," Elizabeth responded, her tone indicating her displeasure at Tyke's flippant remark.

He was instantly contrite and muttered, "I didn't mean—"

"Let it go, Tyke," she heard Lance warn Tyke.

"Well, I've taken up enough of your time," Elizabeth said. "It was a pleasure to meet you. If you'll excuse me, my grandmother is waiting," she added coolly. Not waiting for a response from Gavan and ignoring the nagging question of why or how he came to be at the hospital, she moved hastily toward the hospital's entrance, keeping her focus ahead of her even when Gavan fell into step beside her.

Intent on ignoring him, she missed his subtle nod at his brother, cautioning Lance and Tyke not to follow. A moment later, breathing heavy from the brisk pace she was keeping, Gavan asked with a laugh, "Are you in a hurry to see your grandmother or to get away from me?"

"Maybe both," she replied glibly.

He sighed and she gave him a sidelong glance. Their eyes caught before she quickly looked away.

"If I were you I guess I would feel the same," he admitted. Heart pounding in apprehension over what he would say next, she actually quickened her pace. Realizing she had no intention of pausing to even catch her breath, Gavan caught her arm and gently halted her retreat. With a lopsided smile, he said, "I realize that I botched dinner in a way that is inexcusable, but I'm asking you to accept my apology."

Elizabeth was speechless, bewildered by his interpretation of the disastrous evening.

Gavan mistook her silence as skepticism. In a quandary over how to fix her escalating distrust, he released her arm, ran his hand over his short hair, and said earnestly, "I came on strong. I didn't give you a moment to digest what was happening. But I never intended to upset you. Just tell me what to do and it's done." He grinned sheepishly, adding, "But don't ask me to give up."

Stunned silence followed and then, recklessly, he whispered, "Give me an opportunity to wow you, Elizabeth."

CHAPTER 11

Elizabeth was moved beyond words. Torn between a whiff of relief and a blast of excitement, she could only stare at him in disbelief. He wanted to wow her? The magnitude of the plea sank in and a slow smile curved her full lips even as she tried to contain her delight. Until that moment she had not allowed herself to dwell on the why behind her agitated state. Her pride had been at stake from the moment she agreed to have dinner with him up to the moment she saw him in the parking lot.

She was no longer able to ignore the nagging truth that she simply dreaded his rejection, certain that meeting her in prison-issued clothing was enough to deter any romantic interest. Theirs had not been a traditional meeting. He had not approached her for a date. He was an attractive charming man intent upon meeting a so-called convict. There was no ambiguity as to his intent. From the start his interest had been in her association with Mikel Wilkins and nothing else. Could she have been wrong? Was it possible that he was not prejudiced against the where and how they met and was interested in her as a woman and not just another character in his novel? Oh, she was not foolish enough to believe he wanted anything more than material for his book, but who knew what else could happen?

As they stood staring each other down she wished she was not so attracted to him. She had fought it from the start mostly because she was certain the feeling was not mutual, but also because she had never experienced such a strong and instant connection with any man before. It scared the living wits out of her.

But, she reminded herself with delight, he said he wanted to wow her.

Wow!

He was nervous, too. Elizabeth was fascinated by the discovery. *My,* she thought in awe, *I have been blind indeed.* The newfound realization boosted her confidence.

"I don't know what to say," she finally breathed.

Gavan eased with her response. Encouraged he said, "Saying yes would be a good start."

"Then yes. But only if you can do the same for me."

"You want to wow me?" Gavan teased, grinning as the elevator door opened and several people got off. Elizabeth used its arrival as a buffer to cover her flustered reaction to his teasing and hurried inside without responding. Gavan stood between the open doors, using his body to block the door from closing.

"You don't want to wow me?" he asked in mock disappointment. Elizabeth flicked a glance at him before a smile curved her lips at his comical attempt to appear downhearted.

"I don't know about all that. I hardly know you," she said coquettishly, feeling suddenly flirtatious and enjoying herself.

"Just what I would expect you to say, Ms. Wilkins," he responded, putting on a facade of exasperation, but his eyes lit up at the playful banter. The elevator bell gonged several times and Elizabeth laughed.

"Gavan, you're blocking the door from closing. Are you trying to keep me from my grandmother?" Elizabeth asked.

Her munificent smile gave him pause. For a moment he could only stare in fascination at the transformation it created. She was even more beautiful.

"Well?" she probed.

Jarring himself out of the enchantment her smile elicited, Gavan joined Elizabeth inside the elevator and carelessly pressed the button for the third floor with a wayward smile. But Elizabeth, preoccupied with the discomforting realization that he had known exactly which floor to choose, looked away from him.

Unaware of the change in her, Gavan said playfully, "I wouldn't dream of keeping you from her." Then he added, "Besides, I'm headed the same way anyway." Too late he realized his mistake.

"So it seems," Elizabeth responded softly.

Her smile faded, her body went rigid. Gavan sighed, and briefly lowered his head. He'd done it again. When had he become such a dolt?

"I would have mentioned it, Elizabeth, but the opportunity never presented itself. I didn't expect to see you here. And when I did, I was hoping—"

"You don't have to explain your actions, Gavan," Elizabeth said, cutting him off. "You're here to see Anne. I should have known but like you I was a bit distracted. I didn't even connect . . . I thought you were looking for . . . well, never mind. My mistake. I won't make it again." She raised her chin even and gave him a tight smile. It was a far cry from the carefree grin they had shared moments earlier.

"What mistake? What is it, Elizabeth?" Gavan asked. "If you don't want me to see Anne right now, it can wait. I don't want to upset you again."

Elizabeth leaned against the wall, sighed, and avoided facing him as she fought to come to grips with the highs and lows she had experienced in a matter of minutes.

Gavan was confused by her indignation. Was it so bad that he was there to visit Anne Wilkins? Was she protecting her grandmother or herself? he wondered. Whatever it was, he should have stuck to his plan of action and kept away from Elizabeth. He could have handled their impromptu meeting in many ways, rather than following her and antagonizing her. Now she was displeased with him again. At a loss for words, he was thankful at their swift arrival to the third floor. He stepped aside, a silent surrender. The prudent thing to do was leave. He could meet with Anne Wilkins another day.

Elizabeth was rattled and barely able to contain her fury with Gavan. She couldn't wait to escape the cramped elevator and reach the sanctuary of her grandmother's room. The doors opened at a maddening crawl and the moment she could, she exited, brushing against Gavan's arm as she did so. She jerked aside. Their eyes locked and she bumped against the wall in her haste to flee. Gavan caught her by the arms, steadying her. Then he hesitated, a frown creasing his forehead as his gaze roved over Elizabeth's head and landed on a twin version of her.

As if in a daze, he let his hands fall away. Staring beyond Elizabeth, his attention thoroughly captured, he left the elevator. She trailed behind him. His look of stunned disbelief gave Elizabeth pause. She looked over her shoulder, having little doubt what and who he was watching with such intensity.

The last person she wanted to see was heading toward them. She wasn't ready to face her. Not here and especially not with Gavan present. A moan ached to escape

Elizabeth's throat, but instead she raised her chin and made direct eye contact with Liberty Sutton.

Liberty Sutton and her fiancé, Jarrett Irving, were fast approaching them. There was nothing Elizabeth could do but wait for them.

"Elizabeth." Liberty smiled, her conviviality sincere. Jarrett was less affable, his stance noticeably protective of Liberty.

Elizabeth tried to smile and failed. "Liberty Sutton," Elizabeth murmured. "I had no idea you would be here."

"I came to see Anne. When I called I was told she was being released. I wanted to see her before she left. She's doing so much better," Liberty added with genuine relief.

A moment of uncertainty passed between the ladies when Liberty's gaze fell on Gavan. She didn't blink, nor did her eyes widen, but she smiled and said, "Hello. Are you with Elizabeth?"

"Yes," Gavan answered flatly. "I'm Gavan Ward." He was eyeing with keen interest the woman whose life had been turned upside down by the Wilkinses. She didn't appear distressed. To the contrary, his impression was that she was taking the situation in stride.

"Excuse my manners," Elizabeth apologized. "Mr. Ward, this is Liberty Sutton and her fiancé, Jarrett Irving. Mr. Ward is an author."

"Nice to meet you, Mr. Ward." Jarrett offered his hand to Gavan. Gavan accepted it. He had fallen way down the approval pole with Elizabeth. She was refusing to use his name again. His jaw was rigid but he managed to say, "Gavan will do."

"Gavan Ward. How nice," Liberty said politely.

Gavan couldn't help a smile at Liberty's response. She could not have been less impressed by the tangential information Elizabeth had given them. But it did create a perfect moment to bring up *The Wilkins Affair*. Besides,

Elizabeth was uncomfortable and Gavan wanted to relieve her of her awkward position any way he could.

"I guess I should explain. I'm planning to write a book surrounding Mikel Wilkins and his mad grab for the family treasure," Gavan said lightly. He was rewarded by instant interest from both Liberty and Jarrett. Elizabeth was relieved to no longer be the center of their attention.

"Really?" Liberty murmured thoughtfully. "Is this a collaborative effort, Elizabeth?"

"Unauthorized at best," Elizabeth answered frankly.

"It sounds fascinating," Liberty said.

"Good, because I was hoping I could interview you about what happened," Gavan said quickly.

"Oh, now that's different," Liberty wavered, giving him a wide smile. "I didn't mean I want to be a part of it."

"No rush," Gavan said smoothly, thinking it wasn't far off from Elizabeth's initial reaction to him. Look alike and think alike. He was intrigued. "I have to be in New York for a few weeks. But when I get back in town, unless you plan on coming to New York before then, maybe we could talk? By then I would have spoken with Mrs. Wilkins."

"I didn't know you were leaving. I thought you were having dinner at Henry's," Elizabeth said impulsively, then chided herself for being so obvious with her disappointment.

"Yeah, I forgot about that when Henry mentioned it," Gavan admitted, omitting the fact that he was so flustered by Elizabeth he would have forgotten his own birthday had Henry asked. "I have a few things including some book signings that I have to take care of," he added.

"You don't have to explain. That's your business," Elizabeth said quickly. Her tone was sharper than she intended. Nerves. She had to get them under control.

Gavan frowned at Elizabeth's brush-off. For a moment they had made a connection. But it had only been a moment and he was lost as to how to get it back.

"Jarrett and I didn't mean to intrude," Liberty said, breaking through the fog that had shrouded Gavan and Elizabeth as they once again became engrossed in one another.

Gavan pulled his gaze from Elizabeth. Giving his attention to Liberty, he said with smooth persuasion, "You're not intruding at all. Elizabeth is on her way to see her grandmother and I'm on my way out. But I do hope you'll take time to consider my request. And, like I said, I won't be in town for a bit so hopefully when I get back you'll agree to talk to me about the book. It won't be slander either, I assure you," Gavan added with a broad grin.

"She'll think about it," Jarrett said briskly.

"Jarrett!" Liberty hissed, her irritation that he had spoken for her evident in her tone.

Gavan decided it was an opportune moment to exit. He pushed the elevator button and considered Elizabeth as he waited for it to arrive.

"I've detained you long enough, Elizabeth. See to your grandmother and I'll be calling soon to finish our discussion. It feels as if I'm back to square one," he added with a rueful smile.

"I'm not sure what that means," Elizabeth murmured.

"I'm betting you do," Gavan suggested. "I'll see you soon?" Elizabeth didn't respond and he sighed. The elevator arrived and he got on it, saying to Liberty and Jarrett, "Well, Jarrett, Liberty, a pleasure to meet you and I hope we'll have a talk real soon."

"Same here," Jarrett said.

"Maybe," Liberty said with a smile to take the edge of her terse response. Gavan nodded, giving Elizabeth a last yearning glance before the elevator doors separated them. He had the sinking feeling that she would find any excuse to avoid him and he could not understand how something as simple as his meeting Anne Wilkins had so upset her.

Liberty considered Elizabeth with a questioning gaze. Elizabeth was alarmed by it. It didn't help when Liberty turned to Jarrett and sweetly asked, "Would you mind giving me and Elizabeth a moment alone? We'll be in the waiting room."

Jarrett hesitated, uneasy at leaving the two women alone, but he agreed. "I'll wait for you here."

"Thanks, hon," Liberty said, then gave Jarrett an affectionate kiss on the cheek, silently forgiving him for his imperiousness with Gavan Ward, before leading Elizabeth to the waiting area.

Elizabeth had never felt so humbled in her life. With feet that felt weighed down by a ton of steel, she followed Liberty to the small waiting area and politely sat across from the woman who was identical to her in every way except by blood.

"I never thought you were guilty, Elizabeth," Liberty began reassuringly.

"Jarrett did," Elizabeth pointed out. She crossed her legs and raised her chin with regal aplomb. Liberty noticed, hesitated, and wondered fleetingly if she should assume a like profile. She decided not to attempt such a farce. She was a simple woman from an ordinary background. Mikel had given her the history of the Wilkinses, and Liberty would come across as gauche and drab if she imitated Elizabeth.

"Maybe," Liberty responded, choosing to cross her ankles instead.

"No maybe in this one. He still does, most likely," Elizabeth retorted. Agitated, she rocked her right foot and

Liberty's gaze was drawn to the pretty pink sandals. Liberty had worn blue jeans and a white pullover hoodie top and white Nikes. She wondered how she ever fooled anyone that she was Elizabeth Wilkins.

"He's protective of me," Liberty explained softly.

"Completely understandable," Elizabeth said, glancing away uncomfortably.

"I am not your enemy," Liberty said. "I've grown very close to Anne and I don't want a misunderstanding between us to come between Anne and me being friends."

Elizabeth laughed humorlessly. "Misunderstanding? No, I can't see how it would come between you and Anne."

"Normally, it wouldn't. But isn't she going to stay with you for a while?" Liberty queried, not catching the irony in Elizabeth's voice.

Elizabeth's eyes widened in surprise at the news. "I . . . we hadn't discussed it."

"She said she was staying with you," Liberty insisted.

"Then I guess that's her intent," Elizabeth conceded, but she was upset. Playing nursemaid to Anne was the last thing she needed, but under the circumstances, how could she refuse her?

"Elizabeth, I know what Mikel did. None of it made sense. I knew you were in danger and I want you to know I'm glad you're free. I'm glad your nutcase cousin is put away, but I believe you when you say you had nothing to do with it."

Elizabeth stared at Liberty for a while before uncrossing her legs. She leaned forward and asked in a harsh whisper, "How can you suggest you believe me when you were in the car with me? Don't you recall my taking the money out? That's what got me in trouble."

"And it was strange too. In hindsight I could tell you were nervous."

"It could have been just doing the crime that had my nerves on edge, Liberty. Not innocence."

Liberty was silent, then asked with a lowered gaze, "Then are you saying you're not innocent? Are you admitting you were a part of the scheme, Elizabeth?"

"No. I'm just having difficulty understanding your motives. I *know* I'm innocent. I know Mikel forced me to help him. I was there when he held you hostage because I was being held as well. I know he's a creep and so much worse. But you . . . you have no reason to believe in my innocence or forgive my part, Liberty. So, why are you doing this?" Elizabeth's expression was stoic, her gaze direct, but her voice trembled with the threat of tears and Liberty wanted to hold her, to explain she understood and that all was forgiven. They had both been used and traumatized and Liberty wasn't about to blame herself or Elizabeth.

"I told you. For Anne. But believe it or not, Elizabeth, I'm glad you're free. And I do believe in your innocence. Now," Liberty added, standing with a note of finality, "we can be cordial or you can make this situation tense. But I want to visit Anne when I return—"

"Return?" Elizabeth inquired, standing as well.

Liberty glanced down the hall toward the elevator Jarrett had followed Gavan on, and then looked at Elizabeth again. "Jarrett and I are getting married tomorrow. It's been a long time coming. We're going on a short honeymoon, because of Jamal and everything, but when we get back, if Anne is still with you, I was hoping to visit. Not every day but every now and then and I didn't want any bad vibes between us. I'm willing to let it go, forget about it, as much as can be forgotten of course, and move on. For Anne's sake but frankly for our own peace of mind as well."

"I guess I mistook your intent, huh?" Elizabeth said, giving her first genuine smile.

"Uh-huh, you did." Liberty laughed, then impulsively hugged the woman that she had impersonated less than a week earlier.

CHAPTER 12

Anne was fully dressed, her miniature-sized handbag pressed against her chest, her green eyes staring impassively at the television set that hung precariously from the ceiling of her hospital room. Elizabeth hesitated at the door, taking in her grandmother's frailness with dismay. When last she saw Anne, the paramedics were taking her away. Since then she had been so caught up in her own desperate affairs, it never occurred to her that Anne would have changed.

But she had. Her short blond hair had lost its luster and was now more gray than blond. She had lost weight, too, although understandable with the notoriety of hospital food as a diet. And her liquid green eyes, when they peered at Elizabeth, were less fearsome and had a dullness that had not been there before.

Elizabeth managed to refrain from expressing her shock. She cringed inwardly both from the impatient pinched expression on Anne's face that was a clear indication she could expect a harsh exchange and the cryptic voice, the only familiar aspect of her grandmother, that filled the room with a cantankerous rendition of the hospital's poor administering.

"Repeatedly I asked the nurse to check on that ridiculous television set. I swear it's going to fall any moment. And what has she done? Nothing." Anne considered her grandchild with her usual impartial perusal that never indicated approval or displeasure. "May I inquire what took you so long, Elizabeth?"

It was more a reprimand than an inquiry, but Elizabeth obliged her, calmly kissed Anne's pale cheek, then gave a vague explanation for her delay. "I was delayed by several unexpected visitors. I see that you are ready," she added, not wishing to explain further.

"I've been ready for days," Anne retorted testily. But she didn't rise. Instead, her gaze searching, she asked, "Did you see Liberty Sutton? She was just here."

"I saw her," was Elizabeth's noncommittal response.

Anne frowned slightly at the blaisé answer as Elizabeth picked up her belongings, which were absurdly two bags' worth of items she had collected during her stay, then pointedly waited at the door. Anne watched her granddaughter with open curiosity. She had questions about Elizabeth's release, her intentions with the company, and why she had not called. But, seeing the nurse who she personally felt was incompetent and crass, she chose to refrain from further comment until they were alone.

Nurse Mary, a young, full-figured Hispanic woman, gave Elizabeth a wide pretentious smile. "Good morning," Mary said with false brightness, her brown eyes darting from Elizabeth to Anne, then back to Elizabeth. "I'm Mrs. Wilkins's nurse, Mary. I don't believe you've signed in. She's expecting her granddaughter, but if you could sign in, I'll be glad to let you continue your visit."

Elizabeth chafed at the nurse's overly flamboyant cheerfulness and responded with an exaggerated artificial perkiness, mimicking the nurse, "Actually I am her granddaughter, but thank you, Mary. If you can sign her out, that would be all."

Oblivious of Elizabeth's ridicule, Mary lost the smile, her eyes blinked rapidly, and she said, "You're her granddaughter?" From the moment Anne had gained consciousness right up until that morning, Anne Wilkins had complained and harangued the nurses and her doctor. Mary was thrilled that the bitter, old woman was leaving, but it didn't outweigh her shock that the lovely and pleasant-looking young woman before her was related to Anne.

"Is that a problem?" Elizabeth retorted, all pretense of pleasantries gone. She recalled with some misgiving her grandmother's words upon her arrival and for a moment she worried that her grandmother had not been treated well. But then she dismissed the concern. Anne would never allow anyone to treat her less than well.

Mary didn't appear to have heard Elizabeth. She was too intent in examining Elizabeth's and Anne's differences. Anne was an elderly, frail, blonde-haired white woman, with pale wrinkled skin, keen green eyes, and a mouth so thin she appeared grim even when she smiled. Elizabeth was a tall, dark-haired black woman who despite her light coloring had no resemblance to the aging woman. Mary had a difficult time digesting that the two were related and peered closer at Elizabeth. Then, eyes brightening as if she had made a major discovery, Mary snapped her fingers and said, "Of course, you're adopted."

Elizabeth gaped at the nurse's boldness, glanced at her grandmother, then shook her head in incredulity. The nurse was fake and brazen in her ignorance. Ignoring the erroneous observation and allowing her exasperation to reveal itself, Elizabeth said, "My grandmother is ready to leave. Where do we sign?"

Mary, to Elizabeth's astonishment, actually took the hint and with a mumbled "I'll be right back," hurried to the nurses' station to ready Anne's paperwork.

It wasn't uncommon for people to express surprise or even disbelief when Elizabeth and Anne claimed relations, but few were as crass as the nurse and Elizabeth was not in an indulgent mood. She had to do enough explaining to last her a lifetime; besides, it was inconsequential what anyone thought regarding her grandmother. Then Elizabeth paused, an image of Gavan invaded her thoughts, and she wondered if Henry had explained her relations. Knowing Henry, she was certain Gavan had no idea about her parentage or family beyond Mikel's scandalous crime. He was going to be in for a shock, much as the nurse was experiencing. A whisper of a smile curved Elizabeth's mouth at the thought that Gavan was going to be in for a shock when he discovered her grandmother was a southern, white woman.

"I'm glad to see you still have your sense of humor," Anne murmured, not missing the slight change in her granddaughter's demeanor.

Elizabeth sighed, took hold of Anne's bony arm, and after tucking it in the nook of her arm, slowly guided her grandmother from the room. Halfway to the nurses' station, Mary reappeared pushing a wheelchair with a folder in the seat. Elizabeth was cajoling despite Anne's huffed complaint that only invalids needed wheelchairs.

"It's hospital procedures, Anne," Elizabeth said patiently. She helped Mary settle Anne into the seat.

"Bah! I'm ready to get out of here. Have you moved my things to your house, Elizabeth? I told Sonya I wanted to stay with you."

"I found out this morning. Nothing's been done,

Anne. But don't worry. I'll see to it once you get settled in," Elizabeth answered.

Anne breathed a heavy sigh, drawing Elizabeth's gaze. "Are you all right?"

"No, I am not. I am furious about all of this. As soon as I can, I want you to take me to see Mikel. I intend to tell the rascal just what I think about him."

"Rascal? Don't you think you're being a little kind?" Elizabeth scoffed. She walked a few steps ahead and pushed the elevator button, but she heard Anne's harsh reply.

"Bastard then," Anne reaffirmed. Then she glanced slyly at Elizabeth and Elizabeth tensed instinctively. "Whatever you want to call him. Now, have you heard about Gavan T. Ward?" Anne inquired.

"Of course. He's an author," Elizabeth answered with seeming nonchalance, but her heart pounded rapidly and she couldn't fathom where Anne was going with her inquiry.

"An author who wants to discuss a book about my life." Anne was silent and Elizabeth waited, knowing there was more to come. The nurse led them onto the elevator and it wasn't until they reached the lobby when Anne finally added, "I won't allow it. I was flattered, naturally, but I will not have strangers ogling my life. I won't have him interviewing you, either."

That was so like Anne, Elizabeth thought rancorously. She didn't ask, she ordered. Well, it wasn't Anne's choice if Elizabeth chose to indulge Gavan. Annoyed, Elizabeth wondered what Liberty Sutton found so appealing about Anne. For that matter, she wondered at Anne's genuine affection for her young neighbor. Even before the Mikel incident, Anne had taken a liking to Liberty. It had gone unnoticed by Elizabeth, but now she wondered why. Anne never expressed more than a passing interest in anyone since her son, Elizabeth's father, passed years earlier. Liberty was an enigma that Elizabeth could not grasp.

Of course, Elizabeth rationalized, Liberty hadn't known Anne long and she certainly wasn't around often enough to experience Anne's arrogance or demanding nature. The truth was, there was nothing warm about Anne, not even when she was giving. Elizabeth knew firsthand. She was often the recipient of Anne's generous gifts, but that fact didn't ease the void the lack of affection created. As a child, Elizabeth used to be confused that this unapproachable woman who barely allowed herself to smile or offer any warmth was ostentatiously passionate at giving gifts. As a woman, Elizabeth accepted the situation. It was Anne's way of showing affection. Well then, so be it.

"When he calls you, you just tell him no," Anne added.

Clearly Anne had no idea that she had already met Gavan, let alone given him far more attention than she had planned. Elizabeth chose not to enlighten her. She simply didn't have the energy to explain the events of the past few days to Anne. She chanced a glance at her grandmother and wondered what she would think if Gavan told her about her outburst during dinner. Anne wouldn't approve, of that Elizabeth was certain.

"I'll get the car," Elizabeth said the moment they were off the elevator.

Anne watched her grandchild rush away but made no attempt to stop her. She purposefully ignored the nurse and focused on her grandchild's distracted behavior. Naturally there was a lot on the young woman's mind and there would be time to talk to Elizabeth, of that Anne was confident. There was nothing to do but allow time to heal the wounds Mikel had wreaked upon them.

"Well, I'll be there to watch over her," she said aloud.

"Ma'am?" Mary asked.

"Nothing," Anne said dismissively.

Elizabeth's familiar car pulled into the driveway. Anne came to her feet, hating that she needed the nurse's assistance to do so, and without another glance at Mary, joined her granddaughter.

"Ready?" Elizabeth asked with a quick smile after her grandmother settled into the passenger seat, fastened her seat belt, and set her purse on her lap.

"As can be," Anne replied. She wanted to say more and to ask many questions, but she could feel Elizabeth's tension. She chose to give her grandchild a little time before questioning her. If it took a few days before Elizabeth opened up, Anne was willing to wait. In compatible silence perfected over the years, they left the hospital.

At last they were going home.

CHAPTER 13

"That was too strange," Tyke rambled, leaning into the front seat to talk between Lance and Gavan. "Did you see that other woman? Lance and I nearly collided when she came down with that guy." Tyke laughed, shaking his head in amazement.

"A bit of an exaggeration, but she did take us for a surprise," Lance said dryly.

"Surprise? Please, I was like wow! One moment she's sharp as a whip and the next she's in jeans and casual."

"We get it, Tyke. Like I said, Mikel clearly knew what he was doing when he chose Liberty Sutton to impersonate Elizabeth. Their resemblance is incredible," Gavan said patiently.

"Yeah. I couldn't tell them apart. It wasn't until we saw that guy that we knew for certain she wasn't Elizabeth."

"I wouldn't go that far. There were distinctions. Let's start with the fact that they could not have been dressed more differently," Lance argued.

"Yeah, that threw me off," Tyke agreed.

"You think?" Lance mocked.

"But I knew for certain when she didn't even see Gavan wave that she wasn't Elizabeth."

"How's that?" Gavan asked, frowning.

"Please, man, the way you two were staring at each other! An idiot could see she was digging you."

"There you have it. The idiot has spoken." Lance laughed.

"She's got a man, so what do I care?" Gavan scoffed, not amused.

"We saw. And that guy looked tough, didn't he?"

"His name is Jarrett Irving," Gavan said patiently. "And everyone next to you is tough."

Liberty and Jarrett came down not long after Gavan left them with Elizabeth. He had dallied around, to Lance's annoyance, unwilling to admit he had no reason to stay beyond a vague hope of seeing Elizabeth again. The interview with Anne was now out of the question. And he wasn't ready to go any further with his inquiry with Liberty Sutton as of yet. When he got off the elevator he had felt like a fool when he caught sight of them and, as Tyke so eloquently put it, they didn't see him. He had even waved. It went unnoticed. Beneath Tyke's observing remarks, he suffered a bout of embarrassment, an affliction he rarely experienced. It wasn't as if he was attracted to Liberty Sutton although she could have been Elizabeth's twin. As Lance pointed out, Liberty was different in small ways from Elizabeth.

Liberty was slightly shorter than Elizabeth, her complexion more golden, and her figure was more curvaceous, so much more so that she exuded a sensuality even in her loose sweatshirt, fitted jeans, and tennis shoes. It was in her slow smile, her slanted brown-eyed gaze, and her sultry, relaxed stride. Had he seen her first he might even have been attracted to her. But he preferred Elizabeth's more inconspicuous appeal. She was chic, her appearance was flawless, and she had a subtle allure that stirred Gavan's curiosity the moment he saw her. Her sensuality was resting below the surface, yet

Gavan suspected if impassioned she would be more than Liberty's equal. He wondered what she was like when she didn't have her guard up. He grinned, realizing he wasn't thinking like a writer.

"Thinking about Elizabeth or Liberty?" Tyke asked, peering at him with a knowing grin.

"Shut up, Tyke," both Gavan and Lance said at once.

The brothers laughed, shaking their heads in amazement at Tyke. He could be the most annoying person and over the years, rather than becoming more subdued, it had increased. He had the unique distinction of having the ability to grate them to distraction. He was a close friend, a result of Lance and Gavan interfering on behalf of Tyke when, during a late night out on the town, they stumbled upon several thugs attacking him. Neither brother had thought about his own safety. They immediately jumped into the fray and moments later the three thugs split the scene, leaving Tyke surprisingly unharmed and in the care of two large men.

Come to find out, Tyke was also a student at the Pacific University of Hawaii. Both Gavan and Lance were attending and they hadn't been able to get rid of him since then.

They got used to his uninvited tagging along wherever they went. They introduced Tyke to many women and as a result, he thought of the brothers as ladies' men. Gavan would be the last person to deny it, but he would never describe himself as a player either. He was an unreformed bachelor and he had no intention of changing his status. He was a young thirty-six-year-old and happy with his life.

And meeting Elizabeth hadn't changed him *that* much. So why was he unable to stop thinking about her?

She was baffling and unpredictable. She laughed easily but had a temper that flared with the same ease.

Initially he had contributed her flustered response to the fact that she had received news that she was free only a heartbeat before they met. At dinner he accepted, too, that she was overcome with emotions that she likely had been forced to keep at bay during her tribulation.

But it was their last meeting that baffled him the most. He was certain he had broken through her reserve. And yet, before he could be sure that he had scored, she rebounded and she shut down again.

He could not imagine what he had done. And yet, in a blink of an eye, she transformed to a reserved, guarded woman again, their lighthearted banter gone.

He was confounded as to why. It didn't help that he had to be in New York in the morning and wouldn't be back for more than a week.

The last thing he wanted to do was allow Elizabeth to build up her guard and declare herself unavailable to him upon his return. He was justifiably concerned. She was dismissive on one hand, engaging on the other.

The only good news was that he had made a little headway, incidentally or not, and he was not going to give up the edge he had gained. It was a shame that Liberty interrupted their discussion.

And ironic.

Liberty Sutton was the person he originally wanted to meet, but meeting Elizabeth had changed everything. For the span of a minute, he seriously considered giving up the Wilkins book idea. What he really wanted to do was wine and dine Elizabeth.

"Did you hear one word I said?" Lance demanded. His brown eyes were keen with insight and Gavan refused to squirm beneath his brother's unwavering gaze.

"No, I didn't. So what were you saying?" Gavan asked with an air of nonchalance that did not fool Lance.

"What time is your flight?" Lance repeated, expressing each word with such clarity that Gavan flinched. Lance clearly did not approve of Gavan's distraction with Elizabeth. Gavan understood but refused to discuss her with Lance.

"No need for that, Lance. I was distracted," Gavan said, then answered, "I'm on the three o'clock flight. I thought I would need the time to interview Anne Wilkins."

"Do you still want the research on Mikel Wilkins?" Tyke asked.

"Why wouldn't I?" Gavan demanded, growing annoyed.

"Call it instinct, but there's more to this book than your usual suspects, Gavan. I've worked with you enough to know the difference," Tyke said.

"Yeah, well, if I change my mind about the Wilkins book I'll let you know," Gavan huffed.

"You two are the testiest brothers on earth. Both of you are up to your necks with women and I got to tell you, it's amusing." Tyke laughed, enjoying the Wards' discomfort.

"I have no idea what you're talking about," Gavan said impatiently.

"No? That woman has turned your head 360 degrees. And Lance—"

"Mind your own business, Tyke," Lance interrupted coldly.

"What?" Gavan asked. A quick glance at his brother's stone expression increased his curiosity. There was a brief uncomfortable silence. Tyke cleared his throat, leaned forward, and whispered to Gavan, "Asia dumped him."

"Tyke!" Lance hissed, his brown eyes hard as granite and full of fury. There was no doubt if Tyke were any other man, Lance would have decked him. Tyke was thankful that they were friends. Nevertheless he sat as far back as his seat would allow.

"You were going to tell him anyway, why not now?" Tyke asked defensively.

"When did this happen?" Gavan asked, undisturbed by Lance's barely veiled violence.

"Last week," Lance grumbled. "It was just a fling."

"Like Maya?" Gavan asked gently. Lance caught his brother's stare, then glared out the window.

"Maya was nothing, I told you that a million times." Lance was rigid with fury. He didn't care that Asia had left. And he certainly didn't want to think about Maya's faithlessness. He didn't blame his brother for what happened. Gavan had no way of knowing who Maya was or how Lance felt about her. But the woman was a painful memory he had thought to forget through Asia.

"Yeah," Gavan murmured. A pang of guilt stabbed his guts as it always did when they discussed Maya.

Maya Ayunga had left a strong and unpleasant impression on Gavan. They met at one of his book signings. She was a full-blooded Hawaiian with big brown eyes and long, wavy hair. They dated for several weeks and he even introduced her to his parents. She was sweet, mild-tempered, and generous in her attention. And he had no idea that she was dating his brother.

Gavan had been shocked.

Lance was furious.

Maya was tearfully repentant.

It was her misfortune that the two men she was seeing happened to be brothers. He and Lance made the discovery when Val, their mother, insisted that it was time Gavan married. She thought Maya was the perfect choice and had a lovely picture of Gavan and Maya to support her reasoning. Didn't they look like a happily married couple? she had said, shoving the picture under their noses. Lance had taken the photo and stared at it in disgust.

Without a word, he stormed from the house and it

wasn't until the next morning that Lance confessed what Gavan had immediately suspected. He didn't admit to loving Maya, but Gavan was certain his younger brother did. Where Gavan was only vaguely upset by the incident, Lance was visibly shaken. They agreed not to tell their mother, Val. It would only upset her. Gavan broke up with Maya and a few weeks later, he was in New York. That was when Tyke told him about Elizabeth Wilkins. He jumped at the opportunity. But his recent episodes with women were not encouraging.

"Well, under the circumstances your grumpiness is acceptable. Not that you're not always out of sorts but today I'll forgive you," Gavan said lightly.

"He'll be over her in a week," Tyke said.

"I was over her before it began," Lance confided.

Gavan sighed. He hated seeing his brother that way and he wondered if any woman could ever have that effect on him. And then the vision of Elizabeth faded from view as the elevator doors shut. It was so final, the imagery. He was going to take care of his business and get back in town as soon as possible.

Two weeks later, bedraggled and frustrated after continuous book signings and meetings with his publisher and his agent, Gavan returned to Washington, D.C. During his stay in New York, he made several attempts to contact Elizabeth. Twice he left a message on her home phone. Once he spoke with her assistant, Sonya Brown. All were unsuccessful. She did return his call once. But he had to wonder if she deliberately called his hotel room when she had his cellular number.

Upon his return his first plan of action was to contact Elizabeth Wilkins and finish where they had left off.

CHAPTER 14

Gavan hoped to hear from Elizabeth. She knew he was back because, like a besotted pup, he had left her several messages the night before and again that morning. She had not returned his call. He had two messages from Henry, one reminding him of dinner on Sunday, another stating his disappointment that Gavan had not come.

He was certain it was a dig when the old man added that Elizabeth had come after all. There was another message from Tyke informing Gavan that he had run into a roadblock regarding Mikel's background beyond his relationship with Anne and Elizabeth. Anne wouldn't talk to him and Gavan was going to have to take care of the matter himself. Several messages were left by his mother and surprisingly, Liberty Sutton had returned his call.

After settling his luggage, he searched the refrigerator for a drink. There was one light beer and two sodas. He chose the soda, sat at the kitchen bar, and then returned Liberty Sutton's call.

"Hello," Liberty answered.

"Ms. Sutton? Gavan Ward here," he said.

"Gavan. How are you?" Liberty asked easily, dismissing with formalities.

"I'm well," he said, adding. "I'll be better if you have good news for me."

"Well, I haven't totally rejected your request, if you consider that good news. Oh, and I got married," she added cheerfully.

Gavan laughed, stating, "That is good news. When did this happen?" he asked.

"Last week. Jarrett and I got married the day after we met you, as a matter of fact. You can now call me Mrs. Irving."

"Will do and congratulations," Gavan said with genuine warmth.

"Thank you," Liberty said brightly. Then abruptly her manner sobered and she said, "But that's not why I called."

"No?" Gavan probed.

"Have you been to see the Wilkinses yet? Have they agreed to the interview?"

"No and no. I only recently got back in town."

"You mentioned that you were going to meet with Mrs. Wilkins this week. And I'm bringing it up because, as I said before, I have no problem with speaking with you. But I'm not inclined to go any further if it'll upset Mrs. Wilkins."

"Meaning Anne Wilkins," Gavan clarified, reassuring himself as he did so that Elizabeth was not married.

"Of course."

"Well," he continued, relieved, "your concern is understandable. But I hope to convince you and the Wilkinses that I mean no one any harm. Actually, I planned to call Mrs. Wilkins once I got settled in, but I don't have her home number. I only had her hospital room information. If you have it, that would be helpful and I could at least let you know where she stands on this."

"No one told you?"

"Told me what?" Gavan inquired.

"Mrs. Wilkins is staying with Elizabeth for a little while."

"No. No one told me," Gavan said, wondering how he was going to manage a visit with Anne Wilkins without upsetting Elizabeth *again*. Then his eyes glimmered with excitement. If Anne was at Elizabeth's home, it was a perfect opportunity to see Elizabeth. She had studiously ignored his last calls, not even attempting to return them. He was being ignored and it was his own doing for not being direct. He should have let her know his interest went beyond his work. If he could get another chance to speak with her, he was going to be direct. He wanted to ask her out and forget about the book for the evening. Liberty's next words served him well and he smiled in approval.

"I have an idea," she declared with enthusiasm. "Jarrett and I are visiting Ms. Wilkins today. Why don't you come with us? We can meet you there and then we can all discuss your project together. I think it'll be more convincing if you were to make your request in person rather than by phone. Don't you agree?"

"I agree," he confirmed but as a precautionary measure, he suggested, "Perhaps you should check with Elizabeth first. She may not appreciate an unexpected visit."

"Elizabeth?" Liberty asked as if he were speaking of a stranger. "Do you think she'd care? I hadn't thought about that, but she's at work anyway. But you needn't worry that we're unexpected. I called this morning to confirm that I was coming by. Even if Elizabeth was home, she wouldn't mind, I'm sure. She knows who you are."

"Indeed she does," he said with a drollery that Liberty failed to grasp.

Gavan sighed, inclined to accept her suggestion. It fit perfectly with his goal to see Elizabeth again, but he was concerned how she would view it. He glanced at the clock. It was well past eleven and he expected Lance and Tyke at any moment. Tyke wanted to go over his notes and Gavan also planned to get his brother's assistance by investigating the Sutton woman's family history. As important as his brother's aid was, Gavan didn't want to miss the opportunity to finally meet Anne Wilkins or another chance encounter with Elizabeth.

If Elizabeth was home, he would speak with her and make his position clear. And if she wasn't there, what harm could it do? Either way, it served his purpose to accept Liberty's offer. He would go with Liberty. "Count me in. Let me ask you this. If I were to bring my associates, would that be a problem?"

"What associates?" Liberty asked.

"My brother and a friend. They often assist me with getting material for my books."

"I can't see why not, Gavan. It's all about the book, right?"

"Yeah," Gavan said slowly. It was all about Elizabeth, truth be told, but Liberty didn't need to know that. "So when are you leaving?"

"In half an hour or so. Do you have their address? You can meet me there."

"I don't have her address," Gavan said. Liberty provided Gavan with Elizabeth's address and directions and promised to meet him at Elizabeth's house.

Gavan hung up the phone, feeling slightly guilty for agreeing to Liberty's suggestion. He could use good judgment and call her back and decline her offer. But the desire to see Elizabeth was too strong. He wanted to see her. He couldn't deny it any more than he could deny his need to breathe.

Elizabeth was appalled. From across the room, she chanced a glance out the window and froze. She had just exited the kitchen, a tray with a bowl of fruit and tea for Anne in her hands. With tingling instincts, she moved toward to the window. Vehicles were approaching her house. She didn't recognize either the Mercedes or the Jaguar that pulled into her driveway. But she recognized Gavan's all too familiar face and the impact was vertiginous. The tray shook precariously in her hands and she promptly set it aside before swiftly returning to the window. With a trembling hand, she gingerly shifted the curtain to get a better view of him.

Gavan got out of his Jaguar and stood glancing over her property, his stance confident, his visage piercing even from the distance that separated them. The passenger door opened and two more gentlemen Elizabeth immediately recognized as Lance Ward and Tyke Miles stepped outside the car. Before she could catch her breath, the other car's door slammed and Elizabeth shifted her attention from Gavan, his brother, and Tyke. To her dismay, Liberty and Jarrett stepped out of their car, looking cheerful and energized.

What were they doing here? And why were they all together?

"What is it, Elizabeth?" Sonya asked, picking up the tray Elizabeth had deposited on the table. She came up behind Elizabeth and peered out the window. Elizabeth dropped the curtain and turned so sharply that Sonya nearly toppled the tray's content in an attempt to move it out of Elizabeth's way.

"What is it?" Sonya asked, alarmed.

"He's here," Elizabeth managed to whisper.

"Who?" Sonya asked, confused. She looked out the

window again. Her eyes were instantly drawn to Gavan's tall physique. Leaning against the car behind him were two other men. They didn't follow as Gavan approached Liberty and Jarrett. Sonya had no doubt whom Elizabeth was so worked up over. "Ah, the infamous author, I take it," she cooed, recalling Elizabeth's rendition of how she had met Gavan T. Ward, how handsome and utterly insufferable he was, and then her subsequent silence that followed for nearly two weeks.

"Did you know they were coming? Did Anne?" Elizabeth asked breathlessly.

"I don't recall Anne mentioning your author was coming today," Sonya said, referring to Gavan as the they in Elizabeth's question. "Anne did say she was expecting him to call. It appears that he chose to come with Ms. Sutton. That's Mrs. Irving now, isn't it? Well, perhaps she's giving him that interview he's so dead set on getting." She chattered on, all the while watching as the three moved up the walkway.

"What? Who gave her that right?" Elizabeth demanded, not hearing anything beyond that Liberty had invited Gavan Ward to her home. In her outrage, she forgot any benevolence toward Liberty.

"Anne, no doubt. She did say Liberty was coming by. I'm sure I told you before you left this morning," Sonya said. She was intrigued. Elizabeth's outrage over her unexpected visitors was completely out of character. Elizabeth was not an ungracious woman. Keeping her eyes on the door, Sonya monitored the change in Elizabeth, certain the issue was Gavan and not Liberty. Her young employer was smitten. She could only wonder how Gavan felt about Elizabeth.

Elizabeth flung the door open. She vaguely recalled the mentioning of Liberty's expected visit. But Liberty had failed to inform any of them that she was bringing guests, a grave faux pas under the circumstances. Her sudden presence stopped her visitors in their tracks and they all stared up at her, but it was Gavan that Elizabeth's eyes were drawn to. He was like a magnet and she was unable to resist a slanted inspection. He was always so neat and perfectly packaged. He wore a loose-fitting long-sleeve gray shirt tucked neatly into a pair of darker gray slacks. He carried the gadgets that she was beginning to realize he was never without, a cell phone in his shirt pocket, a Blackberry strapped to his belt. It somehow added to his appeal and she wished he wasn't so incredibly charismatic.

Standing a few feet behind Jarrett and Liberty, with eyes gleaming, Gavan greeted Elizabeth with a sheepish grin. It was as if he saw right through her surreptitious inspection of him. Beneath his steady gaze she flushed, experiencing a tangle of fascination and vexation. How he flustered her. It had been that way from the first. But she was determined to put aside her infatuation and ignore the sensations that he awakened. Her erroneous interpretation of his flirtatious exchange at the hospital, despite his friendly overtures and easy smiles, evidenced his interest in her as solely work related. He was there for all the wrong reasons and she would not forget it again.

She pulled her enamored gaze from Gavan, glanced at Lance and Tyke with a slight nod, then considered Jarrett and Liberty with a tottering smile.

"Liberty," she said with an impressive act of courteousness after her abrupt appearance. "I wish I had known you were bringing someone. We're not quite prepared." Her feigned politeness was hidden by a schooled expression of impassiveness. But her speech was strained and she wanted to wince at the sound.

Someone? He was reduced from Gavan to Mr. Ward

to Someone. What next? Gavan's grin weakened and all that remained was a self-mocking smirk.

Liberty was suitably contrite. The chastisement was deserved. Gavan had even warned her of the possibility, but she had not expected Elizabeth to be home. And she did not expect that, if Elizabeth were home, she would be upset by their visit. She was wrong. Elizabeth, in spite of her cool demeanor, was visibly vexed and it was all Liberty's fault.

Guilty, Liberty kept her gaze averted from Jarrett. He too had warned her not to ignore the possibility that Elizabeth might take offense at having uninvited guests. He had even advised her that there was more to Elizabeth's and Gavan's relationship than either was letting on. And Liberty, impetuous as ever, had not listened. Not only had she dragged Jarrett to Elizabeth's home but she also invited Gavan, and judging from the tension exuding from the pair, she suspected that Jarrett was right.

But there was nothing to be done. They were here now.

CHAPTER 15

"I am so sorry, Elizabeth. I had no idea you would be here. I know this is a rude surprise for you intruding on your home this way," Liberty apologized.

"It's not an intrusion," Elizabeth corrected. "Just a surprise."

"I know. But Jarrett and I are married now and . . ."

Elizabeth gasped, her eyes widened, and for the moment, Gavan's presence was forgotten. "How could I have forgotten? Congratulations!" she said with such pleasure that Liberty grinned and Jarrett chuckled in response.

Buoyed by Elizabeth's enthusiasm over her marriage, Liberty tossed Jarrett a private smile, then said, "Thank you, Elizabeth. I'm really happy and that's just it. Anne insisted that we come by today after I told her the news. So, here we are."

"Yes, but you drove *him* here, too." Elizabeth literally pointed at Gavan, then hastily dropped her hand disconcerted beneath his slow, languid perusal.

"Actually, I drove myself." She shot him an exasperated look.

"Of course. I meant you found your way here because

of Liberty," Elizabeth explained and grew more discomposed at the implications of her statement.

Gavan grinned innocently, pleased that he had her attention. She was so determined to ignore him after that first cursory acknowledgement of him that he was inspired to get her attention any way he could. Their parting, although not a warm good-bye, had not been that sour and yet she was displeased with his presence.

A sudden unpleasant thought assailed him. Perhaps she was entertaining guests already.

Although Tyke had made no mention of a male in Elizabeth's life, she could be seeing someone else. Maya had taught him that lesson well. Until that moment it had never occurred to him to consider it. He had been presumptuous in his own vanity to expect her to welcome him without inhibitions. Disliking the idea that her rejection could be anything more than her fear of having to discuss his book, he narrowed his eyes and happened to catch Lance's glance.

The mocking gaze didn't massage Gavan's ego. Lance was no fan of any woman these days. He would not be impressed upon by his brother's brooding. Still, he couldn't control the worry he felt and asked Elizabeth, "Are you entertaining someone? I could come at another time . . ."

"No. I'm alone. I mean, it's just Anne and me and . . . and Sonya," she stated quickly, flustered by the inquiry. Where in the world did he get the idea that she was entertaining?

"Then it's my poor timing and judgment that I must apologize for," he said, schooling his features to hide his relief. His voice was full of warmth and charm and caressed her from head to toe. She nearly came undone and took a deep, steadying breath.

"Mr. Ward—" she began warily.

"Are we back to that? Is Gavan so unpleasant, *Elizabeth*?" he interrupted, emphasizing her name.

Elizabeth hesitated, wishing Liberty and Jarrett were not witnessing the recalcitrant exchange. "Gavan," she said, obliging him.

Then speaking as if she were chastising a child, she scolded him. "Did I not express my position on your book?"

"You did," he confirmed.

"And yet you are here?" she asked, raising her chin in irritation.

"That I am," he agreed with a big smile.

Elizabeth took a deep breath, exasperated. "You're uninvited."

"And for that I apologize," Gavan said quickly, stifling his frustration at his failure to engage her as he had done at the hospital. He needed to be alone with her long enough to explain his position. But as of yet she had not allowed any of them to enter the house. Bemused, he wondered if she would really turn them away. "I was hoping to change your mind."

"My mind is made up or are you confused?" She didn't intend to give him the opportunity to respond and was preparing to dismiss him when she remembered Liberty and Jarrett. She hesitated, giving Gavan the opportunity to capture her attention again.

"But I am confused. What is it that you want, Elizabeth?" he asked softly.

Elizabeth flushed, certain he was referring to more than his book. He wanted to know if he should stay or go. How could she answer such a question? "I *want* no part of your book, Gavan. My life is private. I thought I made that clear."

"I see," he murmured. He seemed to stand taller,

more broad, his gaze direct, and then added, "I should go."

Lance and Tyke got in the car when Gavan headed toward them. They, like Liberty and Jarrett, had overheard snatches of the conversation. These were enough to imply Gavan was leaving.

Elizabeth was instantly contrite. Gavan's retreating back was more devastating than she could have imagined. Throwing caution to the wind, impulsively she cleared the space between them. Ignoring the curious eyes upon her, she tapped Gavan's shoulder, capturing his regard and halting his stride. He turned to her, his eyes fathomless.

With her pulse fluttering wildly, she said, "I didn't mean you're not welcome. You're here to see Anne and I have no right to turn you away."

"But I'm uninvited," he mocked, more aware of her light touch than he cared to be.

"Yes, but that is hardly the same thing. I'm sorry, Gavan, I've been rude. Please, come inside." She attempted a smile.

Gavan studied her a moment, his gaze searching, and then he nodded, but the teasing light was gone and his face was so impassive Elizabeth was concerned. She felt awful. She swallowed her regret and added, "They do not have to wait in the car, Gavan. They're welcome to come in." She was referring to Lance and Tyke, and Gavan almost laughed. He'd forgotten they were even there.

"Give me a moment," he said, then had a private conversation with his brother. A moment later, to Elizabeth's astonishment, Lance got in the driver's seat and left.

"What . . . how will you get home?" she asked.

"He'll be back," was his confident response.

"I see," Elizabeth murmured, then hurried ahead of him and led her guest inside the house.

"I apologize that bringing him was a problem, Elizabeth. Anne gave no indication that it would be when we discussed his interest in interviewing her. I was unaware of how adamantly you are against the book and apparently him," Liberty said, her tone unintentionally loud enough for Gavan to hear.

Elizabeth didn't respond. She didn't dare. Anything she said could be misinterpreted and with Gavan within earshot, she would not take the risk.

Jarrett observed Gavan's bemusement and chuckled, the look of pure misery on the author's face indication enough that he had heard Liberty. After Elizabeth's about-face, Gavan was and looked absolutely confused. Jarrett could imagine how he must feel. He had gone through similar misunderstandings with Liberty before she admitted that their love could not be conquered. He whisked Liberty to the courthouse and got married the moment she said yes. He was determined she would never again slip away. Glancing tenderly at his new wife, he decided despite her impetuous nature that it was the smartest decision he had ever made.

"I guess we're allowed inside now," he said.

"Think I should go home?" Gavan wondered aloud.

"I wouldn't leave yet," Jarrett recommended. Then with a shrug, he added, "But you have to make that decision for yourself."

Gavan lagged behind in a moment of indecision before following Jarrett.

"Since I was coming to see Anne I thought it would be all right if Gavan came along. He wanted to meet with both of us, so I thought, let's make it simple. I guess I'm trying to apologize," Liberty was explaining to Elizabeth when Gavan entered the house.

"I apologize for my behavior as well," Elizabeth murmured. She was instantly aware of Gavan's presence and followed his path from her front door to the center of her foyer where he hung back, his easygoing stance gone, the carefree rogue nowhere in sight.

She sighed in regret. Again she had made a spectacle of herself. Since he had emerged onto the scene, it seemed overreacting was becoming the norm for her. It wasn't that she wanted him to leave. She scarcely thought of nothing but him during the time he spent in New York. Whether she was working or resting, involuntarily her thoughts would stray to Gavan.

But she had resolved not to call him after the embarrassing encounter at the hospital. Despite her resolve, he on the other hand had no qualms about calling her. Twice she was present when the line rang and listened as he left brief messages, her heart singing that he had called. She had succumbed to his persistent calls and returned one of them. Ironically, he was not available and she had been able to suppress the urge to call him again.

Now that he was here, standing in her home, looking incredibly handsome, she worried she would never be able to ignore him. It occurred to her that she had missed him. Shaken by the realization, she regarded Liberty for several seconds while she regained her composure, then murmured, "May I speak with you a moment?"

Liberty tossed a wary glance at Jarrett and at his subtle nod, she stepped aside with Elizabeth. They didn't go far and Liberty realized the distance was to get them outside Jarrett's and Gavan's hearing range. Curious, she turned to Elizabeth and waited for her to speak.

Elizabeth clasped her hands together. "I didn't mean to react so strongly out there. I've been through a lot. . . ."

"Of course, we all have," Liberty agreed.

"But it's no excuse. You've been wonderful to Anne, and I want to apologize," Elizabeth continued.

"Elizabeth—" Liberty attempted to interrupt again, but Elizabeth wouldn't allow her.

"Please, Liberty, hear me out. I want to tell you that I am sorry, too, that you had to go through that ordeal with Mikel. He was always hateful, but I never guessed the depth of his anger."

"Let's be real, Elizabeth. Who would guess something like that? Please, you don't have to apologize for his craziness," Liberty said emphatically.

"Yes, I do," Elizabeth said firmly. "The moment I saw you and suspected what Mikel did to Anne, I could have warned you that he was, well, crazy. But I didn't. I was naïve and it caused you a great deal of trouble. Wait, please let me finish," Elizabeth pleaded when Liberty opened her mouth to protest again. "I'm embarrassed by all of this, but I am grateful to you for looking after my grandmother. Had you not been there . . ." Her voice caught as she tried to stifle a sob.

Liberty gave Elizabeth's shoulder an encouraging squeeze, saying softly, "It's been a trying time for everyone, but I understand where you're coming from. I'm glad Anne is all right as well."

Elizabeth nodded her agreement, and inevitably her gaze strayed to Gavan. He was looking right at her. Her pulse jumped in response and she had to swallow to breathe. Even across the room he had the ability to overwhelm her with his presence.

"So am I," Elizabeth managed to respond. Dragging her attention back to Liberty, she added, "And I'm glad you're here. Anne will enjoy your visit and maybe, despite everything, we could become friends?" It was a question, one that moved them both.

Liberty grinned impishly, easing the tension between

them, and gave Elizabeth an impetuous hug. "I suspect
we'll be friends or at the least, tolerant of each other."
She laughed.

"At the very least," Elizabeth agreed, her smile more
serene, no less enthusiastic.

Although she and Liberty were of a different breed-
ing, Elizabeth found Liberty's unpretentiousness re-
freshing. They might look eerily alike but together they
were like night and day. Elizabeth decided their dis-
similarities were complementary and she returned Liberty's hug with genuine affection and relief. As she did
so, she raised her gaze and her breath caught. It was as
if Gavan had never taken his eyes off of her. Their eyes
locked and neither could pull away. Then Liberty pulled
free, stepped aside, and the spell was broken.

Unbalanced by the lengthy contact, Elizabeth murmured, "Anne's in her room. I'll check in and see if she
would rather come down or have you come up for your
visit."

Disturbed at how aware she was of Gavan's vigilance
in following her retreat, she hurried up the stairway and
down the long hallway, not stopping until she was outside Anne's bedroom and safely out of his sight.

CHAPTER 16

"She's upset that he's here, Anne."

Anne's bedroom door was ajar and Elizabeth paused at hearing their conspiratorial whispers, particularly since she was the topic under discussion. Her advocate's irritation was heard in the hissing wheeze that accompanied her words. Elizabeth took a tentative step forward, not intending to eavesdrop, but Anne's response gave her pause.

Anne was dismissive. "Nothing upsets her."

Elizabeth exhaled a weary sigh. Anne couldn't have been more wrong, Elizabeth thought. Her face was flushed, her hands shook, and her temples throbbed, all compliments of Gavan's arrival. She could have laughed if it weren't so *upsetting*.

"Well, this does," Sonya countered staunchly. "You should have warned her that he was coming."

"I don't see what all this howling is about, Sonya. Besides, I told her weeks ago that he wanted to meet me," Anne pointed out.

"Did you tell her he was coming here?" Sonya persisted.

"I cannot see what difference any of this makes. She is simply going to have to get over what happened.

Mikel is locked up, for life, I'll wager. Kidnapping? My God, what that boy wasn't willing to do to bring this family down. But never mind him."

"Yes, never mind Mikel," Sonya stated flatly. Anne had a knack for avoiding a subject distasteful to her. It left Sonya with little doubt that Anne was aware of her error in judgment. "Let's discuss your guests below. Are you going to give him the whole family history and embarrass the poor child more than this ordeal already has done or are you going to take your grandchild's feelings into account and send him away?"

"I haven't decided what I am going to do. I am only discussing his book. Liberty wanted to consider it and I agreed," Anne said with growing impatience.

"Liberty is a sweet, girl, Anne, but *Elizabeth* is your grandchild and she wants no part of this book," Sonya ranted, nearly apoplectic in her growing frustration. Nearly thirty years in Anne's employ and the woman hadn't changed one bit. She didn't deserve Elizabeth, Sonya thought sourly.

"Oh, calm down, Sonya. How do we know what Elizabeth wants? Does she even know? She certainly hasn't discussed it with me. Why, she hasn't once mentioned Mikel or Mr. Ward's offer to interview us. All I've heard from Elizabeth is how are you feeling, Anne? Do you want tea or coffee, Anne? I'll check on you in a little while, so get some sleep, Anne. But never, not one word or mention of the trauma she went through," Anne argued.

"Perhaps she isn't ready to share the experience," Sonya retorted.

"Perhaps she's all right with sharing but needs a push," Anne came back.

"A push? She's distraught. And she doesn't want him here." Sonya was adamant.

"Well, why not? She doesn't even know him, why should it matter to her?" Anne replied.

Elizabeth smirked at that remark. Oh, she knew Gavan all right. Anne had no idea. "Trust me, Sonya, whatever decision I make, she'll be fine with it," Anne added flatly.

"If you had seen her, you wouldn't be so sure. I'm telling you she's not ready to talk about Mikel. It's too soon," Sonya stated, a note of finality in her voice.

Feet padding across the floor alerted Elizabeth to Sonya's approach. Attempting to adopt a mask of insouciance, she pushed the door fully open and with a purposeful stride, strutted right by Sonya, who stood momentarily dumbfounded by Elizabeth's presence, and went directly to her grandmother.

"I see Sonya has informed you that we have guests," she commented. Her arms were folded across her chest, her stance reproachful.

Anne had the grace to redden. Propped up in bed, her back cushioned by several large pillows, her silver-gray hair covered by a white scarf and her face pale without a stitch of makeup, she appeared frail and weak. But Elizabeth knew better even as she thought how much her grandmother had aged. She yielded her stance only slightly.

"You were eavesdropping," Anne accused.

"No need to give me that look. I didn't mean to eavesdrop. I happened upon you two talking about me and decided to listen in," Elizabeth said boldly.

Sonya smirked an "I told you so" at Anne. "Do you want me to send them away? I could tell them Anne isn't feeling well after all," Sonya offered.

"No, Sonya. That would be rude. For the record, to keep you two from carping about me behind my back again, I admit that I am upset. However, it's not what either of you think," Elizabeth clarified. It was Anne's turn to tout her triumph and she smiled broadly at Sonya.

Sonya ignored Anne, her brown eyes becoming narrow slits as she squinted at Elizabeth, a signal that she was worried. "Do you mind sharing what it is that's bothering you? If it's not Gavan's book, then what is it? Liberty?" she inquired.

"It's nothing to worry about, Sonya. I wouldn't dream of interfering with either Anne or Liberty's plans. And Liberty is welcome here," Elizabeth added carefully.

Sonya stared at her young employer for several moments before nodding in resignation.

"Sonya, will you bring them up?" Anne asked, her tone authoritative now that she had Elizabeth's support.

"In a jiffy," Sonya said sarcastically.

"Sonya," Anne called again, halting Sonya's departure.

"Yes, Anne?" Sonya inquired.

"Give us a moment before you send them up." Sonya's face softened at the request. Anne could be hard as flint, but Sonya suspected she was going to apologize for her role in trampling Elizabeth's peace of mind. Nodding her approval, Sonya left the room, giving them privacy.

"Sit, Elizabeth." Anne patted the edge of her bed. Elizabeth obeyed albeit not without a defiant glare. She clasped her hands in her lap, raised her chin, and she considered her grandmother. Anne rolled her eyes, undaunted by the mutinous glare. "Well? You'd better say it before they get here. What is it?"

"There is nothing," Elizabeth scoffed. Then relenting somewhat, she added, "I haven't spoken of Mikel, Anne, because it's over. That's all. I don't care to keep hashing over it. I've tried to tell that to Mr. Ward."

"So you're holding it all inside," Anne concluded.

Elizabeth was wistful but no less reluctant. "Perhaps."

Anne sighed. "Your father was the same way."

"You rarely speak of him," Elizabeth whispered, startled that Anne would bring up her father.

"It hurts to do so, so I don't," Anne admitted.

"Exactly how I feel about what Mikel has done to us," Elizabeth asserted.

Anne was thoughtful. She murmured, "It was appalling. Are you all right, Elizabeth? I should have asked weeks ago but . . . well, are you all right?"

Elizabeth squirmed at the question, then froze beneath Anne's unexpected gentle touch on her hand. It was an extremely intimate act for her grandmother. Uncertain how to react, Elizabeth raised her gaze and tacitly considered her grandmother.

Anne recognized the silent question hovering in Elizabeth's eyes and was assailed with regret. She regretted that even now, with her body weighing her down, she could not give Elizabeth what she wanted most. Affection, uninhibited acceptance, and tenderness. It was a weakness she had endured with her son, Elizabeth's father. But she and Elizabeth had an understanding and always had. Anne did not have a demonstrative style, but she loved Elizabeth. She showed it every way she could.

"It was worse than any nightmare I could imagine," Elizabeth confided.

"But you're free now," Anne said, consoling her.

"I never doubted I would be released. After all, I'm innocent." Elizabeth sighed. "But it has been a whirlwind. I felt so alone." She turned to Anne, the desire to fling herself into her grandmother's arms and receive the hug she so desperately needed overwhelming. But years of stern discipline kept her at arm's length. She gave Anne a warm smile instead.

Anne was aware of Elizabeth's restraint and considered her granddaughter gravely. "I am not the austere woman that you think I am, Elizabeth. I admit that I insisted you call me Anne before you could even say a full sentence. And, I'll be the first to acknowledge that I am neither openly affectionate. However," she said, her tone curt to cover her indignation at what she interpreted as censure from Elizabeth, "you have been my world even before your father died. You can think I am cold—"

"I do not think you're cold," Elizabeth denied quickly.

Anne nodded emphatically, refusing to ignore the truth. "You do and it's understood. Your father thought the same thing. Lord, Elizabeth, your mother thought it, too. I . . . I am a woman of my era and I can only tell you that . . . that . . ."

"Yes?" Elizabeth queried, holding her breath expectantly.

"I can only tell you that I care deeply about you, Elizabeth. Deeply," Anne finished, unable to express the words Elizabeth had been on the edge of her seat to hear.

Elizabeth sighed, resigned that Anne had given her best in that moment. "I know you do, Anne." Elizabeth suspected Anne had intended to say more, perhaps something with more warmth, more love. It didn't matter. Anne was Anne and there was nothing she could do about it. She looked squarely at her grandmother, adding vehemently, "I hate what Mikel did to you, Anne. He was angry with you. He said it often enough, but who would have expected him to go so far? He was crazed when he thought you were going to cut him off. I tried to convince him that you would never bring him to such a state. I failed miserably."

"You can't blame yourself for his stupidity," Anne huffed. "He always hated you, too, Elizabeth. Always did, truth be told. And I think you know that."

"I always thought it was because I'm black . . . because

my mother was black. But in this day and age it's rather obtuse, isn't it?" Elizabeth suggested.

"Yes. But we're talking about a very stupid person, aren't we? He always has been and always will be," Anne added staunchly, but she looked away, as she always did when Elizabeth mentioned her mother. Elizabeth noticed and stiffened. If for only a moment Anne would discuss that which was so glaring, the fact that she never cared for Elizabeth's mother, then maybe, just maybe they could learn to express themselves more openly rather than leaving so much unspoken.

"I don't think Mikel ever forgave me for accepting you in the family, Elizabeth. Oh, he was always sullen and plotting how he could get back at me. Although I will not defend that idiot, it was an accident when he hit me."

"It doesn't excuse him, Anne. Everything that followed that momentous moment was deliberate," Elizabeth pointed out.

"Yes, it was," Anne agreed. "I guess it was the turning point for Mikel. He lost it. The question is, did he ever really have it all together?"

Anne never liked Mikel. He had always been a bitter, brooding boy who was quick to anger and selfish as well. She firmly believed that all of his life was leading up to his imprisonment. The past two years were the icing on years of verbal and mental abuse her nephew had inflicted upon their family.

Mikel blamed Anne for his mother's weakness and early death. He blamed Anne for Elizabeth's birth, as if it were Anne's fault that the only woman her son had ever loved happened to be inappropriate for marriage. Even after Lorna Sanders confessed that she was pregnant with Earl's child, Anne had tried to get her son to marry elsewhere, to consider his family responsibility and not marry one of the maids. But Earl had refused.

He was devoted to Lorna and wanted to marry her and didn't care what anyone thought, including his mother. It was a time of rebellion, a residual affect of the sixties freedom movement, and Earl fully embodied it. But Anne battled with Earl, refusing to bless such a union, even while she worried that the impulsive couple would elope with their newborn child. But then Elizabeth's mother died. Elizabeth was only two years old and Earl retreated from society with the loss of his love. He declared he would never love again.

Anne discredited the claim as dramatic at the time, but he kept his vow and there was no one after Lorna Sanders. It was as if Earl had died with Lorna and even the child they had conceived and had adored to the point of exasperation for Anne was forgotten. He was despondent and never the same again.

Anne was left with no choice but to look after Elizabeth's well-being. Was it Anne's fault that she had little time for her nephew? A nephew who had given her nothing but heartache from day one? She had done what she could for both children. There wasn't anything to be said for Mikel's shortcomings and she refused to suffer guilt for his actions.

"He won't be giving us any more trouble, not from where he is now," Anne said flatly.

"I'm grateful that he didn't harm Liberty or her son," Elizabeth said, recalling that Liberty was waiting to see Anne. And Gavan was with them. Elizabeth stood sharply, glanced at the door, then said absently, "I've got to do something to make it up to her."

"Rest assured, Elizabeth. Liberty is made of strong stuff, she'll get over this, if she hasn't already by the looks of things, and she'll be fine. Just as you will," Anne said. "You both have the same spirit and strength. You'll be fine," she added confidently.

"I should let Sonya know you're ready. They probably think we've forgotten about them by now," Elizabeth said. But the door opened before she could reach it. Liberty rushed into the room, Jarrett close on her heels, and she went straight to Anne, bent over her, and gave her a warm hug.

Anne was surprised by the contact and her eyes caught Elizabeth's for a split second before, stiff and uncertain, Anne returned the embrace. Elizabeth smiled, thinking Liberty broke all of the rules when it came to the Wilkins family. A light smile curved her full mouth and her eyes twinkled with amusement at Anne's uncomfortable position. It was that image that gave Gavan pause when he entered the room.

"Liberty and Jarrett. Congratulations and who have we here?" Anne asked when Liberty finally freed her. All eyes fell on Gavan, who had entered the room directly behind Jarrett. Boldly he stepped forth and answered Anne.

"Gavan Ward, ma'am." Politely he offered her his hand. All the while, he avoided glancing at Elizabeth. It didn't matter. When she moved from the door to stand at the foot of Anne's bed, he knew exactly where she was. He felt her eyes on him and sensed when she had looked away. He was so aware of the presence, it was as if he were the wire and she were the surge that charged him.

He barely managed to introduce himself properly to Anne he was so caught up in the gentle picture Elizabeth had made in her uninhibited state. She had been smiling, ever so slightly. No tension. No guarded facade. Just a smile and he was captivated by it.

Seeing her thus strengthened his resolve.

They needed to talk and he wouldn't give up now. Although admittedly, his dropping in uninvited—because he really could not count Liberty's invite as legitimate—

had been a bad idea, if his guess was right, that she was refusing to speak with him because she anticipated another discussion on Mikel Wilkins, it would behoove him to clear the air between them without delay. The truth was, Elizabeth, not Mikel or Liberty, had become his main interest. And his interest had nothing to do with his novel.

"Ah yes, the infamous author," Anne hailed him, redirecting his thoughts to her. She looked him up and down before saying softly, "At last we meet."

CHAPTER 17

"I'm glad to finally meet you. I hope you're doing better," Gavan said politely.

"I am, thank you," Anne answered regally. Then she looked closely at him, her scrutiny taking him off guard, but he stood still for the inspection. When she was done, she said, "You don't look like an author. An actor or model, maybe, but not an author."

"Oh, he's an author all right. I've read one of his books," Liberty chimed in brightly.

Anne nodded, her gaze never leaving Gavan's face.

"And so you heard about Mikel's foolishness and came seeking a story." She didn't ask, she confirmed.

Gavan nodded.

"And you expect that I would grant you permission."

"It's my hope that you'll agree to an interview, yes," Gavan clarified. He didn't actually need their permission to write his novel, but he chose to keep that information to himself for the moment. Experience had taught him that the more cooperative the sources involved, the better his book.

"Well," Anne said, glancing at Elizabeth as she spoke, "I've had time to think long and hard about your work,

Mr. Ward. Unlike Liberty"—she tossed Liberty a gentle smile—"I haven't read your work. But I'm concerned about the content. So, I don't think it would be fair to Elizabeth to encourage further interest on your part."

Elizabeth was stunned. What in the world was Anne doing? Gavan glanced at Elizabeth, his expression suggesting that he thought she had Anne pressured into backing out of the book. She wanted to deny but stood firm beneath his frowning gaze. He turned back to Anne and replied with caution.

"As I informed Elizabeth, I am not interested in slander, only the truth. She's a free woman. I have nothing to gain by sullying her name or anyone associated with Mikel Wilkins. I hope you'll reconsider." He was disappointed and didn't attempt to hide it.

"I doubt that I will," Anne said with a note of finality in both her tone and dismissive shrug.

Again, Gavan hesitated in his response. The information on the case, at least, was public. Anne's permission was not needed, but he preferred her point of view. She had history that no one else could provide. He didn't want to resort to gathering details wherever he could. Probing around to get information for his books was a normal aspect of his research. Tyke was gathering data on Mikel and Lance was looking into Liberty, but snooping into Elizabeth's past without her consent was distasteful to him. He wanted a confirmation, acceptance, and would do whatever he could to get them to agree.

He decided to be patient. He would retreat for the moment. "I understand. I have no desire to push either you or Elizabeth, especially right now while you're both recovering from your ordeals."

Anne smirked, her thin lips tense. "Is that a canned response you give to all of your prospects?"

"I'm always sincere, Mrs. Wilkins," Gavan said impassively.

"Well, my grandchild is upset. I don't expect that my answer will change. Neither will Elizabeth's," Anne said firmly.

"I haven't said that I'm exactly opposed to you giving an interview," Elizabeth said carefully.

"But you are upset over all of this," Anne insisted.

Elizabeth was visibly uncomfortable. The unexpected confrontation between Anne and Gavan exaggerated the strain existing between herself and Gavan. She feared she would snap at any moment.

During the discussion, Liberty had remained silent. She had no idea that Anne could be so cold and blunt. Liberty wondered why neither Anne nor Elizabeth was inclined to consider Gavan's request. Jarrett was stoic, keeping his expression bland. His only concern was Liberty. And right now, she didn't look happy. He was ready to end the visit and come back when Gavan was not around to create tension.

Gavan lowered his eyes, hiding the spark of annoyance that surged at Anne's rejection and subsequent inclusion of Elizabeth in her decision. And if Liberty stayed true to her earlier testament that she would follow Anne's lead, then Anne's rejection would also eliminate Liberty from giving him an interview.

But Gavan was suspicious of Anne's motives. Either Elizabeth put her up to it, which didn't seem likely in the face of denying being opposed to the interview, or Anne had something to hide herself. Why else would she evade the interview after initially agreeing that she was interested? They weren't involved in Mikel's schemes, so why the resistance? He doubted that Anne's refusal was strictly driven by her concern for Elizabeth's welfare as she claimed.

No. Elizabeth Wilkins's grandmother was a fraud. He could see right through her facade and was not at all fooled. She thought to deny him the interview. And supposing it was to protect Elizabeth, what was she protecting her from? Did she think that there was a chance Elizabeth was not as innocent as she claimed? The observation was discouraging and an unflattering disparagement.

Elizabeth was crestfallen. Gavan wondered if she also questioned her grandmother's motives. He had an impulsive urge to protect her from Anne. But it was unreasonable. Anne meant Elizabeth no harm. There was something else amiss but he would not uncover it today, he grudgingly accepted. Recognizing that he would not get any further with Anne at this time, he considered Liberty and Elizabeth.

They were both watching him. Their common expressions startled him. Their similarity had been apparent from the start, yet he had not actually noticed the uncanny likeness until now. He quickly recovered.

"Perhaps, in a few days once you've had a chance to mull over everything, I could call. I'm only trying to gather your versions of what occurred because I want my readers to have no doubt that Mikel alone committed this crime. But, if after you've considered everything and your answers are still no, then I will concede defeat."

His emphasis on Mikel being the culprit was not missed by Elizabeth. She was certain he was defending her. She was relieved by the idea that he was on her side.

"I already shared what I have," Elizabeth said.

Anne frowned and asked sharply, "Elizabeth? Have you already given him an interview?"

Elizabeth hesitated, looking uncertain for a moment, then said carefully, "Actually, it wasn't an interview. . . ."

Gavan waited, watching her, frowning. She hadn't told Anne about their dinner.

"Then what was it?" Anne insisted, scowling at her granddaughter.

"Dinner," Elizabeth said softly.

Liberty laughed, clasped her hands together, and asked with a wide smile, "So that's it? You and Gavan had dinner, huh? When was this?"

"It was a business dinner," Elizabeth corrected.

"If you say so," Liberty said with glee.

Elizabeth glared at Liberty, then turned to her grandmother, all the while conscious of Gavan's steady gaze. Why didn't he help her out of this?

"It happened rather . . . impulsively. Henry suggested that we talk. So we talked, but it was unofficial. Correct, Gavan?" Elizabeth asked, imploring him with her eyes to get her out of the fix with her grandmother.

Gavan was mute for several seconds before nodding, looking at Anne, and said flippantly, "It was nothing at all. Just a meet and greet and then dinner was over quickly."

Elizabeth didn't miss the jibe and grew flustered all over again.

"I see," Anne remarked, her words tart, her eyes narrowed. She turned her sharp gaze on Liberty. "And you? Are you in limbo about this mockery of a book as well?" Anne asked, her voice sulking as if she knew what Liberty's response would be.

Liberty did not blanch at the unmistakable expectation in Anne's gaze. She knew instantly she could not agree with Anne. She was compelled to know more about the Wilkinses, particularly her own baffling strong resemblance to Elizabeth. She hated to disappoint Anne, but she would have no choice.

Stiffening her spine, Liberty replied with open regret, "I'm not in limbo. I am a very willing participant, although I don't really have anything to offer in regards to the Wilkins history. Just my recent encounter, I'm afraid."

Gavan watched the elder woman with interest, noting the way she seemed not to breathe after Liberty's admission. He peered more closely at them, wishing he had a window into Anne's thoughts.

Liberty held her hands together, her tension obvious. Anne's direct gaze was unsettling, her silence bordering on the side of awkward. Liberty licked her lips and fluttered her eyes, giving Jarrett a silent plea to come to her aid. In an instant, Jarrett was at her side, his arm possessively circling her waist as he drew her near him.

"I do not condone this book," Anne said at last.

Gavan felt a pang of guilt at Anne's defeat, but in the next moment Anne relented with a heavy sigh, "However, I won't fight the idea if Elizabeth and Liberty are set upon talking to you."

Her vivid green eyes were steady as they pinned Gavan.

He was silent. Anne paused, her eyes roaming over the faces surrounding her bed, hesitating ever so slightly when she looked at Liberty again. Then she turned her attention to Gavan and said calmly, "I will expect to be fully involved in all aspects of your story. That includes a copy of the draft you give your publisher. I won't have my family's name muddied with exaggerations and blatant lies. Now tell me, have you met with Mikel yet?"

"No, ma'am. I have not. But I plan to," Gavan answered respectfully.

"Indeed you should," she said with a smirk. "He'll have an earful for you. He hates me, you see. But that doesn't matter. I wouldn't tolerate his arrogance when he was a child and I wouldn't tolerate it when he grew up either. He was just like his mother. Ah, but you'll learn all of that, won't you?"

Gavan nodded, allowing Anne to ramble. She settled back against the pillows, evidently tired. Gavan thought it was more distraughtness than weariness. He sensed hurt in her every word. Liberty had failed to side with her and Elizabeth had unwittingly betrayed her. He spared a glance at Elizabeth. She was so quiet he wondered at it.

"Well, Mr. Ward, you may write your book," Anne said with such haughtiness that Gavan couldn't help an amused smile. "So long as you clarify that I had nothing to do with how that scoundrel Mikel came to be such a mean bastard, I guess I can accept the public's awareness of the facts."

"You won't have to be concerned with that. Elizabeth and I discussed it and naturally, all characters would be anonymous," Gavan reassured her.

Anne's green eyes fell on Elizabeth; then she considered Gavan with grave concern. He was a handsome young man. And there was obviously more between the two than met the eyes. In the two weeks Anne had been at Elizabeth's house, not once had Elizabeth mentioned that she'd had dinner with Gavan. Anne had mentioned Gavan enough times to give Elizabeth ample opportunity to bring up the dinner. But she had avoided the subject altogether.

Anne could appreciate her granddaughter's position if she wasn't concerned over Gavan's sincerity. If it weren't for his eyes, those hazel pupils hinged with heavy eyelashes a woman would die for, she would not feel so uncertain. But his eyes were compelling and honest. And that was the problem. It gave her pause. What would he discover when he began his research on Mikel and the rest of her family?

She closed her eyes. She was tired and there was nothing to be done but accept the inevitable. A thin smile curved her lips and she finally said, "Well, that's comforting to know. Perhaps had you said so from the start, I would have agreed more easily." But she didn't open her eyes after she spoke.

Elizabeth took the hint and waved everyone from the room. Liberty kissed Anne's frail cheeks, then took Jarrett's hands and led him from the room. Gavan had already stepped outside the door and waited downstairs with Liberty and Jarrett. He continuously glanced up the stairway for Elizabeth to arrive.

He had succeeded in one battle. But his real challenge had only begun.

CHAPTER 18

"Are you hungry? Sonya will be with Anne for a while, but I can whip something up," Elizabeth offered, not wanting to rush them out after the rude reception she had given earlier.

"Actually, Liberty and I are running a bit late. But thanks for the offer," Jarrett said kindly, understanding her position and embarrassment and not wishing to impose any longer.

"Yeah. We have a lot to do. Again, thanks, Elizabeth, for allowing us to intrude," Liberty added sweetly, then gave Elizabeth a hug. Elizabeth was beginning to accept Liberty's way but was no less stiff in her response. Such affection. How odd it was to receive it and so frequently. When they separated, Elizabeth asked Gavan, "And you? Have you considered how you'll get back?"

Her lack of a similar invitation to hang around had not gone unnoticed. "I'm considering that among other things," Gavan said with an insinuative air.

"If you're stranded, Jarrett and I would be more than willing to give you a ride home," Liberty offered graciously.

"That won't be necessary," Gavan said, his gaze fixed on Elizabeth.

"Perhaps you should call them. Find out where they are?" Elizabeth recommended, disconcerted. His unwavering scrutiny was unsettling, but she held her own. Nevertheless, she breathed easier when Gavan finally focused on Jarrett and Liberty.

"I don't want to hold you up," he began. "Lance will be back soon. But if you don't mind, and if Elizabeth agrees," he added with a glance at her, "I would like a moment alone with her."

"If you're sure you'll be all right," Liberty said, darting confused glances between Gavan and Elizabeth.

"He'll be fine," Jarrett said bluntly. "We'll see you later, Elizabeth, Gavan." With that, he took Liberty's hand and led her outside.

Gavan and Elizabeth were left standing alone in her foyer. Neither spoke until the sound of Jarrett's engine starting filled the room. No longer able to brave Gavan's steady gaze, Elizabeth crossed her arms in front of her and demanded an explanation. "Well?"

"I want to apologize," Gavan said. He hadn't known what he was going to say when he asked Jarrett to leave them alone; he only knew he didn't want to walk out that door without having conveyed his position to her.

Her eyes widened at his words, but she didn't speak.

"I was rude to intrude on you today. I've been uncharacteristically rude since we met," he added with an honesty that touched her. "I guess I've gotten into some bad habits. I never intended to high-pressure you, but from the moment I saw you, Elizabeth, I knew I would do anything to get to know you."

"What are you saying?" Elizabeth whispered, too afraid of another misunderstanding to assume she understood what he was implying.

"I would really like it if we could start again. I'm asking you out, not to discuss Mikel or your family but to just talk. To go out on a date," he added, feeling awkward beneath her stunned gaze.

"Gavan," she began slowly, choosing her response carefully, "you confuse me. First you're only interested in researching information for your book; then you only want to talk to discuss Mikel."

"That's not true anymore," Gavan said quickly.

"Yes, but then you were at the hospital and I found out you were there to see Anne." Elizabeth muddled through her words, trying to articulate her confusion. She was failing badly if Gavan's frown was any indication. She sighed. "I'm not sure I understand what you want from me, Gavan."

"Neither am I," Gavan admitted. "I won't deny that I want to explore the story of your family. There's something there that maybe even you can't see. But I wanted to focus on what happened to Liberty Sutton, originally. Now I've changed my mind. I'm intrigued by many things, I think."

He paused, watching her carefully as he spoke. "Most of all you."

His declaration was thrilling, intoxicating, and she wanted to wrap her arms around his muscular form from the sheer pleasure his words brought her. But she kept her composure and had to ask, "Why me?"

"I'm attracted to you."

The words rolled off his tongue as easily as liquid and Elizabeth wanted to sit, her legs had gone so weak. She wrestled the desire aside as he continued.

"I think you're attracted to me, too. I don't know what happened to upset you when last we met, but I want you to know, yes, I write books about families engaged or involved in family crimes, but what I do for a living and my interest for you . . ." He shrugged, took a step closer to her, and murmured, "They have nothing to do with each other."

"I can't believe that's possible. Your sole reason for being here was to see Anne," Elizabeth countered. "You could not have known I would be here."

"True, but I hoped you would be. You wouldn't return my calls."

"I've been distraught," Elizabeth said.

Gavan smiled and said softly, "We have to discuss this constant state of distress you seem to be in."

"Is it so strange? I've been through a lot recently. Meeting you has only added to my turmoil."

"I never meant to burden you," Gavan amended, still smiling.

As they spoke, he seemed to have gotten closer, so close now that he was inches away. Her voice softened, her eyes lowered slightly, and she said, "I'm not insinuating that you're a burden, Gavan."

He had to still himself from moving any closer. He was so near to her he could pull her into his arms, which was what he wanted to do from the moment he saw her. But he refrained, took a deep, steadying breath, and asked in a husky voice, "Aren't you?"

Raising her gaze, she considered him. "I'm not sure if I like the idea of my family in one of your books. All indications are that, whether I or Anne or any of us like it or not, you're moving forward. And, in the midst of all this, you want me to forget about everything and go out with you?"

"All true." Gavan grinned, then with a raised eyebrow, asked, "So can I see you tonight?"

Elizabeth licked her lips and shook her head in amazement at him. "You've been like a wild, unpredictable typhoon from the moment we met. You came out of nowhere, looking incredible, startling my senses, and then you expect me to tell you my life story. Now you've changed your mind, a little. And before I can digest all that has happened, you want me to agree to a date with you. How am I to do that?"

"I look incredible?" Gavan grinned, not at all concerned with her rendition of his behavior. Elizabeth's cheeks were hot. She had meant to admonish him, not praise him.

"Yes," she bit out, refusing to retract her statement. He knew full well he was handsome and she would not discuss it further.

"I never meant to overwhelm you," Gavan relented, immediately pacified by her compliment.

She gave him a doubtful look.

He grinned. "Well, maybe a little."

"You succeeded," she admitted. Elizabeth wanted to kick herself. Now he would think she was flirting. She did not want to be a victim of his charms, yet she could not turn him away.

"I startled your senses?" he asked softly, reflecting on her earlier outburst with pleasure.

"Yes. I suspect you make a habit of it to get what you want," Elizabeth muttered, but she was entrapped, her eyes caught in his gaze, and no more capable of turning away from him than a moth to a flame.

"As must you," Gavan stated.

"What do you mean?" Elizabeth frowned.

"I mean you're *incredibly* attractive. I could accuse you of using your appeal to get what you want as well."

"You think . . . you think I am attractive?" Elizabeth stammered.

Gavan was unable to stop his mocking grin. "Are you being coy now?"

She was not. And she was no flirt. She didn't even know how to respond to him. His eyes lit upon her like a smoldering flame and her mind went blank. If he even suspected the rising heat in her, felt the tension building in from head to toe, he wouldn't have to question if she was being coy.

Her gaze dropped to his lips and she envisioned the warm pressure of his mouth against hers. He would be a good kisser. And she was a ninny for staring at his mouth, creating a fantasy just because he said she was attractive.

Nervously she ran her palms over the front of her pants. She needed desperately to get away from him before she did something reckless. He was so near. It would be so easy to glide into him and allow him to feel the fire coursing through her veins at the thought of his touch.

She trembled, compelled to look up at him. He gazed down at her with an expression that was both sensual and desperate at once. She gasped softly, breathless beneath his provocative gaze.

"I think you're beautiful," he confirmed, his voice low, a whisper of promises.

Her imagination soared with wanton visions of the two of them together. She had to get a handle on herself. "Th-thank you, Gavan," she stammered, furious that she was so unable to regain her poise. But his gaze was still holding her, confusing her senses.

"Have dinner with me," Gavan suggested, his words like a soft caress.

The way her body was responding to his nearness, she wondered if he knew she wanted to have more than dinner with him. It was a blessing that he was either ignorant of the need growing in her or too much of a gentleman to act on it. She wasn't so sure she could resist outright temptation.

"What?" Elizabeth murmured, distracted, hot, and overwhelmingly aware of him. His mouth had moved, drawing her eyes to it once more. *He has a beautiful mouth*, she thought, *full and sensual with the promise of pleasure.*

"Dinner. You and I," he repeated carefully, his expression so tense that it dawned on Elizabeth that he was fighting to maintain his composure as well.

"It's not a good idea," she said, tearing her gaze from his mouth.

She stood perfectly still, trying to breathe normally and failing badly.

"Dinner or a date with me?" Gavan asked softly.

"Both," Elizabeth answered. "Besides," she was compelled to explain when he frowned, "I'm not so sure I trust you, Gavan. You could be asking me out just to get my story."

Gavan laughed, his humor so sincere that Elizabeth flushed in humiliation.

"That's got to be the lamest excuse I've ever heard, especially knowing that I have Anne and Liberty's approval to move forward. Besides," he added, leaning into her, his face so close not an aspect of her features would escape his inspection. "Have you looked in the mirror lately, Ms. Wilkins?"

She didn't respond. "Meeting you caught me off guard, too, just so that you know," he continued, undeterred by her silence. "I never expected to find a woman like you when I took on this project. No, it's no trick. I would like to have dinner with you, Elizabeth, not as some covert operation for research but to get to know you. I haven't been able to stop thinking about you since we met. Can you at least give me that?" he added with a huskiness that was hypnotic.

He took another step, closing the little space left between them.

Less than a hairsbreadth away, he was so near her

body tingled from the sensation. She had never felt so wickedly attracted to a man in her life.

Elizabeth's breath caught as she gazed up at him. If he was trying to seduce her, he was doing a fabulous job, she thought and they had not even touched. Her body temperature was rising with shameless pleasure. If he touched her, she would melt. It was shocking but she didn't care. She was caught up in the web, the magic of his spell, and she was unable and unwilling to pull away.

Gavan's eyes lowered. His gaze lazily roamed her face. She was certain he was going to kiss her now. She had the sensation of melting against him even though they weren't touching. She was positive she would have done just that. But the doorbell suddenly rang, its shrill shriek shocking them both.

They jerked apart. Gavan's head shot up. The spell was broken.

"Blasted!" Gavan hissed.

He hesitated, regret flickering across his face as he gave Elizabeth one last sweeping appraisal. Elizabeth opened the door and stared up at Lance Ward.

Lance was no less austere than he'd been at their first meeting. "Ever driven a Jaguar? Well, I have and I'm impressed," he said with sarcasm, his glance skipping from Elizabeth to his brother with a rudeness that caused her to bristle.

"Give me a minute," Gavan said.

Lance shook his head with a firm no. "We've been waiting outside for fifteen minutes," he said, ignoring the furious look Gavan gave him.

Gavan moved around Elizabeth and hissed at his brother, "One minute," before closing the door in Lance's face. He turned back to Elizabeth. She was staring up at him with wide-eyed uncertainty. The moment was gone, but he was not done.

"Admit it, Elizabeth," he said, his voice grown urgent. "You want to see me again and I want to see you. Forget *The Wilkins Affair* and say yes."

He was desperate. If he could have just kissed her, maybe he could think properly. But the desire to hold her, kiss her, and make her forget all of her reservations about him was still uppermost in his mind. If she wasn't staring up at him as if he had two heads and had committed the grossest indiscretion, he would have kissed her. If her eyes weren't wide and full of confusion, he could have turned away. And if she weren't Elizabeth he wouldn't have been so torn that it hurt.

Elizabeth's mouth ached to be kissed. The mere thought that they should have kissed tormented her. She wanted it as much as he. Lance may have broken the spell, but she had the control and she suddenly desired it much too much to allow it to pass.

She reached out, her hands resting lightly upon his shoulders. He was tall and she was forced to stand on the tip of her toes. Before she could think, before she could stop herself, she did what she had yearned to do from the outset.

She kissed him.

Fully, deeply, and passionately on the mouth.

Gavan responded instantly to her invitation, ignoring the flicker of surprise at her action. He crushed her body against his. One hand rested in the curve of her lower back, another behind her head, and he deepened the kiss, tasting her with all the zeal of a man starved. An uncontrollable shudder shook Elizabeth, the intensity of Gavan's kiss potent and yielding her senses.

It was more than he could bear. Her sweet surrender would break his control. Groaning, he pulled away, afraid a moment longer in her arms would weaken him to an embarrassing state.

Elizabeth's eyes were closed. Her lips were slightly parted. And she rested weakly against him, drained by the impact of his kiss.

Gavan breathed deeply of the fragrant scent of her hair. He murmured something and sought to kiss her again. As he did so, the doorbell rang again.

Certain it was Lance, Gavan muttered an oath at his brother's untimely persistence and chose to ignore him.

Elizabeth opened her eyes. They were clouded and groggy from his kiss. Their eyes locked. Her mouth was pleasantly bruised from his potent kiss and she licked her lips. Gavan was entranced.

"Tonight? Say you'll have dinner with me tonight," Gavan whispered. "You can't say no, now."

Elizabeth could only nod.

She had kissed him. She couldn't *believe* she had actually kissed him and there he was, taking it in stride.

She was devastated, mortified, thrilled.

"Six o'clock. I'll pick you up," Gavan said. Then before she could speak, he embraced her again, kissed her squarely on the mouth, if not as passionately, as effectively as before, then released her.

With an effort, she steadied her dazed senses.

Annoyed by his brother's interruptions, Gavan abruptly opened the door prepared to cut his brother to the quick. But Lance had retreated to the car, leaning indolently against it, his arms folded across his chest. Tyke stood at his side, grinning.

"Get in the car!" Gavan barked before he even reached them. He opened the driver's door, then looked back up at the house. Elizabeth was standing in the doorway, watching him.

"Let's go, man," Lance said from inside the car.

Without further delay, Gavan got inside and drove away. But he could still see Elizabeth in his mind's eye, not at the doorway as he had left her, but as she had been in his arms, kissing him passionately and with abandon.

CHAPTER 19

"So what happened?" Lance asked.

Gavan had been with Elizabeth Wilkins for nearly twenty minutes. Lance was forced to cool out in the car with Tyke. When Liberty and Jarrett left Elizabeth's house without Gavan, Lance could guess what was going on inside. Gavan might pretend his interest in Elizabeth was purely business, but Lance knew better. He wondered what Gavan was going to do when he got the news that Maya was in town.

"They agreed to the interview. Well, at least Liberty and Anne did," Gavan answered.

"But not Elizabeth?" Lance queried.

"My dad said she might decline," Tyke added.

"Yeah," Gavan said with a grin. Lance and Tyke glanced at each other, then stared at Gavan.

"You're taking it lightly," Lance commented.

"Yeah," Gavan said again.

"Yeah, what?" Lance probed, impatient with his brother's ambiguous responses.

"Yeah, I'm taking it lightly," Gavan responded with a shrug.

"I've spent the better part of my day waiting on you.

Tyke's been to visit Mikel twice and 'yeah' is all the information you're giving up?"

"Yeah, it is. Elizabeth is the key and I'm trying to convince her to talk to me," Gavan said defensively.

Tyke laughed. "Why don't you just tackle her?"

"I thought Liberty Sutton was the key," Lance said, ignoring Tyke and watching his brother closely.

"She was but not anymore," Gavan clarified.

"So what now? I've looked into the information you wanted on Liberty and there isn't much. But," Lance said pointedly, "if she's not the focus anymore, I guess it doesn't matter."

"What do you have?" Gavan asked, glancing at Lance, his expression serious.

"Nothing," Lance said, mimicking Gavan's earlier tone.

"Lance, what do you have?" Gavan repeated, refusing to be provoked.

"Two things. Let's talk about Liberty first. There's no connection between her and Elizabeth," Lance said flatly. "Liberty's a Washingtonian. She grew up an only child. Had some hardships in her life and has a son from a previous relationship. She recently moved next door to Anne Wilkins and that's when the trouble began with Mikel. She's been seeing Jarrett Irving for about two years."

"I know. They just got married. What's the second thing?" Gavan asked.

"You've got company," Lance said with a bitterness to his voice that wasn't there moments earlier.

Gavan glanced at his brother, then faced the road again. "Company?"

"Maya," Lance clarified, staring hard at him.

"Maya?" Gavan's jaw hardened, his eyes darkened, and

his grip on the steering wheel tightened. "What is she doing here?"

"You tell me," Lance said coolly, but his eyes were blazing daggers at his brother.

"It's over between us, Lance. It has been for nearly two months." Gavan scowled. Maya's timing couldn't be worse.

"Maybe she's confused. She's at your place right now."

"Lance, I broke it off with her. You know that." Gavan was patient. His brother had fallen in love with Maya and although initially he had not understood the depth of Lance's emotions, thanks to Elizabeth, he got it.

Lance was unresponsive. Broodingly he turned from his brother, glaring out the window.

"When did she get here?" Gavan asked.

"A few hours ago, according to her."

"How did you know she was at my place?" Gavan wondered aloud.

"Uh, that would be my fault," Tyke interjected. "When you sent us on our way, I thought since your place is closer to the Wilkinses' we could hang out over there."

"Don't worry, Gavan. We didn't hang around long."

"I wasn't worried," Gavan bit out. Despite his sympathy for Lance, he was losing his patience with his brother. Several minutes later, Gavan sighed and said, "I'll deal with Maya, Lance. So is there anything else I need to know about Liberty?" he asked, changing the subject.

"Nothing thus far. There is no tie between Liberty and Elizabeth, none other than their remarkable resemblance. And that isn't that unusual," Lance answered, with equal desire to get off the touchy subject of Maya's affection.

"You're kidding, right? They could be twins," Tyke remarked, baffled how first Gavan, and now Lance, could not see how exact the similarities between Liberty and Elizabeth were.

Gavan pondered Tyke's words, recalling the image of Liberty and Elizabeth in Anne's room. He had been so aware of Elizabeth that Liberty had only been a blur. But there were some nagging common behaviors about the two women that bothered Gavan. They moved alike, smiled alike. No, they had the same mouth. Liberty's smile was broad and inviting. Elizabeth's smile was winsome and tottering. But the end results were the same. Something was amiss, his gut instincts told him.

"Not twins," Gavan said slowly. "But you're right, Tyke. There's something to this. I know there is."

Elizabeth was in deep euphoria. Sonya had been calling her, but she heard nothing. It wasn't until Sonya tapped her on the shoulder that the enchantment of Gavan's good-bye kiss wore off. Feeling more alive than she had in years, Elizabeth turned slowly to Sonya, a smile curving her lips, her eyes bright with the memory of the feel of Gavan's mouth tasting hers.

"Anything you want to share?" Sonya asked with a smile. She was tickled by Elizabeth's sparkling gaze. She had happened upon Gavan and Elizabeth while they kissed. Discreetly she had returned up the stairs and didn't come back down until she heard Gavan shouting outside the house.

"He kissed me," Elizabeth said dreamily.

Sonya laughed. "You act as if you've never been kissed."

"I haven't. Not like that. Not by him," Elizabeth replied. She sat down, taking a seat on the sofa placed beneath the window, the very window where she had panicked at seeing Gavan.

Sonya joined her. "I thought you detested him."

Elizabeth was thoughtful and answered, "I never detested him. I just found him unsettling."

"And now?" Sonya probed gently.

Elizabeth rested her head on the back of the sofa. She closed her eyes and said softly, "Now I'm . . . debating. I'm having dinner with him tonight."

"When did that happen?" Sonya was smiling now, her brown eyes dancing with delight for Elizabeth.

"While he was kissing me." Elizabeth sighed.

Sonya chuckled. "I had a feeling about you two."

Elizabeth opened her eyes and smiled at Sonya. "And you said nothing."

"I've known you a long time, Elizabeth. You're a very private young woman and rarely have you shown your feelings as you have these past few weeks. Between Mikel and Gavan, I figured you've been through a lot. But I wouldn't dare interfere when you so obviously didn't want to talk about what's been bothering you."

Elizabeth nodded in agreement. "You're right and I appreciate it. I didn't want to talk about Gavan. But now, if I don't it's going to kill me. He's like no guy I've ever known."

"He is exceptionally good looking," Sonya agreed. Elizabeth had dated only a few men and none of them had ever created the dreamy expression that Elizabeth was wearing. Sonya was pleased and hoped that Gavan would prove to be as sincere in dating Elizabeth as he was in researching his book.

"Yes, but it's not just that," Elizabeth murmured. "We connect. Down inside, innately, and I felt it from the start. I couldn't understand it. That scared me."

"Why? It sounds like a beautiful thing."

"To you maybe, but for me it was awful."

"You have to learn to embrace moments like these.

Trust me, child, you don't get my age without experiencing some love and some pain. You take them both as they come. Grow from it but keep living your life and enjoy the good and you learn from the bad."

Elizabeth grinned at Sonya. "Sounds very sentimental, Sonya. Is there something you want to tell me?" she teased.

Sonya giggled, sounding as youthful as a schoolgirl. "Not a thing but heed me well. You and this young man have a bond that doesn't happen every day. Enjoy him to the fullest. I know I would."

Elizabeth laughed, then said, "Sonya, you are shocking."

"And you nearly let a promising man slip between your fingers," Sonya admonished.

Elizabeth sighed wistfully. "I told you how we met? How would you feel, Sonya, if a man seeking you out for all the worst reasons was also the most attractive, compelling man you'd ever met? I was devastated and scared that I was going to act the fool. Actually, I have acted the fool from day one with him."

"But he keeps coming back."

"Yes, he does." Elizabeth was thoughtful before admitting, "And that troubled me, too. Am I research or a woman to him? Until this afternoon, I was research."

"Then he kissed you and now you're having dinner with him."

"I certainly am. And tonight, he'll see me as a woman, not research."

CHAPTER 20

Gavan sat in his car dreading the coming confrontation with Maya. She had to be kidding if she thought he wanted to pursue a relationship with her after finding out that she was also seeing his brother. Correction. Sleeping with his brother, too. It may have been unintentional, as she had tearfully claimed, but it happened. He would never hurt Lance. To keep seeing Maya would do just that.

And then there was Elizabeth.

He had delayed coming home, dallying around, running errands, and going over Lance's and Tyke's information before finally accepting his fate. Maya was at his place, beyond reason, and he would have to deal with it.

If it was an ordinary meeting he would not have been so concerned. But he knew Maya, apparently better than Lance. She would have pampered herself with scented oils, wrapped herself in an oversized towel or one of his shirts. Her intent would be to seduce him, work him into a frenzy, and then wheedle her way back into his life. He could visualize the setting she would have arranged, all carnal and seductive. The thought of Maya naked and waiting for him would have once turned him on. Now it only served to irritate him.

She had played Lance. They all knew what went down. So what did she expect to gain by showing up after all this time?

Their affair was over.

"Gavan," Maya murmured the moment he entered his apartment.

Gavan paused at the door. As he had expected, Maya was lying provocatively on the chaise she had moved under his window. She had thrown a white sheet over it and lay completely naked, a small throw pillow under her head, another set of pillows cradled under her knees. He was very familiar with the position.

Maya was beautiful. There was no disputing that. She was an exotic, dream woman. Her hair was a golden honey color. Long, wavy thick strands spilled over the chaise, grazing the floor. Her body was petite but full in all the right places, her breasts were large for her slender body and firm from a recent lift she'd gotten. The rest of her was all natural, from her flat, slightly muscled stomach to her finely toned, sleek legs. There was nothing he could complain about with Maya's form. But she was the wrong woman.

It wasn't her slanted light hazel eyes that he envisioned when he closed his eyes. It was another beauty with dark brown eyes that held him captive.

Maya's allure was not easy to dismiss, but Gavan was no more turned on than if she had been covered from head to toe with a wool sack. She would have to leave.

He scarcely spared her a glance, tossing his keys on the coffee table before going to his bedroom. No comment, no greeting. Gavan glanced around, then spotted what he was looking for. He picked up his bathrobe, went back to the living room, and tossed it at her.

Maya sat up slowly, pulling the robe with her as she did. For the first time since she had made the milestone decision to try and work things out with Gavan, she became uncertain of her appeal. His reaction was way off from what she had expected.

He should have smiled at her surprise greeting. Smoldering with passion, he should have pulled her into his arms and kissed her passionately. The evening should have ended with her in his bed, in his arms, and back in his life. Instead, he had his back to her waiting patiently for her to cover herself.

She had been so confident in her attraction, her own unique form of persuasion, that failure never occurred to her. Her hazel eyes narrowed. She carefully kept her temper in check. All was not lost. Not yet.

She moved closer to him, her body erotically close to his. Her hands crawled up his back and fell lightly onto his shoulders. She sighed, not allowing herself the pleasure of leaning into him. That would be too daring with the mood he was clearly in.

He pulled away and faced her, his expression closed, his eyes hard.

She raised her eyes up to him, her golden gaze sultry. "I had hoped you'd forgiven me by now." She pouted, puckering her mouth in hopes that he would be enticed to kiss her.

He looked down at her. He couldn't deny that her nearness stirred him. But her eyes were wrong, too light, not the dark intense gaze he'd been drawn to all day. Her height was not quite right, either. She was too short, too muscular, too planned. And her breasts, he never thought he would think this, were far too big. He was imagining his hands on breasts that he knew would fit perfectly in them. He was imagining Elizabeth, her dark, almost raven-black hair spilling over him as she stood bewitchingly before him.

"Gavan? Gavan!" Maya hissed, glaring in anger at Gavan.

She had lost him, the faraway look in his gaze hurtful. His hazel eyes had darkened. He was looking through her as far as he was concerned.

Gavan blinked at her sharp call. "Are you back yet?" she asked derisively.

He focused on her once more. "I would ask why you're here, but it's obvious."

"I've missed you, Gavan." She refused to acknowledge his lack of interest.

"I haven't missed you, Maya. In fact, my brother and I have enjoyed a peaceful two months since you and I ended."

"Oh, that again! I told you I had no idea you and Lance were brothers. I can see now the similarities but trust me, Gavan, Lance has nothing on you."

"Maya," Gavan began with a mocking grin, "if Lance was not my brother it wouldn't matter. I still would have ended this farce with you. The fact remains that you were leading on two men. It's only worse because we're brothers. But what if I had never discovered you were leading some poor guy on? I was close to getting serious about you. That would've hurt."

The emphasis was clear. He was not hurt that they ended. She never really had him. But she had been so close.

Maya flushed, her cheeks blushing to a warm pink. She sat at the table, the robe tightly about her. "I had hoped that with a little time to heal you would forgive me."

"I could never forgive you for what happened. You hurt Lance."

"And you, Gavan. Did you ever care? You keep talking about Lance, but what about you and me?" Maya cried.

"You and I are through. It wasn't cool of you to come here. I'm disappointed that you took it upon yourself to do so."

"Your mother suggested it," Maya muttered.

"What? Why would she do that?" Gavan demanded.

"She thought you missed me. She made me think . . . Never mind. I was a fool to think you had encouraged her to ask me here."

"If it's any consolation, Lance and I didn't tell my mother anything. We had hoped to spare her," Gavan added deliberately. "But if necessary I'll tell her everything tonight."

"No!" Maya gasped, humiliated at the idea of Valerie Ward knowing that she had engaged in a relationship with both of her sons. "It would hurt her, I think."

"I agree," Gavan said coolly. He glanced at his watch. "Maya, I have somewhere to be. I have to do this for me and for Lance. I need you to get dressed and I'll drop you off at your hotel."

"Gavan," Maya moaned, hurt, realizing for the first time that it was truly over between them.

Gavan was adamant. He had his brother to think about. He had finally gotten Elizabeth to see him again and he wasn't about to allow Maya to interfere with his plans. "Had I known you were coming . . . You should have called. In fact, Maya, you should find someone else. Do you understand?"

"Are you serious?" Maya whispered. Her throat was tight with emotion. "I can't believe this." She averted her face from him in anguish. She had all but accepted that it was over until his mother convinced her that she shouldn't give up on Gavan. His mother had wanted this. Maya had been a blind fool to allow her heart to lead her.

She had willfully ignored the warning bells, suppressed images of Lance's rage, and gone after Gavan. But he was not in love with her and he had never been.

"Maya, I'm sorry," Gavan said softly. He laid a gentle hand on her shoulder.

She stiffened, her desire cooled by his rejection. She didn't want him to touch her now, knowing he didn't want her.

"I am too," she whispered.

Wiping her tears away, she bravely looked up at him, her eyes huge as she spoke. "I made the mistake, so I am sorry. I'm glad you spared your mother about me, but I wish I had known. She thought you loved me and I was convinced that she knew more than I. It's a mess and I'm sorry."

"We're both to blame. We can't start again but we don't have to be enemies. Let me give you a ride to your hotel," Gavan said kindly.

Maya shook her head, her hair spilling wildly about her. "I don't have one. I planned to stay here."

"What?" Gavan all but groaned.

Her eyes widened. She had made yet another error in judgment. "I'm not exactly loaded, Gavan. This trip was a gift of your mother's to me. I can change my flight to go back early, but I have nowhere else to stay."

Gavan was silent, thinking of his upcoming dinner with Elizabeth. What could really happen that it mattered if Maya was at his place or not? The small possibility that more would happen between them was so dismal that it was laughable. Fine. He would allow Maya to stay the night, but he wanted her gone first thing in the morning.

"Maya, you can't stay more than one night."

"I'll leave first thing in the morning," she said sadly.

Gavan hesitated, wondering how Henry Miles would

feel about a guest for the evening, when Maya's sob caught his attention. She fled down the hall, slammed his bedroom door, and he could hear her crying within.

"Just what I need," Gavan grunted. He closed his eyes, feeling trapped. If Lance knew Maya spent the night at his place, he would never believe nothing happened between them. If Elizabeth thought there was another woman in his life, he doubted if she would stick around for an explanation. Maya's presence was a burden and he was left with one choice.

He would sleep somewhere else tonight, preferably where there was a witness that he was there. Disgusted with himself for not kicking Maya out when he had every reason to, he picked up his keys, glanced down the hall again, and then left his apartment.

He had a date with Elizabeth and Maya's presence wouldn't stop him.

CHAPTER 21

The scent of lavender enticed him. He breathed deeply. It was her scent. She had worn it the first night they dined. It had haunted him the entire night. When the evening was done, her scent would linger behind and he knew he would think of her constantly.

Elizabeth sat across from Gavan, her gaze often lowered, a smile tugging at her lips despite her attempt to appear poised. They had kissed. It was all she could think of all day. It had not lessened when he arrived and took her to dinner. For once there were no uncertainties to hinder her appreciation of all that he had to offer. She enjoyed the pleasure of his company.

She wondered if it was the kiss.

A secret smile curved her lips.

Of course it was the kiss. It was all about the kiss.

They dined in a quiet restaurant off Virginia's Route 1, not unlike Gavan's previous choice. He was a perfect gentleman and she discovered odd facts about him that went far in explaining why Gavan T. Ward was so unlike any man she had ever met.

"My dad is from Virginia. He owns a house in Falls Church. That's where Lance lives most of the time. My mother is Hawaiian." Gavan had been telling her funny tales of his childhood and pranks he had pulled on Lance. He had mentioned Hawaii in one of his stories and Elizabeth inquired further.

"That explains everything," she murmured, smiling.

"I'm not sure if you mean my looks or my manners," Gavan said.

"Both."

"Fair enough. But Hawaii isn't that different from the States. We eat, sleep, and are merry like everyone else." Gavan laughed.

"How did your parents meet?" Elizabeth asked a few minutes later.

"They were both students at Georgetown University. My dad was also a hopeful young artist. He thought he was going to be the next Picasso. He claims he moved to Hawaii to paint the famous volcanoes. We all know it was to follow my mom. She only did a year at Georgetown, got homesick, and fled back to Hawaii."

"That's romantic," Elizabeth said.

"Maybe, I guess love changed his plans. He gave up art and finished medical school and became a doctor. My mom finished her degree in Hawaii and worked at the local hospital. Then my dad showed up one day. She remembered him. They got married and along came me."

"That *is* romantic," Elizabeth purred, smiling. "So who do you get your good looks from, your mom or dad?"

"How candid you've become," Gavan said with a teasing light in his eyes. "I would guess both. I'm down the middle. Lance got most of my dad's characteristics, his coloring, his height, and his temperament."

"But he looks like you. That would mean you look like your father," Elizabeth pointed out.

"Makes sense to me," Gavan agreed.

He sipped his drink and watched her over the rim of

his glass. She was at ease, mellow, and he was reveling in
her presence. Unlike him, she had changed her entire
outfit. Earlier she had worn a black suit. Now she wore
a gold tank dress covered by a black cardigan. She had
chosen high-heeled sandals that showed off her long,
slender legs. He thought it amazing that each time he
saw her she was more beautiful than the last.

"And you, Elizabeth. Do you look like your mother or
father?" Gavan asked.

Elizabeth hesitated, wondering at his motive. Then
she recalled Sonya's advice and answered quietly, "I'm
not really sure. My parents died when I was very young."

"But don't you have pictures of them?" Gavan pushed,
his tone so casual that Elizabeth chided herself for
being suspicious.

"I do. To tell you the truth, I used to ask myself that
all the time. But I've changed my mind every time I
looked at their pictures. I guess I look like them both."

"They must have been two gorgeous people," Gavan
said, flirting.

Elizabeth flushed with pleasure and, needing something to do beneath his approving appraisal, picked up
her wineglass and drank far more than she intended.

"Do you want to hear something odd?" Elizabeth asked.

"Put that way, yes," Gavan answered.

"When I first saw Liberty it was outside my grandmother's town house. For a split second, I looked at her
and thought, 'My God, Mom?' She is the image of my
mother when she was about our age. I, on the other
hand, like I said, look like both of my parents. Odd,
isn't it?" Elizabeth finished.

Gavan was silent, suspicion growing with her every
word. But he had to be careful. He not only didn't
want to broach the subject of Liberty's parentage too

soon but he didn't want Elizabeth's doubts to return. "That's odd," he agreed lightly.

"It would be scary if I found out she had my mother's same personality as well. Anne sure has taken a liking to her. And that's saying a lot," Elizabeth added.

"How so?" Gavan asked.

"Anne did not like my mother, I suspect. And it's just been me and Mikel for years. I've either been at school or working for Anne. Mikel's was always around, too. Between the two of us, no one could claim her affection. I was as taken aback as Mikel when she asked me to run Wilkins-Zonnick."

"Now let's not start on Mikel again. I don't want you to run away from me again," Gavan said hastily.

Elizabeth grinned graciously. "Don't worry. I'm over it. I was—"

"Don't tell me, I know. You were upset, distraught." Gavan laughed.

"And now I'm enthralled," Elizabeth added easily. She gulped, instantly realizing she had voiced aloud her thoughts. It had to have been the wine. She glared at her nearly empty glass.

Gavan's laugh shifted to a smile and he leaned forward. "With?"

"Everything," she said evasively. "The wine is delicious. The food is fabulous. You have good taste in restaurants."

Gavan chuckled. He sat back in his seat and shook his head at her. "Liar," he accused and she blushed beneath his knowing gaze.

"Tell me more about Hawaii. I've never been there," Elizabeth said.

Gavan obliged her. When he was done, she had a wistful look on her face that prompted him to say, "Maybe you could visit some day."

"Visit you?" Elizabeth queried carefully.

"I hope no other," Gavan said with a smile, but he was thinking of the situation between himself, his brother, and Maya. As casually as he could inquire, he asked, "So are you seeing anyone, Elizabeth?"

"Where did that come from?" she asked. Again, nervous energy prompted her to pick up her wineglass and this time she finished the remains. Her earlier annoyance with it dissolved in the face of Gavan's intimate probing.

"I'm curious. You're a beautiful woman. And yet, there seems to be no man in your life. Is there?" He appeared calm, nonchalant, but he was on edge. With Elizabeth, anything was possible and she was one woman who had put his vanity in check.

"No, there isn't. The last relationship I had was short-lived. It ended months ago," Elizabeth answered with a shrug. She stared boldly at him. "And you? Is there a woman in your life? Maybe waiting for you in Hawaii?"

"No. No one," Gavan answered immediately, ignoring the image of Maya that promptly popped into his head. She wasn't his woman. It had been over even before he found out about Lance. But if he tried to explain that fiasco to Elizabeth, she would never believe him. He could barely believe it himself.

They chatted amicably for some time. Elizabeth shared her memories with Gavan, albeit not as amusing as his. Gavan was surprised to discover she was from Savannah and had been in the area for less than ten years. Unlike himself, she did not stick out like a sore thumb, had no accent, and was as sophisticated as any northerner.

Gavan, through bits and pieces of conversation, put together the puzzle of what it must have been like for Elizabeth growing up with her grandmother and a cousin who clearly despised her.

When she smiled, when she lit up at his light banter, it was as if for the first time, and he wanted to see her that way always, to protect her from men like her cousin, to hold her and show her all of the pleasures life had to offer even if only through a kiss.

CHAPTER 22

At first she was disappointed when Gavan didn't try to kiss her again. He was so polite she wondered if he was regretting that they had shared the kiss earlier that day. Then it dawned on her that he could be expecting *her* to kiss *him*. With the wine warming her, it would have been easy to be so bold. But she didn't succumb to the impulse. She was glad she didn't. At the close of the evening, Gavan walked her to the door and true to his word, it was a real date.

Right down to the good night kiss.

She was on the porch, preparing to say good night. She wanted him to know how pleasant the evening had been for her. But when she paused before opening her door, when she turned to say her speech, her breath caught and she stared right into his eyes.

And she was lost.

He murmured her name. She swayed toward him, the rhythm of his voice a hypnotic appeal to her senses. He took her hands, brought them to his mouth, and planted a kiss in each palm. His cool lips tickled her sensitive flesh. She burned where his kisses landed. He pulled her closer and ever so slowly lowered his head. And then he kissed her.

It was a gentle, tender moment and Elizabeth was moved. It was as if he were giving her a chance to tug free.

She moved closer.

Her eyes half closed, her back arched in silent invitation, and her body molded into his. He released her hands to find the small of her back where he pressed her even closer. And then the faint kiss deepened and it was as if her entire body were on fire.

She shivered, ripples of delight nearly causing her to come undone where they stood. She parted her mouth, seeking the taste of him, wanting him to explore the depth of her.

He did, tasting of her as if she were the sweet wine she had drunk.

And it was intoxicating.

She was feverish for him, her body a quivering mass of expectation.

She wanted him and shamelessly let him know with every subtle hint her body could give. He groaned, in grave danger of losing the little self-control he had. With an effort, he ended the kiss and released her from his embrace. It took every bit of his willpower.

They were both breathless. And they were both unappeased.

For long moments they could do nothing but stare into each other's eyes, fascinated that they could have shared such a strong passion. Then Gavan exhaled a sigh of resignation and pulled her to him again. What harm could another kiss do?

His mouth ravished hers. His hunger trailing a blaze of kisses from her earlobe to her neck, down the length of her shoulder, then upward until he found her mouth again. As he did so, his hands stroked her back in slow, languid movements, steadily increasing the pressure to bring her closer and closer to him. They were so close she could feel his heartbeat, was fascinated by his ragged breathing, and in a mesmerized haze, returned his stare as he ran his hand over her cheeks, his expression awed.

In a tantalizingly slow quest, he traced a path over her smooth cheek, ran a thumb over her throbbing mouth, and then slid his hand down the length of her slender neck. He didn't stop his journey until his hand found her breast.

He paused, barely breathing now as excitement soared through him, and he gave her a chance to stop him.

She was beyond stopping him and her eyes closed, beckoning him to continue. He cupped her breast within the palm of his hand as he kissed her again, pouring weeks of hunger into the act. When he came up for air, her legs were like warm liquid and she held on to him for support.

"God, I could make love to you all night," he murmured.

She laid her head on his shoulder in response. He sighed, fighting the urge to accept her silent invitation. Where could they go? Maya had invaded his home and Anne was with Elizabeth. He glanced at his car and sighed.

Another night, another moment was all he could hope for.

"Go inside, Elizabeth," he said in a husky voice. If he didn't leave now he feared he would stoop to levels that they would both regret in the morning. The backseat of his car was no place he wanted to make love, especially not with Elizabeth.

She appeared confused and hesitant to leave him. Desperate to get away from her before his resolve was broken, he took her keys and unlocked her front door. With a gentle nudge, he helped her inside. Looking at her with regret, he closed the door, forcing himself to leave without a backward glance and saved Elizabeth from succumbing to their mutual desire.

Elizabeth awoke smiling and stretched with the grace of a cat. She sprang from the bed and within minutes showered and dressed. Her hair was still wet as she pulled on her suit. She was feeling lighthearted and decided to be bold. She would allow it to air-dry and wear it loose. Dressed, remarkably refreshed despite the wine she had consumed, she checked on Anne and then went to work, the memories of the evening replaying over and over in her head. At least twice she splashed her face with cold water to cool her heated thoughts.

But she couldn't concentrate. Was she alone or had he gone home recalling their passionate kiss as well? It was barely eight o'clock in the morning. Sonya wouldn't get in until that afternoon. She had enough to do to occupy her mind, but Gavan had completely muddied any plans she had had for the day.

She glanced at the telephone. Was he an early riser? She grinned impishly. She hadn't felt so alive in, why, ever, she thought happily. She picked up the phone and impulsively dialed his number. She had no idea what she would say but, shrugging, decided she would make it up as she went along.

"Hello?" a feminine voice answered.

Elizabeth stood sharply, swallowed, then compressed her lips. *Calm down*, she told herself. It didn't have to be as it appeared. Oh, but she was a fool to call him.

"Is Gavan in?" Elizabeth asked lightly, her tone belying her agitation.

"No, he's not," the woman answered with a confidence that suggested she was right at home.

"Could you give him a message?" Elizabeth asked coolly.

"I tell you what, why don't I hang up and you can leave the message on his machine?" the woman suggested kindly.

"Good idea," Elizabeth said, then asked, unable to contain her curiosity, "And whom am I speaking to?"

"Maya," she answered without hesitation.

"Well, Maya, thank you. Thank you very much," Elizabeth murmured, then hung up. Her temper rose as she thought over the final moments of the evening she had spent with Gavan.

The hot kisses they'd shared. His hands all over her. Her silent invitation and his sweet rejection.

It had all been a sham.

Gavan came awake in a fog, his first awareness the lingering kiss he had shared with Elizabeth, his second thought that he was at Lance's house.

After leaving Elizabeth his discomfort had been grave. He needed more than a cold shower and was resigned to a long, restless night. A cold swim wouldn't have cooled him after her eager response to his caresses. By the time he reached Lance's house his condition was only slightly better.

Lance was moody. Considering that Maya was in town, it was no less than what Gavan would have expected of his brother. Barely a greeting passed between them and Gavan was too distracted to take much notice. He was soon left alone.

Gavan sat. He stood. He paced and thought long and hard about what he was feeling for Elizabeth. He sat on the couch, then lay back on it, his eyes wide open, his thoughts drifting over the delicious sweetness of Elizabeth's kisses.

She freely showed him all of the passion that he had suspected lay beneath her cool demeanor. He had never doubted his prowess, but with her he had been uncertain. Until last night he had only known her to be a beautiful and unattainable woman that stirred his imagination. Now he knew she was much more than that.

And then there was the issue of his research. Unwittingly she had given him far more details about her life and therein suspicions plagued him. How intriguing that Elizabeth and Liberty were close in age, so close that they were only a few years apart. How convenient too that Liberty never knew her mother, according to Lance. And with Elizabeth's mother's death, it left many possibilities about Liberty's true parentage.

Sighing, he sat up. Even if he was right about Liberty, now was not the time to bring it to Elizabeth's attention. It would set him back where he started from and he didn't want anything to come between them, to dampen what had turned out to be a fruitful evening.

He was into her and he saw no way around it.

At nearly forty years old, he had kissed more women than he could count. But none had taken his breath away, left him shaken to the core, and crept under his skin and stayed there the way Elizabeth had.

A piece of silverware clattered to the floor and Gavan looked up. He stared directly at Tyke's wide-mouthed grin. It was disgusting. Tyke was eating cereal, his manners abominable as he stared curiously at Gavan.

Gavan sat up, the sheet he had tangled himself into falling to the floor.

"When did you get here?" Gavan grumbled.

"About half an hour ago," Tyke said between spoonfuls of cereal. But he was watching Gavan, smiling as he chewed. "So when did you get here?"

Gavan gave an impatient sigh. "I got here last night. Why?"

"No reason. I just find it real funny that the great lover had nowhere to sleep last night. You're falling from my hero list," Tyke said as if they'd been talking all morning.

"I never claimed that ridiculous title," Gavan protested. He bent down and picked up the sheet, throwing it on Lance's sofa before heading for the bathroom.

"Don't have to. It was given to you by all those women you've conquered over the years," Tyke called.

"You got it all wrong this time, Tyke. And let me tell you something. I don't set out to conquer women, Tyke. They know where they stand and I know where I stand," he shouted from the bathroom. He pulled on his slacks, zipping them impatiently, then after splashing his face with cold water, went in search for his shoes.

"Sure, except you know women are always challenged by that. Besides, you get a kick out of watching them use their feminine tactics to change your mind."

"Think what you will," Gavan said with a shrug. He grabbed his shoes and sat down to put them on.

"Can't help what I see," Tyke responded, then finished off his cereal.

"Where's Lance?" Gavan asked, ending the discussion before he lost his temper.

"He didn't say. I think he's still fuming about Maya," Tyke said.

Gavan shook his head regretfully, then stood up. "I slept here just so that he would know nothing went down between us. I don't want Maya. She knows that without a doubt."

Tyke smirked. "Tell Lance, not me."

"By the way, did you find out anything else?"

"No, but I believe Lance did," Tyke said, pouring himself yet another bowl of cereal.

"Did he happen to say what it was?" Gavan inquired with measured patience.

Tyke pursed his lips, stared into the air, and said, "Not really, only that Liberty's uncle was from Savannah or something like that."

Gavan froze, stared blankly at Tyke, and said, "Tell Lance he can catch me at home."

With Maya?" Tyke asked with a sly glance.

"Cool it, Tyke," Gavan said, his tone bored. "Maya's gone, so don't start any trouble." Then he slammed out of the house, the only indication that he was even annoyed.

CHAPTER 23

By the time Gavan got home, he was convinced beyond a doubt that Elizabeth and Liberty were related. Now he had only to prove it. Thinking about their probable relationship had effectively doused a turn-on that he had been unsuccessful at completely dousing on his own.

A note from Maya was on the table when he entered his condo. He skimmed the brief words with mounting relief. She was gone. It was understood that it was over. Would he please say hello to Lance for her? She never meant to hurt anyone. And she loved him still.

Gavan set the note on the counter. Her words were sad, leaving him torn between relief and guilt at the way their affair had ended. But there was nothing else that could have been done. Not only was his brother more important to him than a fling, but he was so tangled up inside over Elizabeth, she was the only woman he wanted.

He went through his usual routine and checked his answering machine as he switched clothing. He was buttoning his shirt when Anne Wilkins's voice carried over the machine. He paused, listened intently, and seconds later he was calling her.

She had said it was urgent that they discuss Elizabeth.

He worried that she had witnessed their public display last night. Then as quickly as the thought occurred to him he dismissed it. Anne would have interrupted had she seen them, of that Gavan was sure. He wasn't sure what could have gotten her so worked up, but he would find out.

"Good morning," Gavan said pleasantly.

"May I help you?" Anne questioned sharply.

"Yes. This is Gavan Ward. We met yesterday. Do you remember me?" he asked cautiously.

"I called you," Anne harped. "Of course I remember you. I'm not senile, Mr. Ward."

"I never meant to imply that you were," Gavan said, trying to make amends.

"So when do you plan to interview me and what are you doing to Elizabeth?" Anne asked bluntly.

Gavan was momentarily taken off guard by her bluntness but smoothly answered, "I was hoping we could meet at your earliest convenience. Just say when. As for Elizabeth, Mrs. Wilkins, I am doing nothing that should cause you concern."

"But it does. Elizabeth's not an emotional woman. Since I've heard of you she's been nothing but emotional. What did you talk about last night?" Anne demanded.

Gavan was calm but his blood was boiling. Anne Wilkins was rude and overbearing and she was, unfortunately, the grandmother to the first woman he had thought about long term. "I think it fair to suggest you speak with Elizabeth on that," he said carefully.

"Fine. I expected you would say that. So are we to have dinner, too, or will this be by telephone?" Anne inquired.

Gavan lost his patience, scowled, and retorted, "Mrs. Wilkins, you called me. As I said, I am flexible but you're—"

She interrupted his rant. "Yes, yes. Well why don't you come over now."

Gavan's eyes narrowed and he was about to decline when instinct pushed him to accept. "Will half an hour suffice?" he asked, wanting to inquire if Elizabeth would be there. Would she be the new uninhibited Elizabeth he had discovered last night or the coolly reserved majestic woman unmoved and untouched by his presence? He would accept either gladly.

"So what would you like to know, first?" Anne asked a half an hour later.

Gavan was sitting on the couch, Anne on a huge overstuffed chair. She had chosen the family room and the stuffiness of the fireplace. Gavan thought she must really be sick to have the fireplace lit in the middle of the afternoon on a warm day. He had to remind himself not to tug at his shirt's collar.

"You could start by telling me what you know about Liberty," Gavan answered.

"That won't be much."

"Let's give it a try anyway," Gavan urged.

"Liberty Sutton, Mrs. Irving, that is, moved next door to me only a month after I moved into the house. Elizabeth and I were investors and I decided that I wanted to stay in the residence. That's when I first met Liberty."

"Did you notice her resemblance to Elizabeth then?" Gavan wondered.

"No, not Elizabeth. Her mother, however, popped into mind. If she weren't so young I would have thought she was Elizabeth's mother resurrected."

Gavan leaned forward, his elbows on his knees, his chin resting on the arch of his hands. He was incredulous. Elizabeth had made the same connection. "And that didn't strike you as curious?" he asked.

"Why would it? Lots of people have twin features

and aren't the least bit related. Had it not been for Mikel I would never have questioned it any further." Anne fell silent and Gavan was deceivingly quiet. He was watching her and had no doubt that she suspected as he did that Liberty was related to Elizabeth.

Anne waited as did Gavan and finally she eyed him with a brief approval. "I guess . . . I'll admit, Mr. Ward, that I suspected they were related the moment I met Liberty."

Gavan was surprised by the admission. "Did you tell them?"

"Of course not," Anne huffed. "Why open a can of worms? And what if I was wrong, would they not suffer more? Besides, how could I know that Mikel would notice the resemblance and use it against all of us? No one could know such a thing. I thought to leave well enough alone. It's been nearly thirty years since Lorna passed away. What's to be done?"

"Uncovering the truth, for one thing. Bringing together two women who have the right to know if they are family," Gavan said sternly.

"I see," Anne murmured. She hesitated, considering her frail hands, before offering Gavan a wry smile. "Then I will tell you all that I know, but if nothing comes of it I don't want either of them to know what you're up to. Understand?"

"I'm not a private investigator, Mrs. Wilkins, but I'll do my best," Gavan answered calmly. But he was on the edge of his seat with anticipation. Would Elizabeth really appreciate his interference should Liberty prove to be her sister? He hoped so. At this point his curiosity with the women's likeness and his desire to please Elizabeth had become one.

"I can't believe it's been almost thirty years," Anne began, her voice breaking for the first time. Gavan flinched, unable to contain his stoicism beneath her

unexpected distress. Then she regained her composure and Gavan was relieved. He might not like the
Wilkins grandmother, but he certainly did not want to
cause her to have a breakdown.

"Elizabeth's not thirty yet," Gavan pointed out.

Anne eyed him, her green eyes cool, before she smirked
and said, "No. She's twenty-nine as a matter of fact. But
it was nearly thirty years ago that Lorna came to my
home."

"Lorna?" Gavan asked.

"Elizabeth's mother," Anne explained. "She was a beautiful young woman, as you can imagine by looking at
Elizabeth. At the time, I thought she was actually a lot
younger than she was. Alas, she and my son met, fell in
love, and she got pregnant," she added in a sudden rush.

"Lorna wanted to get rid of Elizabeth. I heard her say
it. She didn't want the child," Anne said harshly. Her
green eyes grew as dark as a stormy sea. "I was extremely
angry and disappointed in both Lorna and my Earl."

"Earl was your son?"

"Is. I like to think he's still with me," Anne said.

"Of course," Gavan said softly, trying to curb his
burning questions.

"Earl was a good boy. I had never had any problems
out of him. It wasn't until he met Lorna that he ever
thought to disobey me. He wanted to marry her. I was
completely against it. I regret it now. Oh, don't even
think it was because she was black. Although that may
have had some play on my decision, it was more because
I did not and never could trust that young woman." She
frowned fiercely in memory. "Did you know she was
almost fifteen years younger than my son? She turned
his head and he never recovered. He grieved her until
the day he died. That is why, Mr. Ward, I have regret for
not supporting his affection for her. I broke his heart."

Anne fell silent, her eyes misting. She blinked but no tears spilled forth. A moment later her eyes were as dry as if no emotion had momentarily wracked her.

Gavan watched Anne, careful not to show her just how moving her confession was.

"Well." Anne sighed, finally composed enough to speak again. Her expression had hardened. "That's about all I have for you."

"Is it so implausible that she could be Lorna's daughter?" Gavan asked.

"Anything is possible, I guess, except Lorna claimed to have no other living relatives. Not a soul. And remember, Liberty is older than Elizabeth. Lorna was with me for a while. It seems very unlikely that I would have missed a whole pregnancy."

"Or so Liberty thinks. Remember? Anything is possible," Gavan repeated. Anne didn't comment.

"So where did she come from?" Gavan asked bluntly. Had Elizabeth been present he would have been more subtle, but Anne was not Elizabeth and she was anything but subtle.

"Lorna?" Anne asked. He nodded. "My understanding is she was an only child. Her mother and father died when she was fourteen. She came to the Wilkins family when she was twenty-two, a few years after working on a neighboring property. They were selling the estates. Back then quite a few of my neighbors were selling and moving to Florida or somewhere or another. Lorna needed a job. She didn't want to leave Savannah and so my housekeeper took her in."

"You didn't hire her?" Gavan asked, surprised.

Anne offered him a crooked, thin smile. "No, I didn't. But you must understand. The estate I inherited was a vast bit of property. My housekeeper not only lived on

An Important Message From The ARABESQUE Publisher

Dear Arabesque Reader,

I invite you to join the club! The Arabesque book club delivers four novels each month right to your front door! It's easy, and you will never miss a romance by one of our award-winning authors!

With upcoming novels featuring strong, sexy women, and African-American heroes that are charming, loving and true… you won't want to miss a single release. Our authors fill each page with exceptional dialogue, exciting plot twists, and enough sizzling romance to keep you riveted until the satisfying end! To receive novels by bestselling authors such as Gwynne Forster, Janice Sims, Angela Winters and others, I encourage you to join now!

Read about the men we love… in the pages of Arabesque!

Linda Gill
PUBLISHER, ARABESQUE ROMANCE NOVELS

P.S. Watch out for the next Summer Series "Ports Of Call" that will take you to the exotic locales of Venice, Fiji, the Caribbean and Ghana! You won't need a passport to travel, just collect all four novels to enjoy romance around the world! For more details, visit us at www.BET.com.

SPECIAL OFFER! 4 BOOKS FREE!

www.BET.com

A SPECIAL "THANK YOU" FROM ARABESQUE JUST FOR YOU!

Send this card back and you'll receive 4 FREE Arabesque Novels— a $25.96 value—absolutely FREE!

The introductory 4 Arabesque Romance books are yours FREE (plus $1.99 shipping & handling). If you wish to continue to receive 4 books every month, do nothing. Each month, we will send you 4 New Arabesque Romance Novels for your free examination. If you wish to keep them, pay just $18* (plus, $1.99 shipping & handling). If you decide not to continue, you owe nothing!

- Send no money now.
- Never an obligation.
- Books delivered to your door!

We hope that after receiving your FREE books you'll want to remain an Arabesque subscriber, but the choice is yours! So why not take advantage of this Arabesque offer, with no risk of any kind. You'll be glad you did!

In fact, we're so sure you will love your Arabesque novels, that we will send you an Arabesque Tote Bag FREE with your first paid shipment.

* PRICES SUBJECT TO CHANGE.

YOU'LL GET 4 SELECT ROMANCES PLUS THIS FABULOUS TOTE BAG!

Visit us at:
www.BET.com

THE "THANK YOU" GIFT INCLUDES:

- 4 books absolutely FREE (plus $1.99 for shipping and handling).
- A FREE newsletter, *Arabesque Romance News*, filled with author interviews, book previews, special offers, and more!
- No risks or obligations. You're free to cancel whenever you wish with no questions asked.

FREE TOTE BAG CERTIFICATE

Yes! Please send me 4 FREE Arabesque novels (plus $1.99 for shipping & handling). I understand I am under no obligation to purchase any books, as explained on the back of this card. Send my free tote bag after my first regular paid shipment.

NAME _____

ADDRESS _____ APT. _____

CITY _____ STATE _____ ZIP _____

TELEPHONE ( ) _____

E-MAIL _____

SIGNATURE _____

Offer limited to one per household and not valid to current subscribers. All orders subject to approval. Terms, offer, & price subject to change. Tote bags available while supplies last.

Thank You!

AN085A

ARABESQUE

Accepting the four introductory books for FREE (plus $1.99 to offset the cost of shipping & handling) places you under no obligation to buy anything. You may keep the books and return the shipping statement marked "cancelled". If you do not cancel, about a month later we will send 4 additional Arabesque novels, and you will be billed the preferred subscriber's price of just $4.50 per title. That's $18.00* for all 4 books for a savings of almost 30% off the cover price (Plus $1.99 for shipping and handling). You may cancel at any time, but if you choose to continue, every month we'll send you 4 more books, which you may either purchase at the preferred discount price. . . or return to us and cancel your subscription.

* PRICES SUBJECT TO CHANGE

THE ARABESQUE ROMANCE BOOK CLUB
P.O. BOX 5214
CLIFTON NJ 07015-5214

THE ARABESQUE ROMANCE CLUB: HERE'S HOW IT WORKS

PLACE
STAMP
HERE

the property but she also ran all the domestic business, with weekly accounting to me, of course."

"Of course."

"I am not really sure how long Lorna worked for me before I actually met her. She was not in the main house. I only recall having seen her once or twice before that night when I happened upon her and Earl. By then she was already far along in her pregnancy."

"Did you ever doubt . . . did you ever wonder if Elizabeth was actually Earl's?" Gavan asked cautiously.

"No, I did not," Anne said, clearly annoyed. "And if I had, my doubts would have been quickly alleviated with just one look at Elizabeth. She's the spitting image of Earl. Except her eyes, of course."

"Her eyes?"

"She has her mother's eyes. Dark, long, and almond shaped. Beautiful eyelashes. I'm sure you've noticed Elizabeth's eyes, Mr. Ward?"

Gavan nodded. He had noticed more than her eyes, had looked beyond their depth, but he wasn't about to share that with Anne Wilkins. "I see. It could be then that Liberty was born before Lorna came to you."

"I've thought of that."

"And if she were, then we need only look into Liberty's background," Gavan concluded.

"It may be helpful. Just so that you know, I wanted to know more about Lorna after I discovered she was pregnant with Elizabeth. I checked into her story and found it to be true. Not only were her parents dead, she had no other living relatives that I could find, other than on her father's side."

"How so?" Gavan asked.

"He had a whole other family of uncles and cousins. Lorna's mother had no one," Anne explained. "So, that just leaves Lorna's father as a possibility."

"Well, there you have it. If Liberty isn't Elizabeth's sister she could still be a part of her family. Liberty's family is probably from Lorna's father's side and therein lies the resemblance. I don't think that's so unusual. Do you?"

"Lorna's father was not from this country, Mr. Ward. Neither of his parents, uncles, or cousins has ever set foot on American soil. He came here after his parents died. He was alone and searching for work, and then he met his future wife. Like so many others, they were dirt poor and broke. They couldn't afford the one child they had, you know."

"Where were they from?"

"St. Thomas Isles," Anne answered.

"Wow. And Liberty isn't from there, is she?"

Anne shook her head in response.

Gavan sighed. "Then, that leaves us where we started."

"Exactly."

Anne's satisfaction irked Gavan. He would have asked her more questions but the front door opened and Elizabeth entered, stopping dead in her tracks when her eyes fell upon Gavan.

He smiled, pleased to see her, his eyes falling on her mouth with pleasant memories. She remained stoic, her gaze direct and unwavering. She was neither the cool, regal Elizabeth he had first met nor the impassioned woman he knew last night.

She was furious and he had no idea why.

CHAPTER 24

"What are you doing here?" she demanded. She closed the door, set her purse on the table near the entryway, and walked right up to him. Gavan stared up at her, surprised. He came to his feet, an uncertain smile hovering on his face.

"Good afternoon, my dear. I take it you didn't have a pleasant day," Anne said dryly, capturing Elizabeth's attention.

Elizabeth dragged her gaze from Gavan and looked at her grandmother. "How are you feeling, Anne?" she asked.

"Better. I'm so glad you asked," Anne mocked.

"I'm sorry, Anne. I had no idea you were entertaining someone."

Gavan flinched at the someone reference. There was definitely something amiss. "I have no idea what's happening here," he said, glancing between the two women.

"Neither do I," Elizabeth bit out. Her chin was raised, her nose flared, and her lips compressed. She was flushed with anger. Gavan was thoroughly baffled.

Anne sighed and slowly stood up. "Perhaps you two need a moment alone?" she suggested.

"No, thank you, Anne. If you're through with your discussion, he'll be leaving now," Elizabeth said coldly, ignoring Gavan's probing gaze.

"Thanks, Anne, we could use a moment alone," Gavan said with an audacity that enraged Elizabeth.

Anne considered Gavan thoughtfully. He was a big man but harmless, she decided. Her granddaughter would be fine alone with him. Whatever the problem was, they were two adults and didn't need her interference. Besides, she was exhausted and needed to rest.

"I want you to leave," Elizabeth bit out the second Anne was gone.

"And I will as soon as you tell me what's going on," Gavan stated tightly.

"What's going on is that you are a liar. That's all that I have to say," Elizabeth huffed. She turned to walk away and Gavan caught her arm, swinging her back around to face him. His hold was gentle but effective in keeping her from escaping him.

"What have I done or said to upset you so?" he asked.

"What was I, another conquest?" she blurted, her hurt profound.

"No. I never thought of you that way," Gavan denied.

His confusion was escalating. She was furious. He was dumbfounded. What had happened? Then it slowly dawned on him. Only one thing could have gotten her so riled up, and he swore under his breath.

"Elizabeth," he began cautiously.

She yanked her arm free and glared up at him. "You lied. You've been flirting with me and coming on to me for weeks. And I fell for it. And then I kissed you and I'm so very mad that I did."

"I haven't lied to you, Elizabeth. If you'll just listen," Gavan attempted to explain.

"I will not. I don't trust a word you say. God," she sobbed, "I can't believe I kissed you."

"I'm glad you did. I'm glad everything that has happened happened. I didn't lie to you about anything," he insisted.

"Then who was the woman who answered your phone this morning, Gavan? Your sister?" Elizabeth suggested derisively.

"It's a long, complicated story, but I swear to you she is nobody."

"Oh my God. Where have I heard that ridiculous line before?" she scoffed. "That's the best you can do?"

"It's not what you think."

"Then she is your sister?" Elizabeth mocked but she wished, she hoped, oh, she wanted it to be so.

"No," he said, dousing her last shred of hope with the simple statement. "She's no one. I wasn't there last night, Elizabeth. I was with—"

"You don't have to explain anything, Gavan. I accepted a date and I kissed you. No big deal. But you didn't . . . Why did you have to lie about her?"

"I did not lie," Gavan hissed. How could he get her to understand? What woman would? He felt defeated. It was worse than if he had told her about Maya to begin with. Now what was he going to do?

"But you didn't mention you had a woman staying with you. That's as good as lying and you well know it!" Elizabeth accused.

All the while she was tormented. They had shared moments that she had begun to believe were real. From the start he had affected her. From the start he had taken her where no man had ever had her. Why couldn't she have discovered his deceitfulness before she got caught up in wanting him so badly? And then, after she had kissed him so freely, so passionately, and so trustingly, she had to find out he was not all that he claimed to be.

"Elizabeth, I didn't know she was coming. I got home and she was there. We'd been dating for a while, yes, but it's been over for months. How the devil was I supposed to know she would take it upon herself and come back?"

"Okay, so tell me this," Elizabeth snapped. "How did she get in? If she was so unexpected, why didn't you make her leave?"

"She had a key. I forgot about it, frankly. But I didn't stay there last night. Do you really think I would have after being with you? Come on, Elizabeth. She came without warning and I stayed at Lance's house. She left this morning."

Elizabeth was silent, her doubt expressed in her dark gaze. Gavan was compelled to explain in greater detail. "It's an ugly situation, Elizabeth."

"Indeed it is," she muttered.

"You're not following me." He sighed. "Maya and I broke up months ago. She took it upon herself to come here and I sent her right back home."

Elizabeth hesitated, his sincerity unsettling. But even if it were true, how could she move forward? "I find that hard to believe."

"You wouldn't if you knew why we broke up. She was seeing my brother and me. Neither Lance nor I knew about it. When we found out it was instantly over. And frankly, to tell you the truth, Maya and I were only a fling, nothing more serious than that," Gavan added, his frustration elevated by Elizabeth's insistence that he was lying. It looked bad but the truth was the best answer he could give.

"I'm not a womanizer, Elizabeth. I don't want her. She knows it. And I've made it very clear that I have someone else in my life and that it's absolutely over between us."

Elizabeth had a moment of uncertainty at his confession. She lowered her gaze, then asked tentatively, "Someone else?"

Gavan nodded, sensing she was relenting. He took a step to her and ran a gentle hand over her cheek. "Yes. Someone else. You. I don't want anyone else, Elizabeth. I've known it for weeks, but until yesterday I had no idea where you stood. Please, don't let this come between us."

"There is no us," Elizabeth said dejectedly.

"Like hell there isn't," Gavan retorted. He pulled her into his arms, held her close, and whispered, "I have never held a woman, kissed a woman, or wanted a woman like I want you, Elizabeth. And I'm betting you feel the same way. That makes us us!"

Elizabeth swallowed. Contact with Gavan had a way of fogging her thoughts. If he didn't let her go soon she was going to ignore her good sense and then where would she be? With a sob, she made a feeble effort to escape him. Gavan's response was immediate.

He kissed her. It stopped any further efforts she might have made. He dragged her down to the couch, his kiss deepening, the weight of his body crushing her into the softness of the cushions. "There is no other woman," he murmured between kisses. "Only you. Elizabeth, I'm yours. Have me," Gavan pleaded. He kissed her chin, her neck, her eyes, and then found her mouth again and she was stirred by his desperation.

She wanted to believe him. She needed to believe him. He was everything and more than she had hoped for, but she couldn't just accept his answer. Another woman, after the great passion they had shared, had answered his phone. She needed time to digest his reasoning, his intention.

"Gavan," she murmured, trying to regain her senses. It was so hard to think with him kissing her so gently, so diligently, and so deliciously. She squirmed and he groaned, but she managed to gasp, "Gavan! No. I need time."

He groaned and with eyes hooded with desire, he released her, sitting up to allow her room to move. Shaken, wanting him more than he could guess, she separated from him, putting enough distance between them so that she could think clearly.

"I need time, Gavan," Elizabeth repeated, her voice shaking.

"You don't believe me," Gavan sighed.

"I do," she said quickly, then added, "At least, a part of me, but I can't . . . I need a moment. You have to understand."

Gavan nodded, understanding but disappointed nevertheless. "I have to assist Lance with a project he's working on. A quid pro quo of sorts for all he's been doing for me. But I'll be back in a day or two. Please say I can see you when I get back?" He was gritting his teeth. He had never begged to see a woman before. With Elizabeth he was experiencing a lot of firsts and he wasn't sure what to do. He only knew he didn't want to leave. He especially didn't want to go out of town right in the middle of their spat. But she was tying his hands. He had no choice but to beg.

"You can let yourself out," she answered, ignoring his question.

"Elizabeth," Gavan repeated sharply, "can I see you when I get back?"

"Maybe," she answered, then averting her gaze, she hurried up the stairway. Gavan wanted to go after her. He would have if it weren't for Anne being upstairs as well. The bedroom door slammed and he released a pained moan.

Accepting that they had come to a truce, dazed by the

sudden letdown, Gavan went home. He wondered how on earth he was going to straighten out the mess Maya had gotten him into. And why, of all women, Elizabeth had to be the one things were so complicated with.

CHAPTER 25

Elizabeth never called. Gavan had driven Lance crazy. He rushed him through his business and got home in less than two days. He called Elizabeth the moment he got in. She didn't return his call. He was disappointed to the point of sleeplessness.

He could wait. He had no choice. If she needed a few more days, he would give them to her. But he wasn't about to allow her to forget the connection they had shared. Every day for three days he sent her flowers, morning, afternoon, and evening. He added a box of chocolates saying *don't forget me* to one of his gifts. Another day he sent a plush teddy bear with a note that he was missing her terribly. On the third day he sent a bottle of wine, a picnic basket full of fruit, cheese, and crackers, and a handwritten card asking her to please have dinner with him.

Elizabeth was thrilled with his persistence but resisted giving in, determined to make her point.

Sonya told her she was being foolish. Did she think he would go through that many changes just to "hit it" as the young people would say?

Anne was silent on the subject, but Elizabeth suspected her grandmother thought she was being foolish as well.

The picnic basket was the turning point. She missed him, too. It was so lonely with him away. She had gotten used to his presence. She would find herself touching her lips, dreamily recalling the sweet pressure of his kisses. She would laugh aloud recalling moments when he had teased her. And she regretted that she had allowed a moment of jealousy to push him away. She promised herself she would call him before she left work. Maybe even surprise him with a gift. And then, perhaps they could get back to kissing and maybe even more.

Gavan rolled onto his side, one leg dangling off the bed. His alarm had gone off three times. Each time he ignored it. His mood was bleak. As they had been every day since they met, his first thoughts were of Elizabeth. Only now he groaned. None of his gifts had stirred her to so much as call or send a note. Nothing.

He got out of bed and caught a glimpse of himself in the mirror. He looked a mess. If Elizabeth could see him now she would have good reason to run. He got up, showered, and brushed his teeth. Afterward he shaved and was about to dress when the phone rang.

His head shot up and he stared at his reflection. It had to be Elizabeth. He grabbed the phone, took a deep breath, and tried to sound calm.

"Hello?" he answered, hoping it was Elizabeth. It wasn't.

"Hi, Gavan. How are you?" Liberty said brightly over the line. She had no idea how melancholy he became at hearing her voice.

"I'm fine, Liberty. And yourself?" Gavan asked, his voice laced with disappointment.

She didn't notice. "I'm well, thank you. I was calling because Anne said you already interviewed her."

"If that's what she wanted to call it," he said.

"She said a few things that had me, well, concerned."

Liberty's hesitation distracted Gavan from his glumness. He became attentive and probed further. "As in?" He would have contacted Liberty earlier but he had been too consumed with Elizabeth to think about his research.

"My resemblance to Elizabeth. Truth be told, I never thought twice about it until you came along. And then you and your brother, although you look alike, have less of a resemblance than Elizabeth and I. Isn't that strange?"

"Just a bit," Gavan agreed, careful to allow her to come to her own conclusions.

"Yes, well, I'm recalling Mrs. Wilkins's reaction when she and I first met. I thought the woman would have a stroke there on her doorsteps."

"What happened?" Gavan asked.

"She appeared shocked to see me. She stopped dead in her tracks. She backed into her door. Actually, she scared me. I didn't know what was wrong with her. I thought maybe she was having a stroke. At the time, I was moving into my place. I recall I dropped one of my boxes. Anyway, I went up to her, to see if she was all right. But she didn't answer. She just stared at me as if . . . as if she had seen a ghost, or even more odd, as if she knew me."

"Did you feel as if you knew her?" Gavan queried.

"Not at all. But, well, I called you, Gavan, because like you, I too want to know . . . need to understand or learn why Elizabeth and I look so much alike."

"That's fair," Gavan said.

"When I met Mrs. Wilkins she told me that I had the uncanny resemblance to a woman she once knew, but I didn't think much of it then. I am not even sure if she recalls saying it."

"Did she say who that woman was?" Gavan asked gently. He didn't want to upset Liberty, but if Anne had said that much to her, why hold back?

"No, she didn't. But I thought she meant Elizabeth after we met. We certainly look alike enough. But now I feel it was someone else. And Mrs. Wilkins, she's not saying."

"I don't have answers for you, Liberty, if that's what you're looking for." Gavan was gentle and kind, but he would not speculate without proof.

"I understand. I'm not expecting anything more than the truth. I just want to make sure that if you do find out anything at all, anything unusual, that you'll be honest with me. I need to know. I want to know the truth, no matter how painful," Liberty said.

Gavan was thoughtful; then he said, "Tell me about your parents. Lance said you were raised by your uncle or something."

"My grandparents, not my uncle. My mom and dad died when I was an infant."

How interesting, Gavan thought. Elizabeth had a similar tale. Of course, Earl had only recently died in Elizabeth's latter years, but she had lost her mother when she was barely a toddler.

"I vaguely recall something about a car accident but I can't be sure. I really never asked my grandparents. I was so young and my grandmother died when I was about seven," Liberty continued.

"Do you remember her?" Gavan asked.

"I remember a sweet old woman. That's it."

"And your grandfather?" Gavan continued.

"He moved to Savannah when I was about seventeen. He kept saying it was time to go home, after Grandma died. I had a choice to go or stay in D.C. with my great-aunt, his sister. I chose to stay here."

"Where is your great-aunt now?"

"She died about five years ago. It's just me, my son, and my grandfather," Liberty answered.

Gavan was silent. Savannah was Elizabeth's hometown.

Someone had to know about Elizabeth and Liberty. He had everything but evidence that the two women were sisters. If there had been any room for doubt before, he had none now.

They had to both be Lorna Sanders's daughters.

He supposed that Lorna got pregnant and having no means to tend for a child gave her up. But Lorna claimed to have no relatives in the States, according to Anne. If all that Anne said was true, Lorna would have had no reason to fear telling Anne the truth. But then Liberty was older than Elizabeth. It didn't make sense. Why would Lorna hide Liberty from Anne and Earl if Earl was the father? Did Earl even know that Lorna had, perhaps, gotten pregnant by him before? The problem was, Lorna could have slept with anyone and gotten the same results if her genes were strong enough. What he needed was a picture of Lorna Sanders and Earl. He also needed to find Liberty's grandfather.

Gavan promised he would disclose everything he uncovered. Reviewing his notes, he thought of Elizabeth.

For the first time in several days he thought of Elizabeth without worrying about himself. Instead, he was worried about her. How could he protect her from a potentially painful discovery? And, if he could, would she even let him?

CHAPTER 26

Elizabeth chewed slowly. She and Sonya chose to eat lunch on the terrace at a local restaurant. It was a beautiful day and a fabulous opportunity to celebrate. Anne was going home today. Elizabeth had been so happy to hear the news she'd invited Sonya to lunch. By the time they left Elizabeth's office, Elizabeth's elation had dimmed.

Ever since she decided to call Gavan she had been unable to reach him. She called his cellular phone first. He didn't answer. She called his condo. He didn't answer. And then she tried to find his e-mail address but was confounded if she knew what she'd done with it. She even considered calling his brother on the number he had given her when he went out of town on that fateful day. But recalling Lance's sternness, she pushed the thought aside, finally leaving a message on both Gavan's cellular phone and home phone.

It was very unsatisfying not to be able reach him. She had made a choice and she was ready to share it with him. During the days she had been avoiding Gavan, she used the time to learn more about him. She skimmed through several of his books and even purchased two with interesting titles. She read and reread his biographies. All this had only served to make her miss him more.

Sonya knew Elizabeth well. Their table was for two. They sat close enough to almost hear each other breathe. And yet Elizabeth had fallen into a distracted silence. It did not go unnoticed. Sonya was convinced that her young employer was beyond help where Gavan was concerned. Feeling sorry for Elizabeth but famished, Sonya cut into her chicken and ate heartily, glancing from time to time at Elizabeth, then at her plate.

Elizabeth took no note of the subtle hints hidden in Sonya's glances. She was distracted and every now and then when she caught Sonya's eyes, she would smile. It didn't reach her eyes and Sonya grew exasperated.

"Why don't you try calling him again?" Sonya asked between bites of food.

"I'll look desperate." Elizabeth sighed.

"Oh no. We can't have that," Sonya exaggerated. "*No*, not after days of flowers and candy and gifts and love notes, you wouldn't want him to think you actually care."

"You're taking it the wrong way, Sonya. I left him two messages. He'll get one and he'll call. I'm not worried about that," Elizabeth said. Her tone was tired.

"Then what is it? If you expect him to call please tell an old woman what's got you so down?" Sonya insisted on knowing. It may have been ages since she'd dated, but Elizabeth was the one unschooled in the how-to-date category.

"I can't say," Elizabeth said.

"You can't say or won't say?" Sonya inquired.

"I . . . I don't know," Elizabeth whispered. Then she rested her elbows on the table and her chin on her hands that she clasped together. She looked at Sonya for several seconds before she whispered so softly Sonya wasn't sure she heard her, "I think I'm in love with him."

Sonya smiled. Then she laughed. She laughed so hard that Elizabeth sat back and scowled at her. "I wouldn't have told you if I thought you would make fun of me."

Sonya shook her head, caught her breath, and said with a wide grin that made her small eyes narrow even more. "Child, I'm not making fun of you. But a blind fool could see that you were falling for him. If it weren't against my beliefs, I would venture to say you fell in love the day you met him."

"That's a stretch," Elizabeth said dryly. "But," she offered, "I definitely thought he was attractive. I remember he made me so mad, Sonya. I was like, who does this guy think he is? And even while I was mad, he would make some remark that would make me laugh or smile at least. He's funny. He's handsome. He's charming. He's smart."

"Now don't get carried away. I'll give him handsome. And yeah, he's charming. But after what you told me, he's not the smartest man. If what he said is true about that woman he wasn't smart not to take his key and he certainly wasn't smart to leave her in his house knowing he was going out on a date. To leave himself wide open for speculation from you was foolish. Why, I wonder if his brother knows."

Elizabeth was patient and said, "I believe I told you, Sonya. His brother knows. It explains why there was so much tension between them when I first met him. The poor guy must think every woman that wants him will want his brother."

"Which poor guy?" Sonya asked, confused.

"Lance. Gavan is far more interesting and handsome. Don't you think?" Elizabeth responded.

Again Sonya laughed, shaking her head in her mirth.

This time Elizabeth grinned. "Yeah, I guess that was rather biased of me."

"Just a little. Ah, and look who's here," Sonya suddenly whispered, a smile curving her mouth.

"Who?" Elizabeth asked even as she looked over her shoulder. Her breath caught at the sight of him. She half stood, then sat back in her seat again.

Gavan casually approached the table, his eyes pinned on Elizabeth. His expression was void of any emotion, but he felt ill. She was eating and laughing as if she didn't have a care in the world. As if *she* had not been sleeping late, staying up all night pining over him the way that he had been over her. Why did he have to pick now to fall in love?

He nearly tripped over his feet. In love? Was he in love with her? She was a complicated mystery. A little voice suggested that that was exactly it, she was bewildering and exciting. Maybe it was meant to happen to him this way, swift and hard.

His gaze swept over Elizabeth as if he were seeing her for the first time. Her raven-black hair was pulled back in a sleek bun, her skin was dewy soft, reminding him of a golden sunset, her cheeks were flushed, and she looked incredibly happy, at least she had before she saw him.

It was as if she didn't have a care in the world. And it was very obvious that she was not missing him.

He felt like a fool because now he accepted what he had not allowed himself to consider before.

He was in love with Elizabeth Wilkins.

She captured his heart, his soul, and was the very air he breathed. Every other thought was consumed with her. He was not going to give her up. Not without putting everything that he had to offer on the table first. He was only glad that it was her elderly assistant and not some guy sitting at the table with her. He wasn't sure how he would have handled *that.*

Elizabeth dropped her fork. He was there. They had talked him up and there he was, a bronze Adonis. Her Adonis.

She continued to stare at him as intently as he was staring at her. His gaze lowered to her mouth and she shivered, a rush of excitement throbbing through her at the memory it inspired.

She drank in the sight of him. It was a wonder that every woman present wasn't gawking over him. Appreciating him from head to foot, she was awed that he could make a simple black T-shirt and black jeans look so good.

Her pulse quickened when their eyes met. And then she realized with a jolt that he was not pleased to see her. He was actually angry. It was in the set of his jawline, the stillness of his gaze, the depth of his hazel eyes.

He had not gotten her message and she could only imagine what he must think.

"Mr. Ward." Sonya smiled. "Have a seat," she added facetiously when he took a chair from another table and sat with them.

"My brother and I were finishing lunch at the restaurant next door. Then he pointed across the way and why, it's Elizabeth," Gavan said lightly, but his eyes were intense, steady, and Elizabeth wanted to fidget.

"Well, it's too bad that you're finishing. You and Lance could have joined me and Sonya," she said with more ease than she was feeling.

"How nice to see you're not ill or anything," Gavan murmured to Elizabeth.

"Why would I be ill?" she asked carefully.

"I thought, Elizabeth must be ill. After all, I haven't heard from you, but you sure as hell have heard from me. Or did you get the flowers I sent?"

"I got more than flowers," Elizabeth murmured.

"And they meant nothing?" Gavan asked, half afraid of her answer but wanting a resolution now rather than later.

"Gavan," Elizabeth whispered, very aware of Sonya's presence, "they meant everything. They were beautiful and I'm sorry that any of this happened."

That got his attention. She was sorry? He hesitated, then with a glance at Sonya said in a muttered grumble, "You've thoroughly confused me, Elizabeth."

"Join the party," Sonya teased.

"I'm curious, Elizabeth," he began cautiously. "Where are we?"

"Where? At a restaurant on Twentieth Street," Elizabeth answered with a small smile.

"You know what I mean," Gavan accused.

"We're at square one," Elizabeth answered less flippantly.

Gavan gaped at her in abject disbelief. "That far back? Come on. Do I deserve that?"

"All right, maybe not that far back," Elizabeth relented. Gavan smiled and she responded with an impish grin.

"You're a very stubborn woman," Gavan finally said with a sigh.

"Maybe I am. But I intended to call. I just couldn't get up the nerve to admit that perhaps I, once again, overreacted."

"Elizabeth, I thought you called him," Sonya interjected, surprising them both with her presence. They had all but forgotten she was there.

"I did," Elizabeth corrected. "I left you a message at home and on your cell phone. You didn't get it?"

"Today?" Gavan asked.

"A few hours ago, yes."

"I met up with my brother earlier this morning," Gavan said as he opened his cell phone to check his message.

A moment later he gave Elizabeth an apologetic smile. "Indeed you did call. I don't know how I missed it."

"It happens," Elizabeth said amicably. She was content to see his expression soften, his eyes gleaming with the teasing light she had come to love. Love?

Her eyes widened at the thought. She stared at Gavan so intently that he asked, "What is it, Elizabeth?"

"N-nothing," she stammered. Sonya looked at her sharply but didn't interfere. Trying to get her wits about her, Elizabeth asked, "So what now? Are you still planning to write this book?"

"I'm not sure. I'll have to see where the information leads," Gavan answered. "I do want to share some things with you, Elizabeth."

"Oh?" she asked, but her thoughts flashed to the many kisses he'd bestowed upon her. She flushed at the thought.

Completely unaware of the train of her thoughts, and the fact that they had mirrored his own from the second he saw her, he said, "I've already spoken with Liberty and have some rather interesting leads. We should talk about them among other things." His eyes trailed over her possessively and she suspected just what other things he had in mind.

"I agree. I'm helping my grandmother to get settled in tonight, but tomorrow night I'll be free," Elizabeth answered, feeling breathless beneath the visual caress he'd given her.

Gavan couldn't help but grin. "You're tucking your grandmother in?"

Sonya laughed, the image his question brought forth hilarious to her. Elizabeth glanced at her and she attempted to curb her humor.

"I meant she's moving back home. She doesn't like the idea of needing anyone."

"Is that a good idea? She seems so frail," Gavan said. He imagined Anne trying to get around in a town house alone. It wasn't a pleasant thought.

"She'll be fine. She likes her independence," Sonya answered for Elizabeth. "Besides, Elizabeth tried to convince her to stay. She wouldn't hear of it."

"I see," Gavan said.

Lance stared at Gavan from the street corner, prompting Gavan to stand up. Understandably, Lance was impatient, but Gavan attributed much of Lance's intolerance to his ongoing brooding over Maya. He was becoming as sour as an old, grumpy man.

"I'd better go, Elizabeth." He leaned over and kissed her on the edge of her mouth. It was enough to cause her head to spin. He simply took her breath away and he wasn't even trying. "I'll call you later. We can decide where you'd like to meet then."

"Yes. Until then," Elizabeth said with far more enthusiasm than she had intended.

CHAPTER 27

"Anything you want to share?" Lance asked once Gavan joined him.

They were walking to Lance's car. Lance had come over after Gavan talked with Liberty to compare notes. It was extremely peculiar what he had uncovered. But Gavan wasn't ready to share his information with Elizabeth. Not yet.

"No," Gavan said. He had been smiling, thinking of Elizabeth. She'd forgiven him. He had done nothing wrong, but it mattered not. She had forgiven him and that was all that mattered. At Lance's question, his smile faded. He had no desire to share his feeling with Lance.

Lance studied his brother, then jutted out his chin. "You must think I'm blind and dumb."

Gavan glanced at Lance. "How so?"

"You're falling for her," Lance said. He was almost accusatory.

"What if I am, Lance? What's wrong with that?" Gavan demanded.

"I would think that after that stunt Maya pulled you would be more careful," Lance barked.

Gavan scowled then. "Elizabeth is nothing like Maya."

"No? Well, I thought Maya was special, too. But she wasn't, was she?" Lance asked, his tone full of contempt.

Gavan's instinct was to get angry and defend Elizabeth. He refrained. Lance was lashing out at him. But Gavan knew his younger brother's heart was broken. It was going to take a miracle to get his brother to trust women again. Gavan could only be thankful that he had not become as disillusioned as Lance after the Maya mess.

"I'm curious, Gavan. When are you going back home? You know, as in Hawaii?" Lance asked after a while.

"I hadn't thought about it," Gavan admitted. But now that Lance had brought it to his attention, he needed to, he realized. He wasn't even sure if Elizabeth understood that Hawaii was home for him.

"You may want to let her know," Lance said firmly.

"Yeah," Gavan agreed. Leave it to Lance to put a damper on high spirits.

"You're serious about her?" Lance asked.

Gavan was thoughtful. Yeah. He was serious about Elizabeth. He'd had nearly a week to ponder on his feelings. He wasn't getting any younger, and although that had never concerned him before, he doubted that he would ever find a woman as interesting and lovely as Elizabeth. And he now knew he was in love. That changed everything.

When he didn't answer, Lance gave him a sidelong glance and smirked. "I'll take that as a yes."

"Take it any way you want," Gavan said easily.

"I'm wondering too," Lance continued, nonchalant in the face of Gavan's growing discomfort. "Have you told her about her mother?"

Gavan was silent. Lance was really giving him an earful. No, he hadn't told Elizabeth that they suspected Lorna of having two children and shooing one off to relatives that even Anne didn't know existed.

Lance was gloating. While Gavan had spent nearly four days moping and waiting for Elizabeth's call, Lance had gathered more information. Gavan told him what Liberty had shared with him. But Lance had discovered some additional interesting facts that Liberty either failed to mention or was not aware of. They couldn't be sure if Earl was also Liberty's father, but they suspected that her grandfather would know. And Lance knew where to find him.

Robert Sutton, Liberty's grandfather, had gone back to Savannah years earlier. He left an old forwarding address and Liberty had given a photo of him to Lance. He looked nothing like Elizabeth or Liberty, but he was their best lead. He was the only possible link between Lorna Sanders's past and present and as he had not been to Washington, D.C., in over seven years, Gavan was debating if he should go to Savannah or ask Lance to do it for him. That, he decided, would depend upon Elizabeth.

"I'll tell her soon," Gavan said.

"I hope she doesn't blame the messenger," Lance said dryly.

Gavan made no comment. The Wilkins story was proving to be far more complicated than he first thought. It went way beyond a disgruntled nephew and spoiled granddaughter, as he had initially interpreted them. If Lance was right, it could very well prove to be the breaking point for him and Elizabeth when she heard the news.

Elizabeth fluffed out her soft fur throw, sat in her full-sized chair, and kicked off her slippers. She had changed from the suit she had worn earlier into a sundress. She relaxed her head against the back of the chair, adjusting her position several times before finally feeling comfortable. After assisting her grandmother to settle back into her home, she was restless.

Taking Anne home had proven more of a hassle than usual. Anne had insisted they visit Liberty and Jarrett. Elizabeth found the idea distasteful. She didn't have anything against Jarrett, it wasn't his fault that he was so perceptive, but she had no desire to be in his presence. She had no recourse but to agree when Liberty was exiting her house just as they pulled into the parking lot, Jarrett by her side.

As always, Elizabeth could not get used to the twin-like resemblance she and Liberty shared. It was obvious that in some way they were related. Elizabeth asked during one of their long evenings together following their first meeting with Gavan if she and Liberty could be sisters.

Anne insisted they were not sisters and it was impossible for them to be twins. After all, she was at Elizabeth's birth. And to confound the situation even more, according to Liberty, she was two years older than Elizabeth. That ended any possibility of shared parentage. Lorna had died when Elizabeth was a little more than two years old.

Liberty had greeted Elizabeth as if they were old friends. She sensed Liberty's pleasure at believing they had some real relationship, but Elizabeth was careful. It could turn out to be a wild-goose chase, merely a strange coincidence and nothing more.

That was where she and Liberty were as different as night and day. Liberty was generous and expressive. Elizabeth was cautious and filtered every word with care.

Liberty had chatted away about her conversation with Gavan and how she had been remiss in not realizing the wealth of information she had to share. Of course she told Gavan all she could think of. He was very inquisitive. He was very smart.

Elizabeth wondered at Jarrett's calm in the face of

Liberty's idolization of Gavan. He didn't seem at all bothered, where she, Elizabeth, was resentful with the time Liberty had spent with Gavan. It didn't matter that it had been
by telephone. She was thankful when the couple finally
parted, promising to have dinner with them soon.

It wasn't that late. And that was unfortunate. Now that
she was done helping her grandmother, now that Sonya
had gone home and she was in the house alone, all she
could think about was Gavan.

The week had proven to be long and tumultuous, full
with highs and lows that she hoped would not repeat any
time soon. During the day, she had spent long hours delv-
ing through tons of paperwork due to Mikel's scheming.
Sonya had been instrumental in keeping their investors
from divesting. But legally they were required to inform
all of their clients of the potential risk they encountered. Only two of their clients were concerned. The
others after a few inquiries were appeased and Elizabeth
got through the end of the week without too many eco-
nomic impacts.

Then there were the evenings. And she would have
nothing but time on her hands and Gavan's gifts staring her in the face.

Elizabeth considered watching television, perhaps
the news. She had not kept up with the news since getting caught up with her cousin's outrageous scheming.
She hoped fervently that he was simmering with regret
for causing her so much anguish. Of course, had it not
been for Mikel she would not have met Gavan.

She smiled, tickled by her wayward thoughts. Gavan
had a way of slipping into her mind as easily as he had
slipped into her life. And just as sure as his presence had
effected her, so too did thoughts of him. Her eyes closed
and she allowed her thoughts to drift over their first kiss
and how it had been wickedly long and sultry and sexy.

He was such a good kisser. She could only imagine that he was good. Her eyes popped open and she grinned. She was becoming wanton and it was all Gavan's fault.

In good spirits yet suddenly tired, Elizabeth got up. She was going to bed. There was nothing to do but that. She wasn't focused enough to read. Music might help. Something mellow and soothing. She was in the mood for peace and quiet.

Placing the wrap on the chair she vacated, she searched for her remote and set her CD player. Satisfied with the sounds filtering through the house, she was about to cuddle back in her chair when the doorbell rang.

She stared at the door. Most of the lights were out, but she couldn't see out the window. She couldn't even see the car. But she knew it was Gavan. Somehow, deep inside, she had expected him to come tonight. He had all but hinted that he would.

Trying to curb a smile, she answered the door.

Gavan stared at her as if he had not expected an answer. That ended her attempt to control a smile and she actually grinned. He followed suit.

"Tomorrow is hours away. I've missed you too much to wait."

CHAPTER 28

"Oh, you really know how to turn on the charm, don't you?" Elizabeth inquired, challenging him. Her voice was light and carefree, but she was quivering inside.

"Only for you," Gavan said with a widening smile.

Now what was she supposed to say to that? Unlike him, she wasn't used to light bantering and easy flirtations. She licked her lips and tried desperately to come up with a witty remark. Too late. He appeared amused and leaned toward her. "Are you going to have me stand out here all night?"

"Oh," she murmured, stepping aside.

He entered, pausing in the center of her foyer to listen to the mellow sounds escaping the stereo. He stepped into her family room and took note of the wrap carelessly hanging from the chair. He could imagine her there, curled up in her chair, her hair spilling over the chair, her eyes closed. He cooled his imagination and took a seat on the couch.

"What are we doing, Gavan?" Elizabeth asked softly, coming to stand in front of him.

"Dating," Gavan answered. And then he said, "Except,

I've never dated anyone like you before. And I can't stop thinking about you."

It was true. She had completely and thoroughly invaded his every waking thought, and even his dreams. He had dreamt of her the evening before. He awoke sweating, frustrated, and determined to come to her if she continued to refuse to call him.

His eyes ravished her and had he touched her, she could not have responded more.

He reached for her hand and gently tugged her until she was sitting beside him.

Elizabeth swallowed slowly, trying to catch her breath. She was enthralled by his words, mesmerized beneath his gaze. How could she not be when he was so near, so charming, and so very tempting? He wanted her, yes. She wanted him too but she recognized that it was so much more than that. If only she could tell him. She couldn't, but how she wanted to admit it, to say it, to express herself in a way that words could never fulfill.

She resisted the urge to lick her lips. The motion would be all too telling of just how nervous she was. With a voice not so blithe anymore, she asked, "You can't?"

"No, I can't," he repeated. "You intrigue me, Elizabeth."

"I do?" she murmured, her eyes wide.

With his hand firmly planted on the back of the sofa, Gavan leaned into her, his gaze searching. "You do," he said in a husky voice, telling just how intrigued he was.

Elizabeth reacted to his nearness. The provocative whisper of his words sent thrills through her body, causing her to shiver slightly. Transfixed, his words emotive, his presence persuasive, she slowly closed her eyes.

Gavan responded to her silent invitation. Their lips touched. It was a tentative kiss. He brushed her mouth with his, taking his time exploring her. Then he pulled away and Elizabeth moaned, her mouth tingling from the contact they had shared.

"Look at me, Elizabeth," Gavan whispered.

She did.

His hazel eyes were blazing with feelings he was trying to control. She was within his grasp. He wanted nothing more than to kiss her fully, to inflame her with desire until she lost her composure and called out his name. But Lance's words halted him and he forced thoughts of lovemaking from his mind. He held his body in rigid control.

She waited, watching him closely. He wanted to say something and she refused to panic. *Whatever it was, let it be okay,* she prayed.

"You're so beautiful," he said with such yearning that Elizabeth really did panic. She snapped out of her trance and scooted a small distance from him.

"What is it, Gavan? What's wrong? Why are you . . . what's going on?" she asked.

"Nothing's wrong," Gavan said, wanting to ease her mind. She stood and he patted the seat. "Sit with me. Let's talk."

"Yes, let's," Elizabeth said, slightly miffed. Was he playing a game?

"I have something to tell you," he finally admitted.

"I knew it," Elizabeth gasped. "What is it? Please, don't keep me in suspense, Gavan."

"It's not my intention. It's about your mother. Lance and I have uncovered some interesting details about Liberty Sutton."

"Irving. She's married now," Elizabeth said.

"Of course. Well, based on her past, an ambiguous one, we strongly believe that she is Lorna's daughter."

Elizabeth gasped and Gavan went on, determined to explain it all to her.

"That's the main belief, but there are other possibilities. Lance and I happened to believe Lorna is the best bet. I'm going to Savannah—"

"When did you decide this?" Elizabeth interrupted, surprised.

"Today. It won't be for a few weeks, but Lance and I think it would be a good idea to get down there," Gavan continued easily. "I wondered if you would like to come as well. I think there is where we can get the final pieces of the puzzle. And . . . find out more about your mother."

"What more do you need to know about her?" Elizabeth asked. It was surreal what he was saying. She had suspected, but it had been easy to ignore it when Anne denied the possibility. Now Gavan was saying it was not only a possibility but a strong probability.

"Liberty is older than you. She's thirty? Thirty-one? But your mother died when you were only two. Something's wrong. Either Liberty is actually years younger than she thinks she is or Lorna . . . she didn't die when Anne claims she did."

"That's ridiculous, Gavan," Elizabeth exclaimed. "Why would Anne lie?"

"I have no idea," Gavan said, taking her hand and stroking it as he spoke. He wanted her calm, rational. "Maybe she didn't know. Anything is possible."

"You think my mother is alive?" Elizabeth murmured. The reality of the implications sank in.

"Not necessarily. But maybe she didn't die the way you've always been told. Come with me, Elizabeth. I'll be your strength, but now that we've uncovered this much do you really want to let it go?" Gavan asked gently.

"And that's why you are here?" she asked. "I can't. I can't do it."

"Why not? It'll be for a few days and I'll be there with you the whole time."

"I'm afraid . . . no, not afraid. I don't know." Elizabeth sighed, closed her eyes, and wanted the questions whirling in her head to stop.

"Elizabeth," he began cautiously, "you can't hide from this. And you won't have to go through it alone. Whatever we discover down there, whatever happens, I'll be by your side."

"Gavan," she sobbed. Then, unable to stop sobbing, she tried to turn from him. He wouldn't let her and laid her head on his shoulder, rubbing her back in slow, circular motions, soothing her the way he would a small child.

"I'm sorry," he whispered. "I know it's overwhelming. I know."

"I'm sorry," Elizabeth sniffed, embarrassed that her tears were saturating his shirt.

"Don't be," Gavan said, smiling down at her. "I'll bet you haven't cried since your cousin's attack. Have you?"

"Just a little," she said, trying to laugh, but it was shaky.

"I didn't want to tell you about Lorna," Gavan admitted.

"I suspected. It's not a completely new idea, it's the reality that it could be real, that we could finally know the truth, that caught me by surprise."

"As it would anyone. But you won't be alone. I'll be there with you."

"It's asking much of you," Elizabeth said, staring at him with uncertainty. Could he be any more generous?

"It's nothing. And I would do anything for you," Gavan said emphatically.

Elizabeth was overjoyed by his emphatic declaration. Feeling suddenly timid, she raised her gaze to his. His eyes were heavy, his mouth parting as if he would kiss her. She leaned into him, encouraging the moment. Tenderly, almost reverently, he kissed her. This time he didn't only graze her mouth, he kissed her deeply, his mouth exploring her as if it were the first kiss.

"Elizabeth," he murmured.

"Uhm," she responded, pulling his head back down when he lifted it to speak.

"I want more than a kiss," he groaned.

Her eyes flew open. They were so close she could see the green, gold, and gray specks that made up his hazel eyes. She was afraid to speak, to break the spell encircling them. She could only nod.

"Do you understand, Elizabeth? I don't just want to kiss you. I don't just want to make love to you," he said, his voice husky and barely audible.

"I want to make love to you, too," she whispered, misunderstanding him. She thought he must not have understood her because he shook his head.

"Yes, Gavan," she said breathlessly. "I'm saying yes, too. I want to make love to you."

He pulled her into his embrace, his muscled chest a solid wall, a luxury she was not shy to take advantage of.

"I know, but you're not understanding, Elizabeth. I want to protect you. I want to be here when you need me. I'm not asking you to make love to me. I'm asking you to marry me."

CHAPTER 29

Gavan didn't move. He had no idea what he was doing. He had not intended to propose. But once the words were spoken he, he realized he actually meant them. He wanted a lifetime. And there was no turning back now.

He wanted forever. He had never felt that way about a woman. She was witty, astute, and spirited, and every intuition in him knew she was a prize he could not let go.

He felt a surge of panic. He was besieged with dread that she would not accept him, that she would turn him away. He should have made love to her first, then professed to love her. He was convinced she wanted him the way he wanted her. And she loved him, too.

Elizabeth was stunned. Had she heard him right? He wanted marriage? She couldn't breathe. She was dreaming and she couldn't shake herself awake. For the life of her she didn't know what to say or do. Marriage? He wanted marriage? She blinked and took a long, shaky breath.

She couldn't marry Gavan. Why shouldn't she? she thought wildly. She had never felt so connected, so enamored with a man in her life. He was everything she could dream of in a man. He was intelligent, strong, and virile. And there was no disputing his handsomeness. He was independent as well. And he wanted her because . . . well, because he wanted her. Why not? she thought, exhaling heavily.

"Elizabeth?" he whispered urgently.

"I'm confused," she said.

"I am too," Gavan confessed.

"We hardly know each other," Elizabeth whispered, trying to keep a rational head despite the heady sensation his proposal gave her.

"What we know is enough—"

"No," Elizabeth said.

"Why not? I know I want you like I've never wanted another woman, Elizabeth. You are beautiful—"

"Which is hardly a good reason to ask a woman to marry you, Gavan," Elizabeth lectured softly.

"I mean in ways that go beyond the physical appeal. I think you know that."

"I can't. We can't," she protested, breathless beneath his endearing words.

"Why can't we? I know what I want and I want you. Forever." Gavan was adamant. He was in love and he would convince her that they belonged together if it took all night.

She gasped. His words had a powerful impact. He meant it. Every word.

"I do. It's crazy but I would be crazier to let you get away." He laughed, not at all uncomfortable with the conversation. "I want you, Elizabeth, and I think you want me, too."

Elizabeth couldn't respond, her words were caught in her chest. He wanted her. He had said enough but, but not once had he said "I love you." And that, more than the suddenness of his proposal, kept her from succumbing to his persuasive appeal.

Before she could think of the right words he kissed her, his tongue deep and searching, clouding her thoughts and her will to think.

When he released her, Elizabeth felt faint. She held on to him. She laid her head against his chest, the sound of his heartbeat soothing, imploring her to respond.

"Marry me, Elizabeth, and I will make you happy. Don't think, don't try to rationalize it," Gavan murmured in her ear.

"Gavan Ward," Elizabeth finally said, smiling at the handsome face hovering above her. "I do believe you are the most impulsive man I've ever met."

"And a grown man," he said in all seriousness. I know what I want and—"

"I know. You want me," she finished for him. She was smiling, but it was wavering. Was he even aware that he never claimed his love for her? Passion was great, but passion didn't sustain a couple during hard times. She was in love with him, but she would not fess up to it. How could she when he spoke of passion and lust and wanting? And she could not marry him.

"And then what? We discover day by day what a mistake we made rushing into marriage?" Elizabeth said. She was being sensible, she decided, but his dejected gaze saddened her.

"We discover day by day just how right we are for each other. I'm nearly forty, Elizabeth. Why wait? What are you looking for?"

It was a good question. One that Elizabeth could not answer. Marriage had never been her focus. She had been so busy doing her grandmother's bidding she had not thought about her future. She had dated. She had known men who made her smile, but not the way Gavan did. She had been kissed, but never with the intensity that Gavan stirred. And she had never thought she was in love before.

Until now.

Until Gavan.

She wasn't looking for anything. She wanted him as surely as he wanted her. But she could not bring herself to accept marriage. If it failed soon after, as so many marriages she knew did in the first few years, it would break her heart.

Gavan was still hovering above her. Elizabeth reached behind him and pulled his head down, raising her own until their lips touched. She hadn't answered his question, but suddenly he didn't care. She might have resignations now, but he wouldn't give up. He would ask her every day if he had to until she gave in to what was meant to be.

He pulled her to him, relenting at last.

"I want you," he said huskily. He was speaking beyond making love, she knew, but her body quivered in anticipation and she encouraged him onward.

She shivered with delight when he swept her up in his arms and nibbled at her earlobe. In his arms, she was completely uninhibited. She mimicked his artful kisses and was rewarded by his groans. He sat up, lifted her effortlessly from the couch, and sat her on his lap. She gazed at him in wonder, watching as his eyes roved over her from head to toe. He reached for her, caressing her face with the palm of his hand. He ran his finger over her mouth before slowly traveling down her neck and resting on the curve of her breast. He paused, capturing her gaze.

"Elizabeth," he said.

She couldn't speak and waited as he, one button after another, undressed her. She shivered.

"Are you cold?" he asked huskily. She shook her head no. Nimbly he slid her arms free of the dress and lifting her slightly, he tugged it free. Elizabeth's eyes followed its featherlight descent to the floor.

"I wanted to make love to you from the first," Gavan murmured, his eyes full of admiration and gleaming that caused her to quiver ever so slightly. Intimately, his gaze slid over her, caressing her pert, full breasts and the length of her long legs with a heat that caused her to burn with desire.

Elizabeth could only hold on to him as his head lowered to taste of her. She gasped at the tingling sensations his probing kisses ignited. He kissed her bare skin from her arms to her chest to the smoothness of stomach. "So soft," he whispered. Then he raised his head and brushed his lips over her breasts.

She reached to remove her bra, but his hand caught hers, stopping her.

"No," he murmured. "Let me."

A moment later she was exposed. With his eyes holding hers, he cupped one of her breasts and then he covered the taut nipple and fully suckled. She writhed beneath the sudden moist warmth that enveloped her and threw her head back, urging him onward.

Gavan moaned, freeing one breast to favor the other. When he was done, he trailed wet kisses up her neck, nibbled on her earlobe, and then caught her mouth in a plunging kiss as he effortlessly came to his feet with her cradled in his arms.

Elizabeth wrapped her arms about his neck and, for the length of time to move from the couch to the plush carpet throw in front of her fireplace, she watched him, bemused by the effect he had on her.

He laid her gently on the carpet, stepped aside, and undressed, his gaze never leaving hers.

She ached for him and thought she would scream if he didn't take her soon.

Gavan paced himself. He had taken his condom from his wallet as he undressed and now dropped it purposely on the floor next to Elizabeth. She didn't notice, her arousal so great it turned him on more.

He was at such a peak that if he didn't satisfy her first, he could very well end their lovemaking before she knew the extent of his desire. She was ready for him, but he wanted to explore her fully. He wanted to remember every inch of her. And he wanted her to never forget their first night making love.

He dropped to his knees, his hands grasped her thighs and squeezed.

He held back with an effort that would have amazed a lesser man. He ached to possess her fully, to plunge into her. Her sweet responses uninhibited as she freely touched him in turn were driving him mad.

He was aware of every part of her.

Her ragged breathing. Her half-closed eyes. Her hips that writhed ever so gently, urging him onward. The tautness of her nipples that begged to be ravished.

His hands trailed upward until they reached her breasts. He fondled and caressed them, then brushed her nipples with his thumbs. She moaned with pleasure.

He lowered his body and circled her nipple with his tongue until it hardened to a ripe peak. He cupped it, squeezing gently as he tasted her, licking and teasing the nipple until she gasped. He lowered his other hand, traveling downward from her breast to her hip to her inner thigh, kneading her flesh, stroking her, driving her mad. When he finally touched her most intimate part, she jerked, immediately responding to the contact.

It was nearly his undoing. She was so wet and ready for him he could imagine her warmth surrounding him.

He wanted her then and there. But he wanted it right, he wanted her to know that theirs was a perfect union and she had to have him forever.

He covered her with his body, kissing her closed eyes, blowing softly in her ears, nibbling hungrily on her neck. He continued his lustful assault on her flesh until he reached her inner thighs. Gently he spread her legs and with a deliberate slowness that left her gasping in wonder his tongue darted a wet trail from her inner thighs until he had reached her most intimate spot. He tasted her, slowly pressing his tongue against her sensitive flesh. She thrashed in near delirium and he had to hold her thighs in his grasp to keep pleasuring her. He didn't stop, tasting of her, pressing his tongue on her until she screamed his name.

Only then did he release her and with trembling hands, he unwrapped his condom, barely getting it on as he tortured himself by watching her. She lay beneath him, her body soft and supple and eager.

Elizabeth was aflame. Her body ached with unquenched desire, blood pounded in her ears, and when he lay against her, the length of his large penis weighing against her inner thigh, her senses whirled in a haze of delight. She all but shoved upward to have him enter her.

He groaned his pleasure and with a swiftness that left her breathless, he entered, her moist heat welcoming him. He plunged deeper and deeper, holding on to her with all the passion he'd been keeping at bay. Bodies entwined in complete abandon, kissing and exploring one another in wonder. They both drew gulps of air when their passion was spent but Gavan did not move off her completely. He drew her closer.

As they lay in each other's arms, reveling in one another, she felt him hardening again and her eyes flew open in awe.

He gave her a sensual smile and her lips parted for him in blissful surrender.

CHAPTER 30

Gavan spent weeks wooing Elizabeth and she consistently resisted his proposal. It only served to make him more determined.

They were at the movies, a chick film, he called it.

"More popcorn?" he asked during a particularly tearful scene. Elizabeth scolded him with her eyes. He sat back in his seat, silent. As he stared up at the screen, his hand crawled over her shoulder, ran up and down her skin, and then gently squeezed.

Elizabeth attempted to ignore the contact, but she soon gave in. She turned to him inquiringly. He was grinning and raised an eyebrow at her.

"You're deliberately trying to distract me," she murmured.

"No, I'm not," he said innocently. "I only was checking if you've made a decision yet."

"Gavan," Elizabeth breathed. He was relentless. She knew what decision he was looking for and she was only moments from giving in.

"Tonight, I'll just have to work harder at convincing you," he promised. Then he nibbled at her earlobe, teasing her senses, and she had to concentrate not to gasp.

A moment later she shot to her feet, glared at him, then took his hand and led him from the theater.

Grinning, he happily complied, curving her into his arms the moment they reached his condo. After the Maya fiasco and with her stubborn rejection of marriage, he wanted her to know that there was no other woman for him but her. He even gave her a key, which surprised her.

"I want marriage. It means we'll be sharing keys." He laughed at her incredulity.

The next morning Elizabeth awoke next to Gavan with a smile. He was already awake, watching her, touching her face with an adoration that caused her heart to flutter wildly.

"What is it?" she asked.

"I'm wondering what I have to do to get you to say yes, you'll marry me," Gavan answered honestly. It was true. He had no idea what else he could do but continue to court her in every way. They were so perfectly made for each other he could not accept that she would really turn him down.

"I can't," she whispered yet again. It was a line he hated to hear. When they had children, he would make sure they never uttered those words.

He grinned. "What do you think about children?" The question, for Elizabeth, came from nowhere. She was thoughtful.

She chose to turn the tables on him. "Do you want children, Gavan?"

"Yes, but I'm willing to want what you want," Gavan said without pause.

"Ha." Elizabeth laughed. "You either want them or you don't."

"I do, but if you have issues with it, I'm flexible." Gavan was insistent.

"Actually, I do want children, someday." She smiled, the image of small versions of Gavan assailing her. "Yes, now that I am thinking of it, I do want children."

"Good." Gavan sounded relieved.

They rose and dressed, each hating to leave the other. Lance and Tyke were still looking up information on Liberty's family for Gavan. But Gavan was too distracted to even start a draft of the Wilkinses. He wasn't even so sure he wanted to anymore. Besides, he was busy spending his days preparing for his nights with Elizabeth.

Elizabeth had come to look forward to Gavan's daily proposals. As she left her office, she wondered how he would propose to her and if it would be before or after they made love.

"Elizabeth," Gavan whispered, rising from his seat when she joined him that evening at the restaurant. Elizabeth had gotten off from work later than planned. They met at a new restaurant not far from Elizabeth's job. Gavan had already ordered an appetizer and a drink for them both.

Elizabeth was impressed that he chose her drink, an apple martini, and an appetizer of crab dip and chips, two of her favorites. Each day he proved himself by adding another credit to his score with her.

She kissed him on the cheek, then sat down. "I'm sorry that I'm late."

"You don't have to apologize. You're a hardworking woman." Gavan shrugged. It was Elizabeth's first hint that something was amiss. So paradise had its flaws after all.

"Yes, and you're a hardworking man. So how are things in the world of my family?" she asked. She really was curious. Over the past few weeks Gavan barely mentioned her or Liberty's past. She wondered what was going on. Even Tyke and Lance seemed to have disappeared.

"Things are interesting," he said. "As a matter of fact, I was going to discuss it with you this evening."

"Really? How so?" Elizabeth inquired.

"Some discoveries have been made by Lance. We think it would be a good idea if I went to Savannah. I was hoping you would come with me."

"To Savannah as in my hometown?" Elizabeth queried.

"Yes. Did you happen to know that Liberty's grandfather moved there? It's a long shot, but Lance and I think it's a lead we shouldn't ignore." Gavan gave her the information in such a formal way that she watched him closely, uncertain.

"I'll think about it, Gavan. I'm not sure if Savannah is where I want to be when you do find out about Liberty's mother," Elizabeth answered truthfully. Gavan nodded. Beneath his continued stare she glanced at the martini and took a sip.

"Uhm," she murmured. "Very nice. Thank you."

"Anything for you, Elizabeth." There was that tone again and she raised her eyes to him.

"Gavan, what is it? What's wrong?" she asked finally.

"Nothing's wrong. Why would there be? I'm having dinner every evening with an incredibly beautiful woman, inside and out. I'm happy. Are you happy, Elizabeth?" he asked, suddenly intense.

"Yes. The past few weeks have been, well, wonderful," Elizabeth answered.

"Then please tell me, when I say I love you, why can't you say you love me?"

"Well," Elizabeth began slowly, staring at him with wide eyes while she tried to catch her breath. "If you ever said you loved me I would have."

Gavan was surprised by that answer. "What do you mean?"

"You've proposed to me every day for nearly two weeks. Oh, you're so beautiful, Elizabeth. I love holding you, I want you, I need you. But not once did I hear you utter the words 'I love you.'"

"I can't believe that's true," Gavan denied.

She gave him a look that suggested it was very true.

"All right, maybe I haven't said it," Gavan relented carefully. "Has it ever occurred to you that it may not be a phrase I'm familiar with saying?" he asked.

"Has it ever occurred to you that a woman needs to hear it, especially from the man she's going to marry?" Elizabeth retorted.

Gavan paused, watched her closely, and asked, "Is that a yes?"

Elizabeth sipped her martini, deliberately delaying her response. She set it down again and considered him with a half smile. "Yes."

"Good God, that was intense," he said with a whistle.

"Really?" she breathed.

"Is that what this has been about?" he had to know.

"Pretty much." She grinned at his look of disbelief. "I wanted to say yes the moment you asked."

"And you let me think I was fighting a losing battle," Gavan accused.

"No," Elizabeth corrected slowly. "It was a losing battle. I wasn't going to say yes without you saying you love me." Then she laughed lightly. "But I've relented somewhat. After all, you haven't really said it yet."

Gavan was incredulous. "What are you talking about? I just said it."

"No, you said, when I say I love you, not, Elizabeth, I love you." His jaw dropped and he gaped at her. He snapped his mouth closed, leaned back in his seat, then smiled slowly at her. She immediately regretted goading him.

"What?" she muttered.

He came to his feet and with a loudness that caught the attention of restaurant occupants, he clapped his hands once.

"Ladies and gentlemen, please excuse the interruption, but I need witnesses." Elizabeth wanted to sink under the table.

"I love you, Elizabeth. I love this woman right here. Do you hear me, Elizabeth? I love you." Then he leaned over and kissed her. Everyone cheered and clapped and Elizabeth blushed.

"I can't believe you just did that," she hissed.

"Well, that way you'll never forget that you heard me say I love you," Gavan said as he took his seat again, grinning at the stares and laughter he had created.

"Ready to eat?" he asked casually as if nothing had just happened.

Elizabeth was hungry all right, but food was not what was on her mind. "I'm ready, yes. Let's go home."

Gavan set his menu down, caught the waiter's attention, and made haste in obeying Elizabeth's every wish.

"Can I tell you something?" Gavan asked Elizabeth the next morning. It was Saturday, almost ten o'clock, and they were still in bed.

"Yes."

"You have the softest, smoothest skin I have ever touched. And I've touched many—"

"Gavan!" she said sharply.

He chuckled, giving her a roguish grin. "I was just teasing. Really."

She gave him a sidelong look, her curiosity provoked. "Do I really?"

"Yes. And you know what else?"

"No, but it better not be about some past affair," she said.

"The past is forgotten. I only have eyes, and love, for you."

"That was nice," she breathed, his words thrilling.

"I'm only just starting," he said suggestively.

She laughed. "Are you trying to seduce me, Gavan?"

"Uh-huh," he agreed. "Is it working?"

"Uh-huh," she replied, then rolled onto him, seeking his mouth and kissing him again. They made love, the morning sun beaming into the room and caressing their skin as their bodies intertwined. When they were done, Elizabeth lay in Gavan's arms, running her fingers over his hard chest in idle admiration.

"My grandmother may have a relapse when she hears the news," she whispered.

"That we're engaged or that we're going to Savannah?" Gavan asked.

He felt her shrug. "Maybe from both. Definitely that we're engaged."

Gavan lifted his head and kissed her forehead, muttering, "Then we'll have to be gentle when we tell her. Or we don't have to tell her anything."

Elizabeth rejected the idea. "That wouldn't be fair. She'll be hurt if we don't tell her."

Gavan said lazily, "Maybe I could stay away until she gets used to the idea that we're dating. Then you can tell her that it's more than that. We're in love and getting married."

"My grandmother is no spring chicken, Gavan, and you're making so light of this. Marriage is a serious thing," Elizabeth scolded. His kisses were warming her body from head to toe. Soon she wouldn't be able to think clearly at all and they were never going to get out of bed.

"And I'm serious about you," he said and his tone conveyed how sincere he was.

"I'm not doubting you, Gavan," Elizabeth sighed. She cuddled closer to him.

"We could tell her after we come back from Savannah," Gavan offered.

"As if that would change her reaction at all. It might make it worse," Elizabeth scoffed.

"Then, Elizabeth," Gavan said patiently, "it seems we'll be letting her know real soon. Our trip is in two days."

Two days.

Elizabeth was not so thrilled with the prospect of Savannah, although she was thrilled that Gavan wanted her with him. He had insisted upon it. Fearing it would be her undoing to become clinging, she had urged him to go without her. But he wouldn't accept no.

So now she was going to Savannah.

And she had to tell her grandmother she was engaged before she left.

CHAPTER 31

Anne was distressed. Sonya was delighted. Elizabeth and Gavan sat side by side, so caught up with each other that they scarcely noticed either of the older women's reaction to their announcement.

They were at Anne's house. They had arrived with such beaming faces that Anne immediately suspected an announcement, of what she had not been sure. She and Sonya were finishing breakfast and Anne offered the couple coffee. They declined and sat cheerfully across from her and Anne, holding hands and giving each other long, private glances.

"You're getting married?" Anne gawked at them as if they had two heads.

Elizabeth nodded her head, laughing. "Yes, we're getting married."

"Elizabeth," Anne said bluntly, "you haven't known him very long. Are you sure you know what you're doing?"

Gavan wasn't surprised by Anne's bluntness or concern. It had taken him weeks to get Elizabeth to bend and agree to marry him. She had learned her stubbornness from Anne, he decided.

"I do," Elizabeth said softly. She couldn't curb a grin

from peeping forth when she glanced at Gavan. He had been so persistent and romantically engaging that there was nothing she could but say yes. But most importantly he had finally acknowledged what she needed to hear most. That he loved her and she was still high from the sound of sweet declaration.

"Have you two set a date?" Sonya asked, smiling at them.

Her presence made the discussion far more pleasant and bearable for both Elizabeth and Gavan. Anne had a sternness that would have left them doubting themselves. But Sonya's round brown face was grinning at them in approval.

"Not yet but we're working on it," Elizabeth answered, again glancing at her fiancé.

"I was hoping sooner than later. I would marry her today if she would let me," Gavan added.

"Oh, God no," Anne protested. "Give yourselves time. At least a year," she suggested.

"No. I don't want to wait that long," Gavan flatly refused.

Elizabeth put a calming hand on his arm and said to her grandmother, "We haven't decided on a date but it will be soon. Maybe a few months. We're not sure."

Anne raised her eyebrow gracefully at that information but only nodded.

"Do you have a plan? Are you going to get married here? Elizabeth told us you're from Hawaii, Gavan. Will you honeymoon there?" Sonya inquired.

"Now this is where we have agreed fully," Gavan stated. "We want to get married and honeymoon in Hawaii, because as you just said, it's my hometown. I want to show Elizabeth the island and explore it for the first time myself."

"You've never explored Hawaii and you're from there?" Anne asked skeptically.

"That's pretty much the case. I'm familiar with the homeland, of course, but the tourist attractions, besides visiting a few places with my family when I was a kid, never actually held my interest."

"We've been in the district for nearly ten years, Anne. And I have only been to their art museum. Do you know how much there is to do in downtown Washington, D.C.?" Elizabeth asked, mildly defensive.

Anne was stern, her silence speaking volumes. She was not pleased by their news. She felt that Elizabeth was rushing into things. She had been through a lot since her cousin implicated her with his schemes. Then there was Gavan's book he was writing and his premature announcement that Liberty and Elizabeth could be sisters. No wonder her grandchild was emotional. She would be too if every day brought some new trauma into her life. But it was no reason to get married in a rush.

"Elizabeth," Anne said, addressing her grandchild directly, "you've experienced a lot of suffering these past few months. I don't blame you for feeling the need to hold on to something. And," she added with a studied glance at Gavan, "he's a very handsome man, charming, but that will not sustain you."

To her surprise, Elizabeth laughed, nodding in agreement. "I told him the same thing, Anne. We discussed this over and over these past few weeks. But I love him," Elizabeth admitted easily. "And he loves me. And isn't that what marriage is about?"

"Yes," Sonya said brightly.

"No," Anne said, sharply contradicting Sonya. "It is not," she bit out, tossing Sonya an annoyed glance. "Marriage is about two responsible adults coming together because one, they love each other. Two, they *know* what they are doing. And three, they are *prepared* for the ups and downs that *every* marriage has. Four, they can help each other. Five—"

"We get it, Mrs. Wilkins," Gavan said. He wanted to laugh as well but knew it would insult Elizabeth's grandmother. He didn't want to upset her any more than the news had already done. "Marriage is not always easy, but we belong together. And I'm not letting Elizabeth slip through my fingers. I love her and we're getting married."

"Good for you," Sonya hooted, receiving another annoyed look from Anne.

"We had hoped to get your blessing. Elizabeth and I, when the time comes, want you and Sonya to come with us to Hawaii and stay for as long as you like," Gavan said, glancing between the two older women, hopeful that they would agree. Elizabeth had been very worried about leaving them behind and he saw no reason that they couldn't come to Hawaii as well.

Anne was not appeased. She had no intention of uprooting herself and living on some island, but she spared them another speech. "When the time comes, I will definitely be at your wedding. That is all I can promise."

"Fair enough," Gavan said, accepting her rejection in stride.

Anne sighed, her body appearing more fragile in that moment than ever before. She nodded her approval. She could not stop them as she had her son and his love for Lorna. "Well, I hope you two will be happy."

"Of course they will be. Don't be so glum," Sonya retorted, indignant for the young couple. Gavan shot her an appreciative wink.

Feeling as if she had somehow betrayed Anne, Elizabeth went to her grandmother and held her in a hug. She squeezed and whispered in Anne's ear, "Don't worry, Anne. He'll make me happy or I'll make his life a living hell."

Anne scoffed but a smile tugged at her mouth. "You do that."

She patted Elizabeth on the back and then sighed, dislodging her grandchild. "I can't recall the last time you hugged me like that," she said, staring up into Elizabeth's bright face. "You are really happy."

"Yes, I am really happy."

"Then I give you both my blessing. Now sit down. My neck is cramping staring up at you like this," Anne chided.

Elizabeth complied, taking Gavan's hand as she sat.

"Well, whether you're getting married next month or next year, we need to start planning for your big day. Have you decided who'll do it for you since it's in Hawaii?" Sonya asked.

Gavan shrugged and Elizabeth made a comical face. "Not really. I hadn't thought that far."

"And no wonder, as you're rushing into this," Anne couldn't resist saying.

"I would like to help. Perhaps your mother and I could talk, Gavan, and start setting things in motion," Sonya suggested.

"Can you do that without a date?" Elizabeth inquired.

"How naïve. Of course you can," Sonya chided. "You'll need a dress. A guest list."

"It'll be an intimate affair," Elizabeth said quickly. She had a small group of people she would invite. Gavan was another story, but she doubted that he would care. Besides, she preferred subtle events.

"You'll still need a guest list. And since it's in Hawaii, where will your guests stay? How much and what kind of dining will you have at your reception? There are many things to consider, child," Sonya finished.

"I tell you what," Gavan offered, coming to Elizabeth's rescue. "I'll give you my mother's number and you two can talk. She's great at planning and I think she would love to help."

Elizabeth listened as Gavan exchanged information with Sonya to contact his mother. She was in a daze, a happy dream. She was getting married. His weeks of wining and dining her had left her defenseless. She had wanted him, desired him, needed him, but until the night he confessed to loving her and that it wasn't just passion as she had feared, she would not have believed it possible that they would actually be planning their wedding.

Fascinated that this big, strong charismatic man had fallen in love with her, she glanced at him and touched his arm gently. He looked at her, giving her a slow, sensual smile and his gaze sliding over her possessively.

She was awed at how he had so fully captured her heart.

And to think she could spend a lifetime revelling in him.

She was unable to control a slight quiver at the thrill that ran up her spine, the prospect exciting.

Gavan looked at her again. Capturing her unguarded stare, he searched her eyes, his gaze inquiring. Her breath caught. And she was amazed again at how startlingly handsome he was, his open concern riveting. She was warmed by his adoring approval. Ensnared by the potency of his gaze, a bee caught in the honey of his omnipotence, she could not tear her gaze away.

Then like a douse of cold water, Anne hissed, "Elizabeth!"

"I'm sorry, Anne," Elizabeth stammered, pulling her gaze from Gavan.

Gavan grinned and Anne rolled her eyes and repeated her question. "Sonya was asking if you wanted to consider any of our clients on your guest list."

"Yes. Absolutely," Elizabeth answered, trying to smother her humiliation at daydreaming over her husband.

Anne curbed her irritation with her grandchild.

There was nothing to be done but go along with their plans. Witnessing their infatuation made the reality of their intention all the more inevitable. She only hoped Gavan was sincere. The idea that her grandchild could be deceived by good looks and a suave smile was far too unpleasant to even consider.

"So then, I guess it's settled. Now, tell me about Savannah, Gavan. Liberty mentioned you were planning a trip to my hometown. I would think that now that you're marrying my grandchild you would give up on the idea of making a profit at her expense," Anne said.

CHAPTER 32

Gavan didn't flinch beneath her stare although he had to rein in a scowl of outrage that sprouted at Anne's question. He was in love with Elizabeth. And he didn't need to write about the Wilkinses to earn a living. It was a covert insult and he was furious.

"Well? What about your book?" Anne asked. She was cool and composed and deliberately provoking the couple in any way she could.

Gavan considered her with the same cool reserve. One moment she was relenting, the next she was testing their love. It was a test he would not fail.

"We've discussed it," Gavan answered. "Neither of us has any reason to continue the book as it was. I would be far too partial at this stage. But," he added with resolve, "I am continuing to research the facts surrounding Liberty's parents."

"Why? Doesn't that cost you money to do that?" Anne questioned.

"It does, but in this case I have the good fortune of friends and family. Tyke Miles and Lance, my brother, to be exact. Actually, they are going to Savannah with me in a few weeks to help uncover a few things."

"I'm not comfortable with all of those people digging up my past," Anne said indignantly.

"I understand that, but Tyke has always assisted me. He's a great researcher and even better at discretion. My brother . . . well, he's just helping me. I don't know what we might uncover, so they're going."

"I take it you have no problem with this, Elizabeth?" Anne asked stoically.

"I have nothing to hide. Neither does Liberty. She's in agreement as well."

Elizabeth's statement irked Anne. She wondered if Elizabeth was implying that she was keeping family secrets.

"And neither do I," Anne said sharply.

"She didn't say you did, Anne," Sonya tried to explain.

"No one is accusing anyone of hiding information, Mrs. Wilkins," Gavan added, squeezing Elizabeth's hand encouragingly. "But, as I am marrying Elizabeth, she and I agreed that it would be a nice closure to know what Liberty's relationship is with the Wilkinses. If any," he was careful to say.

"How nice," Anne said snidely. "I realize that you two are in love. However, there are things that no family wants revealed. Private things. Family matters. Don't you believe you are being somewhat intrusive?"

"Somewhat." Gavan astounded her by agreeing. "But I will be careful not to be too much so."

"I doubt if you can contain yourself to that degree," Anne retorted. "As with this marriage announcement, I suppose I can't stop this digging into my son's past either, especially not with Elizabeth and Liberty urging you on. I can only hope you will be respectful through the process."

Elizabeth chose that moment to comment, "I suggested

Gavan talk with Mikel before we leave, Anne." Gavan had gotten enough of a verbal beating.

"He'll only have negative comments. Are you sure you want to talk to Mikel?" Anne asked. She especially did not want Mikel's two cents involved with Gavan's venture. "He doesn't know anything more than I do."

"It's been my experience that the very ones you least expect to have information, have a wealth of information to share. He may know something, even unwittingly, that could assist us," Gavan responded with mildness.

Anne Wilkins despised her nephew and would give no credence to anything he had to say. Gavan, on the other hand, had no such qualms. Mikel could be a window into the past. He could not overlook the man's impassioned role in Elizabeth's life. After all, Mikel and Earl, Elizabeth's father, were closer in age than Elizabeth and Mikel. He would have to remember her father and likely Lorna.

If there were any details missing, any hints to gather, Mikel was a good candidate to seek out. Gavan was confident Mikel would be able to recall something of relevance, unwittingly or not.

Who knew what he may have witnessed or heard and took for granted as being of no importance?

Gavan would not be swayed from interviewing him.

Anne sat back, glanced out of her window into her narrow enclosed yard, and stared at nothing in particular. She considered Gavan again and asked, "What did Liberty have to say, Gavan? You are going to Savannah because of her, are you not?"

"Yes. I thought I mentioned her grandfather. No? She has a grandfather not that far from your old estates. Lance is going down ahead of me and Elizabeth. He and Tyke are going to look into finding Liberty's grandfather's address."

"She never mentioned a grandfather to me." Anne all but pouted.

Gavan was apologetic. "I didn't know that. His name is Mark Sutton. His son was Greg Sutton, who married Ursula Bane. According to the information Lance could gather, apparently Greg and Ursula had one child, Liberty Sutton. They died when she was very young, about a year old. Her grandparents took her in—"

"Just like me," Elizabeth murmured.

Gavan nodded his agreement. "Another coincidence?"

"A horribly sad one," Anne concluded, her voice sympathetic yet firm.

"How did they die?" Elizabeth had to ask.

"I'm not sure," Gavan answered slowly. "Liberty wasn't sure. She mentioned a car accident."

"It seems to me, my grandson-to-be, that you may want to check the death certificates and records to look into this. That's a start," Anne suggested, her own curiosity causing her to put aside her dislike of his investigation.

Gavan grinned, unable to resist his next comment. "That, ma'am, is what I do best." *And I'm going to discover why you're so afraid of the past,* he thought, staring at Anne's strained face.

Gavan stood and Elizabeth followed. "Are we leaving?" she asked.

"Yes. Remember, I have to meet with Mikel and then we have a flight to catch in the morning?" Gavan answered.

Anne halted them before they could leave. "One moment please." They turned to Anne as one. "Do you plan to marry before you finish your research?"

What an odd question, Elizabeth thought.

Gavan thought so as well. He hesitated, before answering carefully, "It could be months, even years before the full truth is discovered. In my experience, even the best start can end up a dead end."

"And that means?" Anne demanded.

"I plan to marry Elizabeth no matter what we uncover in Savannah," Gavan said.

"Then let me assist you somewhat," Anne said quietly. She got their attention and continued. "Start with residents surrounding the Wilkinses' estate. I sold most of the estate years ago, but I am sure some of the residences are still there from when Lorna worked for me. At least, I hope they are. I would wager that they can recall Lorna Sanders and they would know if she had another child or other family members. I was not close with Lorna, so there is the chance that she lied to me and maybe my son about her family."

Anne didn't look at Elizabeth when she made that comment. Had she done so she would have witnessed Elizabeth's amazement. "I want closure, sooner rather than later. I don't want my grandchild walking down the aisle burdened by a secret past."

Gavan was already calculating his options. He would contact Lance and have him and Tyke talk with every person on and surrounding the old Wilkins property.

"Then I'll do my best to disclose everything to Elizabeth right away."

CHAPTER 33

Mikel Wilkins was extremely tight-lipped, unpleasant, and derogatory toward anything regarding his cousin. He refused to allow Gavan the interview when he thought Elizabeth would be present.

Gavan assured him that it was only going to be himself. He wouldn't have Elizabeth in the same room with Mikel even if she were agreeable to it. Which she wasn't, but he didn't share that with Mikel.

Correctly, he expected Mikel to be antagonistic. Yet his very hostility had proven to divulge a wealth of information.

The very first thing Mikel did after Gavan explained more fully his intent for meeting with him was to get up and try to leave.

Gavan wasn't surprised. Mikel had no interest in telling of his downfall, of facing his depravity.

Gavan kept his engagement with Elizabeth to himself, careful not to express his interest in her. Mikel slandered Elizabeth's name every which way from calling her insipid to greedy to a whore.

It took all of Gavan's self-control not to reach across the table and slam Mikel onto it. Instead, Gavan remained impassive, his hands quick to make notes with his pen and his eyes lowered, lest Mikel noticed his growing revulsion.

Mikel ranted about Anne, although less vehemently. "I don't hate Anne, you understand. She treated me like a black sheep at times, but I don't hate her," Mikel insisted.

Gavan sensed that unlike Elizabeth, whom Mikel admitted hating, Anne was a thorn in Mikel's side that he wanted to cradle, not eliminate.

"Can you tell me about Lorna and Anne?" Gavan asked.

Mikel's beady eyes narrowed to mere slits as he tried to recall Lorna.

"Didn't she die one night or disappear? I don't remember. I do remember that Anne took that brat granddaughter of hers in and took care of her, better than me."

Gavan paused, curious as to Mikel's choice of words. "Disappeared?" he inquired further.

"Who?" Mikel asked dumbly.

"Lorna Sanders. You said she seemed to disappear one night," Gavan reminded him.

"Yeah," Mikel muttered, then shrugged. "She disappeared."

Gavan looked up. Suspicion stirred him. He watched Mikel, no longer concerned by what his eyes would reveal. "I thought everyone believed she was dead," Gavan inquired carefully.

Mikel laughed. It was a harsh bitter laugh. Then he shook his head. "Yeah? She is," he said firmly, nodding his head with a force that Gavan suspected Mikel would regret later. "She died when Elizabeth was about two or three or something like that."

Gavan frowned and watched Mikel for a moment

before stating, "Disappeared and died are two different things. I'm confused—"

"Aren't we all?" Mikel hissed.

"By disappear, you mean her death was assumed?" Gavan asked casually, ignoring Mikel's snide remark.

"Who knows?" Mikel scoffed. "The woman invaded my home, mine! She had it out for Earl long before he took her to his bed. She thought she was going to get something out of it, I'm sure. She got something all right." Mikel laughed again.

Gavan held his anger in check. "Did you know Lorna then?"

"Barely, but it was enough to know that I didn't like her. She disappeared on the bayou and I say good damn riddance!" Mikel retorted.

Gavan was still. The audacity and cruelty of Mikel's statement was contemptible. It was a wonder that Mikel had not caused Elizabeth greater harm. Gavan concluded that Mikel Wilkins was crazy and malicious. With effort, he reached into his wallet, keeping his face mute. He pulled out the photo of Liberty's grandfather and held it in front of Mikel.

"Do you know him?" Gavan asked.

Mikel gave a quick scan of the old man's face. There was no reaction. After a thorough appraisal of the photo Mikel shook his head. "No, I've never seen him." It was the first normal response Gavan had gotten from the man.

"But does he even look familiar, like someone you know?" Gavan probed, keeping the photo within view.

"No. He doesn't. He could be any black guy."

"He isn't any black guy, he's Liberty Sutton's grandfather," Gavan said, annoyed.

He pressed the photo closer to Mikel. "Does he look like Liberty to you?" Gavan was careful not to ask Mikel if Mark Sutton looked like Lorna Sanders. He knew Mikel would play it up and use it against Elizabeth, if only to belittle her mother.

Mikel shook his head, his eyes glued to the photo now with more interest. "Not really. I didn't think Liberty was much to look at, pretty much the same as Elizabeth . . . Hey," Mikel gasped, his eyes widening. His gaze darted from Gavan to the photo; then a sneer covered his features. "Lorna had another brat? Before Earl had her, too? You're trying to find out if Liberty's her sister!"

"I didn't say that," Gavan said calmly. He put the picture back in his wallet.

"You didn't have to. Yeah, I see the resemblance between that guy and Liberty. I bet he and Lorna were lovers, too. Everyone knew she was a slut."

"I see," Gavan said calmly, but the muscle in his jaw tensed. It took every bit of his self-control not to knock Mikel Wilkins from his seat and slam him to the ground.

"No, you don't see! Anne doted on Elizabeth. Saw to it that I got nothing but some ragged old property. Then she had to sell it all when Earl died, except the house. She thought she was so brilliant, setting up the trust fund for Elizabeth to run. And now that's all that was left. No one wanted to build on her property in Savannah, so Anne came here. I was left out. So you see, had Lorna disappeared with her daughter, I wouldn't be in here, stuck. Locked up like a common thug," Mikel grunted in repugnance, his face crimson with his rage.

Gavan stared at Mikel, willing himself to remain neutral. More to himself than to Mikel, he questioned, "You hate Elizabeth that much?"

"She tore my family apart. She came into the world a problem and look at my life. Yeah, I hate her. I hate Anne, too. Although it wasn't really Anne's fault that her black maid of a whore wanted to lie with my uncle—"

"That'll do," Gavan said sharply. He stood abruptly. He had to curb his rising temper before he found himself spending a night in a jail cell. As far as Gavan was concerned, Mikel Wilkins was only missing a white sheet and a burning cross to express how he felt.

Mikel came to his feet as well, his eyes searching Gavan's face with open curiosity. Then he said in the calmest voice Gavan had heard him use since the interview began, "I don't hate black people. I don't care what you think, either. I just hate Elizabeth. I hate her mother and I hate Earl. Not because of their race, Mr. Ward, but because they stole my life, my rights. I'm going to rot in this prison for the rest of my life because of them."

"Looking for sympathy?" Gavan asked dryly.

Mikel shook his head emphatically. "Justice. I'm looking for justice. I would have had it if Liberty Sutton hadn't been so weak. I was a fool to think she could actually impersonate Elizabeth just because they looked so amazingly alike. They are nothing alike and I'm ruined because of it."

Gavan paused at Mikel's words and gave Mikel one last consideration. "Actually, the fact that Ms. Sutton is so much like Elizabeth is why you're in here. Ever think that had she not been as brave as she was, she would never have contacted her fiancé and exposed your plans? It takes courage to defy an enemy who also happens to have your life in his hands. Elizabeth would have done the same," Gavan added.

"Elizabeth's weak!" Mikel spat.

Gavan's smile was thin and humorless. He allowed his full height and wrath to show. "Elizabeth's my fiancée. If you ever, ever think to harm her again, you'll be thoroughly sorry. Do I make myself clear?"

Mikel's shock was satisfying and before he could respond, Gavan left.

It was a miracle that he had been able to maintain his composure during the infuriating interview. It was mind-boggling the kind of hatred Mikel expressed toward his family. It was dangerous to hate that way. Gavan was just thankful that it would be a very long time before Mikel would be able to even begin thinking about parole.

When Gavan met up with Elizabeth he drew her to him, holding her with a crushing warmth that left her breathless. He buried his face in her hair and murmured her name. She was bemused by the tenderness but accepted it gracefully.

"We should get some rest, don't you think?" he murmured huskily.

She looked up at him and saw the smoldering glaze in his eyes. She smiled, nodding.

"Yes. We have an early start," she teased, then guided him to her bedroom and her bed.

CHAPTER 34

Moss-covered slopes and aged weeping willows covered the expanse of the landscape. It was a nostalgic scene. The long road was manicured with the grace of historical pride, the shadow from the evening sun softening the avenue as Gavan drove into Wilkins Vista Estates.

They had rented a car once they arrived at the airport. It was going to be a long ride, but Elizabeth didn't mind. Lance and Tyke were already at the Wilkins Estates waiting for them, so Elizabeth had hours to spend alone with Gavan.

Elizabeth stared after the long road behind her with wonder. She had forgotten the soothing appeal of the countryside. Gavan had indeed asked her to come with him, proclaiming he wouldn't do it until after they were married if she didn't want to travel with him. She had agreed. Her intuition was as clear as his. She had to go, for their sake, for herself and her parents.

They left for Savannah the next day, taking the early morning flight and renting a sedan from the airport. Liberty had declined. Regretfully she could not leave on such short notice. Gavan had understood and with

Lance and Tyke trailing behind them, they hurried off in search of Lorna Sanders's past.

Elizabeth was thoughtful, recalling with pleasure the night before they had departed for Savannah. She had never been so thoroughly loved. Losing her mother at such a young age had left a void. The disillusionment of her father had only made matters worse. Anne loved her, in her own rigid, controlling way, certainly not in a manner that could compensate for Earl's indifference. She had dated sparingly in the past, impassive with the men of her acquaintance. The few boyfriends she had were a dull memory, their kisses not able to compare with the passion she shared with just a look at Gavan. She had not even realized that she needed an awakening.

Gavan had done it. He aroused a yearning inside her heart, a hunger that she would never again be able to ignore. It filled her with anxiety that she cared so much and had fallen so hard, and for Gavan, a stranger, and yet he was so much more, her lover and confidant, in an instant.

"You all right over there?" Gavan asked. He was at a red light and shot Elizabeth a glance. He marveled at her winsomeness. Her mouth was upturned with a hint of a smile. He was fascinated by her, every little motion she made. The way she walked, her soft but firm speech, her supple body, and the way she melted in his arms were spellbinding. He took a deep breath, forcing himself not to think about their lovemaking. As abandoned as he was with her, he knew that it was far more than her perfection in bed. The instant they had met it happened. Love. She had touched him in a way he could not begin to fathom. And he had never been a man to deny himself what he wanted. And he wanted Elizabeth Wilkins.

"Oh, I'm fine." She smiled. "I was just thinking how strange it is to be back in Savannah. It's been years since I came down here. After my father died, there was no real reason to visit anymore." Her expression became rueful before she added, "Not that we had a real relationship. He was my father and, well, I was Elizabeth, Lorna's daughter."

"You're more than that," Gavan said, with more harshness than he intended. He was so moved by her account of her father's insensitive opinion. He didn't think he would have liked Earl very much. He was not surprised, having dealt with Anne enough to suspect she would have such a cold, uncaring son.

"I know, I know," Elizabeth insisted. "It was just with him that I was ordinary Elizabeth. I think in hindsight that he was the reason I excelled everywhere else. I was a determined young girl, I can't deny that. I was focused on proving my value, that I was worthy of his attention and I guess his love. I wanted him to know that my existence mattered—"

"It does!" Gavan said, angry at the emotional abuse Elizabeth had suffered. He didn't want to hear any more, unable to contain his disgust of the father that denied her what was rightfully hers, his love. He groaned. Like it or not, he could not shut her up, not now. He needed to hear everything, the most intimate details of the Wilkinses' past, if he had any hope of discovering the connection, if there was any, between Liberty and Elizabeth. Elizabeth's father had hurt her and she was still hurting to this day. He cursed old Earl Wilkins, wishing he could erase the past clean. He wanted to hold her, console her, and encourage her. He kept driving. Elizabeth was a strong woman and would be fine. The comedy of it all was that Elizabeth's strength was a result of Earl's disregard. The old man had unwittingly molded Elizabeth into a very capable and very desirable woman.

Elizabeth peered at Gavan, her thick eyelashes shielding her scrutiny. She could see that he was annoyed but she wasn't sure why. She hoped he didn't think she was pining over the past. She knew that such was life and it could not be changed. She dropped her gaze and looked out the window again. It struck her how little they knew one another. She really had no idea whom she was marrying, did she? He was just a name and an incredibly handsome face. Well, he had a perfect body too, a vision of their lovemaking the night before flashing through her mind. And, oh, all right, she thought with growing warmth, he was also charismatic, clever, and well informed. She knew who he was. It was he, on the other hand, who knew frighteningly little about her.

It didn't matter. She wouldn't let it be a problem, not when she had a lifetime to show him who she was. She was attached and couldn't turn back now.

"I'm not upset with you, Elizabeth," Gavan said gently. She was startled, glancing at him in wonder. He read her so well, too well. "I don't think I would have liked your father very much," he admitted. "If he were around, I would tell him a thing or two and how dumb he was to ignore his beautiful daughter."

A whisper of a sigh escaped Elizabeth. She was flattered that Gavan was so emphatic about her father's disloyalty. Her mouth curved into an amused smile. "Earl wouldn't have given you the time to exercise your frustration, I'm afraid." She laughed lightly. "But don't be angry, Gavan," she said, consoling him. "He loved me. I knew that he did. He even said it on occasion. Usually during one of his wistful moments, I guess. More would have been wonderful, but the knowledge was there. That was enough."

"Uh-uh, no, it wasn't. You can live in denial if you like, but if he turns out to be Liberty's father I'm betting those wistful moments were directly related to whatever he forced your mother to do. I'm under the impression that Anne wasn't as familiar with her dear boy's where-abouts and behavior as she would like to think," Gavan said. He had no desire to ruin Elizabeth's pleasant mood, but Earl was no loyal lover or father. The old man did not deserve Elizabeth's loyalty in turn.

"What do you mean?" Elizabeth asked.

"I think Lorna had Liberty before she and Earl were prepared to fess up to their love affair."

"They never confessed, Gavan. Anne caught them," Elizabeth corrected.

"Okay, true. However, if Lorna had Liberty and Earl was, let's say he was in shock and unprepared for the kid, couldn't she have sent Liberty off and gotten pregnant just as quickly? Correct me if I'm wrong, but I under-stand it's very easy to get pregnant again once you've gotten pregnant once."

Elizabeth was quiet, her heart racing. Her mind was spinning. Did Gavan have children? Was that how he knew such a thing? She certainly had no knowledge on the subject. "Gavan?"

"Yes?"

"Do you, do you have children?" Elizabeth asked.

Gavan laughed instantly. "Children?" he asked, glanc-ing at her with amusement. Her expression sobered him. He cleared his throat and said with less humor, "I do not have any children, Elizabeth."

She didn't respond.

"I have interviewed dozens of women over the years, many of whom have children. It's information I've come across on several occasions. It has nothing to do with my personal experience."

"I see," Elizabeth said. She was thoughtful. "I'm afraid we don't know anything about each other."

Gavan nearly slammed on the brakes. He tossed her a worried glance, then stared straight ahead, his hands gripping the steering wheel. "We know enough. Don't have qualms now, Elizabeth. It's settled. I left my mother a message and I know she'll be calling the moment she gets it."

"Is this about your mother?" Elizabeth dared to ask.

"No. It's about you, about us. Damn it, Elizabeth, I have never been in love, but I know that what I feel for you is real. There is no reason to be worried," Gavan insisted.

"I don't agree," she said softly. Her voice was wistful. "And yet, I don't want to wait. It's irrational, irresponsible, and crazy, almost as if it's a practical joke. I don't want to be a lark, Gavan."

"You're not." He was too upset to continue. A lark! Where in the world did she get that idea?

"I realize that," she said evenly. "I only meant I don't want to make a mistake. We should think on this more, I realize that now."

Gavan scowled. He didn't need to think anymore, his heart knew, his mind knew. She was the one for him and that was that. Pacifying her, he said with deadly calm, "Fine. We have three weeks until the wedding day to think on it. If you think you made a mistake before then, I'll understand your rejection."

Elizabeth was annoyed. That was not what she meant and she was certain he knew it. He was being stubborn and bratty because she was not willing to completely ignore the fact that they were both being very rash. "That makes sense," she said coolly. Let him sulk. Mayhap it was for the best.

Gavan stole a quick glance at her. She was angry. She had started this impossible conversation and he was the one feeling the heat.

"I don't intend to give my mother any reason to hesitate.

We'll go on as planned?" It was a question, but Elizabeth knew he was asking for her permission. She nodded her agreement, unable to speak. She had just given him an out and in three weeks he could very well feel completely justified to take it. What had she done?

"Tell me about your mother. We never actually talked about her," Gavan said, smoothly changing the subject.

"I know nothing about her except what you know. She was twenty-two when she came to work for Anne, about twenty-four when she had me. She was a maid. She lived on the property. She claimed no family and no one ever questioned it. She died during a horrible rainstorm. A drowning."

Gavan digested her cryptic response, feeling her pain as she spoke of the woman she had never known. "And your father, not even he knew anything more?" he had to ask even though he knew she was hurting.

"If he did, he never said a word."

"And then there's Liberty, looking so much like you she could almost be your twin," Gavan said casually.

They both froze, Gavan's expression muted, Elizabeth's worried. Twins? Could that be possible? It would explain even more. But Anne claimed she was there when she was born. She told the story on several occasions how she watched Lorna, suspicious of her intent with her son's child. Anne would have known if Lorna had twins. If the years of Anne's rambling had taught Elizabeth nothing else, they proved that Anne would never allow any child of Earl's to be raised elsewhere. No, twins were even more far-fetched than the idea that they were sisters.

"That's not possible." Elizabeth was the first to speak. Gavan nodded. It was a bit much and he didn't want to upset Elizabeth.

"I'm curious about something, Elizabeth," Gavan said slowly.

"Okay?" His tone had changed and she was wary. What outrageous comment was he going to make this time?

"Have you ever been to your mother's grave site?"

"Naturally."

"Do you have a photo of her?" Gavan asked.

Elizabeth released a heavy sigh. "I always wished I had, but I don't. None exist. I can't understand it, but Earl said it never occurred to him to take a picture. She was their maid, after all. And since she came out of nowhere, seemingly, none existed." She fell silent. A few moments later she asked, "Why?"

"I was just curious, that's all," Gavan said evasively. He was sick, his intuition leaning heavily on the very real possibility that Lorna Sanders just might not be a ghost from Elizabeth's past but a very real figure, alive and hidden somewhere. It had first dawned on him during his maddening interview with Mikel. It was only an intuition, but he suspected Anne was involved as well. He was worried that if he was right, Elizabeth would only be more hurt by the desertion.

"I've always been curious and it is my only regret not having any image of her other than my own mirror," Elizabeth admitted, oblivious of Gavan's disturbing suspicions.

"Do you look like your father?" Gavan asked. Somehow, he was certain he had asked that question before, but he was curious about her response.

"Coloring, yes. My hair is as black as his, certainly."

"Nothing else? He didn't have strong genes, did he?"

"Apparently not," Elizabeth replied.

A few minutes passed before Gavan delved deeper into Elizabeth's memory. "What about Liberty? Besides the fact that you two look alike, does she remind you of your father at all?"

"Her eyes," Elizabeth said immediately. "That is where she and I differ. I would have to say her eyes are remarkably shaped like my father's, more deerlike and wider. But that isn't enough. There isn't anything else about her that could be Earl's. I look more like him, but I do not have his eyes. My eyes . . ." She paused, staring at her image in the rearview mirror, recalling her father's words. "My eyes are my own or my mother's. Not Earl's or Anne's."

"And beautiful eyes they are," Gavan murmured, glancing at her again.

She had leaned close to look in the mirror, and now they were merely a breath away. She blinked, then trying to hide the sudden shyness that came over her, sat back in her seat. She was flustered by the heat that smoldered from his eyes. Her body immediately reacted to his gaze and she fought the desire to squirm, so hot and bothered she became beneath his glance. She ached for him and wanted nothing more than to pull over and make wild, passionate love to him, there in the car. Of course, she didn't say a word and impatiently waited for her body to cool.

Gavan forced himself to focus on the road. It had taken everything in him not to act like a lovesick boy and paw her all the way to Savannah. But she was tempting, he thought with a suppressed moan. She had invaded his senses to the core of his being and he was still shaken.

His fascination with Elizabeth was far more than just physical. He never knew a woman could move him the way he was moved by the very nearness of Elizabeth. He knew her scent, the soft fragrance that lightened the air when she was in the room. He could close his eyes and recall the depth of her brown-eyed gaze. He could still vividly recall the silky smoothness of her skin and her gentle touch from their long night making love.

When she was just a hairsbreadth away from him, his whole body reacted. He clung to control with a thread and forced himself to think of anything else, other than the feel of Elizabeth against him.

Her next words were just what he needed.

CHAPTER 35

"That's Mikel's home, over there," Elizabeth said, pointing toward a small mansion.

Gavan glanced over the acres of land and was disgusted. He frowned, his body cooling with the thought of Elizabeth's cousin Mikel. He had met briefly with Mikel before leaving for Savannah. The encounter had proven to be draining and hostile.

"You're scowling. What's wrong?" Elizabeth asked.

"I was thinking about your cousin," Gavan answered.

"That'll do it," Elizabeth said. She didn't want to think of Mikel.

She wasn't sure she would ever get over the ordeal he had put her through. She had Gavan now, a new life, and she wasn't going to let unpleasant memories of her disgruntled cousin ruin it for her.

"You never asked me how my meeting with him went," Gavan remarked gently.

"Let me guess," Elizabeth said, her scorn for Mikel evident. "He called me every name in the book and my mother's memory he disrespected and oh, he also despises Anne."

"Yeah, pretty much," Gavan admitted.

What she must have endured over the years with a cousin like that day in and day out. Elizabeth was hesitant, and then she said calmly of Mikel, "The feeling is mutual. Can we stop here? I need a moment."

It was quiet for the noon hour. When they arrived at Elizabeth's old home, she was amazed at how much it had changed. The driveway was in disarray. Flower beds that had once decorated the front lawn were overgrown with weeds. The porch stairs were crumbling and the sidewalk could have used a fresh pouring of cement. The green paint on the front door had chipped and fallen off completely in some places. The screen was intact but it was so tarnished nothing ever again would give it a sparkling shine.

The house had an air of abandonment. She tried to recall the years of growing up, the racket from the kitchen, the laughter from the children at play. It was a sound that she had no appreciation for when she was a young girl, but now it was nostalgic.

She actually had missed it.

She looked around, her eyes wide as she entered the house that had once been Anne's. Anne had given it to Earl and Earl had left it to Elizabeth, his only heir. Anne had seen to it that Earl left her everything, except for a few charitable items. Where he had ignored her in life, he tried to compensate for it in his death.

It was all hers now. Although she had no intent of returning to Savannah, she was too emotionally attached to the house to sell it. She turned it into a boarding-house. Anne's housekeeper—a woman who most surely must have known Lorna, Belinda Washington—had graciously accepted the position of caretaker and managed the property for Elizabeth.

Elizabeth was waiting for Belinda to meet them in the dining room. She had called. They had arrived just in time for lunch, or so they thought. Elizabeth was embarrassed because she had assured Gavan they didn't need to stop elsewhere to dine.

It didn't help either how Gavan's brother stared at her. He was neither flirtatious nor kind. His gaze harbored on the side of brooding. He was sizing her up, she knew, even though he had barely spoken more than a few words to her since their departure from Dulles Airport. The man was nothing like his brother. Elizabeth pitied the woman who found herself stuck with Lance Ward. Interestingly enough, their friend Tyke was the exact opposite. He was talkative and full of humor. He seemed genuinely fond of Elizabeth. That was a relief because Lance definitely was not feeling her engagement to Gavan. His dark expression made that clear.

Gavan sat beside Elizabeth. He had taken her right hand and tucked it in his own, comforting her with his strength and warmth. It was the only indication she had that he was aware of Lance's disapproval. Lance needed no words to make his opinion clear. She saw it in his eyes, so strikingly similar to Gavan's, the set of his jaw, more pronounced than his older brother's, and the slight flare of his nose as if he was fighting against an inappropriate outburst.

Gavan raised his eyes, looking over Elizabeth's head, when Belinda entered the dining room. His eyes narrowed. She was not what he was expecting. She was in her late forties perhaps. And she was white, her hair silvery, long, and thin. Her eyes were a dark green shrouded by pale blond lashes. She wore no makeup to enhance them, which Gavan thought would have helped her to be at least attractive. She was tall and thin. What was most curious was the fact that she was nervous.

Gavan released Elizabeth's hand and came to his feet. He walked to her and offered his hand. She was wringing hers. With an effort she untangled her own hands and gave him one of them. It was sweaty and Gavan managed to keep from flinching in distaste.

"Ms. Washington?" he asked, stepping aside to allow her entry.

"Yes. I apologize that it took me so long to come down, Ms. Wilkins," she said, fixing her gaze on Elizabeth as she came fully into the room. Lance and Tyke stood up, uncomfortable because she was uncomfortable. Tyke instantly disliked her. They fell silent and with chagrin, Elizabeth realized they were waiting for her to comment. Elizabeth hastily came to her feet, nearly knocking over her chair. Carefully she straightened it, then gave Belinda a gentle hug.

"We understand. It was short notice, wasn't it? Have a seat, Belinda." Elizabeth offered her the chair near hers. Belinda sat, her eyes focused on the table setting.

Elizabeth turned to Gavan. "This is Gavan, my fiancé. And those young men there are his friend, Tyke, and his brother, Lance. Everyone, meet Ms. Belinda Washington, my caretaker and a family friend."

Tyke nodded at Belinda and sat back down. Lance hesitated, glanced from Elizabeth, back to Belinda, then said, "Nice to meet you, Ms. Washington," before taking his seat again. Gavan sat down and looked up at Elizabeth expectantly. Belinda finally glanced up, looking from Gavan to Elizabeth before asking in a nervous whisper, "What's going on, Ms. Wilkins?"

"Oh, it's just the funniest thing—"

"Actually I'm doing an investigation," Gavan interrupted. Their gazes connected and Elizabeth obliged his silent request to allow him to speak.

"Is something wrong?" Belinda gasped. Her hands were in her lap. She nearly pulled the tablecloth in agitation as she wrung her hands again.

"Everything's fine," Elizabeth reassured her, tossing Gavan an apologetic glance. She knew he wanted her to be silent while he spoke with Belinda, but she could help. He'd appreciate her help in the end. Why else would she have come to Savannah?

Gavan nodded, agreeing with Elizabeth, unperturbed by her assistance.

"Are you aware that Mikel Wilkins has been incarcerated?" he asked.

Belinda paled. Her eyes bulged in disbelief. Lance shot to his feet.

"You all right?" he asked, tossing Gavan a worried glance. Gavan frowned, amazed at the reaction of the housekeeper. Slowly her color returned and she took a deep breath.

"Yes. I am sorry," she apologized. She wouldn't look at any of them. "I was not told."

"Anne and I haven't really told anyone yet. Amazingly it was kept fairly quiet. Well, except Mr. Ward knew all about it fairly quickly," Elizabeth said kindly.

Lance's shrewd gaze fell on Elizabeth. "Mr. Ward?" he inquired, his eyes searching as he spoke. She frowned, confused by his question. He raised a mocking eyebrow, an expression Elizabeth found annoying. "Funny you called my brother Mr. Ward when you two are going to be married any day now."

"Not now, Lance, man," Tyke muttered, nudging Lance for his impropriety.

"I meant it in a professional way," Elizabeth said, her gaze darting from Lance to Tyke. They had been discussing her, she could feel it. It was like watching two boys at mischief. At least Tyke was on her side. She glanced at Gavan, hoping he did not have the same reaction as his brother by her formality when she addressed him to Belinda. She was relieved. He was watching Belinda, the use of his name the least of his concerns.

"I see," Lance said coolly, his gaze following Elizabeth. Their eyes locked, his cold and distrustful. Elizabeth blanched in dismay. Lance grimly cut his gaze away. Elizabeth was shaken, uncomfortably aware of Lance's hostility toward her. Like him, she looked elsewhere, fuming at his sneer. It was none of his business that Gavan wanted to marry her. She and Gavan were two mature adults. They didn't need anyone's permission to marry and they certainly didn't need Lance's interference. In that moment, she truly did not like Lance Ward.

"My brother is overly protective, Ms. Washington," Gavan said calmly, his words not very soothing as far as Elizabeth was concerned. Gavan kept his eyes on Belinda. "You seem to be the same way, about Mr. Wilkins, that is. Were you fond of him? I realize you worked here for years, but Mikel must have visited often."

"No, he didn't. It was actually rare. I—I don't recall seeing him that often," Belinda denied quickly. There was a pause before Gavan leaned closer to Belinda, his body brushing against Elizabeth as he did. She caught her breath, ashamed that in such a setting her body would react so strongly to him. She swallowed and moved ever so slightly out of his way.

"I got the impression you were upset that he was locked up. No?"

"No. I'm surprised of course. He's a Wilkins. I don't know why he would have to go to such extremes for money."

Again the room fell silent. This time Gavan looked away, his gaze falling on Lance. Did he just hear her right? Lance nodded, a silent acknowledgement that Belinda was more than surprised by Mikel's incarceration. She had known his crime and no one had told her.

"How did you know that?" Gavan asked, sitting back in his seat.

Belinda looked at Gavan, uncertainty clouding her deep green eyes. "Know what?"

"Why he was locked away." Gavan was patient.

"I . . . I keep up on the news of the family." Belinda was lying. Elizabeth itched to comment but refrained, not wanting to burden Gavan on his job. She stared in amazement at Belinda. The woman must have thought they were all fools. Elizabeth wanted instant gratification now. If she knew this much about Mikel, there was no telling what she would know about Lorna.

"That makes sense," Gavan lied. He needed Belinda as calm as possible. He needed her to slip up as often as possible. His gut instinct warned him that she was a wealth of information, by knowledge or coincidence.

"I was very upset to hear about Ms. Anne's hospitalization," she added hastily.

"It was tragic," Gavan agreed.

"Is she all right?"

"She's doing very well. She's been home for nearly two weeks now. You should call her when you get a moment," Gavan suggested.

"I will."

"You should call Mikel as well, I think he could use the contact," Gavan added casually. As he suspected she winced, grew agitated, and looked as if she wanted to flee. Elizabeth wanted to shake the older woman and insist that she relax. Mikel couldn't harm her.

"I would rather not. I . . . excuse me, Ms. Wilkins, but I confess I never much liked Mikel. He was a terrible young man." That was cause for surprise. Elizabeth had assumed by Belinda's odd behavior that perhaps she and Mikel were close, maybe even lovers. It wouldn't have been far-fetched, it had happened to her mother.

"I understand," Elizabeth replied softly.

"So do I," Gavan reassured Belinda. He tapped his fingers on the table, then casually said, "Actually, Elizabeth and I didn't come here to look into Mikel. What we're trying to explore is Elizabeth's past. Anything you can tell us would be helpful."

"Of course." Belinda was agreeable. "What do you want to know?"

"Lorna Sanders. Do you remember her?"

Belinda froze, swallowed, and stared at her hands. Lance's eyes narrowed, Tyke was bored, but they were all patient as Belinda collected her wits. "I do."

"Do you remember her children?" Gavan drawled. Elizabeth shot him a look. Children?

"I know that Elizabeth is her daughter, if that's what you mean," Belinda answered, her glance at Elizabeth sympathetic.

"It's all right, Belinda. I'm not ashamed of my mother," Elizabeth said coolly.

Belinda sighed, obviously relieved. Gavan was not finished.

"Did you know her other children?" he asked. He spoke as if it were common knowledge that Lorna had more than one child. He wondered if Belinda would take the bait.

Belinda hesitated. She seemed confused. Her frown slowly eased and her expression became bland. "I didn't know Lorna well enough to recall her other children. I thought it was just Elizabeth."

Her answer was a disappointment. Gavan had expected no less, knew the routine with interviews such as these, but he had hoped for more. Belinda Washington had more information and for reasons he could only guess at, she wanted to keep it to herself.

"Can you explain that?" Lance demanded from across

the table. He didn't believe a word Belinda spoke. The woman had shifty eyes, nervous gestures, and more importantly, she kept her gaze averted.

"I . . . I don't know what you're asking. Lorna had Elizabeth, here at the house. I didn't know her that well at all. Anne didn't care for her. I didn't get a chance to really know Lorna. She was rarely in the house after Anne discovered she was pregnant. It was common knowledge. Everyone knew Anne caught Lorna with Earl and after that, Anne despised your mom. I'm sorry, Ms. Wilkins, but that's all I can tell you."

Footsteps were heard outside the dining room. A moment later a houseguest walked into the dining room, rubbing his eyes. He appeared as if he were sleeping, perhaps taking an early afternoon nap. He stopped short at the door when he saw the small gathering. "My apologies. I wasn't aware you were having a meeting." He started to back out. Belinda had turned quickly around when she heard him. In sharp contrast to her nervousness with Gavan, she seemed animated and excited.

"Walt, this is Ms. Wilkins. She owns the house," Belinda said quickly, waving the gentleman into the room. Walt was an older white man, rather scraggly with a thick beard reaching his chest. His eyes were an ocean blue, small in the roundness of his plump face. His skin was a ruddy rouge as if he had been out in the hot sun too long. He appeared to be in his early sixties but that was anyone's guess. When Belinda stood, she was a head taller than him. The way he looked up at her, Elizabeth had no doubt that this houseguest was much more than a visitor.

Walt grinned at Elizabeth, a dazzling white smile that Elizabeth suspected was freshly shined or new dentures. She returned his bright smile. "Ms. Wilkins? Why, it's nice to meet you, ma'am. I've heard a lot about you.

Your mom and my Belinda were best of friends," he said
cheerfully.

Elizabeth's smile faded at his comment. Her eyes lowered and her pulse quickened. What on earth was going
on? Belinda had just confessed to knowing nothing
about Lorna Sanders. And now they were best friends?

CHAPTER 36

Belinda paled and swayed. Both Gavan and Lance came to their feet, rushing to her aid. Tyke sat up.

"Are you all right?" Gavan asked. He was holding Belinda's elbow for support. She nodded. Gavan glanced at Lance, then stepped aside, allowing his brother to guide Belinda back to her seat. Gavan sat beside Elizabeth. They watched Belinda as Lance picked up a glass and poured her some water.

"Drink this," he said kindly, handing her the glass. She accepted, downing the water far too swiftly. Confident that she was all right, Lance sat down again, his gaze watchful.

Walt was in a state of shock. He had never seen Belinda so pale. He looked more closely at Elizabeth, his curiosity tinged with uncertainty. "Are you all right, sweetie?" he asked gruffly. He stood behind Belinda, his keen eyes taking in the somber expressions around the table.

"I'm fine Walt," Belinda answered.

"That water isn't helping. I'll be back in a moment. I have some brandy in my room," Walt offered.

"No. Stay." Her words were so sharp that Walt reeled to a screeching halt. He sat beside her, subdued.

"Ms. Washington?" Gavan said gently. She raised her

eyes. They were tearful. Gavan was saddened by her despair, but he was concerned now for Elizabeth. He had seen her face at Walt's words. She was stricken and he was determined to see her through this. He put aside his sympathy for Belinda and pressed on. "I'm confused, Ms. Washington. I thought you barely knew Lorna. Your friend here seems to be under another impression."

"I . . . admired Lorna. I liked her all right. I exaggerated to Walt about our relationship," Belinda explained hastily.

"Why?"

"She was kind and fun and I thought it was very unfair how Anne treated her." It sounded plausible, but Gavan didn't believe that was the whole of it. Gavan was losing his patience. It was so ridiculously obvious that Belinda was more than capable of clearing up the matter. He wanted to shake the woman. "Were you employed before Lorna or after she came to the Wilkinses?" Gavan asked.

"Before. Yes. It was before, she came about the same time, about six months later, I think." Belinda's nervousness was disturbing. What could she possibly be so upset about?

"Ms. Washington, I am not the police. This is not a criminal investigation. And I am not on a crusade to harm you, either. I'm trying to fathom why you aren't telling the whole truth—"

"I am telling the truth!"

"If Belinda says it's the truth, then it's the truth," Walt said, defending her.

"The truth is, we only want to know if Lorna had other children or family that she never told Anne about," Gavan said, remaining calm in the face of Belinda's rising hysteria.

Belinda appeared surprised. "Wh-why? Wh-what is this about?"

"Seems to me he couldn't be more clear," Tyke grumbled. Lance shot him a disquieting look. Tyke rolled his eyes but kept quiet.

"There's a woman in Maryland. She and Elizabeth have a remarkable resemblance to one another," Gavan explained.

"No," Belinda murmured, shaking her head. Elizabeth sat perfectly still. Belinda was acting so strange.

"Yes," Gavan countered smoothly. "She's the reason we're here. We think that Lorna Sanders had another child. Anne is of the belief that maybe Lorna had a sister or another family member that could explain Liberty's existence. What do you think?"

"I can't . . . I have no idea." Belinda shuddered.

"Were you working the day they discovered Lorna missing, when she died?" Gavan asked abruptly.

"I was here," Belinda whispered. Her eyes filled with tears. She wrang her hands again. "Mr. Wilkins was devastated. I think Mrs. Wilkins was as well. The only person not upset was Mikel. He seemed rather pleased by the notion. He hated Lorna. He hated everyone. Lorna didn't trust him either. If she had not gone away, then he would have harmed her eventually."

"Really?" Gavan urged her. He was excited. She had slipped. She had slipped and wasn't aware of her error. He looked at Elizabeth, wondering if she caught the mishap. He could tell by her stormy expression that she had.

"Mikel was about ten years younger than Lorna, but even still he was threatening. Earl wanted to marry Lorna, you know. He was in love with that one," Belinda continued. Gavan nodded, silently prodding her on. "It was why Anne hated Lorna. She did not want her son married to the maid. She was very out of touch when it came to those things. Not to mention the fact that Lorna was black. That created a scandal in their family. They're all dead now, huh? Except Anne and Mikel." She sighed, sipped her water, and gave Walt a colorless smile, then continued, her remorseful glance at Elizabeth a warning of what was to come.

"It was raining the day Lorna disappeared. I think she was twenty-six. She was in her prime, young and beautiful. She was upset. She and I . . . we had been listening at the door to Anne and Earl. The baby, Ms. Elizabeth, was asleep in Earl's room. That was why we were there, we were supposed to get the baby. Earl had her. Anne was threatening Earl. Well, actually, she was threatening to ruin her own son if he married Lorna. Anne didn't mind the scandal of the child, she even said she loved Elizabeth, but she would not tolerate any more of her son's antics. That's what she had said. But Earl wanted to marry Lorna. I said that, didn't I? But he did. We all knew he was crazy in love with his Lorna."

She paused, lowering her gaze once more. "Lorna was in love with Earl, too. She would have done anything for him. She didn't want him to lose everything because of her. She also knew that Earl wasn't going to give up until she agreed to marry him. She was weakening. But she was scared. She was worried about her baby, too. If Earl lost everything, what would happen to Elizabeth? If they married, they would be shunned. This isn't exactly New York where you can do whatever you want. It's Savannah and back then, a white man didn't just marry the black maid. Lorna decided she had to leave. She told me what she was going to do. I tried to tell her not to do it. I was just a teenager. I couldn't stop her. She insisted it was the only way."

"Are you saying she committed suicide?" Tyke gasped, sitting up in shock as the truth of Lorna unraveled.

Belinda shook her head, huge teardrops streaming down her cheeks now. "No," she choked out. "I'm saying she . . . she isn't dead. She's in Savannah."

Gavan caught Elizabeth before she fell in a faint. He was shaken. He had known, he had suspected. The truth was more devastating than if Lorna had actually died. He carried Elizabeth in his arms and walked to the door. "I need a room to lay her down in."

Belinda hastened to help him. They took Elizabeth to the second floor and laid her on the bed. She moaned, opening her eyes slowly.

"You fainted," Gavan murmured, answering her unspoken question. He sat on the bed beside her. He was angry. Lorna Sanders was alive and she had left her child to fend for herself with an old busybody and a deadbeat father.

Belinda stood in the doorway, uncertainty causing her to stay. Gavan looked at her in disgust, then realized it was not Belinda's fault that Lorna had lied to her daughter, possibly her children about her own death. Her reasons may have sounded honorable, but there was no excuse to leave Elizabeth, none. He smoothed over his expression, sorry for the woman.

"If you don't mind, Ms. Washington, I would like to continue this conversation once Elizabeth and I have spoken. You can imagine the shock she's experiencing."

"Yes. I am sorry. I'll wait downstairs." She hurried away, her footsteps heavy as she raced down the hall.

"I suspected it," Gavan admitted, helping Elizabeth to sit up. He fluffed the two deflated pillows and stuffed them behind her back.

Elizabeth was angry. "She's crazy. I can see it in her eyes."

Gavan stroked her cheek, soothing her with his touch,

his gaze. He smiled, his gentle gaze causing her heart to flutter. "I don't think so, love. She's telling the truth."

"No. She's mistaken," Elizabeth said, unable to accept Belinda's declaration. She took a deep shaky breath. Gavan's gaze fell to her heaving bosom, then rose to her eyes only to drop again to her full trembling mouth. He leaned forward and tenderly kissed her. Elizabeth closed her eyes. The last thing she needed was for Gavan to make love to her now. Her senses were confused enough with the pleasure of his touch clouding her thoughts.

Gavan sighed regretfully, pulling away even as she returned his kiss. Elizabeth's eyes opened and slowly her focus cleared. "I believe her," Gavan said gently, waiting for her to look at him fully before he spoke.

"Why?"

"I suspected it when I first heard how Lorna died." Elizabeth expressed shock at that declaration. Gavan was firm. He continued. "They never found her, Elizabeth. It was a deliberate trail of evidence supporting the assumption that she drowned. She either wasn't dead or she was an incredibly clumsy woman." His rationalization did not soothe Elizabeth.

"If it's true, then she gave me up and Liberty as well."

Gavan ached for her. "Maybe Liberty is not her daughter," he suggested, searching for an explanation that would heal Elizabeth's pain.

"Maybe she died in the bayou," Elizabeth said bitterly.

"Belinda has more answers, Elizabeth. Do you feel up to coming down or would you rather stay here and relax?" Gavan asked, coming to his feet.

"I'm not a coward," Elizabeth said.

Gavan laughed, relieved that she was not going to brood in the room. She hadn't cried. Determined to uplift her spirits, he embraced her, holding her chin up so that he could search her eyes.

"Where have I heard that before?" he teased, the gleam in his eyes causing Elizabeth to flush.

She instantly recalled their initial meeting with humility. She had been brazen and rash and didn't trust him from the start. When had it changed?

"That was bravado speaking," she exclaimed.

"Uh-huh. And it's not bravado now?" Gavan demanded, his lips nibbling at her ears.

Elizabeth gasped. He didn't really want to make love now, did he? She wouldn't do it. Oh, but she could be persuaded.

"No," she gasped, trying hard to ignore the thrilling sensations racing in her veins at his featherlight kisses. She pulled away, laughing lightly at Gavan's comical expression of disappointment.

"You're trying to distract me." She smiled and flirtatiously swept past him, dodging his hand intent on smacking her rear.

"Did it work?" he called, staring up at her with such longing that she flushed.

She tossed him an affirmative glance, then hurried down the stairs. But her distraction was only momentary. Her smile vanished and her eyes clouded with disapproval the second she saw Belinda.

Her ebony gaze was cheerless. Her nostrils flared ever so slightly as the rage built within her. She no longer felt faint. She felt a burning fury in the wake of all the years she had mourned her mother's death.

And her mother had been alive.

Belinda had known all along.

And now Elizabeth was determined that Belinda was going to tell her everything. Nothing would stop her from finding Lorna Sanders.

CHAPTER 37

Gavan had anticipated a grueling game of hide-and-seek to resolve the truth of Lorna Sanders when they first met with Belinda. He by no means anticipated or even dared to hope that his interview would be so extraordinarily revealing. He would have preferred a less dramatic account, given Elizabeth's presence. He suspected that the burden of truth Belinda had been carrying was one she had been yearning to shake.

But the inquiries weren't complete.

Now he had more questions. He thought he knew the why behind Lorna's faked death, but that was only the beginning.

How did Lorna live? Was Earl aware of her deception or did she keep it a secret from him? Was she still alive? And if so, where was she?

Why hadn't she contacted her daughter after Earl's death or even after a few years once Anne was fully involved with the child's life and the risks had passed?

Gavan prayed that Lorna was still alive and not yet a ghost of the past. It would be an even greater tragedy if she was dead now. He paused at the dining room entrance, watching Elizabeth with growing concern.

She stopped short of entering the dining room and he knew that the information they had gathered was beginning to register and sink in. The sadness had only begun. He regretted his decision to bring her along. It had been unfair of him to insist, but their love was so new he didn't want to lose a single day of being near her. Nevertheless, he would have spared her the pain of Belinda's claims.

"Elizabeth?" he murmured, capturing her attention.

She turned to him, her gaze sorrowful. Her lips quivered as if she would say something or sob at any moment. But she didn't.

He inhaled sharply, pained to see her this way. He had done this to her by wanting her by his side. He wanted to console her. But how? What could he say to soften the blow of Belinda's confession?

There was nothing he could say to ease her pain or the subsequent rage she would experience when the magnitude of Lorna's deception finally settled in. He came to her side and took her hands.

"We'll get through this," Gavan whispered.

She took a deep breath, closing her eyes briefly.

"A few more questions, Elizabeth, and we'll leave," he promised.

Her face softened beneath his encouraging words and she nodded. She would get through it. She had no choice but to keep going.

He wrapped his arm about her waist and together they walked to the table, his warmth giving Elizabeth the support she needed to regain her composure. Lance and Tyke discreetly waited at the table. There was no humor, no teasing light in their eyes. The matter of Lorna Sanders had taken an unexpected turn and Gavan sent a silent thanks that neither his brother nor Tyke had made some glib barb that would upset the situation more.

Elizabeth sat at the table across from Belinda in the seat Lance had vacated. It was a pointed statement of distaste. She didn't want to be near the woman she considered a conspirator with her mother. Belinda blushed but remained seated. Walt was at her side, his eyes worried as Gavan sat in his seat once more.

"I just have a few more questions, if you don't mind, Ms. Washington," Gavan said gently. He sympathized with Belinda. She at least had the courage to tell the truth about Lorna. Now she had only to say she recognized Mark Sutton's photo, which he was pulling out of his wallet, or that she knew about the birth of Lorna Sanders's previous child, and they would be done.

"I want to help, I do," Belinda breathed, her voice cracking with tears she was trying desperately to hold back. Gavan could imagine her nearly thirty years earlier, still a teenager. Young and confused, looking up to the older black maid who had captured the heart of their boss's son.

He could see how someone like Belinda could admire a flirtatious, assertive woman that he imagined Lorna to be. He had no doubt about Lorna's personality either. From all accounts, particularly Anne's, he gathered that Lorna lived with a certain amount of freedom. That would have been a part of her coming of age. He could see that freedom in Liberty, if not Elizabeth. There was no doubt. None.

He set the photo of Mark Sutton on the table.

Belinda stared at it, her blank expression not very promising.

Gavan stared at it as well, the image of Liberty's grandfather still puzzling. There was nothing about the man that resembled Liberty, or Elizabeth for that matter. Mark Sutton's eyes, the key as far as Gavan was concerned, couldn't have been more different. Elizabeth and Liberty shared the same eyes, the darkness, the shape, the expression. They were as one. If Mark was truly Liberty's grandfather, then he had to be a relation of Lorna's. The possibilities were endless.

Mark could have been Lorna's father, uncle, or even brother. Lorna could have married before coming to the Wilkinses or after faking her death. None of the possible answers satisfied Gavan's burning question. Why give up Liberty, too, because he held on to the belief that Lorna was Liberty's mother?

But was Earl her father? He was no longer sure.

The problem was the pictures that Elizabeth had of Earl didn't help. He could see a slight resemblance to Liberty but nothing concrete. Where Elizabeth was definitely her father's child, Liberty must have been her mother's image. And yet, Liberty and Elizabeth looked so very much alike. And no one had a picture of Lorna.

"Have you seen him before?" Gavan asked after a few moments had passed, giving her time to take in the image of Mark Sutton. Walt was staring at the picture, frowning, his curiosity overtaking his worry for Belinda.

"No. I don't think I have," Belinda answered with sincerity. She looked from Gavan to Elizabeth. "Who is he?"

"He's the grandfather to a woman I believe is my sister," Elizabeth explained.

Belinda blinked. "What sister?"

"Are you aware if Lorna had another child?" Gavan asked, studying her.

Belinda shook her head, her confusion obvious. "No. She never had another child."

"Did you talk often, then? Do you still communicate?" Gavan asked, barely able to hide his growing excitement. This was the break they needed.

"Not often. Not anymore," Belinda said, oblivious of the agitation filling the room. "When Lorna first left, she would write me. I had to hide and read the letters. She didn't want Anne to discover her secret. She wrote under two names. She never used her own."

"What were the names?" He was beside himself with excitement.

Belinda shrugged, answering, "Ursula Bane, sometimes Greg Sutton."

Lance nearly came to his feet. Gavan did. "Sutton?"

Belinda jumped in a panic. Walt dove in front of her, spreading his short body protectively over her.

Elizabeth sprang to her feet as well, her heart hammering wildly against her chest. It was too much. To have all their answers fall so quickly into place was unbelievable.

It was surreal. She felt light-headed again.

"Sit down, son, you're upsetting my gal," Walt shouted, his voice loud from apprehension at Gavan's bizarre outburst.

He had no wish to have to deal with this big man. If Gavan intended harm toward Belinda, Walt knew he would be no match.

Gavan grinned, reached over, and good-naturedly squeezed Walt's shoulder, causing Walt to wince, before he sat down. He slapped his leg and shook his head, his laughter startling them. "This is unbelievable. No way. I can't believe this," he said.

Lorna had outwitted Anne all along.

Elizabeth continued to stand, staring in bewilderment at Gavan. She hadn't understood what transpired, but she was going to find out. If he didn't explain himself soon she was going to burst.

Lance sighed. Gavan had put together the puzzle of Elizabeth and Liberty. As if anyone could ever have doubted.

Lance wasn't impressed. It was easy enough to guess after one look at the two women.

"What's happening?" Tyke demanded.

Tyke was confused by what had taken place. He stood by Elizabeth, watching Belinda and Walt.

Walt was straightening himself, gingerly sitting back in his chair.

Belinda was multiple shades of pink and bright red spots. She had just had the shock of her life.

Tyke blinked, amazed at her bright, spotted coloring, even more so as it faded back to a pale pink.

"Sit down, Tyke. You too, Lance. Sweetheart, I'm sorry," Gavan said to Elizabeth.

She sat down, not taking her eyes off him.

"I think we'll only be here one night after all," Gavan said with a smile. When they were all seated, Gavan turned to Belinda, heedless of her nervousness.

"A few months back, Elizabeth Wilkins and Liberty Sutton met. Mikel Wilkins noticed right away how much they looked alike. That's what this is about. They looked so much alike that we wanted to find out how that was possible. You see, not only do they look alike but they have like mannerisms and behaviors that normally can be attributed to family. Liberty Sutton never knew her mother. As with Elizabeth, her mother died when she was very young. Now that we know Lorna did not die that fateful night, I'm betting that Liberty and Elizabeth are in fact sisters. When you named Mr. Sutton, well, it stands to reason that he is likely the same Sutton who raised Liberty. She was kind enough to loan the picture of her grandfather to us."

He pointed at the picture with relish, his expectations high. "I think this man is or was either in a relationship with Lorna or was possibly even her father. Whoever he was to her, when she became pregnant again I think she sent her daughter to him. By who, I can't begin to guess, but one thing is for certain, there is little to no doubt that Lorna Sanders is Liberty and Elizabeth's mother."

"Really?" Belinda breathed.

"That surprises you and yet you knew she was alive," Gavan said dryly.

"And alone," Belinda said pointedly. "Lorna had no family. I know it. I would send her money in the beginning, whatever I could spare. Then a few years had passed and she began sending money to me, to pay off her debt. I told her she didn't have to, but she insisted. She said it was payment for keeping her informed about her daughter." She looked at Elizabeth.

"You spied on me?" Elizabeth frowned.

"Never," Belinda said emphatically. "I only told her what was common knowledge. I was the only one that knew she was alive. I told her you were well taken care of. And true to her word, Anne took you in. I told her you were doing very well for yourself."

"Did you?" Elizabeth hissed, half rising from her seat.

"Did you tell her I cried often for the loss of my mother? Did you tell her I didn't really know my father even though he was always here? Did you tell her how I would have given up everything to have her? Well, did you?" Elizabeth demanded. She was fighting tears that threatened to escape.

The room was in an uncomfortable silence.

Belinda swallowed, looking away in discomfort.

Gavan glanced at Elizabeth, willing her to be stronger. Again, he thought it was a mistake to bring her, to expose her to the pain of the past.

Lance stared, too, surprised with her outburst. She was at least a woman of some feeling. Not cold and heartless as he had thought, as Maya had proven to be.

"I told her what I knew," Belinda muttered.

"Can you please tell us what you know now?" Gavan asked quickly, before Elizabeth's fury became full-blown.

"It's been a weight I've carried for years. I'm glad that it's no longer a secret," Belinda admitted.

"Sounds to me like all anyone ever had to do was ask you and the truth would have been known long ago," Lance suggested casually.

Elizabeth shot him an impatient look. Gavan ignored him.

"Do you know where she is?" Gavan asked flatly.

He wanted to get Elizabeth out of that house. The expression on her face was killing him. She needed peace and he wasn't going to dawdle around a moment longer than necessary.

"No." Belinda's tone was sad.

"You wouldn't," Lance snorted.

"Lance, please. Let Gavan finish," Elizabeth pleaded with him.

Lance shrugged and fell silent. He was impatient and had no talent for investigating. Gavan had asked him and Tyke along with the expectation that the process was going to be draining. He expected to interview dozens of Lorna Sanders's acquaintances. It appeared he needn't go any further than Belinda Washington. Lance and Tyke weren't needed and Lance wanted to go home.

"When was the last time you heard from her?" Gavan continued.

"I'm not sure . . . it's been years." Belinda looked up sharply. "It was after Earl died. I haven't heard from her since then. She just stopped writing and calling altogether after that. I thought . . . I thought she was heartbroken."

Again everyone fell silent, digesting this last bit of news. Even Lance didn't have a comment. Elizabeth lowered her eyes, fighting tears. She fully understood what Belinda was implying. After Earl passed away, Lorna no longer cared, about the Wilkinses or about Elizabeth. She wished she hadn't heard that cutting detail.

"Where was she when you heard from her last?" Gavan's voice was cool now.

He knew Belinda's assumption had hurt Elizabeth. He would have kept her away had he an inkling of the depth of how informed Belinda was. For the hundredth time he berated himself for having been selfish and lacking good judgment when he asked her to come with him. But he was afraid to end the interview with Belinda and give her time to realize what she had done. No, he had to keep going and milk her for every bit of information she had.

"West Virginia," Belinda said.

"West Virginia?" Elizabeth inquired dubiously.

Belinda frowned, sat back, and closed her eyes.

They waited, impatient, as she collected her thoughts. It was only a few moments and then she opened her eyes and, still frowning, her thin lips pursed in contemplation, said, "Maybe not. She could have been in Georgia still or North Carolina as I recall. I don't remember. She was always on the go. She worked for several people over the years."

"Do you know the names of any of the people who employed her?" Gavan asked, having pulled out his notepad. Now it was getting complicated. His initial elation was fast fading as he realized that Lorna Sanders could very well never be found if she didn't want to be.

"She worked for the Jameses for a few years. But that was when she first left here. Uh, then there was the Harpers. A family by the name of Wilbertson. I remember them because of the Wilkinses. Oh, and the Schultzes."

"And the Suttons? Did she work for them? Or were the Suttons her family?" Gavan asked.

"Why, she worked for the Suttons first. That was why she used their last name when she wrote me. I thought I told you that," Belinda answered, glancing from Gavan to the picture.

"No, you didn't," Gavan said firmly, but his heart nearly dropped at her blasé response.

"Whatever Mark Sutton was, he was not her father. Lorna had no family, Mr. Ward," Belinda said. She was thoroughly upset by Elizabeth's reaction to the news of her mother.

She kept her promise to Lorna for nearly thirty years and in the blink of an eye, she had divulged all that she knew. She sighed, knowing the truth of blabbering was that she was worried about Lorna. Belinda had no way of knowing where Lorna was or what had happened. It was more than three years now and Belinda blamed her grief on her failed discretion.

"Ms. Washington," Gavan said kindly, "is there anything else at all that you can remember that could help us? I imagine Elizabeth would like to find her mother now."

"I don't know anything else. If I did I would tell you," Belinda said. Her face was forlorn. She looked from Gavan to Elizabeth.

"Just so that I got it straight," Gavan continued, drumming his fingers on the table, his gaze fixed on the caretaker. "Lorna Sanders is not dead. She faked her death to protect her daughter and Earl, correct?" Belinda nodded. "She kept in touch with you, swearing you to secrecy, I presume, while you kept her abreast of her daughter and Earl's lives. She wrote you periodically . . . By the way, how often did she contact you?"

"Not often. About twice a year. She only called more frequently during the last few years before Earl died."

"Okay. So she contacted you either by writing or calling. And she never once mentioned another child?"

"No." Belinda was firm.

"And Mark Sutton is not her father but her employer?" He needed to be absolutely sure for Liberty's and Elizabeth's sake.

"Yes. She went to work for him fairly soon after leaving the Wilkinses. It didn't work out. None of her jobs did. I don't think she was very happy anywhere."

"But she continued to use the Sutton name when she wrote you?" Gavan pushed.

"She never stopped, right up to the last letter. She always wrote under Sutton."

Gavan was quiet.

Belinda swallowed, uncomfortably aware of the eyes on her.

The doorbell rang and everyone looked up. The timing was a relief for Belinda and Walt. It was disappointing for Elizabeth. Belinda didn't move. Her employer was still Elizabeth, and she had no desire to upset her any more than she already had. Then Gavan nodded, smiled at her, and extended his hand. She took it and he gave her a firm shake.

Gavan smiled at Belinda. "I know you have to get that. I want to thank you for your time. I imagine this was difficult for you."

"It was," Belinda confirmed, darting her gaze across the table to Elizabeth. She was a fool to admit anything about Lorna.

Gavan picked up the photo of Mark Sutton and carefully placed it in his wallet again. He chanced a glance at Elizabeth, fearing her reaction over the events they had been through. He was relieved. She appeared unperturbed, holding it together. He became thoughtful, pondering over the whopping information he had gathered.

In the midst of the madness surrounding the speculation of Lorna Sanders, his conclusion was remarkably simple.

The Suttons had adopted Liberty as their child, probably at Lorna's request. Gavan suspected it was an unofficial adoption. But if Liberty was older than Elizabeth, others would have known about her, especially Belinda. That meant that Lorna got pregnant after she left the Wilkinses. Or . . . He paused, his eyes falling on Elizabeth. Lorna was already pregnant when she ran away from Wilkins Vista Estates.

He was very still, fearful that any action on his part would give away his thoughts. He came to his feet without a sound, averting his gaze from Elizabeth while he collected his wits.

Elizabeth caught every movement, her eyes widening with concern. Gavan was upset and was trying to hide it. She watched him with dread. What now?

"What are you thinking, Gavan?" she asked. She stood slowly.

"I'll tell you in the car," he said.

He ignored her frown at his evasiveness. He was being careful. Not that much more could upset her, but he didn't want to alarm her again. He had a revelation, but he wasn't going to say it here.

CHAPTER 38

Lance came swiftly to his feet at seeing that Gavan was about leave. Belinda and Walt had all but run from the room, leaving their guests alone. Lance looked at Elizabeth, stopping her from joining Gavan with a firm hand on her shoulder.

"Would you mind? I want a private word with Gavan," he said. Before Elizabeth could reply, he ushered Gavan from the room. The two men stopped just outside the door, their voices low and inaudible, even with Elizabeth straining to hear.

Tyke grinned, watching Elizabeth with amusement. She hid her anxiety well. She wanted to know what Lance was discussing with Gavan and he had no doubt she would find out. He was amazed by her, too. She was much too subdued for the type of women who dallied with Gavan. Unabashedly staring at her, he decided she rivaled Maya's beauty. She wasn't sultry and exotic like Maya, but she was nevertheless appealing to the eyes.

Unlike Maya, Elizabeth was utterly oblivious about her appeal. She wore very little makeup, her long hair was modestly pulled back in a chignon, tidy and neat. She wore a white sundress that hugged her figure in a demure sense. She was almost angelic in her beauty. If it weren't for her bold gaze, her sleek but curvy figure, and her amazingly pleasant voice, Tyke would have wondered how Gavan ever found the courage to propose. She was absolutely nothing like the shameless flirts that swarmed around Gavan.

Elizabeth swallowed, only noticing Tyke's avid attention on her when she gave up trying to hear Lance's urgent whispers. She was torn. She wanted to get up and demand to be a part of the conversation. She couldn't. The discussion was between brothers and it could very well have nothing to do with her. Then she felt Tyke's eyes on her and was startled. He was so engrossed in his speculation he had leaned forward. She went from being annoyed to amused.

"I have pictures you can have," she said lightly, the look she gave him mocking.

He laughed, unperturbed by her sarcasm. He sat back and continued to inspect her. "I never really looked at you before now."

"Do you approve?" she asked, unconcerned by his opinion.

"Hell yeah. But I am surprised," he added.

She raised a delicately arched eyebrow. "About?"

"You and Gavan. What else? Why the sudden decision to marry? You two don't even know each other." He voiced exactly what she was thinking. She had no answer. She only knew that she wanted Gavan and she was willing to give marriage a try. She smiled, shrugging at the irony of his question.

"I think . . ." She paused. "I think you'll have to ask Gavan."

"Ah, spoken like a true wife-to-be." Tyke laughed.

"Have you two been friends long?" Elizabeth asked, changing the subject, her gaze darting to the door where she could see Lance's back. She willed Gavan to look over his brother's head. He didn't, his gaze intent as he listened to Lance. What were they discussing?

"Almost all my life. He saved my behind in elementary school. It was four of them, so don't get me wrong. Ever since then, I've been his best friend," Tyke said proudly.

"I see. What do you do?" she asked, turning her full attention on him then. Tyke was momentarily stunned, her direct gaze vivid and breathtaking. She had to have the most gorgeous eyes he had ever seen. The depth and serenity was overwhelming.

"Well?" she asked, frowning faintly when he didn't respond.

"What was the question?" Tyke repeated embarrassed. He was not going to act the fool again over Gavan's woman. He had already made an imbecile out of himself for Maya. But, man, why did Gavan have to get all of the good ones!

"What do you do? Are you a writer as well?" she asked patiently.

"No. I assist Gavan from time to time, but I actually work with my dad," Tyke answered.

She wasn't listening anymore and he followed her gaze with a sigh.

Gavan was returning, tall and handsome and overpowering the room.

"Ready?" Gavan asked. He was unsmiling. Elizabeth nodded, glancing from her fiancé to his brother, a worried frown on her face.

"Yes. Where are we going?" Elizabeth asked, trying to ignore Lance's frown.

"I thought it would be a good idea to get out of here, grab a meal," Gavan said, guiding her from the dining room toward the front door. Elizabeth shrugged, giving him a sidelong look.

"Are they coming?" she asked casually.

"No."

"Good," Elizabeth agreed. Her tension eased at the realization that she would not have to sit through a meal with Lance brooding and Tyke gaping.

"Have any ideas where we can go?" Gavan asked, strapping on his seat belt.

"Oh, now you ask." Elizabeth laughed.

"I just realized we hadn't seen a place to stop since leaving downtown."

"There are places, quaint, quiet but nice. There's a seafood restaurant at the hotel just about ten miles out."

"Seafood it is then," Gavan concluded. Lost in thoughts from the day's events, they drove in compatible silence.

"I'm in shock," Elizabeth said aloud.

"As you should be," Gavan said promptly. "Who wouldn't be?"

"I can't think of a single person who wouldn't be," she admitted.

Her mother was alive. That in itself after having gone all of her life believing she was dead was enough to take a person over the edge. But not Elizabeth. Yes, she had fainted. But she pulled herself together and he was impressed that there were no further hysterics from her.

The circumstances certainly called for them. He had tried to prepare her for the worst. But he could not have guessed that Lorna was still alive. He didn't even suspect it until they got to Savannah.

He expected the information to come together in trickles, enough so as to give Elizabeth time to adjust to the news. But he had no time to prepare Elizabeth. It was utterly implausible that Belinda Washington would divulge the truth with little to no urging.

"My mother abandoned me," she whispered. Gavan realized he could have spoken too soon. He glanced at her, frowned, then turned his gaze back on the road.

"She was protecting you," he replied.

"I don't agree . . ." She paused, averting her gaze and staring out the window.

"Elizabeth." Gavan sighed, hating the forlorn look in her eyes.

She turned away from him, gazing out the window. Dry-eyed and bitter, she whispered hoarsely, "I would rather not talk about it, Gavan."

Gavan understood and didn't push her.

She needed time.

Gavan was hardly surprised to see how empty the restaurant was. It was not yet the dinner hour, but they were open. He was starved and grateful to be seated. He took one look at the menu and grimaced. It wasn't the kind of fare he was using to getting, but he would grin and bear it.

"Know what you want?" he asked Elizabeth, staring down at his own menu in disappointment.

"A salad," she answered.

"I thought you were hungry," he teased.

"I never said I was. I wanted to get away from the house, though," she said. She had actually been famished all morning. Her earlier breakfast had been hurried and unsatisfying. But after Belinda's tale she had lost her appetite. She only agreed to go to a restaurant to get away for some peace of mind.

"You should eat." He was genuinely concerned.

"I am, a salad," she said calmly.

He was about to argue the point when the waiter came to the table. He gave in and looked closely at his menu. Nothing was appealing. He finally ordered the steak, deciding they couldn't ruin that, could they?

"Starving?" Elizabeth asked, a small smile playing on her lips once the waiter had gone.

"Pretty much." He was hesitant, and then determined, he leaned across the table and took her hands. Elizabeth didn't resist, knowing what was to come.

"I'm sorry about your mother." He gave a short laugh. "Ironic, isn't it? We're not supposed to be sorry when someone is found alive."

"She is dead, Gavan," Elizabeth said softly.

"Elizabeth, you'll have to accept the truth someday." Gavan was gentle.

She tugged her hands to free them. He wouldn't relinquish his hold, compelling her to look at him.

"I accept the truth. A woman named Lorna Sanders had me, abandoned me and my father, and lived happily ever after on her own terms. She died a long time ago," Elizabeth whispered, her gaze lowering as she spoke.

"Elizabeth—"

"No," she said sharply, her eyes blazing as she stared at him. "No, Gavan. You have no idea what she has done, what this lie has done to me. God knows what Liberty is going to think when she hears about this. I am . . . hurt. It hurts to think that I was so unimportant to her, so not special." Tears welled in her eyes and Elizabeth snatched her hands free this time, swiping angrily at them.

Gavan's hands were still in the middle of table. Softly he said, "You're very special. I knew it the moment I saw you. Why do you think I can't get enough of you? Lorna made a mistake." He paused. Then he took a chance and told her what he suspected.

"I believe that it had nothing to do with you not being important and everything to do with the fact that you are important and always have been important."

"You can say that because it's not you," she protested.

"Maybe," he acknowledged. "But I can also say it because I believe it and I think deep down inside you do too. Lorna sounds to me like a frightened young woman. She was alone, Elizabeth, and afraid to lose everything. I'm betting she didn't even know she was pregnant when she ran away," Gavan continued, catching his error too late.

Elizabeth looked sharply at his words. "What are you saying? What do you mean pregnant?"

He paused, sitting back in his seat now. He had to make a quick decision, tell her what he suspected or lie. Too much was at stake to lie. "I think your mother was pregnant when she ran away," he repeated. "I don't think she knew and I think that frightened her. She probably didn't get far. Lance is looking into any families with the name Sutton in Savannah, the surrounding cities, and the whole of Georgia if he has to."

"That's why they didn't come with us?" Elizabeth breathed.

"Yeah. He suggested it. He and I came to the same conclusion. He pulled me aside because he didn't want to upset you further. I agreed that it would be helpful if he looked into the Suttons."

"I see," Elizabeth murmured.

"Anne gave me information as well," he admitted.

Elizabeth nodded, calmly accepting the possibility that her own grandmother may have known. "What did she tell you?"

"About the Suttons. She heard it from Liberty, of course. I think somehow Lorna got Mark Sutton and his wife, who were much older than Lorna, to raise Liberty as their own. Liberty called Mark her grandfather so he must have allowed her to believe that she was his grandchild, and that her parents died when she was an infant. She never had a reason to suspect differently."

"And so Liberty and I have lived separate lives so that my mother can have her own," Elizabeth scoffed.

"She stayed in contact," Gavan said.

"Not with me!" Elizabeth huffed.

"Not to your knowledge. I'd bet she's been around. I agree with Lance. I think she may even know where in Savannah. I think your mother has always been close," Gavan suggested.

Elizabeth swallowed at his statement, glancing around the near-empty restaurant with curious eyes. No woman was in sight. It was fanciful and sweet of Gavan to so steadfastly attempt to comfort her, but in her heart she didn't believe Lorna had stayed around, at least not for her. Earl Wilkins was her motivation from the beginning to the end. Hadn't Belinda all but confessed that bit of news as well? Lorna stopped writing and calling the day Earl died. That was proof enough for Elizabeth.

"Why are you defending her, Gavan?" Elizabeth asked morosely.

"I'm not defending her," Gavan said gently, reaching for her hands again. This time Elizabeth didn't resist. He turned her palms upward and kissed them. "I hate to see you hurting like this. I would never have brought you with me if I could have predicted this. I feel guilty for pressing the subject, and that's saying a lot because I never feel guilt about doing my job." He smiled ruefully and Elizabeth laughed lightly, her response encouraging him. "I can't change what's happened, but I promise you, Lance and I are going to find her and discover, at the very least, if you and Liberty are sisters. As I said I was going to do. I won't be able to convince you of anything different about Lorna, not tonight or maybe even ever."

Elizabeth nodded, soothed by his statement. She

took a deep breath, gave him a shaky smile, and said softly, "Are you regretting your proposal now?"

"Hardly," he said, shaking his head for emphasis. "I have never been happier in my life. And I mean that, Elizabeth. You have brought a whole new meaning into my life. I don't regret anything. Well"—he shrugged—"except asking you down here. That I wish I could take back."

"Don't," Elizabeth said. "You could not have known this would happen. We were looking for proof that Liberty is my sister. How could you or any of us know that we'd discover so much more? I don't blame you for that, Gavan."

He hadn't thought it possible but he loved her even more in that instant. "Then you'll still marry me?"

"Nothing could change my mind," she responded.

Impulsively he rose from his seat, pulling her up with him. Elizabeth gasped, too late grasping his intent. He kissed her. She didn't reject him, thoroughly enjoying his ravenous kiss. He had intended only a light kiss, but as he embraced her, common sense fled.

Reluctantly he released her.

She swayed from the heady sensations clouding her senses.

He grinned, helping her to sit, his gaze full of triumph.

She didn't notice. She was basking in the aftermath of his kiss. The few attendants in the restaurant were forgotten. And for the moment, her mother's strange past was forgotten as well. All that she could see was Gavan.

Elizabeth's ardent response and unguarded desire for Gavan stirred him. He exhaled a sigh of satisfaction. The evening wasn't going to be a complete disaster.

He wondered if she would always want him so.

God, he hoped so.

"More wine?" he asked. His smile was meaningful and full of promise for what was to come.

CHAPTER 39

"Thank you, Gavan," Elizabeth murmured.

Gavan had dutifully distracted Elizabeth all evening.

"I don't think I have any stories left, not any interesting ones anyway," Gavan said later in the evening. Elizabeth had delayed leaving the restaurant as long as she could. He knew what she was doing and had obliged her for as long as he could. The restaurant was closing before she finally accepted that they could not sit there all night.

Returning to her childhood home, she had closed her eyes and he thought she was asleep. Somewhere between the restaurant and arriving at the house she sighed aloud. "Will things ever be the same again?"

"Nothing stays the same, Elizabeth. But remember the old adage, life is what you make of it. You'll get through this and I'll be by your side all the way."

A smile curved her mouth, but she didn't open her eyes. It wasn't until they were leaving the car that Gavan became concerned. Had she imbibed too much wine? She stumbled. Once was enough. He reached for her and encouraged her to hold on to him. Her head was resting on his shoulder, his arm was draped over hers absently caressing her arm, and together they walked up the stairway.

The door was unlocked. He opened it, stepping aside to allow Elizabeth to enter. She paused in the doorway and the light from the house cast a soft silhouette over their forms. She looked up at him, her eyes sparkling with mischief.

"On Christmas Eve Anne would have a party. Someone always put mistletoes throughout the house, but it was the mistletoe in this doorway that always inspired my imagination."

"Did it?" Gavan asked, staring down at her with an increasingly hungry gaze.

"Yes. Kiss me, Gavan. Kiss me right here. I want—"

She didn't get to finish her speech. His mouth possessed hers in a breathless siege. He kissed her thoroughly, drawing her to him as his need grew stronger. She could never grow bored with his kisses. She wrapped her arms about his neck and stood on the tip of her toes, returning his kiss as boldly, learning from him that which no other man had ever taught her. She could feel him swelling with need, his heaviness testing the boundaries of her imagination.

"Let's go to our room," he said gruffly, overcome with desire for her.

"Uhm," was all Elizabeth could respond.

Each time they touched it was like a new beginning. She couldn't think, his presence was so potent. He was like the sweet wine she had consumed all evening, only far more intoxicating than any sensation she had ever experienced.

"Come on," Gavan said, then lifted her into his arms and carried her up the stairs. She protested, feeling lightheaded and very aware of how much wine she had consumed. She was at once self-conscious.

"I can do it, Gavan." Elizabeth laughed lightly.

"I know you can, but I'm in a hurry," Gavan said. Then for emphasis he nibbled at her ear. She squirmed in his arms and his need increased to dizzying heights. He paused on the steps, willing his self-control to return.

"Put me down. I got it," she said, breathless now. With a sigh, he carefully set her on her feet.

She hurried down the hall. She faced him the moment she reached their bedroom. The sight of him made her catch her breath. He had paused at the steps and had watched her hasty retreat, his gaze hooded with desire and lust and love.

Was it the wine making her see things? No. And if it was, she didn't care.

She returned his long gaze, watching him with a boldness that moved him closer and closer to her. She felt like a vixen, playful and desirable beneath his heated gaze. Her slender form relaxed, her smile inviting him to finish what he had started.

He reached her and she raised her head to keep contact with him. In doing so, she leaned against the door for support. His eyes roved over her with unbridled desire. She wanted him, that much he knew, but what game she was playing, he wasn't sure.

But he was very willing to oblige her.

Very.

"Elizabeth?" His voice was husky with eagerness.

Elizabeth gazed up at him, no longer toying with him. With the heat in his eyes, his exceptionally muscled frame looming over her, all thoughts of leading him a merry chase vanished.

Wordlessly, she wrapped her arms around his neck. Their eyes locked and she slowly stood on her tiptoes while drawing him downward. She didn't stop until their lips touched, her eyes boldly imploring him.

He groaned, his eyelids grown heavy with passion. Hers fluttered closed and she kissed him, deeply and luxuriously, savoring the feel of his hard body straining against hers, the sweet pressure of his mouth as he allowed her to lead him. She felt him harden against her thigh and shuddered with anticipation. His hands slid down her back, stopping when he reached her buttocks, where he held her and pressed her against him, incredibly molding their bodies even closer.

"Want to take that into your room?" Lance drawled, strolling past them without a second glance. Tyke chuckled but didn't say a word either.

Elizabeth was stricken, appalled at being caught.

She squeezed her eyes shut, waiting until Lance and Tyke were no longer in the hall. When she opened her eyes she stared right into Gavan's dark hazel hypnotic gaze. His expression was sensual, his gazed hooded, and it was as if he had already taken her, his eyes had darkened so from the desire she had ignited in him.

He was completely unperturbed by Lance's mocking comment.

"Gavan," she murmured.

It struck her that he may not even have heard Lance. She was enthralled, her lips curving with pleasure. She had never been so unbalanced by a man. And Lord knows no man had ever been so captivated by her. It was breathtaking and . . . very sexy to be in his arms.

"You haven't changed your mind?" he asked even as his hands continued to stroke her buttocks, pressing her against him.

She couldn't speak. She had not changed her mind.

He smiled, the look of pleasure in his eyes warming her insides. He picked her up, so swiftly she didn't have time to object. He carried her into their room and with the heel of his foot, closed the door.

Elizabeth was excited, amazed by Gavan's strength. She was no little girl, she thought, yet he carried her as if she weighed nothing. He didn't release her but sat on the bed, cradling her in his arms. She felt languid and supple in his arms, enjoying the feel of him, watching him with open curiosity. He took his time, his eyes caressing hers as he began unbuttoning her dress.

She was compelled by his gaze, aroused by his deft removal of her clothing. Her dress unbuttoned, he slid it off her shoulders. His hands barely grazed her skin, yet she burned where they traveled. Her head was still cradled against his arm and she aided him as he removed her bra and seconds later her panties followed.

He searched her eyes, then allowed his gaze to devour her fully.

She shivered, waiting to see what he would do next. He stared at her breasts, full and taut beneath his hot gaze. He reached for her bra and she trembled. He looked at her and dipped his head, kissing her deeply.

Elizabeth closed her eyes, relishing his lovemaking. His tongue explored hers, dipping and tugging at hers until she was gasping. He kept making love to her mouth, trailing his tongue over her bottom lip before tasting her chin and cheek with a pressure that caused her skin to tingle. She sighed, allowing her head to roll back as she gave him more room to explore the sleekness of her neck, her collarbone, and farther until his mouth found his destination. She gasped, bucking slightly when his tongue circled her nipple. Still holding her, his hand cupped her breast and his tongue explored her nipple until it was peaked to full bloom. She squirmed, wanting to touch him, frustrated with the arousal he was creating within her.

She gripped his leg with her free hand, silently spurring him on. Gavan groaned, then began greedily to suck and pull at her breast, no longer teasing the nipple. Elizabeth nearly cried out, dazed by the sudden warmth and pressure of his mouth against her. Then she felt him lift her from him and a moment later she was laid upon the bed.

Her eyes fluttered open and she stared, mesmerized as he quickly stripped. A condom in hand, he leaned his knee into the bed, the old mattress groaning under his weight. He hesitated. Elizabeth smiled. The noise didn't matter. It was all the encouragement he needed. Deftly he put on the condom, then was beside her, pulling her into his arms.

She touched him, her eyes fastened on his bulging arms, his magnificent abdomen, and lower where his manhood proudly protruded. Her caress paused and her eyes swiftly rose to his again. He grinned, pleased with her reaction, kissed her again, pulling her fully into his arms, her soft body molding into his.

He leaned his weight on one elbow, his free hand stroking her flesh. He cupped her breasts, dipping his head to kiss them, turning her body slightly to reach all of her. His hands fondled her skin, massaging her until she quivered. His hands trailed down her waist, over her hips, and down the length of her thighs, where he paused. Her breath caught when he gently spread her thighs, his hand exploring the heat of her moist flesh, indolent, leisurely stroking her until she moaned.

She slipped her arms free and pulled his head closer. He buried his head into her neck, hungrily tasting of her. She wrapped her legs over his, encouraging him to take her. She didn't want to wait any longer. Torturously, he took his time, his mouth tasting again her breast, kissing her flat abdomen, and trailing a kiss to her thighs.

"Now," she breathed, unable to stand any more.

Gavan squeezed her, kissing her body as he traveled

up the length of her until he was fully covering her. He grabbed her arms, putting them around his neck before taking her, his strokes deep, pressing against her throbbing pelvis. She held him, raising her hips, meeting him with each thrust. The action drove him crazy.

"Elizabeth," he groaned in ecstasy.

He drew her up to him, his hands gripping her hips as he plunged into her, his pelvis rubbing against hers with repeated friction until she gasped and fell back, quivering wildly.

She grabbed the sheet, twisting and arching in continued ecstasy from the pressure his body created. Gavan held her, pressing her to him as he came to his own fulfillment.

He buried his head between her breasts, drained, then rolled beside her, pulling her into the curve of his body.

Sated, exhausted, they slept.

CHAPTER 40

Lance was starving and bored. Gavan and Elizabeth had come back to the inn, obviously tipsy from their early evening dinner.

The meal Belinda fed them at the inn had been horrible. Tyke, never one to care about the quality of his meals, had eaten with relish, the bland food not an issue for him.

Lance had refused to eat, drinking three cups of black coffee by the time the ordeal of being polite ended. He had retired to the old study, impressed with the piano and many books that lined the wall.

Shortly afterward Tyke joined him.

"Gavan needs our help finding Lorna." Lance's comment was given without looking at Tyke.

"Sure. It isn't as if I have anything else to do. And I'm getting paid, right?" Tyke said without hesitation.

"You'll get paid," Lance said dryly.

Lance was about to leave Tyke and try and get some sleep when they heard Gavan enter the house. Lance had gotten up to greet them, only to be stopped by Tyke's quick shove.

"Look," Tyke said.

Lance did and scowled. Standing in the doorway, Gavan and Elizabeth were deep into a kiss, oblivious of the world. He stepped back into the study, but Tyke continued to stare.

"Get in here, Tyke," Lance ordered. Elizabeth was a beautiful woman, but Maya had been as well. He was disturbed by Gavan's infatuation such as it was. He refused to accept that Gavan was truly in love. Perhaps his brother felt the need to come to Elizabeth's aid, but love her? After what Maya had done to them? Lance was incredulous.

"I guess we won't get any more ideas out tonight," Lance said loftily, then sat back down.

"Seems so," Tyke agreed, grinning. "She's hot, hot, hot . . ."

"And my soon-to-be sister-in-law. Remember that," Lance said sternly. He might not approve of his brother's marriage, but he wasn't going to allow Tyke to disrespect anyone in his family, inlaw or not.

"You didn't let me finish, Lance-a-lot," Tyke mocked. "I think she's hot, but I think she's smart as well. I would never have given Gavan credit for having good taste beyond the physical appeal he usually goes for. I'm impressed."

"I'm sure Gavan will be pleased." Lance's voice was dry.

He was distracted, waiting to hear the lovers leave the hall. He and Tyke both heard their laughter as they went upstairs. Lance gave them a few more minutes before he felt confident that they were in the privacy of their bedroom and he could go to his room. He tossed aside the book he had been holding, not recalling a single word from it, and left the study. Tyke, like a loyal shadow, was close behind him.

"Where are you going?" Tyke asked.

"Where else? To bed," Lance responded, taking the stairs two at a time.

"It's kind of early for that."

"It's been a long day and we won't get anything else out of Gavan tonight. Get some rest. We have a bit of exercising to do tomorrow." Lance had reached the top of the stairs.

"Exercising?" Tyke wondered aloud.

"Trying to snuff out Lorna Sanders, not literally exercising," Lance said impatiently.

Then he came to an abrupt halt, Tyke nearly colliding into him.

Tyke stepped around Lance, curious to see what had caused the sudden halt. His eyes bulged and a wicked grin spread his mouth. Gavan and Elizabeth were locked in a passionate kiss, oblivious of the world.

"Think they're in love now?" Tyke whispered with a chuckle.

"Yeah, maybe I believe I do," Lance said coolly.

The couple was oblivious of all except each other.

Lance narrowed his eyes, stomped his feet noisily, and walked toward them. His room was three doors from Gavan's. He didn't have much choice but to keep going. And with Tyke beside him, there was no telling what embarrassment he would put Elizabeth through.

The problem was neither of the two moved even after he made an exaggeratedly loud approach. He shook his head, amazed that they could be that oblivious. As he passed them, he drawled, "Want to take that into your room?"

He didn't look back, swearing inwardly at his brother for making love to his fiancée in the middle of the hall. He slammed his bedroom door shut.

That ought to wake them up!

Two hours later, Lance was still awake. The house was silent. He could hear the crickets and night sounds outside his window. He yawned, unable to sleep. As was the case since Maya had visited Gavan, thoughts of her invaded his peace.

He sighed, disgusted with his weakness, with her memory. He didn't want to think of Maya and he didn't want to resent his brother for his happiness.

Restless, he paced the room until he stood in front of the window. He flung it open, inhaling deep gulps of the night air. He was taking in another deep breath when he saw them.

Belinda was bent over, taller than the person she was speaking with. The other person looked up at the house and nodded. Belinda turned away, walking quickly to the house. The other person turned the opposite direction, leaving.

Suspicious of Belinda's intent and knowing his imagination could very well be running away with him, he watched the retreating figure. He cursed the darkness of the night. They were so deep in the South, streetlights were used sparingly. Then the retreating figure turned around and for a moment she was illuminated by the spare light, the spot she had chosen to look back at the house ideal for his viewing.

She was a petite woman with long wild hair. And he wondered if she could be Lorna Sanders.

He was perfectly still, afraid she would see him if he so much as breathed.

Moments went by. He had to do something. She was here. He was certain Belinda had lied. She must have contacted Lorna the moment she left Elizabeth. Was she planning to stare all night or did she intend to make her presence known? Lance had the sickening feeling she had no intention of being seen by anyone, particularly Elizabeth. He debated what to do.

Gavan would be furious if Lance let Lorna elude them without attempting to keep her near. Lance,

unlike Gavan, didn't feel he had the right to interfere.
It wasn't his fiancée, his book, or his life. He blinked.
She jumped, the movement momentarily placing her
in the soft light that spilled from the house. Her gaze
fell sharply on him as if she felt the movement. His
breath caught, his eyes widening in amazement. The
woman was the splitting image of Liberty Sutton and yet,
she looked like Elizabeth, too. It was her eyes, Lance
hastily decided. Her eyes were clearly Elizabeth Wilkins's.

The woman took a step back, once again engulfed in
darkness.

Lance was galvanized into action, the decision made
for him with the certainty that she was indeed Lorna
Sanders. He hurried from the window, tossed open his
bedroom door, and ran down the hall, yelling Gavan's
name as he dashed through the halls.

He heard Gavan shout his name but didn't pause lest
she escape. Reaching the front door, he raced outside.
He ran around the side of the house, his pulse quickening. He heard other footsteps and knew they were
Gavan and Tyke following.

He didn't see her. He turned in a circle, bent over as
he tried to catch his breath.

"What's going on?" Gavan demanded, his voice booming and winded in the quiet of the night. He only wore
his boxers, his feet bare.

Lance didn't get a chance to respond.

"Who's that?" Tyke asked loudly, pointing at the
slight figure racing through the path toward the road.

Lance immediately took off after her, Gavan fast on
his heels, bare feet and all. Within moments they
reached the woman. Attempting to stop her, Lance
grabbed her arm and swung her around, nearly causing her to fall in his haste.

Gavan's large frame saved her. He helped her to

right herself and was about to release her when she yelled at him, furious with being manhandled. She demanded to be released, trying to pull her arm from Gavan's firm grasp.

Gavan wasn't sure what to do. He had never encountered a situation like this. He couldn't just hold the woman. He had no idea what was going on.

Then he got a good look at her face and took a sharp intake of breath. At first he had thought she was a younger woman, the shadows of the night confusing him, but a closer examination showed her age. Her hair was silvery. Her skin was showing signs of aging albeit with grace. She was still very beautiful. But it was her eyes, her long, deeply brown almond-shaped eyes that blew her cover.

He had no doubt that it was her.

Lorna Sanders.

His appalled expression caused her to falter. He released her, his dismay real. She looked away, her eyes darting from Lance to Gavan and Tyke back to Lance.

"Who do you think you are?" she demanded angrily, her voice shaking with exhaustion from the sprint.

"Lorna Sanders?" Gavan asked, ignoring her question.

She flinched but quickly shook her head.

"I believe that woman died years ago," she said calmly.

He was watching her closely. The shock had worn off, and his expression was now only mildly curious.

"Then who are you? Her ghost?" Lance mocked.

He was doubled over, catching his breath, his eyes rolling over the older woman with annoyance. She didn't appear winded at all.

"I'm none of your business, that's who I am," she retorted.

She had been petrified when she saw the young man

watching her from the window. She didn't know what to expect but made haste to get away.

She was absolutely stunned that he had the audacity to give chase. Belinda had warned her to be careful. But she had wanted to see for herself. It had been so long since she'd seen Elizabeth. She thought a glimpse wouldn't hurt. She had spied her child many times and no one had ever been the wiser. And now these oafs had caught her and Lord only knew what mess they would create.

"Ma'am, whoever you are," Gavan said between clenched teeth, his patience worn thin, "do you have a car or something to get you out of here safely? It's pretty dark to be out here alone."

Perhaps if he could change tactics, she wouldn't battle with them and would return to the house. Gavan could only hope, but she didn't take the bait.

She eyed him coldly, knowing full well he knew she was Lorna Sanders.

"I know how safe I am. I was doing fine, in fact, until you dimwits chased me down. Do you own this place now? Is that it?" she asked, her tone scathing, but Gavan could hear the urgency in her question even though she tried to cover it with anger.

"No. Actually, your daughter, Elizabeth Wilkins, owns it," Gavan said, nonchalant in his response. He was searching her face as he spoke.

"I do not have a daughter," she said emphatically, staring him directly in the eye when she spoke.

"There. You see? It's all clear. She doesn't have a daughter," Elizabeth said scornfully.

Gavan turned sharply at Elizabeth's statement. Seeing the strained look upon her face, he knew that she had witnessed everything.

Gavan was worried by her rigid control. She had approached them unheard in the chaos, her arms full with a robe and shoes for Gavan. She handed them to him, her smile brave.

He hesitated, then gratefully took the items, pulling on the robe and shoes without tearing his gaze from Elizabeth.

Lorna started, too. The women faced each other, their silence long and deliberating.

Lorna lowered her gaze first.

"I didn't want it to be like this," she said, her voice choked with suppressed tears.

Elizabeth was unmoved. Lorna's eyes filled with tears and she shivered, the night suddenly cold, her daughter a true stranger.

"How did you expect it to be?" Elizabeth asked, sounding only vaguely curious.

"I don't know. I never expected anything," was Lorna's heartbreaking reply.

Neither spoke. Lance suggested they return to the house.

"Elizabeth?" Lorna asked.

Her voice was full of uncertainty now. Gone was the angry woman, bent on fighting off her attackers.

Before them stood a haggard, lonely woman, weak with exhaustion, years of pain, and hours of misery with the knowledge that her daughter now knew the truth. She wasn't going back without Elizabeth's approval. She held her breath, waiting for her daughter to respond.

Elizabeth was calm and composed. But her eyes were full of disgust and a touch of misery. She gazed at her mother, so stoic, so still it was as if she were looking through her. Then she calmly turned her back to Lorna and walked back to the house.

Her answer resolutely no.

CHAPTER 41

Gavan gave Lorna a pitying look before hurrying after Elizabeth. He stopped her in midstride, standing resolutely in front of her. He frowned, watching her closely, knowing her stoic expression was a cover for the deep turmoil she was experiencing. "You can't leave it like this," he whispered urgently.

"Yes, I can."

"Elizabeth—"

"No, Gavan. You heard her yourself. She doesn't have a daughter. She's been denying me for years. I see no reason to change it now." Elizabeth firmly pulled free out of Gavan's grasp and hurried to the house.

"In the morning, then," he whispered, more to himself than Elizabeth. She heard him and kept walking. The morning would be no different. She did not have a mother.

Gavan turned to Lorna again. She hadn't moved since Elizabeth walked away. It dawned on him then that she was tired, not just from her encounter with Elizabeth but most certainly from years of hiding and lying. He wondered just how long she had followed Elizabeth. If she had always been there, a part of Elizabeth's life just as she had been tonight. He suspected that it was the case.

"She hates me," she said quietly, to no one in particular. Gavan started at her unexpected dejection. He nodded, grudgingly agreeing with her.

"She'll get over it," he offered.

She shook her head wildly. "No. I don't think she will."

Gavan didn't know what he should say. He didn't know this woman. She had hurt the woman he loved. He couldn't side with Lorna Sanders when all he wanted to do was protect her daughter. He sighed, his gaze falling on Lance.

"You should stay at the inn tonight," Lance suggested, coming up behind Lorna and gently taking her arm. She swallowed and shook her head, furiously fighting her tears.

"No. I'll go. She wants it that way," she said, her earlier bravado returning.

Lance hesitated, catching Gavan's eye. They were both stumped as to what to do.

Tyke, clueless as usual, said loudly, "Yeah, right."

All eyes fell on him, Lorna's wide with surprise. She had forgotten the man was there.

Tyke grinned. He cleared his throat and added directly to Gavan, "Your fiancée does not want to lose her mother again. Any idiot can see that."

"And you are an idiot," Lance said coolly.

"Maybe," Tyke said, undeterred. "But I think Ms. Sanders should return to the house. In the morning, it'll all be straightened out."

"Don't be naïve," Lorna said, staring at Tyke as if he had two heads and was yet growing another. "Thirty years can't be straightened out overnight."

"Sure it can," Tyke said confidently. "I saw how she looked at you and how you looked at her. Trust me, I'm good at helping other relationships, not my own, of course, but others'—"

"Stop rambling," Lance snapped.

"Right." Tyke laughed. "I just think if you leave now you'll only make it worse. Stay at the inn, see Elizabeth in the morning, and tell her what happened and why. Right, Gavan? Help me out here, you're the writer. Isn't it true that a little confession goes a long way?"

"Yeah, maybe," Gavan agreed carefully. He wasn't so sure he wanted Lorna under the same roof as Elizabeth, not just yet. He wouldn't turn Lorna away either if she chose to try to reconcile with her daughter. It was a matter out of his hands. He felt helpless and didn't like it.

"I don't know." Lorna was uncertain, her gaze falling on Gavan.

"It has to be your decision, Ms. Sanders," Gavan said evenly.

"Belinda said you're working on a novel about the Wilkinses," Lorna began cautiously.

"Something like that," Gavan responded.

"That's how you discovered that I wasn't dead?" Lorna queried.

Gavan shook his head, a hint of a smile curving his lips. "Actually, I had a hunch from the start, but it was Belinda that cleared it up for us."

"She hated lying for me all these years."

"As she should," Lance said firmly.

"I hated asking her to. I loved my daughter. I still love her. I never wanted to leave her behind, but it really was the only way." Lorna was urgent now. "By the time I got on my feet, by the time I was able to take care of her with any kind of confidence, she was nearly grown, almost eighteen. I couldn't interfere then, not after lying for so long. Do you understand that I kept silent for her?"

"I gathered that." Gavan was kind. He never doubted

for a moment that from Lorna's point of view, leaving Elizabeth in the care of the Wilkinses was the best recourse. Convincing Elizabeth of that was another matter. And then there was Liberty. His eyes widened. She had said daughter, not daughters.

"Are you coming?" he asked gently.

He offered her the comfort of his arm, quelling any hint of guilt at helping Elizabeth's mom. Tyke was right. They just needed to clear the air and a reunion, tearful and happy, was imminent. He sighed, tucking Lorna's arm in his, hoping they could resolve the past.

Elizabeth watched them from the window. She wasn't surprised to see Lorna enter the house. A pang of relief that Lorna had not left assailed her and she was annoyed that she could care after all.

She turned from the window and sat on the bed, her eyes closed in depression. Hadn't she always fantasized that her mother was alive? That it was a horrible mistake? Now it was true and she was an emotional wreck. She wanted to run below and hold her mother, cry on her shoulder, and promise that they would never be separated again. She couldn't. Lorna Sanders deserved to be punished for what she did to Elizabeth, what she did to Liberty Sutton's life.

Oh God, she had forgotten all about Liberty. Did Lorna deny her, too? And Liberty's son, he had a grandmother. It was a mess. A total fiasco. She groaned. She should never have allowed Gavan to write his stupid, invasive book. Look what he had done. It was his entire fault.

Her eyes popped open at the thought. She swallowed and shook her head in denial. No, it wasn't his fault. If it hadn't been for him she would never have known or even suspected the truth, but it wouldn't have changed the fact that Lorna Sanders was still alive. Gavan only opened the portal to the truth, he didn't create the problem. She could see that Gavan was hurting, too. She wanted to soothe him, reassure him that she was fine.

She couldn't hear anything below, but she knew they were there, talking to Lorna, talking about her. Despair overwhelmed her. She was not going to come down. She was not going to give Lorna Sanders a chance to come up with some outrageous explanation as to why she left, lied. It was clear by Belinda's words that Lorna never cared for Elizabeth or Liberty; only Earl had mattered. Nothing could change that fact.

She laid her head on the pillow, not bothering to undress as she slid under the sheet. She doubted if she would be able to get back to asleep although she was lethargic in her despair. She closed her eyes, her back to the door, and she fell asleep within moments.

CHAPTER 42

Gavan offered Lorna a seat in the same study Lance had used earlier. It was the most private area and he wanted to be alone with Lorna.

"Guys, if you don't mind, I'm going to sit with Ms. Sanders. Go on up and I'll inform you in the morning what's happening," Gavan said to Lance and Tyke.

"No problem. I'm drop-dead tired now," Lance said, then yawned for emphasis. He smacked Tyke on the back and gave him a shove toward the steps. "Come on, big guy. Time for bed," he teased, knowing it would annoy Tyke to be spoken to as if he were a kid.

"Take it easy on her," Tyke said.

Gavan entered the study and paused. Lorna appeared frailer by the moment. Her face was averted and all he could see was the barest of her profile, her long hair fairly covering her face from his view.

He sat down in the chair across from her, leaned forward, and rested his elbows on his knees, his large hands clasped together as he considered her. "Elizabeth's upset."

"Do you think I can't see that?" Lorna frowned.

"I think you have a whole lot of explaining to do

and I think you should be prepared to tell her," Gavan said, not unkindly.

"She won't let me." Lorna sighed.

"You have to give her a chance," Gavan urged her.

"She'll never forgive me," Lorna murmured.

"Perhaps. We can't know what she'll decide, but at least give her a choice. Let her decide this time what course to accept."

"I wouldn't know where to begin," Lorna whispered.

"Start from the beginning. Why did you leave?" he asked. It wasn't his intention to get a confession from her, but suddenly the words flowed forth and she couldn't seem to stop them.

She held nothing back.

"I heard Anne threaten to disinherit Earl one night when they were arguing about me. She wasn't going to leave him one penny if he married me," Lorna told him.

"I loved Earl. I really did. And I loved my baby, too. I was so upset that day. It was raining and I was impulsive when I decided to run. At first I was going to just leave and not tell Earl where I was. Then I realized he would look for me. He loved me, us. Me and Elizabeth. He adored his little girl. I didn't want to see him separated from her. I couldn't take her with me. Besides, I had nothing. No family, no friends. Nothing. Why should I have taken her from her father to starve her and have her struggle?"

Gavan nodded, encouraging her to speak.

"I went out to the bayou and it was then and there that I decided I was going to fake my death. I tore my skirt, pulled my hair, and dropped off a shoe, then waded into the water and swam across. I wanted my trail to lead to the water. In hindsight, it wasn't such a good fake death, but I was a black woman, no one was going to delve too deeply into what happened to me."

Her tone grew resentful with that reality.

Gavan was sympathetic.

"I hitched a ride downtown, got a job as a maid at the Savannah Inn, and that was when I met Mark Sutton."

"So you did remain in Savannah?" Gavan exclaimed, for the first time interrupting her.

Lorna nodded. "For a little while."

She looked away, her gaze full of remorse. "I discovered I was pregnant just two months after I faked my death. I . . . I didn't know what to do. Mark was so understanding and kind . . ."

"Was he in love with you?" Gavan asked gently. Again, she nodded. He wasn't surprised.

"He offered to help. He asked me to marry him. Can you imagine?" She laughed lightly. "First Earl, then Mark, two completely different men, both wanted to marry me? It was tempting, so very tempting. But I couldn't. Not only did I not love him—I was still desperately in love with Earl—but I couldn't hurt his fiancée."

"That was kind of you," Gavan said, not without a hint of sarcasm.

Her temper flared and she glared at him. "I am not a cruel woman, Mr. Ward, contrary to what you may think of me. I love Elizabeth. I never meant to hurt anyone."

Gavan was motionless. He leaned forward. "And what about the other child, Liberty Sutton? Did you love her?"

In a voice barely audible she asked, "How did you know about her?"

"How could I not? She's the spitting image of you and Elizabeth," Gavan scoffed.

"But . . ." She hesitated, looking at him with uncertainty. "She and Liberty don't know about each other. How could you know?"

Gavan sat back, considering Lorna before answering, "It seems your correspondence with Belinda was lacking.

Your daughters met a while ago. What do you think sparked the idea that there was more to your disappearance than met the eye?"

"That's impossible," she gasped, ignoring his question. "How could they meet?"

"Remember Mikel Wilkins?"

She scowled, her eyes dark with loathing. "I remember the racist brat. He hated me. The feeling was mutual."

"He saw Liberty, kidnapped her, and forced her to impersonate your daughter. They looked so much alike, you see," Gavan said, ignoring her outraged expression.

"He didn't hurt her?"

"No. She was terrified but she survived. They both survived. Elizabeth was accused of helping Mikel in his scheme. For a few days they even locked her up."

"Oh God."

There was real pain in her eyes and Gavan felt a tinge of remorse. He had been cold and callous, but she had seemed so nonchalant he realized deep inside he wanted her to suffer, if just a little. He was repentant.

"She was released, Ms. Sanders. She was safe and treated well while inside, if that's any reassurance."

"It's none. I can't believe they locked up my child." She shuddered.

"The charges were dropped. The irony is that had they not locked her away she and I would never have met," Gavan continued. "I thought I was going to do a story on the Wilkinses, Anne and her son and Elizabeth. I thought she was guilty at first. I took one look at her and I knew she would never stoop so low."

Lorna was watching him now and asked her own question. "When did all of this happen?"

"A while ago."

Lorna considered Gavan with her own appraisal. He was a big man but gentle and he was in love with her daughter. He would protect her and give her the affection and love that Lorna had never given her, that she knew Earl had sadly lacked in showing her. She was consoled by that.

"When did you find out you were pregnant again?" Gavan asked suddenly, his blunt question catching her off guard.

"With Liberty?" Lorna asked, disconcerted by the abruptness of his question.

He raised an inquiring eyebrow. "Are there others?"

"No. Of course, not." She sighed.

"I didn't think so."

"Oh." Her tone was irritated now. "Well, did you know that I didn't know I was even pregnant until a few months after I left Earl?"

"As a matter of fact, I suspected that was the case," Gavan responded.

She was quiet, considering him with displeasure. "I don't owe you anything, Mr. Ward."

"You certainly don't," was his easy reply. "You do owe Elizabeth and Liberty Sutton something, however. Honest answers for starters."

"You're engaged to Elizabeth. What do you have to do with Liberty?" Her voice was wary now.

"Liberty wanted to know as did Elizabeth why they had so much in common. And it was inevitable once they met that their bloodline would be discovered. Did you know that Mark Sutton left her alone with his sister when she was just seventeen?"

"I knew," Lorna admitted. "I was angry with him. He had promised he would never leave her. Just a year before he left her I had pondered telling Liberty the truth. I didn't like the way Mark was living. His depth of poverty had grown over the years and he no longer cared. I think in his own way he had loved his wife. When she died, he gave up."

"And he couldn't have you either. Maybe that was a part of his despair."

Lorna swallowed, uncomfortable with the topic. "I never loved him. He knew that. But I thought he was smart. I was impressed with everything he had, his house and his land. He was engaged to Mary and he had a bright future. I was so confident everything would be fine. He had offered to keep Liberty, at first, until I was able to get my life together. But Mary, his wife, had Liberty believing she was her grandmother and that their supposed children, Greg and Ursula, had died. How could I come into her life with such a tale having always been the truth for her? I was outraged when Mark first confessed, but he convinced me it was for the best. He told me he would not let any harm come to Liberty."

She was near tears but she didn't cry.

She looked at Gavan, a wide smile curving her mouth as she spoke of her youngest daughter.

"I named her Liberty because I was hoping she would have the freedom to live and love the way I never did."

Gavan understood.

"I kept in contact with Mark for years. She was fine. He assured me that she was well taken care of. I admit, there was a time when I was worried. Years after I left, when Liberty was only six, he lost his house and his land. He moved to D.C. and I didn't hear from him for several months. That was a frightful time. His wife hated me and I thought maybe that was it. Then I heard she had died and I hurt for him. He was so depressed."

"And Liberty?"

"He insisted she was okay. He and his sister were caring for her. Once I suggested visiting. He said the moment Liberty saw me she would know I had to be her mother. She and I are the spitting image, not like Elizabeth, who looks more like Earl."

Gavan was only partially placated. Lorna didn't seem to be such a gullible woman, but perhaps she was. She was certainly weaker than he liked. She had given up both of her children with the hope that their caretakers would be able to care for them better than she ever could. He sighed. How wrong she was to think they would prefer guardians with money rather than their own mother. How sad for Lorna to have paid such a huge price for the sake of love.

"I'm curious, Ms. Sanders," Gavan started. "Why did you leave Mark's employ? Why didn't you just stay on as the maid? And where is he now?"

"Okay . . . first, I don't know where Mark is. I haven't heard from him in years. He just seemed to have disappeared. He may be in Georgia or anywhere." She sighed, took a steadying breath, then continued. "I did stay with Mark, as a maid of course, at least for the first two years. I was there with Liberty, her mother in every sense. But Mark was having financial problems. He let everyone go. Mary saw to it that I was on the list. I didn't mind. I was a maid and was confident I would find other employment. I left with that intent, to get another job and then Liberty. But, as I said, Mark convinced me otherwise. By the time he gave up the struggle of not losing his property, four years had gone by and Liberty had forgotten me. That was my fault. It's all my fault." Then she did the unthinkable and began to cry.

Gavan came hastily to her side, pulled her to her feet, and cradled her, his large body overwhelming her slight frame. When she had cried her full, she sniffed and pulled away.

"You are kind, Gavan. Don't hurt my daughter," she

sobbed. Then without looking at him, ashamed that she had broken down, she hurried from the study.

Gavan let her go, hoping she would not leave the house, afraid that it was exactly what she would do.

A few moments passed. He didn't hear any doors open or close. He couldn't guess where she had gone.

Only the morning would tell.

With a heavy heart he entered his room. Elizabeth was asleep, fully clothed and curled on the bed. He studied her, worried how she would be come the morning. There was no telling if she would break down and cry or be the indifferent woman she had portrayed tonight.

Tired and drained from the roller coaster the day had presented, he undressed and lay beside Elizabeth. He reached for her, wanting to fall asleep with her in his arms. But he hesitated, debating if he should chance awakening her by undressing her or allowing her to sleep as she was. He decided to risk it.

She did not budge from her deep sleep. No doubt the consumption of wine and the shock of first hearing and then discovering that her mother was actually alive had overwhelmed her. He cuddled closer to her until their bodies were snug and warm. In the morning he would tell her all that Lorna had shared with him.

Hopefully she'd be able to forgive Lorna. But, although he sympathized with Lorna, Elizabeth was the woman he loved. Whatever happened, he would be on her side.

Content with his decision, he closed his eyes and slept.

CHAPTER 43

Gavan stared at the note Lance handed him with concern. Elizabeth was dressing upstairs. He'd come down ahead of her and met Lance's and Tyke's grim expressions with instant dread.

"What?" he asked.

He sat at the table. The aroma of the southern breakfast Belinda had prepared for them was far more appealing than the dinner Lance had experienced the night before. But Gavan didn't touch his meal. Not after Lance slid the two folded notes across the table at him.

"There are two notes. One is for Liberty and one for Elizabeth. It's from Lorna," Lance said. His tone was unusually kind and Gavan all but groaned.

"What's from Lorna?" Elizabeth asked as she joined them in the dining room.

She appeared remarkably well rested and unaffected by the night's dramatic turn of events. She sat beside Gavan and poured a cup of coffee, the slight shake of her hand the only indication that anything abnormal had taken place.

Gavan and Lance looked at each other before Gavan answered her. "Lorna has left you a note."

Her wide-eyed gaze so full of apprehension that she was trying desperately to cover moved him.

"Can you handle this right now? You don't have to read it now. Frankly, Elizabeth, you don't have to read it ever," Gavan said with fervor.

She stared at the note he put in her hands. She set it on the empty plate beside her coffee, then folded both her hands in her lap and stared at it.

"I'll read it now," she finally murmured.

Lance lowered his head. He had been so caught up in his own anger it was only just beginning to dawn on him what Elizabeth Wilkins was going through. He was guilty of adding to her discomfort and wanted to make amends. But how could he? He could only offer a truce and that was lame in itself.

Lance watched his brother's constant protective gaze on Elizabeth. Gavan had allowed Lance to brood and even be rude for weeks. It was Gavan's way of apologizing for a wrong he never committed to begin with. Neither of them could have known what Maya was up to. Lance pursed his lips.

Now it was his turn to be the supportive brother.

"She's gone," Elizabeth murmured as she skimmed over Lorna's letter, then reread it several times over.

Again Lance and Gavan glanced at each other. They both had expected Lorna to flee. She was as wary as a frightened rabbit when they caught her trying to escape last night. They doubted Elizabeth would ever see her again.

"She says she's sorry for what has happened," Elizabeth went on. "She asks that I forgive her." A note of derision laced her voice. "She realizes that she doesn't belong and will not interfere. She's congratulating us on our marriage. God, what an awful woman," Elizabeth muttered and tossed the note onto the table. Before Gavan could reach out a comforting hand she jumped up and stormed from the dining room.

Gavan was close behind her.

"I could go look for her," Gavan said. He was holding Elizabeth, rocking back and forth with her. She wasn't crying, at least not on the outside. Gavan wished that she would. It would have been better than holding it in.

"No. Leave her. She's irresponsible and always will be," Elizabeth murmured.

"She loves you." Gavan was matter-of-fact.

Elizabeth pulled back a bit and looked up at him. "You believe that?"

"Yes, I do," Gavan answered, adding, "She did what she felt was in the best interest of you and your sister. She left you both with people she thought would take care of you. You should be thankful, too, Elizabeth. You got the better end of the deal growing up in a bit of luxury compared to Liberty's hardship."

Elizabeth appeared rueful and shook her head slowly. "I don't know about that, Gavan. Liberty is carefree and one of the happiest women I have ever met. She takes life in stride and is not afraid to go after what she wants. That had something to do with her childhood, I'm sure. Just as I'm hesitant and reserved has a lot to do with uncertainties in my childhood."

Gavan considered her words, then pressed his lips to her forehead and whispered, "Why don't you do something carefree then?"

Elizabeth smiled, assuming he meant making love. "As in?" she asked with a content sigh to be held by him.

"Marry me," Gavan murmured.

Again Elizabeth drew back and looked at him. "I already said yes, didn't I?"

"You said yes, but I can't get you to lock down a date. Say you'll marry me now. We can be in Honolulu in no time."

"Gavan. Now is so . . . it's too soon," she tried to reason with him.

"No, it's not. Take a lesson from your mother and your sister and jump on the train now, Elizabeth. Why are you allowing time to slip away? I love you. You love me. With all that has happened I've certainly learned from it. Come away with me. Meet my family and let's get married. I can get my parents to arrange everything we need. You need only say yes."

He was so persuading and she was so overcome with the need to hold on to something real and permanent and . . . yes.

Yes. "Yes, Gavan. I'll do it," she said.

"I'll do it," she repeated, grinning.

"Finally." Gavan sighed with feigned exhaustion. "I'll get our tickets and we can be in Honolulu in three days."

"Three days!" Elizabeth exclaimed.

"Well, yeah," Gavan said patiently, not understanding her concern. "I'll need a little time to close a few things. I'm sure you'll need to make arrangements, get a temporary assistant to keep your office going while you're away. And then there's Anne and Sonya and we have to invite your long-lost sister—"

"Slow down, my head is spinning." Elizabeth laughed, stopping him with a gentle hand on his mouth. "You're not supposed to be so involved. That's my job."

"I'll take on any job to have you, Elizabeth," Gavan said with such sincerity that she stretched upward to kiss him, first on his chin, then his mouth.

"Keep it up and everyone will wonder what happened to us," Gavan murmured huskily.

"Let them wonder," Elizabeth whispered, wrapping her arms around his neck and, closing her eyes, kissing him deeply.

CHAPTER 44

"*Aloha kâkou!* Elizabeth and family," Val called the moment she spotted her sons and their guests coming through baggage claims.

"She's offering you a very warm hello," Gavan whispered in Elizabeth's ear. Elizabeth smiled brightly in turn, admiring Gavan's parents instantly. They were warm, friendly, and beautiful people. And there was no question where Val's sons got their good looks and charm.

She was a handsome woman. She was tall, full figured, slightly overweight but not unpleasantly. Her hair was dark and wavy, near her hips. She was no young girl, but she was a very attractive woman. She hadn't dressed for the occasion either. She wore faded blue jeans, an even more faded yellow T-shirt, and well-worn tennis shoes. She was very relaxed and very friendly.

Gavan's father, Robert, stood quietly at his wife's side, allowing her to gush over Elizabeth while he simply smiled at her. Finally, when Val finished fawning over the beauty of her daughter-in-law to be, Robert bent over and gave her a gentle hug. Elizabeth was breathless at the sight of him. He was a doctor? She was speechless, wondering if his patients found him intimidating.

He was an awesome figure of a black man. His presence commanded authority although he was a gentle being beside his wife. He was broad and strong, nothing like the image Elizabeth had envisioned. Gavan had described his father as kind, gentle, and very amicable. A lighthearted man, he had said with a smile. She expected someone with a less furious expression, a less dominating figure.

This man, tall and broad with his dark brown skin, made even more pronounced with the constant tanning of the Hawaiian sun, did not appear gentle at all. Except for his girth, he reminded her instantly of Lance. They were the same coloring, the same build, albeit Lance was more slender, and even had the same stoicism. Had he not smiled, had he not embraced her so affectionately she was certain she would have cowered beneath his massive presence.

Elizabeth was amazed at Gavan's family. They made her feel welcome as if she had been expected for years. She was extremely relieved. She had not known what they would think of her, latching onto Gavan so quickly and shamelessly. She was prepared for the worst, expecting to be treated in the same manner Lance had done since he was told about the engagement.

"Welcome to Honolulu, my dear," Gavan's mother breathed, guiding Elizabeth from the baggage claims depot. "I'm so excited and pleased that you and Gavan are getting married here."

"Me too," Elizabeth breathed.

Val led them to their waiting sedans, briskly giving instructions to the drivers. Elizabeth was amazed at the woman's thoroughness. She was all sweetness with Elizabeth and Anne and formal with the drivers. She reminded Elizabeth of Sonya, especially when Elizabeth was younger.

The drive to the Wards' home was breathtakingly scenic. Gavan's family lived on the island of Honolulu. It was his mother's people. His father moved to Hawaii in the sixties and finished college on the island. He met Val and they married a year later. Val was proud to share her family's history, even hinting at a certain lineage with Queen Ka'ahumanu, one of Hawaii's most influential queens, known as the woman who changed a kingdom.

Robert was quick to say that bit of information was up for debate. They laughed easily over it, but Elizabeth was inclined to deem Val secretly believed it.

It was a pleasant surprise to be embraced so warmly by his family. And Elizabeth was thankful too that Val had taken a liking to both Sonya and Anne, despite Anne's austere disposition.

Sonya had ridden with Lance and Tyke. Jarrett, Liberty, and her son, Jamal, were also passengers with Lance. Gavan's parents had thought of everything, driving two cars two the airport and handing the keys for the second vehicle over to Lance.

Elizabeth had at first worried that Liberty would feel as she had when she discovered the truth about their mother. Liberty's only regret was that she didn't get a chance to meet Lorna. She was far more understanding than Elizabeth could ever be, but then that was Liberty. It was a facet of her sister's personality that she was fast getting familiar with.

That left Anne and Elizabeth alone with Gavan, his mother, and his father. Elizabeth understood why they asked Anne to ride in their vehicle, but she wished it were Sonya's pleasing smile and plump warmth next to her.

During the ride, Gavan couldn't stop looking at Elizabeth. Her experience with Lorna had broken her heart and he ached to ease her pain. He wanted to heal her heartache. Since that fateful night in Savannah, he held her constantly, suppressing his own desire to show her compassion and warmth. He was careful when they kissed, gentle in his touch, and silently conveyed his concern.

The flight to Hawaii had been long and arduous, but Elizabeth had slept through most of it, her nearness a temptation that he fought for eleven hours. She had no idea what she did to him, to his self-control. When they arrived in Hawaii, her expression of awe pleased him, her hug reassured him, and he again was confident that she shared his inexplicable desire to be with her.

And not once had she mentioned Lorna.

For the first time in several days she appeared genuinely happy. His homeland had managed to boost her spirits and he was proud of it.

Val sat across from Elizabeth, her son on her right. Robert sat across from Gavan, Anne's small frame in between him and Elizabeth. The sedan was large, but with Gavan's large bulk it felt small and cramped.

Gavan appeared amused, thinking Anne had never been so disconcerted in her life. Elizabeth was quiet, politely responding to his mother's questions.

Their eyes connected and each time, Elizabeth would flush and look away. He was amused but obliged her by averting his gaze as well, listening to his mother ramble on with all of her plans she had already made.

"It won't be a large wedding, Elizabeth. I thought something more intimate, among family and our dearest friends, would be more appropriate."

"It sounds very sweet," Elizabeth agreed.

"Well, don't say it like that." Val laughed. "It's your wedding. You're supposed to remember this day forever. I remember mine. It was beautiful, wasn't it, Robert?"

He nodded, gave Elizabeth an encouraging smile,

then went back to looking at his paper. "And you are going to be a lovely bride. Did you get your dress?"

"Yes," Elizabeth answered, forcing herself to concentrate.

"Fabulous. I'm so excited. I never thought this boy would marry. Look at you, nearly forty. I didn't think you would ever find the one for you." Val nudged Gavan.

"Oh, I found her," Gavan said pointedly, the look he gave Elizabeth causing her to react with nervousness.

Val laughed heartily at Elizabeth's response to her son.

"Good. And I want grandchildren right away. You do want children, don't you, Elizabeth?" Val asked.

Elizabeth flushed. "Gavan and I have talked about it. Eventually, yes."

"Eventually? Now's the time, sweetie, while you're young and energetic," Val said firmly.

Elizabeth grinned, noting Gavan's discomfort with amusement but feeling sorry for him all the same. His mother was very animated and Elizabeth liked her. She expected a lot more blunt moments to occur before the wedding date. And she planned to tease Gavan relentlessly.

They'd been traveling for days, it seemed to Elizabeth. From Savannah to Maryland. And then two days later they were packed and on their way to Hawaii. The flight was half a day's trip and by the time Gavan and Elizabeth were able to get to bed, they were both too exhausted to slip away and meet.

Val put them in separate rooms, insisting that she was too old-fashioned to allow them to sleep together before the wedding. Gavan and Elizabeth glanced at each other when she made that announcement, both realizing it would be weeks or even their wedding day before they could be together.

Val intended to keep them separated and she was an early riser. Each morning she skirted Elizabeth away on one errand after errand. By nightfall, Elizabeth was exhausted.

They were so many things to do.

She had to pick out the cake, decide on her hair, and needed to visit a few locations for their honeymoon.

Val insisted they needed to be away although Gavan had said they would stay in Hawaii; there were more islands than Honolulu to visit. They needed to be utterly alone for at least a few days. They went shopping, buying new clothes and perfumes and jewelry, all at Val's insistence that it was a new start and she had to pamper herself.

It was such a whirlwind of activity that Elizabeth hardly had time to think. And then, suddenly, the day of her engagement dinner arrived. She realized with a start that she had barely thought of her mother since she had landed in Hawaii. Elizabeth shook Lorna from her thoughts, refusing to dwell on her.

Her wedding was in two days.

Two short days. The expectation was at once frightening and exciting. She loved Gavan. He made her feel so special and so alive. She had never loved anyone the way she loved him. She was fascinated that such a feeling could exist.

Again her mother entered her thoughts. She fleetingly wondered if that was the way she had loved Earl. She couldn't have. She would never have left him if it were so.

Everyone was downstairs waiting for her to come down for the dinner, but she needed another moment to subdue her emotions. From the moment they arrived she had been constantly attended on and always kept away from Gavan.

His mother had planned for Elizabeth to stay with her while Gavan was expected to stay at his own apartment.

Gavan adamantly refused, insisting he should stay at

the house as well. Then Lance and Tyke joined them. Val suddenly had a houseful and every room was occupied.

It was a huge house. Six bed rooms, all furnished and laid out in the Hawaiian style of eloquence and color. The room she had been given was between Gavan's parents' room and the guest room where Anne and Sonya were staying.

Jarrett and Liberty were given the large guest room because of Jamal. Lance was on the main floor. The room Anne and Sonya took over was his old room. Tyke was next door to him and Gavan stayed in his old room at the back of the house.

His brother had teased that when they were younger, Gavan had insisted on that room for its privacy and now it served to isolate him from the rest of the family. Gavan was not amused.

A wistful smile played on Elizabeth's lips. She had not been given a chance to breathe, let alone think about her future with Gavan. She wasn't afraid, strange as it seemed. She wasn't worried that they would discover just how different they were. She trusted that their love, so powerful and sincere, would help them through every trial. She prayed for what his parents had and what her parents would have had.

She stared at her reflection, her eyes tearing at the thought of her parents. She would not think of Earl and Lorna. Not now. She swiped at her eyes, then quickly fixed her makeup. She considered her reflection and blinked with pleasure.

She hardly recognized the made-up woman in the mirror, thanks to Val and her wondrous makeover. She had taken Elizabeth to a spa two days after they arrived, insisted she get the works including a massage that did wonders to relieve the tension in her shoulders. She had gotten a manicure, pedicure, body waxing, and facial.

She was treated like a queen and could see how Val kept her youthfulness.

Elizabeth had been amazed that Val was in her early sixties. She wouldn't say exactly how old she was, but all the same she looked fantastic. Now Elizabeth was reaping the benefits and was impressed by her own image. She smiled at her reflection, a little excited at the prospect of seeing Gavan. She had been planning all day to find a way to isolate herself with him. She missed him. It felt as if she had only seen glimpses of him for days. His father kept him so busy on one errand or another.

And it was all deliberate.

The parents thought keeping them separated would make their wedding day even more blissful. The few times they found themselves alone, on the brink of a kiss or an embrace, somehow Val would appear insisting she was doing this to help them keep their romance alive until the honeymoon.

Elizabeth was sure she didn't want their assistance.

She had no doubt she would be as lustful for Gavan after they married as she was right now. Her body had experienced his loving and she wanted to be near him now, not later. She wanted to kiss him, to cuddle up to him and make sure it wasn't all a dream.

Sighing, she dabbed on a soft shade of mauve lipstick, patted her hair, and stepped away from the mirror. She had never looked so . . . alluring. She smoothed her dress down, feeling very sensual in the snug black sheath dress she had chosen. Val had agreed that it was a perfect dress only after Elizabeth pointed out that it was softened by the pink lace trimming. Her heels were black with pale pink, another item she rarely wore. Her legs were bare, but the fresh waxing gave them a shimmer that was silky and smooth. She felt very pretty, very womanly, and very ready to see Gavan.

Her pants and conservative shirts had been set aside, tucked away by Val, no less. Her closet was now lined with feminine dresses, pretty blouses, and the pants that she was allowed were very figure flattering. Her mother-in-law-to-be was making sure her son had reason to get her with child. She flushed at the thought, again remembering her plan to corner Gavan and sneak away with him.

She picked up her matching purse, then hurried from the room. She was late and they were waiting for her. They were going to dine out with Gavan's family and some of their guests. But she had every intention of turning Gavan's head.

When she was done, she doubted if he would still be too exhausted to sneak away. With a mischievous twinkle in her eyes, she entered the foyer, a wide smile ready to greet her hosts. It froze in place.

Standing at the bottom of the stairs was her mother.

CHAPTER 45

Gavan was distraught and had utterly lost his patience with his parents. His father kept him out for hours, running fool's errands and deliberately stalling with various last-minute chores.

They were doing any- and everything to make sure he was too exhausted to do anything but sleep by the time he got home.

And it was, coincidentally, always past the midnight hour when they got home. Twice he stole into Elizabeth's room. Each time she was sound asleep, Val having ensured that his future wife was too exhausted for any late-night rendezvous.

It wasn't that he didn't appreciate what his parents were trying to do . . . Actually, he didn't appreciate it.

Not one bit.

They weren't helping him. They were frustrating the situation.

He didn't want to only make love to his future bride, as his mother so blatantly stated. He wanted to see her, to talk to her, to get lost in the depth of her brown eyes.

He dressed carefully for the evening, at his mother's request.

She had a special engagement dinner planned for them. Somehow she had managed to pull several of his friends and family together for the occasion.

Gavan was impressed, the list of guests a mix of family he had rarely seen over the past twenty years. Under other circumstances, he would have anticipated the opportunity to see his family with pleasure.

Tonight he was full of gloom. This dinner was yet another means to keep him from Elizabeth.

He adjusted his bow tie, glaring at it in annoyance. He wasn't exactly a bow tie kind of man.

Grimacing, knowing his mother wouldn't approve, he undid the tie and the top button of his heavily starched shirt.

He felt a thousand times better.

He looked over his black suit with appreciation. It was a tailor fit, largely a requirement due to his massive build. His mother would at least be pleased that he had worn cuff links and his black dress shoes. He was clean shaven, his hair freshly cut. He was getting married in two days and he was more than prepared.

Mulling over how he could possibly gain a moment alone with Elizabeth, he left his bedroom, his eyebrows furrowed in deep thought.

The murmur of voices floated through the house. Gavan hastened to the foyer to meet up with Lance, Jarrett, and Tyke.

"What? No dirty jeans?" Tyke guffawed the moment he saw Gavan.

Gavan scowled, in no mood for Tyke's teasing. "I thought I heard Elizabeth." He was expected to tag along in the car with Lance, Jarrett, and Tyke. Everyone else was riding with his father. He wanted to at least have a moment with Elizabeth before they departed.

"You're lovesick," Lance said, shaking his head as if he

were ashamed of his brother. But Gavan wasn't fooled.
Lance was finally happy for him. Gavan wasn't sure
when the turning point occurred, but somewhere between Savannah and Hawaii, Lance's temper cooled
and he became less hostile toward Elizabeth.

Sitting on the bench near the front door, Lance appeared bored, his expression bland. He wore gray slacks
and a gray pullover shirt and he eyed Gavan with a smirk.

"And here I recall you saying you'd found the one
when you met Maya last year," Gavan retorted. He was
instantly contrite at the pain that filled Lance's eyes.

"Sorry, man. That was a low blow," Gavan said quickly.

Lance shrugged. His hazel eyes cleared just as quickly
as they had clouded. Amazingly enough since arriving
in Hawaii, Maya had not crossed his mind. He wasn't
even angry anymore. Lately he found himself wondering about the little woman he had seen hurrying away
from the courthouse. Someday he was going to ask
Elizabeth about her, but for now he was content to be
alone. "Don't worry. It's an old wound. I'm healed."

"Here they come," Tyke said loudly, distracting the
brothers with his booming voice.

Robert led his wife and their guests into the foyer. Like
his eldest son, he wore a black suit with a starched
white shirt. Unlike Gavan, he wore a neatly set bow tie.
He looked uncomfortable.

Val, on the other hand, was a vision in her gold-spun
evening dress and long, flowing hair. She wore a pale
yellow headdress, one she had acquired in her youth.
It suited her coloring and her cheerful demeanor. She
would have made a stunning entrance walking side by
side with her husband had Anne's much shorter and
slight frame not made the threesome appear somewhat comical.

Anne had chosen a tan pantsuit and white flat shoes

that reminded Gavan of a nurse's outfit. She wore a white formal hat with a single tan ribbon. She had even put on lipstick, Gavan noticed. Sonya stood beside Anne, decked out in a purple long skirt suit and a wide-brim hat that sat on her big hair precariously. She grinned at the group, pleased with her outfit.

"Mrs. Wilkins, Sonya, you both look so beautiful," Liberty gushed.

"Thank you, child." Sonya brimmed with pride.

"Thank you, Liberty," Anne said with a half smile that was huge for her.

"And look at you, Mrs. Ward. What a lovely dress," Liberty said brightly, appraising Val's dress with a light whistle.

"*Mahalo!*" Val smiled. "This dress was made years ago and I can still fit it," she added with delight. She stepped around Liberty, her husband right behind her.

"It was beautifully done," Liberty acknowledged.

The foyer was abuzz with separate conversations filtering through the room. Lance and Tyke were throwing barbs at one another. Liberty graced Anne, Sonya, and Val with tales of her honeymoon a few months earlier. Gavan was standing beside his father, not even pretending that he was listening to anyone or anything as he stared up the stairs in anticipation of Elizabeth.

It was no wonder that no one heard the front door open.

Liberty was the first to see her. She was rendered speechless, barely breathing at the sight of a slight woman gingerly entering the foyer, her purse clutched against her bosom, her eyes wide and searching until they fell on Liberty with a shock.

They each knew instantly who the other was.

CHAPTER 46

Gavan had told Liberty everything. His sympathy was appreciated, but she felt more for her mother's loss than her own. After all, she had been without her child for years at one time.

It only hurt to think that her mother wasn't willing to even try to make amends for the past. Unlike Elizabeth, Liberty was not averse to reuniting with her mother. She didn't care about the past. Her son and Jarrett had taught her well that only the present and future mattered. Her own dramatic experiences with first losing her son and then getting him back had humbled her.

She didn't know Lorna, but she felt love for the stranger that was her mother. If only she could get Elizabeth to feel the same.

Gradually, all conversation ceased as one by one the family became aware of Lorna Sanders's presence. She appeared small and timid safely huddled against the door, her purse and a small bag her only possessions. Val was the first to react, completely unaware of who she was. The woman had walked right in. Fortunately for her, the alarm wasn't on.

"May I help you?" she demanded. She glanced from Lorna to Liberty, then back again.

"Yes. I'm—"

"Lorna Sanders," Liberty whispered, walking past Val to stand directly in front of Lorna.

Gavan was jolted from his searching of the stairway at Lorna's presence.

"What are you doing here?" he asked. It wasn't gracious, but he was in shock. He was getting married in a few days. He wanted nothing to come between him and Elizabeth.

He knitted his eyebrows at Liberty's calm acceptance. He and Lance exchanged looks, but neither moved or spoke. It was between mother and daughter.

Jarrett was uncertain for once. Liberty didn't appear upset, but he was unable to deduce what she was feeling, she was so motionless. She had chosen not to discuss her mother from the moment she was informed Lorna was alive. Jarrett had thought she was dismissing Lorna from her life. He could only assume that he had been wrong. He waited, prepared to assist Liberty if she needed him.

Lorna's gaze was searching as she measured her daughter. She saw no rejection, only a remarkable young woman that was her identical image almost thirty years earlier. And, unlike Elizabeth, Liberty did not express disgust but awe at the sight of Lorna. Lorna was awed herself, her tense features relaxing as she stared at her youngest child that she had barely known.

"Liberty?" she breathed, taking an uncertain step forward.

Liberty smiled. Her eyes filled with tears, and then she wrapped her arms about her mother and held her tightly.

"Yes," she murmured, her voice catching on a sob.

"Liberty?" Jarrett said from behind her. "Jamal's on the stairs," he explained, giving her a contrite grimace at interrupting. Liberty pulled away from Lorna and stepped aside, glancing up the stairs as she did so. Her smiled widened at the sight of her son sitting on the steps, watching her. She waved him forward. He came, not stopping until he was in front of her. She took his hand and turned him to Lorna.

"This is my mother. Your grandmother, Lorna Sanders," Liberty said with such ease that Lorna felt weak with relief. Jamal smiled up at his grandmother, his two missing front teeth not an issue.

"Hello," he said politely.

Lorna was pleased at the boy's encouraging reception and bent to give him a hug. "You're dressed up handsomely," was all she could think to say.

His grin broadened. "Ms. Elizabeth is getting married. We're celebrating."

"Did you get dressed all by yourself?" Lorna asked.

Jamal pointed to Anne. "No, Mrs. Wilkins helped me."

Lorna's face fell and she stood up and faced Earl's mother.

"I'm rather good with children, don't you think?" Anne asked calmly.

She had come around Jamal and Jarrett so that she could get a better view of Lorna. It was obvious to her that Lorna had not even recognized her. She was angry, furious with Lorna for showing up at the Wards' without an invitation. And after what she had done to Elizabeth.

"I didn't mean to intrude," Lorna said softly, old animosity surfacing at the presence of Anne. She glanced at Lance Ward, who smiled encouragingly at her. He had warned her it wouldn't be easy when he'd called. But she had gotten on that plane and come anyway. There was no turning back now.

"Well, you are," Anne snapped. "Elizabeth doesn't want you here. Not after what you've done."

"I'd like to hear her say it," Lorna responded cautiously, her moment of relief gone. Her gaze darted uncomfortably over the faces of the Wards before landing on her daughter's fiancé.

"She'll be down in a moment." Gavan answered her unspoken question.

"And I don't want you here when she arrives," Anne reiterated harshly. She was angry, not just for Elizabeth but for the grief that Earl had suffered the rest of his life because of Lorna.

"Just a moment, Mrs. Wilkins," Liberty interrupted, her own tone sharp, her arm protectively pulling her mother closer. "I'm very happy my mother is here. I don't consider her presence an intrusion at all."

"Well, I do," Elizabeth said coolly, her expression bitter as she stared at her mother from the stairway.

All eyes turned toward the stairs.

Lorna's heart dropped at the sight of her eldest daughter. Elizabeth was furious, there was no mistaking it. Before Lorna could react, Gavan rushed to Elizabeth's side.

"You okay?" he whispered. She nodded, her gaze never leaving Lorna's face. Gavan was doubtful but like a protective fortress, he guided Elizabeth down the few remaining steps, troubled at the lack of emotion.

"Elizabeth," Lorna whispered, stricken by the contempt she saw in her daughter's eyes. She had expected no less, but she had hoped, she had prayed that Elizabeth would soften during their separation.

"I thought you had run away again," Elizabeth said coldly.

"I know you're angry—" Lorna started.

"You don't know that," Elizabeth retorted. They were

face-to-face now. "How could you know anything when at the first sign of conflict, you run?"

"I didn't run this time," Lorna defended.

"Then what do you call it, *Mother*?" The word was said with such venom even Liberty gasped.

"Elizabeth!" Liberty said harshly. "Don't you think you're being a bit cruel?"

"You don't understand," Elizabeth retorted, then immediately flushed at Liberty's raised eyebrow.

"She's my mother, too," Liberty pointed out. "And unlike you, I have had a much harder time. Don't forget, my son was taken from me. I know what she's going through. I forgive her. Trust me, you'll get over the pain. What matters is she's here now and she wants to be a part of your life, our lives."

"Well said," Lance agreed, praising Liberty.

Elizabeth fell silent, Liberty's words achingly true. She did want to forgive her mother, to understand what she must have been through, gone through. But Lorna Sanders was no child when she had Elizabeth and Liberty. She was a grown woman, capable of making smart decisions if she wanted to. Elizabeth's face hardened.

"It's my wedding, Liberty. And I don't want her here," Elizabeth said coolly.

No one spoke.

Even Val was uncertain what to do.

Then Liberty sighed and said calmly, "You're right. It's your wedding." She looked at her mother, her gaze tearful, her smile tremulous. "Are you at a hotel?"

Lorna nodded, too emotional to speak.

"Jarrett and I will take you back. Give me a moment. I'll get Jamal dressed," Liberty said, then headed for the steps.

Anne went up too her, grabbing her arm. "What are you doing?"

"I'm going with my mother." Liberty pulled free and started to walk again.

"I'm your grandmother," Anne hissed. "Have I no say?"

"No," Elizabeth answered for Liberty.

Liberty paused, staring at Elizabeth, unsure if she had heard her correctly.

"Don't go." Elizabeth sighed. "I've been rash. I'm distraught. I . . . She can stay if Ms. Ward will have her."

She had already lost her mother, she thought, she didn't want to lose her sister when they were only just beginning to know each other.

Liberty hesitated, glanced at her mother, then calmly nodded. "We need to talk."

"Now?" Lorna asked breathlessly.

"What did you expect, Lorna?" Anne snapped, her anger causing red blotches to tinge her cheeks. "You always were rash in making decisions. First with lying to my son, then with faking your death and leaving these poor girls to fend for themselves. And now this! I lost Earl . . ." Anne's voice choked and Elizabeth was afraid that Anne was going to be ill, her face was so flushed. "I lost him a long time ago, years before he died. The day you died."

"I'm sorry, Anne. I am. I never meant to hurt him. I thought he would move on. That it would be best for everyone if I no longer existed. And I didn't want Elizabeth to be poor and homeless, the way I was when I came to you, when I found Earl. I loved him. I did, but I loved my children and I couldn't let their lives be ruined because of me. Do you understand?"

"Yes. I understand but I do not approve," Anne said firmly, her composure back as she stared bitterly at Lorna.

"In hindsight neither do I. But I left myself with little choice the moment I left the house. It started and I couldn't seem to put things right again. And I never would have," Lorna added emphatically, turning to her daughters imploringly.

"I never would have, had you not come looking for me. I didn't know I had a chance with either of you. I lost you both, for years, and when I found you again you were both grown with your own problems, your own happiness, your own lives. I thought I lost you in Savannah. And then Mr. Ward called me and told me to come to you, that a daughter needs her mother. So I came. I knew you were getting married and that I might never get a second chance like this. I had to come. I had to tell you that I love you. I always loved you," Lorna said, tears spilling down her cheeks. "Oh, Elizabeth, please forgive me," Lorna cried.

"I never meant to hurt you, not like this. I was wrong, wrong, wrong. I can't make up for the past, I can't make up for the time we lost, but I can be here for the future, however much time I have left can be yours, all yours. Please, just try to forgive me."

Elizabeth was torn, looking from her mother to Gavan. He saw what was coming before she even knew it was coming. She fought against sobbing and averted her gaze. Gavan came to her side, holding her, comforting her.

"It's okay to cry," he whispered for her ears only.

"But I'll ruin my makeup," Elizabeth sniffed. Gavan smiled.

"You'll still be beautiful to me," he said gently.

"I don't know what to do," she whispered.

Neither did Gavan.

And that was the problem.

As he held Elizabeth, his family and her family watching the scene between mother and daughter, his gaze fell on Lance.

"Lance?" he asked. All eyes turned to Lance. "Are you the Mr. Ward she's speaking of?"

At his words, Elizabeth pulled free and stared up at Lance. Her eyes were clear, but she sniffed. She was no longer angry with her mother, but she certainly had a few words for Lance Ward if he had dared to interfere with her life.

He seemed to guess her thoughts, because he gave her a sweeping bow.

"I guess I am," Lance said easily. His nonchalance irked Gavan, but then Lance explained himself, giving up all pretense of ignorance. "It occurred to me in Savannah that things ended badly. And why wouldn't they? The confusion and emotions were elevated. I thought, give them a few days, a week or so, and perhaps things will get patched up."

"Did you now?" Gavan bit out, annoyed with his younger brother.

"I did. With you two lovebirds being on an emotional roller coaster, I decided to butt in."

"Oh, you did, did you?" Elizabeth hissed.

"I did," Lance said so cheerfully that Jarrett and Tyke actually grinned. The sisters shot them a look and they quickly sobered.

"We didn't need your help," Elizabeth argued.

Lance shrugged. "Maybe you didn't, but tomorrow, a week from now, someday you are going to thank me for butting in."

"I thank you now," Liberty said softly.

"*'A'ole pilikia.*" Lance nodded to Liberty, then walked to Lorna. He wrapped his arm about the elder woman's waist and gave her an encouraging squeeze. Still holding her, he looked at Elizabeth and Gavan and said, "This woman did what she had to do. Isn't that right, Ms. Sanders?" He paused, looking at her.

"Yes," she mumbled.

"You see? Liberty can understand because of her

own similar problems, but you, Elizabeth, you've never experienced losing a child."

"I don't need to experience it to know it's painful." As soon as the retort was out she knew what Lance was getting at. She flushed.

"Exactly." He grinned and Elizabeth was surprised. He'd barely even smiled at her, let alone grinned before. He was really enjoying himself. "However, I do owe you a bit of an apology. I thought it was a mistake, a crazy idiotic mistake for my brother to marry you, and so soon after meeting you. But I was wrong and I'm happy for you and Gavan. Now, the problem is, if Gavan wasn't so in love, if he wasn't so caught up in making sure you're happy at any cost, he would have realized that what would really make you happy is reconciliation with your mother. So, here she is. All yours. Granted, I didn't expect her until tomorrow—"

"I took the first flight out," Lorna explained, her eyes large in her consternation. He had made her promise not to tell how she knew and then he blurted it out on the first hint that they knew it was him.

"Understood. At any rate, she's here, we're all dressed. I think this is as good a moment as ever to get to know the family. We are all *Ohana*, aren't we?" He pinned each of them with a deliberate gaze, daring them to deny their status. No one countered. "So, as a family, we should go to that engagement dinner, don't you agree, Mom?" Lance asked, looking at his mother for approval.

She was staring at him as if he had two heads. For nearly a year he had been full of gloom and doom, refusing to speak of the pain that was so obviously tearing him up inside. Now he was cheerful and helping, actually helping his brother. She shook her head in amazement. At his frown, she quickly nodded her agreement, confounded by his performance.

"Gavan?" Elizabeth looked at Gavan, her uncertainty clear.

"I want you to be happy. For the rest of your life my goal is to make sure you're happy, Elizabeth. But I agree with Lance," he added cautiously. "I think Lorna should sit with us and you three should get to know each other. Don't you think it's time?" He smiled at her, dazzling her.

Elizabeth sighed heavily. Everyone was looking at her as if she were the guilty one.

She didn't look at her mother because if she did, she would cry. She was at a loss. To give in would be to accept all the wrong that Lorna's absence caused. But to deny Lorna was the same as denying her sister, or her husband-to-be, and she didn't want to be the selfish one. It would only be dinner. An evening with Lorna and in the morning, another day and time they would talk.

"I can't make any promises," Elizabeth murmured. "But I'll acquiesce to Lorna joining us for dinner."

"Thank you, Elizabeth," Lorna murmured.

CHAPTER 47

The chatter was nonstop and Elizabeth had a difficult time keeping up with the conversations at her table.

Val had chosen a rather popular tourist spot for their rehearsal dinner. The restaurant was huge with four floors. The Wards' party was on the second floor and took up the entire expanse. Glass windows made up the wall and the sight of the ocean was in full view. The dinner was totally chaotic, the number of guests—that Val had claimed would be a small gathering of friends and family—an enormous clan.

Elizabeth focused on the crashing of the waves against the beach to ease her delirium.

She was overwhelmed by the size of Gavan's family. His mother had three sisters, all married with two to three children themselves. She had two brothers, married as well, but only one had kids, five. They were all grown. No children had come though. Robert's younger brother was there with his wife, who was pregnant. His other two brothers couldn't make it to the island on such short notice. They would be there for the wedding.

Elizabeth, again, was separated from Gavan. This time she hardly noticed, so intense was her conversation with Liberty and Lorna. They talked most of the evening, engrossed in each other's details about their past.

A few times Elizabeth would catch Sonya's look of approval and smile. She would feel Gavan's eyes on her and give him a reassuring smile as well. It wasn't as bad as it could have been with her mother at the table. And for that she was thankful.

She glanced once at Lance, her surprise hero, and gave him a smile that he accepted as a truce and forgiveness for his intrusion. He nodded subtly at her and then continued with his loud conversation with the men surrounding him.

Initially other family members would interject, asking questions of their own, but Val's subtle hint that the threesome should be left at peace took no time to settle in.

Elizabeth listened intently to her mother's tale. She was still a maid, currently living with the Schultzes, her employers in Savannah, just miles from the Wilkinses' old estates. She often slept at the Wilkinses' as Elizabeth and Anne hadn't been there in years. It was the closest she could come to reliving the glorious days she had spent with Earl.

Liberty insisted her mother had to quit. She was too old to work so hard. She could live with Liberty. Elizabeth agreed but offered to buy her mother her own house instead.

Liberty and Lorna stared at Elizabeth, gawking at her offer. Elizabeth shrugged. She was financially set for life. Her father had at least seen to that. She owed her mother a home of her own.

Gavan watched his fianceé and mother from across the table. He was pleased to see them talking so amicably. He was worried it would never happen. He felt content and had to smile to himself. He was almost paternal in his emotions.

His eyes roved over Elizabeth at the thought. There was nothing paternal about how he felt for Elizabeth. He had to look away. Just watching her could arouse him and that would not do. His cousin was speaking to him. He was hard-pressed to pay attention, his gaze falling repeatedly on his lovely wife-to-be.

"Admit it. Keeping you two away from each other has enhanced your libido," Val whispered into her son's ear.

She was sitting on his left, his father next to her, and his aunt, Val's oldest sister, on his right. Clearly, Val could see his every move. He shifted, uncomfortable beneath his mother's knowing gaze.

"Mom," he started, exasperated, "has it ever occurred to you that you can be a little too personal with your questions?"

He sighed, shaking his head in amazement at his mother. He accepted defeat in the face of her stubbornness. She had no idea how very willing he was to give her all the grandchildren his wife could bear, but he kept the thought to himself.

His eyes fell back on Elizabeth. This time she returned his gaze, a teasing smile curving her lips. He was captivated, the gleam in her eyes causing him to come fully out of his seat before he even realized he was standing. He quickly sat back down, his eyes never leaving her face. He could handle a few more hours or the whole night if he had to, but there was no doubt, if his instinctive reaction to Elizabeth was any indication, that he could not wait another day to see Elizabeth.

Lorna noticed the strain on Gavan's face and smiled, staring down at her plate in discretion. As she did so, she felt the pull of Anne's gaze. She looked up, the burning anger in Anne's eyes unmistakable. Elizabeth may have forgiven her, but it had no effect on Anne.

Anne had moved from her seat beside Liberty to sit

next to Lorna. Lorna had been so engrossed in watching her daughter, she hadn't noticed. Now the two women measured each other. Finally, Anne spoke, her voice low, her words for Lorna's ears only.

"I hated you all of these years," she said. Anne's mouth had barely moved, but Lorna heard her clearly.

Lorna swallowed before responding, "I thought it was best to go."

"It was," Anne confirmed. "But I didn't want you dead. Earl didn't want you dead."

"I did it for Earl, for Elizabeth," Lorna insisted.

"Oh, nonsense!" Anne hissed, leaning closer to Lorna. "You did it for you. You wanted to be a martyr. Well, you were. I lost my son the day you left. I had to fight to keep Elizabeth. She was so withdrawn and sad all of the time—"

"Because of Earl's lack of interest. Belinda complained about it in the beginning," Lorna accused.

"That foolish girl didn't know what she was talking about," Anne retorted. "Earl was brokenhearted over losing you. He thought you were dead, Lorna. If you had simply run away, left the child and him, he would have gotten over it eventually. I would still have cared for Elizabeth. You didn't have to fake your death."

"I did and you know it," Lorna insisted. Her eyes were hard chips of anger, the uncertainty and guilt having vanished as a flurry of hushed words poured from her. "You would have denied Earl his livelihood. You and I both know it's true. And had I not faked my death he would have come for me. I would have given in and my daughter, my child would have been desolate—"

"She would have been happy, Lorna. Because she would have had you and her father. And her sister for that matter," Anne added.

Lorna fell silent. She had second-guessed herself for

years. By the time Elizabeth was a teenager, she realized beyond a doubt that she had made a mistake. But it was too late, she kept telling herself. She couldn't come back. Earl had changed, drastically, and would never love her the way he once had. Elizabeth would hate her, too.

The truth was, had it not been for Gavan's inquiry, she would never have been brave enough to come forward. But the past had been unmasked and she could only make amends the best way she knew how.

She nodded her agreement with Anne, surprising her. "You're right, Anne. Isn't hindsight a wonderful thing? You can always see the past so clearly." She smiled. "I was young and foolish and impulsive, too. I didn't think it through, but I . . . I did what I thought I must at the time. Elizabeth didn't turn out so bad, either. You taught her well. Belinda always praised your efforts."

Anne was mildly appeased by the compliment. She would never approve of Lorna's manufactured death, although a small part of her understood. She would always blame Lorna for the loss of her son, too. In time, maybe she could forget and even forgive a little. Tonight, she could only call a truce. If Elizabeth was willing to start fresh, then Anne would honor her granddaughter's choice.

"She turned out beautifully," Anne said.

They looked at each other and in unison smiled, their silent understanding putting their past differences aside for the greater desire to see Elizabeth's future secure and happy.

"Both of my daughters are," Lorna amended. Anne nodded, but she knew she would always be partial to Elizabeth and told Lorna so. They fell into an amicable discussion about the two young women, their voices still very low, the tension faded from their slender shoulders.

Liberty noticed the moment the fire went out of

their debate and she sighed, relieved. She and Elizabeth had been watching the exchange, unaware that they both had been barely breathing in worry. The sisters' gazes locked, their relief evident as they exchanged a smile. A new beginning had just occurred and they were determined to make the best of it.

Dinner lasted well into the evening. By the time the guests left, Val's household was exhausted and impatient to get home. They all dispersed, barely a word of good night as they entered the house. Soon the house was silent.

Gavan was restless, his body unused to the abstinence his mother's interference forced on him. He paced his room, frustrated with his growing needs. He was not used to denying himself and it struck him that he had no desire to call anyone else.

He wanted Elizabeth.

Only Elizabeth.

He needed her, to hold her, make love to her, be near her. He was going crazy with the time they had spent apart.

He sat up, no longer caring that she was only a door away from Val and Robert. He was going to get her and bring her to him. He swung open the door and was thunderstruck and elated, to see Elizabeth standing there, her hand poised as if she was about to knock.

"Elizabeth!" he cried.

"Hush," Elizabeth said quickly at his outburst, looking over her shoulder before hastily entering the room. She closed the door and leaned against it, her hands behind her still on the doorknob. Gavan gazed down at her, frowning only slightly at her attire.

She had come to his room fully dressed. The only difference was her heels were replaced with lace sandals. She even had her purse. She obviously did not have a seduction in mind. She grinned, her eyes twinkling mischievously. She clearly guessed his thoughts.

"I missed you," she breathed.

His eyes lit up. "Does that mean—"

"No," she interrupted firmly. "I will not disrespect your mother like that."

Gavan took a step back, massaged his temple as if he had a headache, and groaned. "Great. I sure as hell wish you didn't care, because I got to tell you, I never honored—"

"Please," Elizabeth interrupted again. "Keep the past in the past. I don't want to hear about your nights in here."

He grinned, properly chagrined. "Sorry." He pulled her to him, holding her closely to his body. "I wish we were getting married tomorrow. Frankly, I wish we were married right now."

"So do I," she whispered, kissing his earlobes, breathing into his ears.

"Lord, Elizabeth, don't do that," he warned, and squeezed, causing her to gasp.

"Don't do what?" she teased, reassured with his response. Her tongue darted out and she dabbed his earlobe before gently nibbling it.

"I thought you wanted to respect my mother's wishes," he groaned. He pressed her to him and she felt him swelling even as he held her.

"I do. That's why we need to leave, right now," Elizabeth said, flustered by the reality of his response. He froze, stepped back so he could look into her eyes, and narrowed his gaze.

"Where do you want to go?" he asked.

She grinned impishly. "Would the beach be too wanton—"

"No, it wouldn't," Gavan said quickly.

"Well." She sighed heavily, enticing his imagination. "No, that won't do. Can't you get us a hotel?"

He grinned, then embraced her again, this time kissing her fully, no longer content with just holding her. When he was done they were both breathless. "Am I marrying a bad girl?"

"It all depends on what you consider bad," she responded easily.

He groaned again, his body responding to her barb instantly. "I have a condo. We can go there," he offered. She nodded, having forgotten that small fact he'd divulged. The adventure of sneaking out of the house was exciting, not to mention that they were going to finally be alone again.

"Let's hurry, Gavan," Elizabeth urged. Her excitement incited him. He rushed around the room, dressing quickly. As he dressed, Elizabeth watched him, a teasing smile curving her lips.

"You are an incredible man," she murmured. He didn't say a word, only quickening his haste to dress.

"I think I loved you the moment I saw you," she continued. He paused, just long enough to look at her in awe. He had felt the same way. She grinned, fully understanding him.

"Gavan?" she called softly.

He was putting on his shoes. "Yeah," he answered, more a groan than a word.

"I want you," she said, her voice low, husky, her gaze ardent. Gavan thought he would go crazy if she didn't stop talking. He told her so.

"Elizabeth, if you don't stop teasing me, you'll have me all right. Here and now. Let's go," he said. Then hand in hand, they left his room, Elizabeth's light laughter filling the hallway.

"I knew you would try this. I saw it in your face tonight,"

Val said calmly, standing on the stairs, Robert at her side. Her husband looked exhausted, his eyes clouded with sleepiness. Val was dressed in pale blue silk pajamas, her hair pinned up, her robe tightly secured. She was quite prepared for her son's late-night rendezvous.

Elizabeth gasped at Val's presence. She was instantly embarrassed and averted her gaze. She didn't like feeling as if she were a wayward teenager creeping out of the house. She hadn't even encountered a situation like this when she was a teenager.

Gavan gave his mother a furious scowl, his frustration mounting. His mother had gone too far. He and Elizabeth were leaving. "Mom," he said in exasperation, "we're going out for some fresh air." Her presence was as effective as a douse of cold water.

For several moments she didn't say anything. Gavan feared she would persist. Instead she shrugged and murmured, "All right. I understand. I only wanted it to be a special day. Your wedding is very important to me. Good night, then. Robert, are you coming?"

Robert gave Gavan a sympathetic look, then obediently followed his wife up the stairs. Gavan watched them go, his vexation with his mother mounting. He was positive she was faking for the express purpose of creating guilt in him and Elizabeth. He refused to take the bait. Thankful to be rid of his mother, he turned his attention on Elizabeth.

"Ready?" he asked gently.

Elizabeth couldn't look at him. "I think I should go back to my room."

"No!" he shouted. She stared at him. He softened his tone. "No. She does that kind of crap all the time. Don't let her get to you. Please, Elizabeth. Don't change your mind now."

Elizabeth was hesitant, then guilt-ridden. She wanted

to be alone with Gavan just as much as he wanted to be with her. She glanced up the stairs and wondered if Val would think she was immoral if she ran off with Gavan. It wasn't as if they were eloping.

Gavan sensed her indecisiveness. He became desperate and said in an urgent whisper, "Come with me, Elizabeth. We can be back before anyone awakes."

She had to smile at that. She licked her lips, nodded her head, and then smiled, her eyes voluminous in her bright face, "If you can promise we'll be back, I'll go."

"I promise," he answered. Before she could change her mind, her took her arm and went out the front door.

They were getting in Gavan's car when the car alarm blared.

Elizabeth jumped. Gavan groaned.

He shut off the alarm and slammed the car door. What else could go wrong this night?

"This was such a bad idea," Elizabeth groaned, no longer feeling seductive.

"Hardly," Gavan rebutted. "I should have thought about it days ago." He drove out of the parking lot, tossing Elizabeth a promising look.

"You won't think it's a bad idea in half an hour."

CHAPTER 48

Gavan opened the door to his condo. Like a school-boy, he resisted the urge to skip and shout with joy as he entered. He barely closed the door before he pulled Elizabeth to him and began kissing her. She was more than willing to return his passion. He lifted her in his arms, still kissing her as he carried her to his bedroom, knowing without looking where he was going. He kicked his bedroom door open, causing it to bang against the wall from the force. A woman screamed and he nearly dropped Elizabeth in his shock.

"Who the hell are you?" he demanded. Elizabeth stared at the bed, shocked to see Shannon lying in Gavan's bed.

"Shannon?" she cried, stunned.

Gavan released her and Elizabeth slowly walked to the bed. Shannon pulled the covers up to her chin, obviously nude beneath the sheets. Gavan was frowning fiercely, oblivious of the woman's discomfort. What was she doing in his place, his bed? He was furious.

"Elizabeth, what in the world are you doing here?" Shannon breathed.

"What do you think?" Elizabeth hissed. She shot Gavan a look of disbelief, then stared at Shannon again.

Shannon gasped, finally realizing what Elizabeth thought.

"Oh no. No. It's not what you think. Your mother-in-law and Anne wanted to surprise you. They brought me here. They didn't want you to see me until the wedding. You two are supposed to be at the house," Shannon said in a flurry of words.

Like a stalking panther, Elizabeth paused, eyeing her best friend in wonder. Then she broke into a brilliant smile and sat on the bed. "I must be in love because I was ready to rip you a new one. I thought . . . Oh, never mind what I thought. Thank God I was wrong."

"I concur. You were way angry. I've never seen you so ready to pounce before," Shannon admitted.

"I was devastated. First my mother shows up and then you. But I'm so glad you're here." Elizabeth laughed, then hugged Shannon.

"And not your mother?" Shannon asked. She had been fully informed of Lorna Sanders's existence through Anne. She was first shocked, then happy for Elizabeth. Anne was not so pleased, but Shannon had faith that the mother and daughter and Elizabeth's newfound sister would manage to become one big happy family.

"I'm becoming more receptive. It'll take time," Elizabeth answered.

"Time makes everything better. . . ."

"Or worse." Gavan scowled at them. He wanted Shannon out. It was the middle of the night and he knew he couldn't very well kick her out.

Elizabeth looked up and gave him a regretful smile. "Maybe this was just a bad idea."

"Maybe Shannon can sleep on the sofa," Gavan retorted.

"No—" Elizabeth started.

"I don't mind," Shannon said quickly.

"I do, Gavan. She's my friend. I can't do that to her," Elizabeth said firmly.

"Elizabeth, come on. Look how far we've come," Gavan pleaded.

"It needn't be here," Elizabeth insisted.

"Then where? It's almost three o'clock in the morning. Do you want to check into a hotel at this hour?"

"No, I think we should just go back."

"Great!" Gavan huffed, then stormed from the room. He sat on the sofa in his living room and stared at the television screen. He didn't bother to turn it on. He was too furious to move.

Elizabeth sighed, coming to her feet. "Gavan and I haven't had a chance to be alone since we've arrived."

Shannon frowned, her slender eyebrows knitting together. "Really? Why not?"

"His mother is of the belief that we should wait until we're married before making love again."

"What's wrong with that?" Shannon asked.

"Nothing. Except Gavan and I miss each other. I miss him," Elizabeth emphasized.

"That's so romantic." Shannon smiled.

"Not if you were in it," Elizabeth declared.

"I can leave, Elizabeth. I don't mind. I just got here this morning. A hotel would be fun," Shannon offered brightly.

"No. I don't want you to stay at a hotel. Besides, it's late. Gavan will get over it. I'll more than make it up to him on our honeymoon," Elizabeth said softly.

"Ooh . . . I heard that." Shannon laughed.

"Gavan and I are going to leave. I want you to have your privacy. We'll talk tomorrow," Elizabeth said, coming to her feet.

"We can't. You're not supposed to know I'm here until the wedding," Shannon said, sitting up.

"I can't leave you on your own for two days. That wouldn't be right," Elizabeth said.

"Why not?" Shannon scoffed. "I have plans. I'm in Hawaii, Honolulu. There is much to do. Sailboating, visiting the volcanoes, touring, shopping . . ."

"Okay, I get it. Actually, I envy you. I haven't gotten a chance to enjoy the sights. I've been so busy preparing for the wedding."

"I'll make up the loss for you." Shannon grinned.

"I bet you will. Don't go overboard. I'm going to leave and try to soothe the beast."

"Indeed. Didn't I tell you there was something about the two of you?" Shannon teased.

"I think, honestly, Shannon, that I knew it the moment we met. It was just there. Just like that I gave up my heart. I'm still reeling from it."

"I'm so happy for you. And I'm glad I made it in time. I wasn't so sure I would."

"I'm glad you made it, too. Bye, girl," Elizabeth said, then hurried for the door.

"Oh, Lizzie, my mom sent her congratulations. She's proud of you, she said."

"I'll call her when things calm down. I promise." Then Elizabeth hurried from the room to find Gavan. She found him asleep on the sofa, his light snoring an indication of how exhausted he was. She smiled down at him, then softly padded back into the bedroom. She peered through the doorway.

Shannon leaned up on her elbows, her eyes knitted together again in the familiar habit she had when confused. "Is something wrong?"

"He's asleep. I don't have the heart to wake him. I'm going to get us a blanket, but I wanted to warn you that we're here. I'll be sure to wake him early in the morning so that we can get back to the house before Val or the others awake."

"Poor guy. All that energy wasted." Shannon laughed.

"Oh, hush and stop being bad. Good night, Shannon." Elizabeth smiled.

"See you at the wedding," Shannon called before Elizabeth closed the door.

Elizabeth breathed a deep sigh of satisfaction.

Their wedding day. It couldn't come fast enough.

CHAPTER 49

Elizabeth was a beautiful bride.

She had originally chosen a suit for the occasion, the short notice and fast betrothal leaving little room to decide on a more formal gown.

Val was adamantly against it.

She had dragged Elizabeth to the boutiques in downtown Honolulu, spending hours in one shop until they found the perfect dress, one that Elizabeth fell in love with instantly. It was a white satin strapless gown with a trail at least six inches long. A small satin ribbon snapped around the front, softening the lines of her dress while accentuating her bosom and bare shoulders. Val helped her to choose a sheer white veil lightly sprayed with silver roses. Her hair had been pulled back in a neat chignon, a silver and white crown her only adornment. She was a perfect picture of serenity and happiness.

Gavan stared in awe as she strolled down the aisle. When she stood beside him, the ceremony was a distant blur as he drank in her loveliness, content at last to know the day had come.

They exchanged rings and then the pastor announced they were man and wife. He could kiss his bride.

Gavan did so with relish.

He held her close to his chest and kissed her long and ardently, his mouth hungry for the taste of her.

"Gavan!" his mother hissed, a smile pasted to her face at her son's enthusiastic kiss.

Regretfully he pulled away, his eyes soaking in every image of Elizabeth. She was smiling, her eyes slightly closed from the long kiss.

"Congratulations, son," his father shouted, patting him on the back with a loud whack.

The congratulations poured in. Soon they were surrounded and they both thanked their guests, their eyes straying to one another repeatedly.

Elizabeth was smiling at Gavan when Shannon came from behind and tapped her shoulder.

"Congratulations!" Shannon cried, then kissed Elizabeth on the cheek.

"Thanks, Shannon. Now you have to take that leap of faith," Elizabeth said.

"Nah. It'll be years before I find the right man, unless there's another like Gavan. He's wonderful," Shannon added.

"There is always his brother," Elizabeth suggested, her gaze falling on Lance, who had his hand on Gavan's shoulder while they talked with other members of their family.

Shannon followed her gaze and visibly shuddered. "Not likely. He's very unapproachable. But keep scouting for me. I'm off to Atlanta, but we're going to have to get together soon. You'll call, won't you?" Shannon seemed doubtful and Elizabeth squeezed her.

"I'll call the moment I get to Maryland."

"You're coming back to Maryland?" Shannon was surprised.

"Only for a bit. Gavan lives in Honolulu, but he travels

back and forth to New York and Virginia so often that we haven't decided exactly where we want to settle down yet. I'm so deliriously happy, I don't care where we choose, but it'll likely be Virginia. Considering that Anne, Sonya, and Lorna are getting up in age, they may need us."

"Understood. I think your mom wants to see you. Take care and congratulations again," Shannon murmured, then stepped aside to allow Lorna to speak with her daughter.

"Congratulations, Elizabeth," Lorna said quietly. "You're a beautiful bride."

"Thank you," Elizabeth said, unable to add "Mother" to her vocabulary as readily as Liberty had.

Lorna smiled. Her eyes were full of happy tears for her daughter. "I think you two are going to be a very happy couple."

Elizabeth glanced at Gavan, another smile curving her lips. "I can't seem to stop smiling," she admitted.

They fell silent, and then Lorna impulsively took Elizabeth's hands. "Now is not the time to talk, but I want you to know I meant every word I said the other night. I want to make up for the lost years. Oh, I know we can never recapture the past, but the future, Elizabeth, the future can be so bright. It will be bright," she corrected. "I want you and Gavan to have plenty of babies. I want to shower them with all the years of love you and Liberty deserved. I love you, Lizzie Wilkins."

Elizabeth impulsively wrapped her arms about her mother, embracing her for the first time, and whispered in her ear, her voice urgent and sincere, for Lorna's hearing only, "I don't know you. But I've always loved the knowledge of you. I suppose I can learn to love the real you, too."

"That's all I could ask for. Thank you," Lorna nearly cried.

"Now, no crying," Sonya said, having shamelessly listened to their private conversation. Her own eyes were moist with unshed tears.

Elizabeth laughed, releasing her mother to hug Sonya. A few feet away Anne stood, watching, her eyes no less bitter, but she appeared so lonely and frail. Elizabeth motioned to her and Anne came forward.

"I still love you, Anne." Elizabeth laughed and before Anne could react, she gave her grandmother another hug. Anne was content. She would have to learn to accept the new Elizabeth and all the emotions that came with her new openness and affection. After all, her grandchild was genuinely in love.

"You're crying?" Anne asked once she was free.

"My tears are joyful ones." She laughed.

"I hope so, Elizabeth, because it's your wedding day. Sunny and bright," Liberty said, coming up behind Elizabeth with Jarrett and Jamal at her side.

Elizabeth turned to her sister with a brilliant smile. "It certainly is and I'm too happy for words."

"Then you two made up? For real this time?" Liberty asked, seeing her mother's genuine contentment. Her eyes darted from Lorna to Elizabeth.

Elizabeth nodded. "For real."

"Ooh, Elizabeth, I think your new husband is seeking you out." Liberty laughed, raising her gaze over Elizabeth's shoulder to stare at Gavan as he approached them.

Elizabeth grinned and turned swiftly around to greet her new husband. Her eyes were inviting, her smile sweet. "So we did it," she said.

"We did it," he agreed.

"Did I tell you how beautiful you are?" Elizabeth asked, grinning. Gavan rolled his eyes, but his mouth was still curved in a smile.

"Please don't call me that, it'll make me blush," he whispered teasingly.

"Then you'll be even more beau—"

"Uh-uh, don't say it. Besides, did I tell you yet?" Gavan asked.

She frowned, confused. "Tell me what?"

"You are the most beautiful woman I've ever met." His expression was grave, serious.

"Then you haven't met a lot of women," Elizabeth said lightly, but she was shining inside. He was too wonderful.

"That's the truth." He laughed. Elizabeth gave him a light punch.

"Now none of that. I could turn out to be a jealous woman after all," she retorted.

"I'll never give you a reason to be jealous, Elizabeth. I'm yours and have been from the day we met."

Elizabeth swallowed convulsively, unable to think of words to say. Gavan grinned, pleased that he affected her so passionately. He extended his hand and she automatically accepted it. He pulled her closer, then kissed her cheek before whispering against her lips, "Want to make a run for it?"

Elizabeth bit her lower lip, glanced up at him, then with a mischievous gleam in her eyes, nodded. "I'd love to."

"Then come with me," he whispered.

Grinning, defiantly ignoring the guests that began to approach them, they raced like children from the church, eventually creating a stir as everyone realized they were making their escape. A cheer of encouragement filled the church, Lance and Tyke the loudest in the crowd as they watched the lovers escape to their utopia. Shannon waved, nearly tumbling backward from the movement. Lance caught her, then hastily released her and continued to shout, *"A hui hou! A hui hou!"* *Till we meet again,* in Hawaiian.

Breathless, Gavan and Elizabeth scrambled into their waiting limousine and hastily closed the door. Gavan pulled Elizabeth into his arms and smiled down at her.

"Aloha wau iâ òe," he whispered. Elizabeth looked into his eyes, smiling, certain the softly spoken words were those of love.

"That was beautiful, what does it mean?" she asked.

"I love you, what else?" He laughed.

"I love you, too, Gavan T. Ward." Elizabeth laughed. Then, mindless of the guests that waved to them and the driver that awaited their direction, they began kissing again, their hands groping and searching each other like starved lovers.

The driver grinned. He drove from the church to the reception. He pushed the privacy button to shield the lovers from his view and took the long route.